Ann Sophia Stephens

Phemie Frost's experiences by Mr. Ann S. Stephens

Ann Sophia Stephens

Phemie Frost's experiences by Mr. Ann S. Stephens

ISBN/EAN: 9783743367784

Manufactured in Europe, USA, Canada, Australia, Japa

Cover: Foto ©Andreas Hilbeck / pixelio.de

Manufactured and distributed by brebook publishing software (www.brebook.com)

Ann Sophia Stephens

Phemie Frost's experiences by Mr. Ann S. Stephens

PHEMIE FROST'S EXPERIENCES.

BY

MRS. ANN S. STEPHENS.

AUTHOR OF "FASHION AND FAMINE," "REJECTED WIFE," "OLD
HOMESTEAD," ETC., ETC., ETC.

NEW YORK:

G. W. Carleton & Co., Publishers.

LONDON: S. LOW, SON & CO.

M.DCCC.LXXIV.

Maclauchlan,
Stereotyper and Printer, 56, 58 and 60 Park Street, New York.

To

FRANK LESLIE, ESQ.,

ONE OF THE BEST-TRIED AND MOST VALUED FRIENDS I HAVE,

THIS VOLUME,

THE LIGHT AMUSEMENT OF MY LEISURE HOURS,

IS

Respectfully Dedicated.

ANN S. STEPHENS.

ST. CLOUD HOTEL,
NEW YORK, *March,* 1874.

PREFACE.

Thistle down, thistle down, cast to the wind
　　So lightly and wildly, you scarcely can find
A glimpse of it here, or a gleam of it there,
　　As it trembles, a silvery mist, on the air.

Like the wide thorny leaves whence the mother root threw
　　Up its crown of rich purple, bejewelled with dew,
These feathery nothings, barbed, sparsely, with seeds,
　　Must struggle for life with the brambles and weeds.

CONTENTS.

PHŒMIE FROST'S EXPERIENCES.

I.

LEAVING HOME.

 HAVE made up my mind. Having put my hand to the plough, it isn't in me to back out of a duty when duty and one's own wishes sail amicably in the same canoe. I am going to give myself up to the good of mankind and the dissemination of great moral ideas.

Selected by the Society of Infinite Progress as its travelling missionary, with power to spread the most transcendental of New England ideas throughout the world, I shall take up my cross and go forth.

The evening after the Society had crowned me with this honor, I asked Aunt Kesiah and Uncle Ben Frost, who have been working the farm on shares ever since my father died, if they could not make out to do without me for some months, or weeks, or years, just as duty or my own feelings took a notion to stay.

Aunt Kesiah sat right down in the rocking-chair, and looked straight in my face for a whole minute without speaking.

"What," says she at last, "going away from home at your age—a female woman all alone in the world! You and the Society just take my breath away, Phœmie. Where on arth are you a going to ?"

" Well," says I, "it seems to be my duty to seek a field where there is the most sin and iniquity a going on, where dishonesty rides rampagnatious as a roaring lion, and fashion flaunts herself

like a peacock with moons in every tail feather. First of all,
the field of my duty lies in York, that Babylon of cities."

"But whose a going to bear the expenses ? " says Uncle Ben,
who always was 'cute as a miser about money matters. " Duty
is sumtimes rayther expensive."

"The Society," answers I. "The members are a picking up
produce now, I shan't go empty-handed on my mission. All
the members are wide awake about that. Crops have been
first-rate."

".Yes," says Uncle Ben, " I give in there."

"And hens never laid better since chickens were hatched,"
continued I.

" Jes' so," says Aunt Kesiah, " if the pesky creturs wouldn't
run off and hide their nests."

"Hams are plenty, smoked beef ditto, to say nothing of
dried apples. I mean to sell everything at a profit and settle
accounts with the Society."

"I reckon you'll get cut short; up to this time there has
bin lots of talking in that Society. When it comes to giving
—but never mind—we shall see ! "

" There, there, Benjamin, don't you go to pouring cold water
on our Phœmie's missionary work. She is sot on going, so let
her go."

" Is she sot ? " says Uncle Ben, looking at me sort of anxious.

" Yes," says I, " my face is turned to the mark of the prize
of the high calling."

" Jes' so," says Uncle Ben, "got your hand on the prow with
a hard grip? That being the fact, old woman, the best thing
is for you to lend a helping hand and send her off comfortably.
She can try anyhow, though I have a notion that the world
has got to be so wicked since the war, that one female woman—"

"Girl ! " says I.

" Well, girl—may fall short of regenerating the hull of it all
to once. Still there is no knowing what any one can do till
they try."

" When do you lay out to start? " says Aunt Kesiah, all in a flutter.

" Right off," says I.

" By land or water ? "

" Both," says I.

" Oh, dear ! what if you should get shipwrecked, and all the produce and garden sass with you ! " says she.

" There now, don't skeer the girl, Kesiah," says Uncle Ben. " The Sound don't rage to any great extent, neither are the engines alles a busting as a general thing."

" Well, well, if she's sot on going, I'll do my best to help get her off," says Aunt Kesiah, and she goes right to putting lard in a kettle, and while it was a heating, rolled out a lot of doughnuts, which article of food she excels in. For two whole days that good soul devoted herself to making crullers, dough-nuts, and turnover pies, as if she thought I should not find any-thing to eat till I got home again.

Well, by and by the day came for me to start. That tea-party and a prayer-meeting at Deacon Pettibone's house was a season that none of us will ever forget. Mrs. Pettibone, our president, is a wonderfully gifted woman, and that night she seized right hold of the horns of the altar and fairly beat herself. Oh, sis-ters, it *was* a touching time when I drove with Uncle Ben through Sprucehill a bowing from one window to another, for every member of the Society seemed to rush heart and soul to the windows ; and when I found your executive committee on that platform, the tears that had been standing in my eyes just burst out and overflowed my soul.

There I sat on my trunk in your midst, with a bandbox at my feet, and a new satchel, large, plump, and shiny, in my hand, ready to start, but feeling the responsibility of my trust, and the danger of a young girl going forth into the world all alone. No wonder some of you thought I should give up and take my hand from the plough. It was a trying situation. I felt it ; I suffered ; but, knowing that the eyes of all Sprucehill were upon me, I was firm. Yes, even when Aunt Kesiah placed that satchel in my lap, and told me with tears in her eyes to take special care of it, for she did not know what I should do if it got lost.

She said this so loud, and with such deep sobs, that a tall gentleman who stood on the platform with a satchel in his hand, seemed to be greatly affected by the touching scene, and kept close to us till the train come lumbering and snorting in.

Then, sisters, you remember how we fell upon each other's neck, and wept and kissed each other, then tore apart. How I went weeping into the cars leaving the satchel behind, and how Uncle Ben pushed it through the window, telling me to be awful careful of its precious contents so loud that everybody heard, and I have no doubt wondered how many thousand dollars it held. Well, the contents of that bag were miscellaneously precious. I had seen Aunt Kesiah pack it, with a feeling that made me homesick before I left the old farm. Doughnuts, crullers, turn-over pies, with luscious peach juice breaking through the curves. A great hunk of maple sugar, another of dried beef, some cheese, and a pint bottle of cider. It nearly broke Aunt Kesiah's heart because she couldn't top things off with a pot of preserves, but I wasn't sorry, thinking they might be unhandy to carry.

Well, I took the satchel, set it upon my lap, and looked out of the window at you all, as well as I could for crying, till the train gave a jerk that made my teeth rattle, and moved on.

When I lost sight of you, sisters, I felt awfully lonesome and almost 'fraid to trust myself among so many masculine men as filled the cars. Being an unprotected female, with a certain amount of promiscuous property in my charge, I felt a commercial and moral responsibility that weighed down my shoulders till I felt like a camel with an enormous load to carry.

Had I been travelling with nothing but my own self to take care of, the sense of responsibility would have been less; but I could not help thinking that the dignity of our Society was in my keeping, and the anxieties of all Sprucehill followed me swifter than the cars could run or the snorting engine draw.

So I pulled my dust-colored veil tight over my face, and, with my feet planted firm on the floor, sat **bolt**-upright, holding the satchel on my lap with both hands, kind of shivering for fear some man might attempt to sit down **by** me. I couldn't think of this without feeling as if I should sink right through the red velvet cushions that I sat on.

I was so anxious that my heart jumped right into my mouth when that man I had seen on the platform come my way. While he was looking around, the breath stood still on my lips, and I gave my satchel a grip which would have hurt it if such things have any feeling. I have no doubt that the austerity of my countenance scared all the rest of them off, for most of 'em passed on, after giving me a regretful glance; but when he come in swinging his new satchel, so independent, I moved a little; for I knew he was a gentleman by the way he wore his hat— clear back on his head—by the great seal, with a red stone in it, on his finger, and by the heavy gold chain swinging across his breast.

When I saw this man's eyes fixed on my seat so beseeching, I kind of moved a little more and then let my eyes droop downward, determined not to help his presumptuous design to sit by me a single bit.

"Thank you," says he, sitting down close to me, and chuck- ing his satchel under the seat. "If there is a superior person in the car, I'm certain to have the luck and the honor to sit be- side her. Some people prefer to look out of the window, but I would rather gaze on a sweet, pretty face, by a long shot— especially if it does not belong to a girl with airs."

I felt myself blushing all over at this delicate compliment, and observed, with becoming diffidence and great originality, that "beauty was only skin-deep at the best, and not by any manner of means to be compared with Christian piety and high intellect."

The man—he was a stalwart, handsome man ; not pursey like Deacon Pettibone, nor slim to bean-poleishness like the cir- cuit preachers that live about, and only pick up a little roundness at camp-meetings; but tall, and what young ladies call imposing. Well, the man gave me another long look at this, and says he:

"But when all these things jibe in together so beautifully, who is to say which it is that captivates a man's fancy? Not I. It is my weakness to take lovely woman into the core of my heart as a whole; but, if there is one quality that I prize more than another, it is piety."

I blushed with thrilling consciousness of the grace that has been in me so long that it has become a part of my being; but his praise did not satisfy me. One hates to take sweet things in driblets, with a spoon, when the soup-ladle is handy.

"Piety is a thing to be had for praying, fasting, and unlimited devotion. Anybody can have it who grapples the horn of the altar in deadly earnest. In short, if there is anything that everybody on earth has a right to, it's religion. The only aristocracy there is about it, comes when one reaches the high point of perfect sanctification—a state that some people do reach, though it is sometimes so difficult to point out the particular person."

"Ah, indeed!" said he. "But I have penetration, madam, great penetration. Do not torture your sensitive modesty by an attempt to conceal extraordinary perfection from one who can so fully appreciate it, and who grieves to say how uncommon it is."

I said nothing, but dropped my eyes, and sat up straighter than ever.

"Permit me," says my polite fellow-traveller, gently laying his hand on my satchel; "this is too heavy for the lap of a delicate female. Supposing we place it side by side with mine under the seat?"

I held on to the satchel, afraid that he might mash one of the turn-over pies.

"Do allow me. I really tremble to see a person so formed by nature borne down by such a weight," says my fellow-traveller, with great impressiveness. "It isn't to be thought of."

" But—but I don't feel the weight so very much," says I, loosening my grip a trifle.

" But, my dear madam, remember that the life and health of a person like you is of consequence to the whole universe. Remember the siotic nerve."

" The what nerve ? " says I.

" Siotic," says he. " That nerve which is so tender in very pious people. They say that the Pope has been suffering agonies with it."

" Dear me," says I, " is it anything mixed up with a heart disease ? "

" Not at all ; it is a strain upon the great sensitive nerve that runs like a whip-cord from I don't know where down the back of the le—"

Oh ! sisters, he almost had that terrible word out, but I gave such a start and blushed so that he turned it right round on his tongue, and says he with great emphasis, " limb."

" Oh ! " says I, with a gasp of relief, " now you speak so that a modest New England woman can understand. So there is a nerve ! "

" Peculiarly susceptible in religious and intellectual persons," says he.

" Running down the limb ! " says I.

" Both limbs," says he, " which a weight carried on the lap is sure to exasperate if it does not end in kinking up the siotic and crippling the l—limbs."

" Are you a doctor ? " says I.

He smiled.

" A sort of one," says he, and, without more words, he took my satchel and sat it down by his, under the seat, as sociable as could be.

After that, he took hold of my hand, as if he was a-going to feel my pulse, looking sweetly anxious.

" Is there a siotic there ? " says I.

He gave my hand a hard squeeze, and seemed to ruminate.

" It takes a little time to discover," says he, half closing his eyes. " Be tranquil; there is no danger now. The arm has been in one position rather too long; change·was necessary. But this is a change."

Then he gave my hand another squeeze, and, leaning back, shut his eyes entirely.

That minute the engine gave out a sharp yell that nearly scared me to death. The cars heaved a jerk and a jolt, the man on the platform sung out something, and before I could say Jack Robinson, my fellow-passenger made a dive under the seat, dragged out his satchel, and made for the door, bowing as he went, and hustling out something about its being his station.

While I was a-staring after him with all the eyes in my head, the cars gave another jerk, and, splash-bang, away we went, so fast that the man scooting along that platform, waving his hand backwards, seemed to be swimming in fog.

Sisters, I must say that a feeling of lonesomeness fell upon me after he went; his conversation had been so scientific and interesting that I felt the loss.

Besides that, I felt a little hungry, and thought I'd take a bite óf something to eat.   So I stooped down, lifted the satchel to my lap, and tried to open it.

The lock, it seemed to me, had got a stubborn twist, and wouldn't open; just then the conductor came along, and I gave him a pitiful look.

" Please, sir, help me a little," says I; " it won't open all I can do."

The conductor came forward, snatched hold of the satchel, and wrenched it open.

" Thank you," says I, lifting my eyes to his gaze, and diving my hand down into the satchel, for I meant to give him a doughnut for his politeness ; but instead of that luscious cake, my hands sank into a half peck of sawdust packed close in the satchel my fellow-passenger had left behind.

" Look there," says I; "isn't it dreadful, and I an unprotected female ? "

" Was your money in the bag ? " asks the conductor.

"No," says I, putting one hand up to my bosom, to make sure it was safe. "I always keep my money where—no matter, the—the handsome upstart will have a splendid feast of turnovers and doughnuts, besides a lively drink of cider; but as for money, that is in a safe place."

"And your ticket?"

"That," says I, "not being private property, like money, is kept handier."

With that, I took the ticket from inside of my glove and handed it to him.

"All right," says he, "the scamp hasn't made so much of a haul as he expected."

"But he'll have a sumptuous meal," says I, a little down in the mouth; for I was growing hungry, and not a bite left. Just then a boy came into the cars with a basketful of popped corn on his arm. It looked awfully tempting, for every kernel was turned wrong side out, white as snow. I bought a popped corn of the boy, and pacified myself with that till the cars stopped ten minutes, where there was a mean chance to get something more substantial to eat. I went in with the crowd, helter skelter; wrestled my way to a long counter, got a cup of tea which I swallowed scalding hot, and, after a hard struggle for it, carried a wedge of custard pie off with the palm of my hand for a plate, and skivered back to the cars, nibbling it as I ran; for the bell was ringing and the conductor yelling "all aboard!" so loud that half the passengers went back coughing and choking, and muttering some kind of wickedness as they went.

Well, all the rest of my car ride was just like this, only once in a while a little more so, till I got onto the Sound. There a great large steamboat, a quarter of a mile long, took a part of us in, and carried us right out to sea.

HELL GATE.

I was just a little disappointed in that roaring element. The air that came above it was salty and light, and the waves sparkled beautifully, but they did not rage worth a cent.   Still the shores away off on both sides looked dreamy, and we cut through the water so swift that it made me dizzy.

Two or three stylish sort of men seemed as if they were hankering to speak to me as I sat there all alone on deck; but I didn't seem to see it, and they contented themselves with looking at me as if I was the most cruel creature on earth ; which I meant to be.   The loss of one satchel full of doughnuts and things is as much as I can afford on one trip.

By and by that part of the ocean we travelled on kept growing narrower and narrower, till you could see houses on both shores, and splendiferous houses they were, with great meadows a-sloping down to the water; tall trees shading them, and bushes growing together in clumps.   Some were of stone, some of wood, with pointed roofs and cupolas, and great wide stoops, in which you could see people sitting and moving about. Some with spy-glasses in their hands, a-watching us sweep by them like a house afire.

I felt lonesome and almost homesick, but for all that the sight was exhilarating—very.

"Haven't we got almost to New York," says I to the captain; "it seems to me as if the sea was shutting in."

"Oh, we are almost there," says he, "close on to Hell Gate now."

"To what?" says I, almost hopping from the stool I sat on.

"Hell Gate," says he.

"Oh, mercy ! you don't tell me it is so bad as that ?   I knew York was an awful wicked place, but I didn't think an innocent missionary would have to go in it through that gate !"

"It is a little dangerous for sail crafts," says he, smiling, I suppose, to comfort me ; "but you are safe.   We shall go through with a rush."

I caught my breath.

"But supposing *He* were on the watch ?"

" *He!* Who ? "

" Don't ask me; I'd rather not mention his name, being a female who abhors profanity."

All at once the captain's eyes began to sparkle as if he were just longing for a tussle with the evil one.

" Don't be afraid," says he, " I reckon we shall make the gate without much trouble. The blasting won't stop us yet awhile."

" Blasting ? "

" Yes; they'll have the all-firedest upheave there, before long, that ever tore a hole in the bottom of the sea."

" Blasting! with fire and brimstone ? "

" And nitro-glycerine," says he, as calm as skim milk.

" And you mean to take this big steamboat right through it with me on board ? "

He laughed right there in my frightened and pale face.

" I really don't know any other way to reach New York," says he.

" Let me ashore," says I, a starting up, " me and my hair-trunk; I don't care for the produce; it may serve to cool their tongues down there. But put me and my hair trunk on any land. It is all I ask."

" It's impossible," says he.

" But I won't go through that in—that awful gate," says I.

" Why, we are in it now; don't you see the whirl of the waters ? "

" In it now. Oh, mercy! "

I fell down upon my seat, and buried my face in my shawl, shaking from head to foot.

Sisters, that cruel man laughed. O, how hardened he must have got, going through that sulphurious gate.

" I say, madam, there is no danger, we are almost through now."

" Is *he* there? Have you seen anything of his blasting hosts ? " says I under my breath. " Do they mean to fire up just yet ? "

"No, no, we are all safe. Quite through—New York is in
sight."

I let my shawl drop a little, and peeped out. There was no
sign of a gale; the water was a little bubbly and rough, as if it
had been rushing through a race-way, but that was all. ·That
captain of ours must have been on good terms with the old
serpent that keeps the gate, or he never could have got through
so easy. Now that it was over, I almost wished I had found
grit enough to see how it was done. As it was, my eyes were
hid, and I did not even see the awful old gate.

Well, at last I rose up slowly and looked forward. There
was New York City, right before me; just one pile of roofs
and walls with cupolas, pointed fronts, and steeples; looking
through the smoky haze acres and acres of houses, miles and
miles—a whole island laid down with stone. All around it,
just as far as I could see, the water was thick with ships,
steamboats, and small boats, all flying up and down and across,
like living things, each with an errand of its own. There,
along the edges of the city, was what seemed to me like a forest
of dead trees, without a leaf or a sign of greenness upon them.

"Well," says the captain, "you see that we have run the
gate. Never been here before, I reckon?"

"No, never," says I, "and hope I never shall be again."

"I thought things seemed a little green," says he.

"From the Green Mountains," says I.

"Exactly," says he. "Well, how do you like the looks of
the city?"

"Hazy," says I; "dry as tinder. All stone walls, and too
many dead trees about for my notion."

"Dead trees? I have never seen any," says he, a-looking
around.

"Must be awful short-sighted," says I. "Just look down
there; it is like a burnt faller."

He looked ahead where my finger was pointing, and laughed
right out.

"Why, that is the shipping," says he.

" Shipping," says I. " Don't tell me that ! I wasn't brought up in the woods not to know tree trunks when I see them, dead or alive."

" But I assure you those are the masts of vessels. You can see the hulls now."

I did see the hulls, and felt dreadfully; what would the captain think of me ! At once I looked up.

" Yes," says I. " There is no question about it. Those are the hulls of ships, and the others are masts; but I was right."

He laughed : " But you said they were dead trees."

" Just so. Isn't a mast made out of a tree ? "

" Certainly."

" And isn't the tree dead before it can be made into a mast ? "

" Why, yes," says he, and now it was his turn to be down in the mouth.

" Well, then, isn't the edge of the water there chuck full of dead trees ? "

At first the captain sort of choked a little; but the next minute he burst out a laughing.

" Do you want to know my opinion ? " says he.

" Well, rather," says I.

" Well, it's this : Green Mountain or not, if anybody buys a certain lady I know of for a fool, he'll get awfully taken in."

" Shouldn't wonder," says I.

With that, I picked up my umbrella, tied my bonnet a little tighter, took my bandbox in one hand, and followed the crowd across a plank bridge, and got into about the dirtiest road that my foot ever trod on.

" Want a carriage ? Want a carriage ? " I never saw men more polite than the drivers with whips were. It seemed as if they couldn't do enough for me. It really was a strife which should take me in his carriage. Their attentions really were flattering. It was like a welcome in this strange place.

It was like being in a little room all cushioned seats and windows when I got into the great double carriage so kindly offered me.

The cushions were soft as down, and gave so, when I seated myself, that I couldn't help catching my breath. "Where to," says the driver, a-leaning through the window.

"First," says I, "if it won't be too much trouble, I will go somewhere and buy a new satchel; I really don't feel at home without one. Then you may take me to a boarding-house in Bleecker Street. You'll know where it is by inquiring about a little. The name is Smith, and they come from Vermont. Their daughter married and settled on Sprucehill. Smith. You can't help but find them."

"Have you got a number?" says the man.

"No," answers I, "only one family.

"But the house."

"No," says I again. "I haven't got any house, but the old homestead on Sprucehill."

"But Bleecker is a long street."

"Is it?"

"And I must have a number."

"Why, isn't one street of a name enough?" says I, getting out of patience. "What on earth do you want?"

"I want the name of the people."

"Smith."

"And the number of the house they live in."

"Oh, then, houses go by numbers, not names, here in York, do they? Stop a minute!"

Here I took a slip of paper from my pocket-book which Smith's daughter had written, and gave it to him.

"All right," says he, hopping up the wheel, and going to his seat. Then away we rolled, genteel as could be.

I bought the satchel at a store we drove by, and then we went on and on and on, till at last he stopped before a brick house with a good deal of iron about it.

The driver jumped down, ran up the steps, pulled a rusty knob fastened to the door stone, and faced round towards his horses.

A girl I should consider as hired help opened the door.

"Is Mrs. Smith at home?" says I, a-putting my head out of the window.

"Yes," says she.

"I'll get out," says I.

The driver unfolded a lot of steps that had been hid away under the windows. I went down them with a genteel trip. The man had been so polite, I stopped to thank him.

"Three dollars," says he, a holding out his hand.

"Three dollars? What for?" says I, all in a flutter.

"For bringing you here," says he. "Stopping on the way, and so on."

"But you invited me."

The fellow grinned, and held out his hand harder than ever. The help on top of the steps giggled.

"Come, look sharp, I can't wait all day," says he, as pert as a fox.

"Well," says I; "being an unprotected female in a strange place, I can't help myself, I guess; but they do sell politeness awful dear in York. It must be scarce."

I gave him three dollars without another word, feeling like a robbed princess as I did it. Then I took the bandbox and new satchel in my hand, and walked into Smith's boarding-house, about the homesickest creature that ever bore a cross.

II.

PHŒMIE'S FIRST VISIT.

SISTERS:—Some of you must remember my cousin Emily Elizabeth Frost, that married a Dempster ten years ago when most of us were little mites of things sewing our over-and-over seams. She was a smart creature enough, and as her mother was a proper, nice woman, it was reasonable to hope that she could be depended on to

2

bring up her children; for her father was a deacon in the church, and her mother just the salt of the earth. Well, as soon as I got settled in my boarding-house, I took it into my head to go and see Cousin Elizabeth. She hadn't been to Vermont lately, and I'd rather lost track of her; so I gave one morning to hunting her up.

Some useful things can be found in a great city like this. Now, I tell you, amongst them is a great, fat dictionary, crowded full of names, where everybody that keeps a decent house sets down the number, which is a convenience for strangers like me.

I found the name of Cousin Elizabeth's husband, who keeps a bank somewhere down town, the book said, and got into the first street car that went towards the Central Park. After a while I got out and hunted up the number, feeling awfully anxious, for the houses about there were what the papers call palatial— a word we have not much use for in our parts. I just stopped on the other side of the street and took a general survey before I attempted to go in, feeling more and more fidgety every minute, for that house just took me down with its sumptuousness. Such great windows, with one monstrous pane in a sash, and lace and silk and tassels shining through! The front was four stories high and ended off with the steepest roof you ever saw, just sloping back a trifle, and flattening off at the top, with windows in it, and all sorts of colors in the shingles, which they call " tiles " here. Then the stone steps wound up to a platform with a heavy stone railing on each side, and a great shiny door, sunk deep into the wall, was wide open, and beyond it was one of glass, frosted over like our windows on a snapping cold morning, and under my feet was a checkered marble floor. I found the knob of a bell sunk into the door jamb, and pulled it a little, feeling half-scared to death. Then I just stepped in and waited in front of the glass door.

A colored person of remarkably genteel appearance opened the door, and gave me a look from head to foot that riled the old Adam in my bosom; then he muttered something about the basement; but I put him down with just that one lift of my finger.

"Is my cousin, Mrs. Dempster, at home ? " says I.

"I—I'll inquire," says he, as meek as Moses ; "walk in."

Walk in I did.

" Have you a card ? " says he.

"No," says I; "as a general thing cards ain't desirable among relations, nor moral under any circumstances with religious friends. Say that Miss Frost is here—Miss Phœmie Frost, from the State of Vermont. No cards ! "

The fellow opened a door on one side of the hall, and I went through. Don't expect me to describe that room. It isn't in me to give the least idea of it. Great chunks of glass like the hub of a wheel, with crooked spokes of glass starting every way from it, and what seemed like hundreds of icicles falling from them, dropped down from the ceiling. When the negro opened the blinds and let in a drift of sunshine, they turned into a snarl of rainbows that fairly blinded me. Then there was a carpet soft as spring grass in a meadow, and bright as a flower-garden; chairs shining with gold and silk ; marble women, white as milk, with not a thing on worth speaking of, and looking-glasses half as large as our spring ponds.

I turned my looks away from the women without clothes, while that colored person was by; but gave them a skimpy peep or two the minute he was gone. Really, it was dreadful. I would not have believed such things of Cousin Elizabeth.

Oh mercy on me ! while I was looking, in came a gentleman, who bowed, and took a chair, and sat smiling on those creatures just as if he was used to it. Talk of blushing—my face was one blaze of fire.

While I was wondering what I should do, a girl, or what ought to have been a little girl, came sidling into the room, gave me a look as if I'd been a dog in the wrong place, and went up to the gentleman.

"Mamma will be down directly, and has sent me to entertain you," says she, shaking out her short skirts, and almost sitting down on the crimpy hair that half covered them behind. Ah! I see you are admiring our crouching Venus. Lovely, isn't it? The curving lines are so perfect. The limbs —have you observed the foreshortening of that limb?"

The foreshortening of that limb? Mercy on me, I couldn't stand it. Another minute and I should have boxed her ears, for all the blood that burned in my face went tingling down to my fingers. That was too much; so I up and said I would call again, and marched right out of the house. Girls indeed!

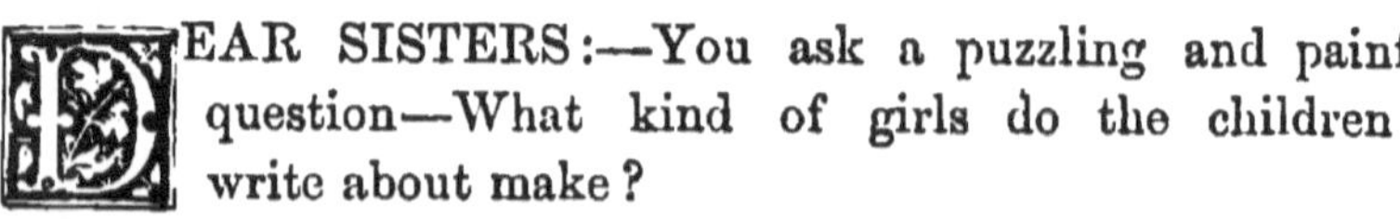

III.

ABOUT GIRLS.

DEAR SISTERS:—You ask a puzzling and painful question—What kind of girls do the children I write about make?

My dear friends, girls—modest, rosy, bright-eyed school-girls, such as you are a-thinking of—are scarce as hen's teeth in this great city, and not to be found in profuseness any-where. They went out with pink calico sun-bonnets, and ain't likely to come in again yet awhile, I tell you! Republican institutions can be carried to a great extent; and our young ones have found it out, and trample down all the good, whole-some old fashions before their little feet quite get out of baby shoes. At this moment I can't find a girl of twelve years old that don't know a thousand times more than her mother, and wouldn't attempt to teach law to her father if he was a judge in the Supreme Court. Yet, it's a shocking truth, the little upstarts don't know how to read like Christians, or spell half their words. The tip-top fashionable school-marms here are quite above teaching such common things as reading and spelling, and turn up their noses at any study that hasn't some "ology" or "phy" at the end of it.

I should just like to have a string of the girls that walk in squads up and down the Fifth Avenue, with short dresses and hair streaming loose down their backs, in a district school-house, with no books but Webster's Spelling-book and the Columbian Reader. Wouldn't I astonish them with science? I guess they would understand the meaning of a spelling-class by the time I got through with 'em!

As for arithmetic, they don't know what it is in these high-falutin seminaries; mathematics is the word; A B roots and squaring circles, as if circles ever would be square. Of course they can't, having been tried and kept round as an O all the time. But these A's and B's, and roots and such like, are considered as arithmetic for girls here; so the end of it is, they can, maybe, tell you how many square feet there are in a building lot, but couldn't add up ten shillings to save their lives; of course they forget how to estimate the square feet for want of having unlimited building lots to work on, while the washing bill and girl's wages and such things, come up every day all through their lives.

What *do* girls learn at the schools?

Oh, a mighty deal that some good women pass half through a lifetime without knowing, and are just as likely as not all the better for it. Some of the lessons are paid for, and some are given free gratis for nothing by the scholars to each other, and what some of them don't know in the way of flirting, drooping the eyes, and things you never dreamed of, ain't worth keeping secret.

"A little leaven leavens the whole lump." That passage has always relieved my feelings about the old patriarchs; for it's a proof that they and their families had raised bread in those old Bible times; and light bread, even if saleratus has to be used, is a blessing on the domestic hearth. For that reason, I'm astonished that bread-making is left to men-bakers here in York. But this passage sometimes puts you in mind

of something beside turnpike emptins. I should like to pro-
mulgate some genuine old-fashioned ideas into these tip-top
schools, where one bold, forward girl with unwholesome ideas
in her head, would set them working like leaven in every
innocent young soul in the seminary. Somehow, more or
less, girls always do manage to give a good deal of knowledge
that isn't set down in the bill, though that is generally long
enough, goodness knows.

I wish you could see one of these bills with the extras.
Now in our district schools, there isn't much chance for the
scholars to get over intimate. They don't sleep and eat and
work together, like canary birds crowded in one cage and huddled together on one roost; the weak don't catch the faults of
the strong, and if they did, the free breezes of our hills would
sweep them away before the poison struck in. Flirtations
do not become a science with them before they can spell
" baker," and they don't often learn such things from their
New England mothers, anyhow.

Well, I would give a good deal to see a genuine girl who
did not think herself a marvel of superior knowledge at twelve,
or had not plunged into a heart disease at the sight of some
hotel lounger at fourteen. I tell you, sisters, these young
creatures have too much liberty; they have no wholesome
growth either of body or mind. They know too much at fifteen, and will know a great deal too little at forty.

The girl of twelve—which is about the age you are thinking
of—has a great deal more assurance than some of our church
members at fifty. Baby boys and girls haven't gone quite out
of fashion, but they are getting scarcer every year, people tell me;
and regular-built, wholesome children are as hard to find here
as green gooseberries in October. I've seen plenty of little men
and women, that couldn't speak plain to save their lives, dressed
out like soldiers on a training day, with short frocks or tunics,
and legs as bare as bare could be; but such boys and girls as
we remember are not to be found anywhere nowadays, I tell
you.

What does all this mean? Just this: Mothers don't trust their young ones out of fashion long enough to grow. Besides, there isn't, only now and then, one who gets acquainted with her own child well enough to know what is good for it. Why, these city women would go crazy to see a little girl, six years old, swing upon a gate or riding horseback on a rusty old farm-horse, gripping the mane with both hands, and sending up shouts of fun if she happened to tumble off. Children, in the natural state, love water, like ducks and goslings. It used to be a sight to watch them, knee-deep in the brooks, with their tenty-tointy feet shining through the ripples, as they hunted for water-cresses and sweet flag-root; but catch one of your new-fangled young ones at anything with so much human nature in it. All the water they see is in the bottom of a bath-tub, rubbed on their skimpy limbs by an Irish girl's hands. Not the mother's. Oh, no! Care of one's own children is too much for a healthy young woman nowadays. Being a professor and member of a church, I want to speak accordingly, and just drop the mothers here. Christian language isn't up to the occasion.

Well, as I was saying, the meanness of these mothers in hiving up their young ones and cheating 'em out of the very best years of life, is enough to make a saint mad. The rough-and-tumble season, which gives a child sound lungs, strong limbs, and a brain that thinks of nothing but high play, is just knocked out of their lives. It's an awful swindle on the poor little things, and I'm not afraid to say it openly and above-board here in my very first report.

If I haven't a right to speak on this subject, I should like to know who has. That's all. I never had a child of my own, which is, perhaps, natural to a state of single blessedness, and so had plenty of time to make other people's children a special-ity. Besides, haven't I kept district school, and boarded round enough to get an inside view of a good many family circles? Haven't I seen droves of young ones, in loose calico slips or cosey-fitting jackets and trousers, coming miles to school, only setting their dinner baskets down now and then to stone a squirrel, or climb up among the burrs of some great chestnut limb which offered to give them a ride to Boston or a trip to Canterbury.

Dear me, I think I see them now running "like split," as they said, to catch up time, with such a lively color rushing through the tan on their faces, hats off, and sun-bonnets flying out by the strings.

There, that's what I call childhood. You and I, sister, know something about it; now don't we? Do you remember that little red school-house where we learned our letters, and the old broken-limbed apple-tree behind it? No wonder the limbs got scraggly; they couldn't stand horse for a whole school, year after year, without some wear and tear, could they?

Well, may be you and I owe to that old patriarch more than we know of. The apples were so sour the pigs wouldn't eat 'em, but they never hurt us. Then the limbs stretching out every which way—weren't they splendid to swing on, and in a hot day the shade was like a tent.

You and I have been tough and hearty all our lives, just as like as not on account of that old tree and the long road home, and the pine woods it ran through, with the good wholesome samp and milk when we got there. There was generally a little red light in the sky from the sunset when we went to bed, and just a streak of rosy yellow when we got up, with dew enough on the grass to wash our faces in before breakfast.

That's what I call life for a child; all out-doors for a playground, good, sound sleep, plenty of wholesome food, three times a day, and always hungry at that. Why, the few years after you begin to toddle, and before you learn to read, if you're properly let alone, are choke-full of happiness that ripples like a brook through your whole life. I say, once more, it's a sin and a·shame to cheat a child out of that which is just God's portion of a human life.

Now I ask you, isn't it probable, between you and I, that

the Saviour picked out just such bright, happy little creatures as these, when He took 'em in His arms and blessed 'em, and said of such is the kingdom of heaven. If the apostles wanted to hunt up one of the kind now, they'd have to catch it in the cradle. Just think of bringing forward one of the little things we meet in the avenues here, to be held up as a monument—all flutings and lace, kid gaiters, pink and blue sashes, long white feathers, and parasols. Yes, believe it or not, I say parasols about the size of a poppy. Oh, don't mention it! The whole thing makes me sick. The children you meet here in York look like little barefooted scarecrows, or else like motto papers afloat.

But are all the little folks you see painted like a dahlia, and pink as hollyhocks. You are asking this question in the Society. I know it. Well, I should rather think not. These whipper-snappers go tipping down the avenues, and ride with their mothers' lap-dogs in the Park, a-looking like their own French dolls, and are about as likely to make men and women.

IV.

MORE ABOUT GIRLS.

SISTERS:—My cousin's little girl has just upset me. Remember she is my own flesh and blood; and genuine honest blood in Vermont is as pure as the sap in our maple-trees, and ought to keep sweet as the sugar we make from it, wherever it is found. Being my second cousin in her own right, I expected to find her a model of what the rising generation ought to be, and went to that house, exalting myself accordingly. I shall find, thought I, a genteel, modest, seemly little lady, polite, and cordially glad to see a relative that wants to love her and exalt her into a pattern and a

2*

monument of female promise. But instead of that, just read my last report, though it must fall short of giving you any idea how heavy my heart was, and how my brain burned with disappointment.

Has female modesty died out since you and I came into the world? or was it burnt over during the war, like the great prairies, where the hot flames parch up all the sweet green grass and the bright flowers, killing them root and blossom, snakes likewise? One thing is certain, my dear sisters in the cause, honesty among men and modesty among women go hand in hand all over the earth. When women degenerate, it is because the moral atmosphere which they breathe is tainted and unwholesome. Something has gone awfully wrong both with the men and women of America in these latter years. The fraud and demoralization of the thing they call " shoddy " has settled down upon our social life everywhere. I shudder to think of it! With a constitution made strong with fresh air from the Green Mountains, and morals consolidated in the oldest congregation of the State, I feel afraid of myself and almost weary of well-doing. It has become so miserably unfashionable to be honest, that people seem to think me crazy when I speak my mind.

Do not start and say that Phœmie Frost is ready to give up her mission ; because she isn't of that sort. Her hand is on the plough—they spell it *plow* here, which takes away half the strength of that agricultural word—on the plough, is she, a female, to turn back because rocks and roots choke up the furrow? Not if Miss Frost knows anything of herself!

Speaking of female modesty, between my little cousin and that marble girl, the poor naked creature seemed to have the most of it. She did scrouch down and try to hide herself behind herself, as if she was ashamed that the man who made her had forgot to cover her up a little. But the live girl did not seem to feel for her a mite ; in fact, I think she enjoyed seeing her scrouch, because of the foreshortenings, you know.

It's of no use denying it, I did feel down in the mouth about this girl; and seeing my duty clear, determined to do it or perish in the attempt.

Once more I stood in front of that "palatial residence," and, with a hand made firm by a powerful sense of duty, pulled the silver knob in the jamb of the door. The same finified youngster came and asked me with his saucy eyes what I wanted there. This time I had written out a square piece of paper, on which he had the pleasure of reading: "Miss Phœmie Frost, Home Missionary and Special Plenipotentiary from the Society of Infinite Progress, Sprucehill, Vermont." "Think," says I, when I handed him the paper, "if this don't fetch them all down a notch or two, nothing will."

And it did!

Yes, I have the pleasure of saying pretension and pomposity do have a wonderful effect here in New York. I don't know whether it was the missionary or the plenipotentiary that brought my cousin to her oats, but rather think it was the latter—having a foreign twang to it, of course, it impressed her aristocratically.

The waiter-man took me into the drawing-room, as he called it, but why, no human being could have told; for there wasn't a sign of drawing paper, pencil, nor painting things in sight. In fact, it was the self-same room that I went into the last time I was there. A little darker and more sunsetty, because the red curtains swept close, and blinds were rolled down under the lace. There was that marble girl, too, a-looking at me as if half-scared to death; but in that light she seemed dressed in a veil of pink gauze, and looked just lovely. There being no man by I really could have kissed her, she seemed so sweet, and so awfully ashamed of herself huddled down as if she longed to creep out of sight.

The door opened, and that fellow came in simpering like a chessy cat, and asked if I would be so good as to walk up to the boudor.

"To the what?" says I.

" To the ladies' boudor," says he, a turning his head, and trying to choke off a laugh. " This way ! "

I took my satchel from a table all framed in gold, and checkered with precious stones, where I had laid it down. Then, bowing my head and lifting my forefinger, told that servile creature to proceed, with an air of command that quenched his saucy smile in no time.

Up the stairs he went, and I followed after ; treading a carpet that gave to the feet like a meadow in its first spring grass. Through an open door I saw my cousin lifting herself up from a sofa, covered with blue silk and open-worked lace. Then she dawdled towards me with one hand out, and the laziest smile you ever saw about her mouth.

" Cousin Emily," says I, " how do you do ? "

" My dear Miss Frost," says she, " I'm happy to make your acquaintance."

Happy to make my acquaintance, and I her first cousin. Did you ever ?

At first I *was* taken aback, and felt as if I should choke. Hadn't I learned that great white creature her letters ? Hadn't I spent dollars on her for slates and pencils, besides taking her to the maple camps when she was a little girl, and giving her no end of sweet sap to drink. Who was it but me that turned down her first over-and-over seam, and gave her a tentie-tointy silver thimble to take the stitches with. I wonder what she did with it ? Now she was happy to make my acquaintance, and dragged a double winrow of worked flounces, topped off with a muslin skirt and scarlet training jacket, across the room to tell me so. Our mothers were sisters ; pray remember that !

" Take that seat," says she, a-dropping down to the sofa as a great white hen turkey settles onto its nest. " How long have you been in the city ? Do you make anything of a visit ? So thoughtful and kind of you to give me an early call."

There I sat, straight as a sign-post, with my satchel in my lap, and both hands on that, riling up like an Irish girl's coffee, and feeling the wrath within me grow stronger and stronger while she settled back and half-shut her eyes, and seemed to be quite satisfied that she had done her best. I could see that her half-shut eyes were turned on my alpaca dress, which was a trifle dusty, and on my cotton gloves, that were clean and whole, at any rate. While she examined them, I took an observation of her. Mercy, how she has changed! Five times the hair she ever had before hung in great, heavy braided loops down her back. There must be some way of making the hair grow, 'specially here in York, that we never heard of. And her figure, which was slim and graceful as the droop of a willow when she married, has swelled out fearfully behind, which makes her seem to stoop, and gives one the most humpy idea of a camel in motion of anything I know, which, being Scriptural, is, I dare. say, the only religious idea she has kept firm to.

"You called the other day," says she. "I was so sorry not to have seen you; but I was dressing to go out. Still, you saw my little girl?"

"Yes," says I, "I saw your little girl; and, to tell you the honest truth, that is what brings me here now. I haven't had a minute's rest since I was here. Why, Cousin Emily, I expected to see a child. Instead of that—"

She roused up at this, opened her eyes wide, and interrupted me.

"Instead of that," says she, turning a great gold bracelet on her arm, and smiling as if what she was saying swelled her out with pride—"instead of that, you found a finished young lady. No wonder you were surprised."

"A finished young lady!" says I, riling into strength. "That is what no child ever can be; and let me tell you, the attempt to force one into such an unnatural creature is abominable. You can polish every bit of the modesty and innocence of childhood out of a little girl; but all that you can get for it is affectation and self-sufficient impertinence, becoming neither to the child nor the woman. Why, cousin, the little creature I saw in your parlor—sent there, as she said, to *entertain a gen-*

tleman—was just an absurdity to him, and to me something dreadful. I asked myself what a child like that would become at forty years of age. Why, cousin, when she is at her meridian she will feel herself at least a hundred and fifty. You have cut off all the bloom and richness of a young life; you have made a dainty little monster of her—swept away all companionship with children, and made it presumption and impertinence when she attempts to force herself among her elders. I could not be so cruel to a dog as you have been to that child."

Cousin Emily woke up now with a vengeance. Her sleepy eyes flashed lightning. "Cruel!" says she. "I cruel to my only daughter? Why, there is not a child in America who has had such care—such abundant chances for improvement. She has been to the most expensive schools."

"Exactly," says I.

"She has had masters at home—music, dancing, the languages—"

"Exactly," says I.

"Things that I never thought of learning she has mastered."

"Just so," says I.

"She had a French nurse before she could speak. No expense has been spared by her father. I never had such chances; and we are determined to give her a splendid education. In fact, she might come out this season, so far as that is concerned; but I have resolved to be rigid—not a day before she is seventeen. Then her education will be complete."

"Her education complete at seventeen! Why, Cousin Emily, a woman's education is *never* complete. At the best schools we get but a dreamy sort of idea of the things we must bring all the faculties of a well-regulated mind to understand in after years. A well-educated woman is one who studies and learns something every day of her life—who thinks about what she sees, and acts upon what she knows."

Cousin Emily lifted up both hands, all covered with shining rings, as if to choke me off. I stopped. Far be it from Phœmie Frost to force the opinions of our Society upon unwilling ears; but I lifted my forefinger in solemn admonishment, and says I:

"Oh, Cousin Emily, Cousin Emily, has it got so that you hold up both hands against common-sense!"

"Not against common-sense," says she, "but against your uncommonly long sentences. Why, Miss Frost, it is like our old-fashioned country preaching."

"Which has died out of your heart, I dare say. Oh, Emily, Emily, what would your sainted mother, my aunt, say?"

This brought the misguided woman to her tears. She sat up on that lace-silk sofa, straight and listening, as I have seen her many a time on the a b c bench at school, when her little feet couldn't touch the floor.

"Cousin Phœmie," says she, "I am trying to do what is right."

"I hope so," says I, with tears of thankfulness in my eyes, for the "Cousin Phœmie" went straight to my heart. But my mind isn't quite equal to more of this conversation this morning. The next time I come this way we shall both be more like our natural selves."

With that I tightened my cotton gloves, took up my satchel, and left that house, feeling that I had paved the way to a good work hereafter.

V.

POOR CHILDREN.

ARE there no genuine children among the poor of New York?

Beloved sisters, your question wrings the heart in my bosom. I asked it of myself this very morning, and resolved to investigate.

I hadn't found a child that could be called a child outside a perambulator, which means a little carriage pushed by an Irish girl, with a cap on, along the avenues. So I took my mission down among the tenement-houses. There I found young ones on the sidewalks, the doorsteps, and in the gutters, thick as grasshoppers in a dry pasture lot, all hard at work, trying to play. But the play seemed more like fighting than fun. Two girls stopped me on the sidewalk, swinging the dirty end of a rope, while another tried to jump it, but only tripped up, and went at it again. Shaking her loose hair, and—yes, I say it with tears in my eyes—swearing at the other two.

I laid my hand on her head, and gently expostulated. She was a little mite of a girl, with a sharp, knowing face. The first word she spoke made my nerves creep. Why, that little thing had the wickedness of an old sinner on her baby mouth, and couldn't speak it out plain yet.

Oh! my dear sister, and you, my friend, in the great course of infinite progress and general perfection, had you been with me, almost broken-hearted among that rabble of children, who will never, never know what childhood is, the last pound of butter and dozen of eggs in our village would be freely given to support my mission here. Barefooted, bareheaded, bare-legged, and, it seemed to be, bare of soul, these little wretches swarmed around me when I kindly asked the baby girls not to swear, all making faces at me. The boys, that sat with their feet in the gutters, flung away the oyster-shells and lobster claws they had just raked from an ash-barrel, and began to hoot at me. One little wretch—forgive me for calling names—not more than five years old, had a cigar in his mouth half as long as his own arm. When I stooped down to take it from him, he gave a great puff right into my eyes, and scampered off, with his dirty fingers twirling about his face like the handle of a coffee-mill.

As a New England woman, whose duty, I take it, is to set everybody right, I wasn't to be put down by a boy like that, but caught him by the collar of his jacket, snatched the cigar from his lips, and flung it into the gutter, where it sizzled itself out. Then I lifted my forefinger as I do in Sunday-class, and began to admonish him. But instead of listening, he got the skirt of my alpaca dress between his teeth and ground a great hole in it, swearing like a trooper betweenwhiles.

Oh, sister! that was a trying season! In less than three minutes the sidewalk was swarming with dirty-faced children. I might as well have been in a wasps' nest. The spiteful imps buzzed around me so—little girls, with lank hair falling over their eyes; lazy boys, swaggering like drunken men, and swearing like troopers; and a woman—the boy who smoked called her mother—who stood on a doorstep, with a hand on each hip, scolding like fury. I kept my finger up. They would not hear a word I said, but I felt it my duty to do that much, when a very gentlemanly man in blue regimentals touched my arm, and observed in the kindest way that things were getting so mixed and unpleasant perhaps I would permit him to escort me round the corner. You know, sister, I always had a power in the lift of my finger. It was wonderfully manifest just as this gentleman crossed the street, and must have astonished him, for the children hushed up at once, and huddled back to the doorstep like a flock of lambs, which was an evidence of moral suasion I take pride in reporting to the Society.

VI.

HE HAS COME.

SISTERS :—As a representative of your august body, I ought now to have been in an atmosphere of royalty —Imperial royalty, which counts at A No. 1, as kings are put down. The young potentate of all the Russias, with all his ships and things, ought to have been on hand a week ago; but he still lingers on the "rolling sea and briny deep," a prey, it is dreadfully to be feared, to sea-sickness—which, they tell me, is heart-rending—and storms which are liable to aggravate the sea-sickness.

I sympathize with that young man in all the depths of my feminine nature—which are getting bottomless from the great need of compassion which human life exhibits to the thinking mind. He ought to have been here when our enthusiasm was at its hottest point. Then he would have had the stormiest sort of a welcome. The soldiers were ready to file out any minute ; the mouths of ever so many cannon were burning to let off fire ; all the ships would have burst into a storm of flags at the first gun. People couldn't but just keep from shouting every time they met each other. But the young man didn't come. He hasn't come yet, and all the enthusiasm is burning down to cinders and ashes. When he does come, I'm afraid it'll be like putting a mess of apples into an oven after the pan of baked pork and beans has been drawn out—half roasted, and hard at the core when you cut 'em.

This is a great country, my friends—in fact, very extensive —but you can't wake it up to an earthquake of enthusiasm about the same person more than once. That prince had better have struck when the iron was red-hot. He didn't, and so I can't tell you anything about him, except that he isn't more at sea than the rest of us. When he does come, depend upon it, there will be an uprising among the females of this great city ; and foremost of her sex will be your representative, faithful to her trust, and ready, with a modest helping hand, to lead this young person into the paths of propriety.

He has come at last, but the bitter-sweet of hope and fear has been given us as daily food for two weeks past, and the wormwood of ceaseless apprehension took the place of the yellow berries, and nightshade darkness settled down upon us. Lovely young girls cried over their ball-dresses of illusion, and wondered if *their* hopes would thin off into the same slimpsy nothingness. Middle-aged ladies, whose hair needs no powder, and whose teeth never ache, began to falter in the dancing steps practised in the private recesses of their own palatial homes, and wondered if their joints were to be twisted and racked into new-born graces, only to settle down into rusty stiffness again without having fascinated the Russian soul out of that princely bosom.

Of course it is right and proper that an opportunity to study the antiquities of a nation should be offered to every potentate and prince that honors our Republican shores by setting his high-born foot upon them, and it is highly proper that first-class specimens should be in readiness the moment he enters a ball-room. That is what people tell me has always been the custom at balls given to princes, and it isn't likely that new rules are to be laid down for the benefit of a lot of girls, any-how. Governors and mayors are not often so young as they have been. As a general thing, their wives are not troubled with an epidemic of youth and beauty. It is an awful omission in the laws, but these dignified chaps can't get up young and dashing wives for the occasion, when a great high potentate from over seas shines down upon us in the dancing way. I haven't a doubt they would like to sacrifice themselves and astonish the world by so doing, but common people would be apt to call it bigamy. So they have to do the very best they can with such wives as they have got, and furbish them up with diamonds, laces, flounces, and a dancing-master, till they answer to begin with.

I don't mean to be hard or sarcastical on this subject, but in these times, when it is so easy for a man to put away his wife, couldn't this official potentate get a temporary divorce just for the occasion, especially if the kingly visitor happens to be young and very fond of dancing. It would give us young girls a chance.

Don't think that I am putting on airs, or that I don't feel reverential when age is mentioned, but Emperors' sons don't come to our free land of liberty every day, and girls are so plenty that old folks ought to stand back. Far be it from Phœmie Frost, on her own humble merits, to build upon opening that ball with the Imperial Duke of all the Russias; but a Society like ours has its social, moral, and scientific claims. As for literature, since my reports have been honored by publication, I must maintain the dignity of the position. If dignity and age is to lead in this grand ceremonial, I have kept school, and—well, yes—no, one could say that I—in fact, as to years, am I not competent to open the ball with any prince that can come across the ocean, be he boy or patriarch? There, that sentence is off my mind, and I can go on without a hitch of the pen.

In other respects I have been silently but surely preparing myself. The Society has been liberal, and most of my savings were in the bank, rolling up interest beautifully, when I came from my childhood's home. Then there was a handsome profit on the donation of eggs and butter and maple-sugar which came in the freight train before I started. I attended to the sale myself at the market, and had nothing to do with that Mr. Middleman people talk so awfully about as a cheat and a general grabber. Well, I dickered the things off at a good price, as I was a-saying, and have got the money safe in my bosom— a hiding-place sacred to myself alone.

Thus lifted above all mercenary anxieties, I gave my attention entirely to the self-improvement necessary to my appearance before his highness as a representative character on whom the eyes of all Sprucehill were fixed. I would say the world— only for the modest consciousness that comes over me when I think of myself as a genius.

VII.

THE FRENCH DRESS-MAKER.

ALPACA does make a first-class dress for our social gatherings and literary circles in Sprucehill, and when puffed out behind, and trimmed promiscuously with flutings, it sometimes has a sumptuous appearance elsewhere; but for a ball, in which one aims to dance with a great grand Archduke of all the Russias—excuse me for saying it, but alpaca is not quite the thing. Doubtful of my own imperfect judgment, I asked a fashionable dress-maker in the Third Avenue, who had "Madame" spelt with an E on her tin sign at the door, and she said: "It wasn't the thing for a lady entirely, by no manner of means," and her tongue had a rich roll to it, which satisfied me that Ireland had sympathized with France in her troubles, to the extent of getting the language a little mixed.

"No," says she, a leaning both elbows on her counter, and a looking at me from head to foot. "Madame should have a *robe de* silk, very complete, with flowers in her hair entirely, and an overskirt to the fore, garnitured with Limerick point."

"An overskirt before," says I, lifting both hands, satchel and all. "Why, every skirt that I've seen in the street, or anywhere else, was puckered and bunched up behind," says I. "Excuse me, but I really couldn't think of wearing 'em in any other way."

The French dress-maker—I know she was French by the letter E after Madam, and because the sign said she was from Paris. Well, she colored up, and looked every which way at first, but then she gave a skimping laugh, and said that I didn't understand French. I—I didn't understand French! I who had studied "French without a Master" as a speciality, with the most intelligent member of our circle, and conversed in the language as directed by that excellent book so fluently that the

pronunciation sounded almost like English nipped off a little !
This was too much.

The clear grit, which lies at the bottom of every New England woman's heart, riled up in mine when that cherished
accomplishment was cast into disrepute.

"Madame," says I, putting a keen emphasis on that E, " I
came here to inquire about the most fashionable way of making a dress, not to give or take a lesson in the languages. Permit me to say I never could submit to wear an overskirt in the
way you speak of—wrong side before—why, it would look dreadfully."

"But Madame does not understand; I speak English so
much in this country that my own language gets knocked into
smithereens. I beg pardon—into confusion. Madame must
be very perfect herself to detect it."

I felt a smile creeping over my lips. Really, sisters, I had
been too hard on the poor woman. It was not her fault if my
ear was so very correct that nothing but the purest accent could
satisfy me. She saw this look dawning upon my face, and I
knew that she felt relieved by the way her elbows settled down
on the counter again.

"If madame will take a chair—that is, repose herself.
Madame—"

"Excuse me," says I, benignly, for I didn't want to hurt
her feelings again. "*Mademoiselle*, if you please."

"Pardon me," says she, humbly.

"Just so," says I, benignly. "Now supposing we go on
about this ball-dress. How much silk will it take ? "

The woman sat and thought to herself ever so long. Then
she counted her fingers over once or twice. Then she said she
didn't exactly know how much, which is the way with dress-
makers all over the world, I do believe.

"But one won't buy a dress without knowing how much to
ask for," says I. "Say twelve yards now ? "

The woman lifted herself right off from the counter, and sat
staring at me.

"Twelve ! " says she, " eighteen at the least."

I felt as if some one had struck me. Eighteen yards for a dress, and gored all to pieces at that !

" Some of your dress-makers in Broadway would want more than that ! " says she, " and send for more and more after that."

I made no answer, but took up my satchel and walked straight out of the door.

Eighteen yards of silk for a dress! The thought of it kept me awake all night.

The next morning I went right up to the palatial residence of my cousin, Emily Elizabeth Dempster, feeling that she would expect me to enter on that subject about bringing up children, which was my duty ; but I was so down in the mouth about that dress, that everything like a moral idea had just swamped itself in those eighteen yards of silk ; and instead of giving advice, I went into that house to beg for it, feeling all the time as if somebody had dumped me down from a mighty high horse onto that stone doorstep, and left me to travel home afoot. In fact, I felt as if coming to that house to ask about ball-dresses, instead of giving instruction, was a mean sort of business. But the ambition of a great, worldly idea was burning in my bosom, and I resolved to press forward to the mark of the prize of the high calling.

Mercy on me ! it is a ball-dress, not a class-meeting, that I am writing about. Oh, my sisters ! is it true that black angels and white angels ever do get to fighting in a human soul, just as they do down South ? If so, they had a tussle in my bosom that morning, and the black fellow came out best, with a gorgeous silk dress a-floating and a-rustling out from his triumphant right hand, and the splendid shadow of a great Grand Duke following after.

Cousin Emily Elizabeth was just coming downstairs, flounced and puffed and tucked up about the waist, till she was all over in a flutter of silk, and lace, and black beads, with a dashing bonnet on her head high enough for a trooper's training-cap, all shivery with lace and bows, with one long feather curling half way round it, and a white tuft sticking up straight on the top, looking so 'cute and saucy.

Emily Elizabeth looked a little scared when she saw me coming in with my satchel; but when I told her what I wanted, her eyes brightened up, and she laughed as easy as a blackbird sings. "Oh, is that all!" says she. "I thought it was about the children. I'll give you a note to my dress-maker. Styles all French, and *so recherché.*" Look in the dictionary, sisters, and you will discover that this means something first-class.

She took out a pencil and a square piece of paper with her name printed on it, and wrote something French, with the number of a house, which I won't give, not wanting any of my friends to be talked out of a year's growth, as I was.

"There," says she. "The cream-on-cream all go to her. She'll fit you out splendidly. Leave it all to her. Good-morning, cousin; I must go; but my daughter is in the drawing-room—she will entertain you."

"Just so," says I, putting the card in my satchel, and making swift tracks for the out-door; "but I haven't time to be entertained."

VIII.

THE GENUINE MADAME.

ELL, I went straight down to that dress-maker's house, and handed the square paper cousin had written on to a lady who was fluttering round among a lot of girls, all hard at work sewing, like bumble-bees in a rose-bush.

She looked at the paper; then she gave my alpaca dress an overhauling with her scornful eyes. Then she began to talk; but, my goodness, her French was awful. I couldn't understand a word of it. Once in a while she would chuck an English word in, and rush on again like a mill-dam.

When I tried to put in a word of genuine French or pure English, she lifted her hands, hitched up her shoulders, and seemed as if she was swearing at me one minute and wanted to kiss me the next. I couldn't stand that.

"How much will you ask—how many yards will it take. *La pre la pre?*" says I, bursting into French.

The woman looked around on her girls, spread her hands as if praying for help, and then, all red in the face, *she* burst into English. Then I knew she did not understand her own native tongue, and gave her a sarcastic smile.

"I find everything. How many yards? Oh, that depends on the idea, the invention. I have it here growing in my brain. The price? Ah, I cannot tell. When the work is complete then we know. There will be crêpe and point—"

"But I don't want points," says I. "Talk in English if you don't understand your own language. The price, the price!"

"Oh, very well, it shall be to your own satisfaction—perfect," says she, and then the creature shook out her hands as if she was shewing chickens from a corn-crib, and before I could say another word she shewed me on to the steps and shut the door.

Well, I went back to my boarding-house, beat out and worried almost to death. Figures are satisfactory to the New England mind ; but when you have only a whirlpool of broken words, ending with satisfaction, with a woman's hands spread out on her bosom, and nothing more, it is tantalizing. But I reckon the figures will come by and by, only I *should* like to have an idea of what they will count up to.

As I was saying in the beginning of my report, ten thousand anxious female bosoms thrilled with expectations every night, and existence dragged wofully in literary and fashionable circles until that auspicious moment arrived when the son of an Imperial Emperor cast refulgence on our Western Hemisphere. But the waiting of us young girls was lonesome, very.

I had done my best. For the first time in my life I had

twisted my front hair into little wire tongs they call crimping-
pins; maybe it was their tightness that held my eyes so wide
open last night. I was trying with all my strength to shut
them, when the sound of a cannon, ever so far off, brought me
up in the bed, with my hand clasped and the heart in my
bosom trembling like a frightened chicken.

"He has come," says I to myself. "Alexis has come. To-
morrow we shall see him—handsome, young, filled with Imperial royalty from the crown of his noble head to the soles of
his patent-leather boots. But will he wear his crown in the
procession, or only keep it for the grand ball. What if he
should rest that crown on the head of some distinguished
American, selecting a literary lady?" This thought impressed
me; both hands went up to my lofty brow. Alas! they only
sent the crimping-pins ploughing across my head with a thorny
sharpness that filled my throat with screeches.

My dress has come home—I am stunned:

Thirty yards of silk, $10 per yard	$300.00
One piece French crape	25.00
Ten yards Brussels point	100.00
Linings	10.00
Making	50.00
Materials	35.00
Silk buttons	12.00
Passementerie, etc.	15.50
	$547.50

I have just recovered from a long fainting fit. They have
taken the crimping-pins out of my hair and deluged it with
crystal water. I am lying on my couch faint and exhausted.
Oh, my sisters, the paths of royalty are beautiful, but full of
thorns. That bill has been enough to destroy all my pleasure
in the visit of the Grand Duke Alexis.

IX.

READY TO LAND.

THE great Grand Duke of all the Russias has been thrown upon our shore by an upheaving of the mighty deep, and is now rocking at his ease in the iron-clad cradle of a great nation. Oh, he had a terrible time. Winds tossed him, storms pitched that noble vessel end foremost into the very bowels of the sea, then hove it up on great mountain waves, where it rocked and tottered and trembled, while the rain washed its decks—rendering mops useless—and the lightning got so tangled in the spars and rigging that you couldn't tell which was rope and which was fire.

Out of all this danger the great Grand Duke was blown upon our shore, with a good deal less fuss than Jonah had when he took to his life-boat with fins and tail, and discharged cargo on a desert shore, without the first chance of an imperial reception, and nothing but an upstart guard to offer him the hospitalities of the country.

Before daylight, Sunday morning, the vessel which bore that noble youth, all weather-beaten as a rusty potash kettle, but grand and majestic after its tussle with the storms, shot out her anchor in the lower bay—for New York has two bays, and two fine old rivers empty into them. The squadron—which means three or four other ships from Russia—had been waiting there till their great iron hearts nearly burst with fear that the imperial vessel had foundered; and when they saw it careering in amongst 'em, they set up a shout that made the very fishes in the bay rest on their fins and wonder what it could mean, for they had never heard Russians before, and it seemed as if the alphabet had been shaken ten thousand times over from as many pepper-boxes, and rained down on the water in one great shout.

Nobody has told me yet how his imperial dukeship took this,

and I haven't liked to inquire too closely. Supposing him asleep in the sweet privacy of his own upper berth, it wouldn't be quite proper, you know, but it must have been soul-stirring to hear those native syllables raining down blessings like tacks and brad-awls on his noble head.

How our imperial guest spent the Sabbath-day is a mystery that Russia and the Russians only can solve. But I am credibly informed that ten thousand upper-crust females betook themselves to secret devotions in their own rooms, in crimping-pins and curl papers, the moment we got news that he was here.

As for myself, I confess—no, our Society is not a confessional, and the secrets of a lady's get-up don't belong to a report for the public eye. So I say nothing on that point.

Sunday night I couldn't sleep a wink; my heart was full of noble aspirations, and it seemed as if some wild Indian of the forest had got his grip in my hair and might scalp me any minute, everything was twisted so tight in that direction. In fact, to say nothing of sleeping, I couldn't have winked to save my life. But I bore it with Christian fortitude, determined to press forward to the mark of the prize. Oh, dear! will I ever remember that this report isn't a class-meeting confession? Well, the morning came, and oh, my sisters, it was pouring cats and dogs. When I heard this, I rose up in bed, covered my face with both hands, and just boo-hooed out a crying. I knew well enough that ten thousand other young girls were weeping like the skies; but that only made me feel worse and worse, for mine has always been a sympathetic heart, and I felt for them—I did indeed.

I did not know what on earth to do. Cousin Emily Elizabeth Dempster had promised to come and take me down to the *Mary Powell*, a steamboat which the committee had engaged to take itself and all its wives and their friends, down to welcome the great Grand Duke, and bring him up to the city.

Cousin Emily Elizabeth's husband was a head cockalorum in this committee, which being the *crème on crème*—excuse French,

it will break in somehow in spite of me—well, which being the
crême on crême that had skimmed itself off from all the common milk of New York society, puffed Cousin E. E. up like—
like a ripe button-ball.

Since my reports have appeared in what the newspapers call
the world of letters—I say it modestly, but truth is truth—
Cousin E. E. has been sweet as maple-sugar to me, I can tell
you. She had her eye teeth cut in Vermont, and understood
that Queen Victoria knew there was one notch above the
crown when she took to writing books. I say nothing; but
there is an aristocracy that cuts its own way through all social
flummery, like an eagle among chippen birds. That is real live
genius; and if New England hasn't got her share of that, I
don't know where its head-quarters are.

Well, I and the clouds shed tears together for a good while;
then I started up. "What if it does pour?" says I to myself; "the Grand Duke has been in storms before this; he ain't
sugar nor salt, to melt at anything less than the glance of a
loving eye. What's the good of being down in the mouth
about a little rain? I'll get up—I'll unskewer my hair—I'll
put on *that dress,* if I die for it." I started out of bed; I
stood before the looking-glass; I began to untwist, to unroll;
I did the corkscrew movement; I jerked—I shook my hair
out—ripple, ripple, ripple, it fell over my shoulders. Then I
rested awhile, and winked my eyes with exquisite satisfaction—
for freedom is sweet both to the head and heart.

I felt like a new creature—a delicious looseness settled on
my temples—a feeling of feminine triumph swelled my soul.
Could he resist the fleecy softness of that hair—the thousand
ripples breaking up the sunshine—only there wasn't any sunshine to break. Not a silver thread was visible; if there had
been several the night before, it was nobody's business but my
own. My arms were tired with continual undoing; but, sisters,
am I one to faint by the way? No, no, a thousand times no.

I began to roll, to braid, to puff; I planted hair-pins in my
head as thick as bean-poles in a garden. Heavy braids—ex-

pensive but lovely—fell down the back of my head; fluff on fluff shaded my lofty forehead. I say nothing; but my literary success, great as it is, has not been more satisfactory than this.

I put on that dress in a great hurry, for Cousin E. E. was at the door in her carriage. How it glistened in the glass! How it swept out on the carpet, a peacock's tail is a trifle compared to it! I tucked it up; I turned the lining inside out, pinned it, puckered it round the waist, and then put on my new bonnet, which looked like a black beehive with a bird perched on the top. Then, with a burning heart, that fairly turned against it, I put on my waterproof cloak and pulled the hood over my poor bonnet.

I opened my cotton umbrella, and went down. Cousin E. E. was waiting, and a tall fellow in half regimentals held the door open. I jumped in as spry as a cricket, and away we went.

X.

DOWN THE BAY.

HE *Mary Powell* lay huddled up close to the wharf, with a great white flag crossed with blue stripes at one end, and the glorious old star-spangled banner at the other. In fact, she was all dressed out in flags. They were soaked through and through till their slimpsiness was distressing. In fact, the steamboat looked like a draggled rooster with no fence or cart to hide under.

The committee were all there, with a whole swarm of ladies in waterproof cloaks, huddled together like chickens in a coop. There were generals, too, with gold epaulets on their shoulders: one that I'd heard of in the war, General McDowell, and some others, that lighted up the deck a little with their gold lace and sword-handles.

She moved—I mean the *Mary Powell.* The sea was gray, the sky was black. Now and then I saw a flag fluttering by on some vessel, like a poor frightened bird searching for shelter, and pitied it. Then all at once bang went a gun. I hopped right up, and screamed out:

" What's that ? "

" The salute," says a gentleman close by me. " A salute for the Grand Duke."

I sat down astonished.

" Sir," says I, " I can't believe it. I—I've been saluted myself before this, and I know what it is. No human lips could have made that noise."

The man looked at me, and puckered up his lips a trifle, as if he were trying to choke back a laugh.

" I'm speaking of guns," says he, " not the sweet little salutes in your mind."

" Oh," says I, " that makes a difference, though I never heard firing off guns by that name before."

" The Grand Duke will have twenty-two of 'em," says he.

" Well, then, I'm' glad it's only the guns," says I, and a great big sigh of relief came up from my jealous bosom.

Then we all went on again, till I heard some one call out that we'd got to heave-to. This scared me dreadfully. I looked around. Which two of all these females did they mean to heave into the vasty deep ? Not me for one. If Russia is barbarous enough to want that sort of cannibal hospitality, I'm counted out.

Shivering with fear, I drew back into the crowd, but watched things like a cat. Drifting through the fog, I saw a little vessel coming close to us, as if she had something to do with this heathen ceremony. The ladies in their waterproofs crowded to the side of the steamboat, as if they rather panted for the glory of being drowned then and there for the pleasure of the great Grand Duke.

I heard a splash, but could not see if any one had been flung over, and when I got up to look, there was a magnificent old fellow, with ribbons in his coat and brooches set thick with shining stones on his bosom, a-coming up the side of the boat. He looks so proud and puffy, that I should have took him for the great Grand Duke, only that he wasn't near young enough.

"Who is it?" says I to the old gentleman.

"Catacazy," says he.

"Cat—what?" says I, categorically.

"Catacazy, the Russian Minister," says he.

"Minister," says I; "do they mean to get up a prayer-meeting on board?"

The old gentleman simmered down the laugh that was on his lips into a smile, and said he thought not.

This pacified me, and I sat still while we went down through the upper bay, which seemed wrapped in waterproofs too, and into the lower bay, which heaved and rolled as if it was half-choked up with sweltering wet blankets. Then we came in sight of the ships, and saw the flags a-battling with the storm; but no one on board seemed to care a continental cent whether New York sent out her *crême on crême* or not. This silence made my heart sink.

Then the minister went to the side of the vessel, leaned over, and swung his hat. By and by a boat came from the great Grand Duke's vessel, in which an imperial-looking man stood upright, like a high-born monarch, and lifted his cap as if it had been a crown.

"It is—it is—oh, yes, it is the Duke!"

This was on every lip but mine. I could not speak; exquisite emotion forbade it.

No one came on board; but the minister with that catish name got into the boat, and then some of the committee, which skimmed itself again, and thickened up its cream considerably.

There we waited and waited.

They came back at last. That young gentleman was not the great Grand Duke. He wasn't coming till next day.

Oh, how we wilted! Some of us almost burst out a-crying. I did not speak; I could not. Ever since we reached the lower bay, I had felt dreadfully discouraged; now a strange sinking of the heart seized upon me—a faint dizziness, an agony of disappointment seemed raging in my stomach. Oh, my sisters! these exquisite sensibilities are a proof of greatness, I know, but the sufferings they bring, no human being but the creature of genius can tell.

I am better. The glorious sight which followed that stormy day has relieved me. I have seen ten thousand flags blazing along Broadway—I have seen three times ten thousand republican worshippers waving their hats and handkerchiefs in acclamations for the son of an imperial despot. I have heard the glorious music of an imperial serenade—I have seen HIM.

XI.

THE GRAND DUKE.

SISTERS:—I have seen him. This hand has been pressed—significantly pressed—by the soft, rosy palm of imperial royalty. If a tablet to my memory should ever be sunk in the walls of our meeting-house, I charge you, dear sisters in the cause, to have this honor cut in Roman capitals deep into the marble; for what is an exaltation to me is glory to the Society, and, in fact, to all Vermont.

I have been on the same steamboat with the great Grand Duke; his splendid blue eyes have looked into mine, and in that glance we grappled each other, soul to soul. He has smiled upon me through the yellow glory of that silky mustache, under which his plump, red lips shone like cherries, ripe enough to swallow, stones and all. He speaks English; reveres genius, and knows that it can never grow old.

I saw him in Broadway, when all the New York militia turned out, which was a training day worth looking at. A snow-storm of handkerchiefs burst out of the windows; ten thousand female hands waved him forward. Shouts rose from the multitude; little children were crowded back into the gutters; women were jammed together on doorsteps and curbstones. In fact, the skim milk of society was compelled to flow in awful narrow channels, while the *crême on crême*—excuse French once more—rolled smoothly through the city in carriages, with royalty leading the way, a regiment of trainers leading him, and a band of music leading the whole..

I saw the whole glorious procession. From block to block I flitted, like some aspiring bird on the crest of a wave. My heart was full, my eyes fixed on one object—that tall, noble figure, with a blue watered silk scarf across his royal bosom, and a half-moon hat, with dipping points, gracefully lifted from his head. He must have been dazzled; he must have been impressed by this proof that republics scorn monarchies and trample them under foot.

I flitted onward through the crowd, waving my handkerchief from a doorstep now and then. That handkerchief the idol of this august occasion seemed to follow eagerly with his eyes, as a sort of beacon light which kindred sympathy impelled him to recognize, for wherever I went he lifted that half-moon hat from his royal brow and smiled. I felt this compliment to the depths of my soul—it thrilled me.

When I lifted myself out of the skim milk, and flowed in with the cream of cream on that stand in Union Square with my cousin and the *élite* of society, he saw me again and recognized me once more, which irritated my cousin's jealousy a little, for she insisted that he lifted his black half-moon to the whole of us. But I know!

I watched the carriage that bore him with a blushing cheek and a beating heart. There was General Dix, a real nice-looking old gentleman, sitting in front of him; there was Catacazy, the ambassador of all Russia, also a nice gentleman as you want to see, with *his* hat off, a-bowing and a-bowing. We flung up our handkerchiefs—we clapped our hands.

The Clarendon Hotel stands near one corner of the Union Square; it has a skimpy piazza in front made of iron, and I've seen bigger hotels anyhow. But it is considered tip-top, and is always brimming over with the cream of cream. That is why Mr. Catacazy took my Grand Duke there. There was such a crowd of folks and trainers that I lost sight of him. By and by out he came into the piazza, and stood right before our aristocratic stand, which was fringed round with red cloth, and over which the star-spangled banner waved itself meekly to the nest of black eagles that streamed out over that noble scion of all the Russias.

I could not see *him* plainly, as my heart panted to, so I borrowed my cousin's glass—a little spy-glass, understand—not specs, which I haven't come to by a long way. Well, I unscrewed the eye-glass, wound it up to the right notch, and brought him almost to my face; and there I stood, choke-full of heavenly satisfaction, all the while *he* looked down on the general training of soldiers that marched stream on stream between him and me.

While my soul was going out luminously through these eyes, Cousin Emma Elizabeth Dempster touched my elbow, and says she :

"Miss Frost, if you've got through with my glass, I should like to try it a little."

I gave it up. Not being long-sighted, the whole pageant was a blank to me after that cruel deprivation, for I could no longer see that imperial figure on the piazza.

My reports are making a tremendous sensation, and I—well, being modest by nature, I say nothing, but a committee, skimmed daintily off from the cream of cream, called at my boarding-house, and wanted me, as a rising star in the literary hemisphere of writers, to invite the great Grand Duke to a private reception, or entertainment, or something, where some that hadn't been on the steamboat could shake hands with him, and others might just touch the extremity of his coat, which they gave me their honor they wouldn't pull—as some high-bred ladies did when he was going from the boat.

I received this committee with dignity, and promised to take their request into mature consideration, as soon as I could learn personally from the great Grand Duke whether he should prefer to have this homage paid by my own sex to the extremities of his coat, or not. I felt for these young ladies. I had experienced the yearning desire that possessed them, and knew how truly irrepressible it was. Had it not inspired the whole committee of reception, their wives, and their children to the third generation? Had it not disturbed fashionable life to its very dregs, and given spice to our weekly literature? Yes, I felt for these young persons, and in a little speech, remarkable for its graceful elocution, gave them encouragement.

XII.

TICKETS FOR THE BALL.

ICKETS for the ball! Sent, no doubt, at the Grand Duke's request. Cousin Emily Elizabeth has got tickets too. We shall go together in the same carriage, and leaning on her husband's arm. Dempster is a handsome man, and really *distingué* looking. Excuse French; an educated person will break into it now and then.

The day has come. Cousin Emily has just sent me a bundle of things, with her compliments—a little box with a cake of lovely white chalk in it; another, smaller yet, filled with a pink powder that looks like ground rose-leaves, and a bottle with something liquid and dark in it, which does not seem as if it was good to drink. What on earth does Cousin E. E. expect me to do with these things?

Ah! pinned to the bundle, I find a letter, beginning " Dear

Cousin Phœmie," and asking me to excuse her, but she sends the things, thinking that I may want to rejuvenate, and perhaps dye, before I go to the ball.

Rejuvenate! Does she mean to say that I'm not young enough? and if I wasn't, how are these things a-going to help me? I know that girls in school sometimes eat chalk and chew gum, but never heard that they got the younger for it. Then the pink powder—well, it's no use calculating about it, especially as she wants me to die after it. I wish Cousin E. E. would ever learn to spell. When a woman dies she does not do it with a " y " as a general thing.

Now what *does* all this mean?

I was doing my hair at the looking-glass, when Cousin E. E. came in, looking like a queen; her blue silk dress was all spotted with gold flowers, and it streamed out half across my bedroom. Over that she wore a long white cloak, with tassels to it, and her hair was looped in with pink roses that were not redder than her cheeks, which would have satisfied me that her health was first-rate, if it hadn't been for the shadows that lay around her eyes, which had grown awfully dark since I saw her at home.

" Oh! " says she, " I am just in time. Came early, thinking you might want help. Sit down; that will do. Now where is the you-know-what—those boxes—you understand? "

Here E. E. flung off her cloak and came to the glass. I declare to you the creature's neck was white as any snow-drift but uncovered to an extent that frightened me out of a week's growth. Her arms, too, were the same, and bare as her neck. She had a narrow pink shoulder-strap, and some lace between them, and that was all; only a string of white stones, that shone like a rainbow now and then, was around her neck and one arm; two or three of the same kind of stones hung down from her ears, and shot out light from her hair.

The whiteness of that neck astonished me, and made me look every which way.

E. E. didn't seem to mind that, but took off her long white

gloves and laid them on the table; then she snatched up one of the boxes, and began to rub a handkerchief that lay on the bureau in it.

"There now; hold back your head a little," says she; "shut your eyes."

Here she began to rub my face and neck and arms with the handkerchief till they looked white as her own. Then she changed boxes, and I could feel her making soft dabs at my cheeks, which tickled a little.

"Now open your eyes," says she.

I opened them wide, she astonished me so; and, as true as you live, she began to tickle them with a tenty-tointy brush. After that she titivated my hair a little, washed her hands with some Cologne water, and snatching up my pink silk dress, which lay across the bed, just buried me in it. I declare it was scrumptious to feel the silk a-rustling round me, and a-settling down on the floor, wave on wave. Well, the bill was a damper, but I couldn't help enjoying it for all that.

"Now," says E. E., a-drawing on her long, white gloves, "just take a look, and let us be off—Dempster is waiting."

I did take a look, right straight in the glass, and couldn't help doing it again and again, the lady I saw there seemed so much like a magnificent stranger to me—so white, so blooming —so—. Forgive me, sisters—I forgot that modesty is a tender blossom that should be encouraged—and I will say no more, only this, Cousin Dempster's neck had a good deal more of it than mine, and that French dress-maker had given me a little chance of sleeves, while her's left them out altogether.

When she spread out my skirt, it half covered the room. All at once she saw just one little spot of rain on it, and held up both her hands.

"Why, you haven't worn this before? Good gracious! no lady in our set ever wears the same dress twice. The idea!"

I felt myself wilting, for she was sarcastic in her speech. Then I up and spoke for myself.

"Yes, I wore it once," says I; "but it was tucked up under

my waterproof cloak, with the lining turned inside out, and nobody saw it—especially the great Grand Duke, who didn't come out of his own vessel."

"Oh," says she, "then it won't be an absolute disgrace to the family if you wear it. I began to be afraid to go with you. There, now, don't look pins and needles at me, but just put something round you, and let us be off, or *he* will be there before us."

That was enough. I huddled up that pink silk in my arms, and in less than two minutes Cousin Dempster's carriage was so choke full of his wife and me, that he took a seat with the driver.

XIII.

THE GRAND DUKE'S BALL.

OH, my! wasn't that ball-room a sight to see? Seats piled on seats, all cushioned with red velvet, and one end curving round like a great red horseshoe, with flags and flowers and shields running below the bottommost tier; a great swinging balloon of sparkling glass poured its light, like July sunshine, down on a crowd of people, that looked more like born angels than human creatures. It fairly made me dizzy to look at 'em from Cousin Dempster's box-seat, which was right in the end of the circle.

After a while I got my senses back, and looked out for *him*. He wasn't there yet, and that gave me a chance to see things. Four more heaps of glass, that seemed as if they had caught fire, hung in the other end of the room, and beyond them was a fountain of water, a-sparkling and a-flashing and a-tinkling in a make-believe garden by moonlight, with live fish swimming in it, and live flowers blooming in piles and heaps around it, and make-believe trees. Half running round the room was a lot of marble posts, with white flower-pots running over with sweetness, and linked together with running vines, that made you feel yourself almost out of doors.

All this was splendid; but there was one spot that everybody looked towards, and I most of all.   Three boxes, cushioned with red velvet, were just chained together with great wreaths of flowers such as I never saw in a garden; but I knew they were genuine because of the scent, which was delicious.   Banners set full of stars and stripes of red and white silk, all tangled in with flowers, hung over these boxes, and right in the centre streamed a white silk banner, on which our old bald eagle and the black eagles of all the Russias flocked together as sociable as robins in a nest.

"There he is !   There he is!"

I started.   I caught my breath, for back of the white flag *he* stood with the light a-shining on his beautiful yellow hair, and a smile on his lips.   Oh, how grand, how tall, how gorgeous ! Everybody was a-looking at him.   The girls around me—always forward, and *so* silly—began twittering together, and looking that way as if he would ever think of dancing with them.   They swarmed around me, as a representative person. They forgot their own trivialities, and rendered me such homage as genius commands from commonplace minds.

"You are an author," said they.   "You belong to the great aristocracy of the world.   Speak for us.   He cannot dance with all of us, but he can look this way through his opera-glass, and give us all a chance of being put in the papers as the beautiful young lady he admired so much.   We appoint you a committee of one.   Address him in our behalf.   Get some memento of him that we may leave to future generations."

The entreaties of these young creatures went to my heart.   I raised my forefinger, which was like an oath to them, and says I:

"Thanks for this honor.   Like a Roman matron I will do my duty.   Wait."

I arose from my seat, and swept, with a dignity and grace

that must have done the Society I represent great honor, around the gallery, and found my way into the private retiring-room of our illustrious guest. It was small but beautifully furnished. My pink silk, as it trailed in, seemed to fill the whole room. In the looking-glass I saw a figure, tall, commanding; I may say queenly—but enough of that.

A person stood near the door and looked in. I lifted my finger; he approached.

"Go," says I, "to the great Grand Duke of all the Russias, and tell him that Miss Phœmie Frost, a committee lady, awaits his presence here."

He started—he smiled—he went.

I drew back and stood against the wall opposite the door. *He* entered, looking a little puzzled. I advanced one foot, then the other, three long paces, as queens do when they act on the stage. Then I sunk down in a profound curtsey, wound myself up again into a royal position, and held out my right hand.

"Great Grand Duke Alexis," says I, "son of an illustrious father and an imperial mother, whom all women love to honor, - welcome to our shores—welcome to the fashion, genius, and beauty embodied in the females of America."

Before I could finish the address to which duty and ever-burning genius inspired me, the great Grand Duke quenched my ardor by a heavenly smile that danced in his blue eyes, and almost broke into a laugh on his red lips. His voice was like over-ripe strawberries when he spoke and said: "The ladies did him great honor; he had not English to express his pleasure, and no power to repay their kindness." This was my time.

"Being the head of a committee of so many young ladies that it is impossible for your Imperial Majesty to dance with the whole, I—that is, these ladies—wish to be represented in the festive cotillon by a person worthy of the occasion. Not the wife of an American potentate, who may or may not have any claims of her own, but a potentate in herself. Not crowned with the shadow of a man's laurels, but wearing her own bay leaves as Tasso did."

Here I felt my eyes a-drooping, and my tall figure bent like a weeping willow. The great Grand Duke saw my confusion, and his smile deepened audibly.

" Say to the lovely committee of ladies," says he—

But I interrupted him, and putting one hand on my heart, observed, with a gentle bow:

" Embodied in me."

Then he smiled out loud again, and says he:

" If the Committee of Arrangement permit, I shall have much pleasure."

With that he bowed and prepared to go out. I drew back toward the wall till the pink silk skirt began to tangle up my feet, and kept my eyes lifted to his face, which was still bathed in blushing smiles. Another step, a low curtsey, and I lifted myself up with dignity while he passed through the door.

I was alone, with nothing but the looking-glass to gaze on my delight. The young ladies had begged of me for a memento of royalty. I looked around. An ivory-handled hair-brush lay on a marble shelf under the glass. I seized upon it, knowing that it had touched his head. I examined it. Imagine my joy—six bright yellow-brown hairs clung to the bristles! Carefully, daintily I picked them out, and, laying them in the palm of my white glove, formed a tiny tress of them—tiny, but oh ! how exquisitely precious !

With this treasure in my hand I went back to my constituency. They crowded round me ; sparkling eyes gazed upon the glorious prize I had secured ; cherry lips kissed it with gushing fervor, and pleaded with me for just a morsel. I secured one lovely hair for myself, and, cutting the rest into tiny bits, distributed them generously. Oh, sisters ! this act endowed me with wonderful popularity among my young companions. We girls should be generous to each other. I was generous, and an orchard full of spring robins could not have chirped more happily than they did while flocking around me. But the dancing began. I stood ready, with my long pink silk skirt gathered half way from the floor. But all at once it dropped from my hand—*he* was on the floor, and another lady clung to his arm. The jealousy of that committee of gentlemen had prevailed. He danced with the Governor's wife.

Did I stand ready to play second fiddle to her? No, no! a thousand times no! Was I not a New England lady? Did I not feel that the literature of the country had its eyes upon me? *He* couldn't help it; the deploring glance that he cast upon me was enough to satisfy me of that. Indeed, his feelings were so hurt that he really could not go · through the figures of the cotillon, but kept dancing every which way, like a man torn with distractions. My heart ached for him. I could not bear to see his distress, and retired with dignity to my seat upstairs and looked on, while my proud New England heart burned with indignation. If I live, that committee of gentlemen shall hear from me again.

XIV.

THE NATURAL HISTORY PHILANTHROPIST.

SISTERS:—He has gone! The luminous star that has shone upon us with such refulgence for the last few weeks, has gone to our beloved " Hub of the Universe," where poets, governors, and other distinguished men of New England are now revolving around him like the spokes of a cart wheel. Mr. Holmes has written him some sweet verses; Mr. Longfellow has greeted him with welcomes. They have given him balls, dinners, and a cold in his face. In short, New England has been true to itself and its climate. When the hub turns on its axle, the spokes whirl and the tires revolve, giving a swift throb to the whole universe. As a New England woman—I beg pardon—young lady, I am proud of Boston, proud of the honor they are doing to *Him*. But after all, the Hub must imitate. We took the crown off.

Before he left, a new and exquisite idea came into my head —some people may think it a little flighty, but you will understand all the poetry it contains. I have a canary bird—for I love birds with all the inborn intensity of genius—so old that his feathers are nothing more than a creamy white. In that particular he—I should say she—being a female, that never sings beyond a chirp, has the gift of silence peculiar to the sex. I got her cheaper on that account. Well, she is almost dove-like in color and in sweetness of disposition. No more lovely messenger from heart to heart could be found in the whole world.

Well, sisters, I took this bird from its cage with my own hands, and I smothered it with kisses from my own lips, which quivered with intensity of emotion. Then I tied a blue ribbon about its neck, and attached to that a tenty-tointy note which contained these lines :

> Farewell, noble prince, my fond heart is gushing
>   With thoughts that no language can ever reveal ;
> With the sweetest affection this warm cheek is blushing,
>   And hopes to my maidenly bosom will steal,
> Of a time when our souls, with united expression,
>   Shall mingle with harmony more than divine ;
> And the priest—be he Greek, or of any profession—
>   Shall bless this poor hand as it clings unto thine.

The paper was of an exquisite rose-color on which I indited this gem. I flatter myself that genius can sometimes write beautifully. It is not just the thing to particularize here, but if that Grand Duke *can* read English he must have admired the sweet morsel which that lovely songster bore to him on the wings—well, of a canary.

I would not send my bird in a cage, because handsome cages are expensive, and do not carry an idea of freedom with them, which our spread eagle might have led the great Grand Duke to expect. Neither would I trust her with a street boy whose hands might be dirty and unsafe. No, I put on my bonnet, locked the bird with his blue ribbon in a box covered with gilt paper, and walked straight down to the Clarendon Tavern, and asked for one of the committee-men.

A tall, grave-looking gentleman came into the room, where I sat waiting, and said he was Mr. Bergh, one of the committee-men, and then stood a minute, as if he was waiting to know what I wanted.

I had heard a great deal about the gentleman's goodness to the poor dumb beasts that are so abused and trampled on, and my heart rose right into my mouth.

" Mr. Bergh," says I, reaching out my hand, " in the name of New England, permit me to shake hands, and thank you for the good you are a-doing to so many of God's own creatures."

The gentleman smiled, and reached out his hand.

" I am glad to hear," says I, " that some old bachelor has left a lot of money to your society. It is just what I would do myself if I hadn't a hope—that is, it may be possible that all the money I have will be needed for a special occasion—as no free-born New England woman would be beholden to a foreign nation for her setting out.

Here Mr. Bergh smiled. You have no idea how much younger he looked when he did smile ; the benevolence that made him a Natural History Philanthropist just shone out from his eyes, and beamed all over his face, till I longed to be—well, say a duck, or something of that sort—that he might save me from oppression.

" Thank you," says he ; " most men want some object in life. You ladies have done so much for humanity that we are content to leave it in your hands, but the poor animals have up to this time escaped compassion."

" Not compassion, but assistance," says I. " Cruelty to animals is mostly confined to men."

" Not exactly," says he. " I have sometimes seen kittens

and pet dogs treated more unmercifully than omnibus-horses, and by innocent children too."

I did not answer. How could I? The remembrance of a trout-brook, with birch-trees hanging over it, and great red-seeded brake-leaves growing thick on the bank, made me shudder. Hadn't I held ever so many kittens under water in that very spot, and shouted and laughed to the other girls—some of you, my sisters, among them—while the poor little things kicked and struggled for life, that was just as dear to them as it is to me? Hadn't I hunted up birds' nests, and driven the pretty creatures distracted by handling their eggs, till at last the nests were broken up? Then didn't I string the cold eggs into a chain, and hang them in triumph over the looking-glass in our keeping-room?

You will tell me, out of the kindness of your hearts, that these were sins of ignorance. Just so; and it is this ignorance, which is sometimes cruel as the grave, that Mr. Bergh is trying his best to enlighten. No child would do a cruel thing if it were made to understand the pain it is giving. Yet, sticking pins through flies, and spearing wasps to the wall, are about the first thing a smart baby learns to do.

Did you ever see a lot of boys going home from school, when a garter-snake, or any other harmless serpent, crosses their path? They know well enough that the poor things do no harm, and are as afraid as death of them; but see the great stones they heave upon the miserable reptile; the shouts they send up, as it writhes, and coils, and fills the air with feeble hisses, trying, poor thing, to save its bruised and broken life to the last.

Does anybody tell the boys that this is brutal cruelty? No, even the Christian mother, who would not do an unkind thing to save her life, forgets that God makes snakes as well as ring-doves, and that pain is just as bitter to the snake as to the cooing bird.

Sisters, we are all wrong in leaving these things to men only. If we did our duty, and taught little children that even thoughtless cruelty is a sin, and that the fun which comes out of pain to any of God's creatures is a crime, there would not be much for Mr. Bergh and his noble society to do. The cruel instincts of a child become ferocious in the man. With such, men can best deal. I thank God that one brave spirit is found ready and able to protect the dumb creatures that are given us for blessings, not for victims.

. While I am writing this, picture after picture comes up from my own past girlhood, and my heart stands still as I remember how ferocious a thirst for fun and ignorance can be in a child. How many sleepy-looking toads I have seen, with their backs all jewels, and their throats yellow gold, that asked nothing but a burdock leaf for shelter, and a few flies for food, crushed to death by boys who thought no harm, and only liked the sport of killing something.

Since then, I have learned that these little creatures are a great help to gardeners, and that wise men foster them with kindness and care.

Once, down by the trout-brook we know of, I saw a lot of children, busy as bees, doing something on the bank, where two or three boys were kneeling, and the rest looking on. Of course I went down to the brook, and, being a little mite of a creature, looked on, half frightened, half wondering.

The boys had caught a great frog, green as grass. He was, I have no doubt, one of those hoarse old croakers, that make one timid about going by ponds and marshy ground in the night, up in our State. Well, they had him down in the grass, and one held him while the other ran a pin through both jaws and twisted it there. There was no fun in this. A lot of doctors cutting off an arm couldn't have been more gravely in earnest. Some of the boys were eight and ten years old; but not one of them seemed to feel that they were doing a hideous thing. I remember feeling very sorry for the poor frog, but it was not till years and years after that I understood the horrible, lingering death these ignorant boys had tortured him with.   Since then I have never thought of that sparkling trout stream, without a pain at my heart.

"Childish ignorance," I hear you say—for some of these boys were your own brothers, and meant no harm.   But what right had they to be ignorant?   They knew well enough that it was against the law to kill one another.   Why were they not taught that the life that God gives to His meanest creature is as sacred as a good man's prayers; unless necessity calls for it, and then it must be taken with as little suffering as death can give?

Sisters, I am in earnest; the missionary spirit is strong upon me.   I wish our Society to take up this subject with interest.   What Mr. Bergh has been doing among men, we must do among the children of this generation.   When ignorance is an excuse for cruelty, you and I and every woman of the land are wretches if we allow a child to sin because it knows no better.   There is no great study necessary to work out a reform here.   The mother who knows what is right knows how to impress it on her children; and if they play at death and destruction, she is the person most to blame.

Don't say that I am writing out one of my popular addresses before the Society—I never thought of such a thing; but when I saw the great Natural History Philanthropist, my heart and mind went right back to you and my duties as a missionary of universal progress, and I sat there in silence thinking over these things till I forgot that he was there.

At last he spoke, and said, kindly enough, "Is there anything I can help you in?"

I started and reached out my hand.

"Mr. Bergh," says I, enthusiastically, "I can help you! All the world over we women work best in the primary department.   You have begun a grand and a noble work among men.   We will begin at the other end, and in that way cut your work down to nothing.   I see a clear path before us. Henceforth I will belong to your Society, and you shall belong to mine.   Is it agreed?"

He sat down by me; his eyes grew bright; his earnestness of purpose inspired me to press forward to the mark of the prize —I beg pardon, the old prayer-meeting spirit will manifest itself in spite of me when my soul is full of a great purpose.

After we had talked on the great subject satisfactorily, he said, all at once, "But you came for some purpose in which I may have the pleasure of serving you."

Then I remembered my bird and its imperial object. Revealing my gold-paper box, I opened it carefully, fearing a sudden flight. Nothing moved. Trembling with dread, I put in my hand; it touched a soft fluff of feathers that did not stir.

My heart sank like a lead weight in my bosom. I looked in; the poor little thing lay in the bottom of the box, with its wings spread out, and its head lying sideways. I touched it with my hand; it was limp and dead. While I had been talking with so much feeling about cruelty to animals, my own little songster—no, being a female she was not that—but my poor pet had been smothered to death in that gorgeous little receptacle.

With my heart swelling like a puff-ball, I turned my shoulder on that good man, and closed my satchel solemnly, as if it had been a tomb.

"Sir," says I, in a voice full of touching penitence, "I feel myself just at this minute wholly unworthy of the mark of the high calling to which I have offered myself. A young lady who puts herself forward to teach thoughtful kindness to the young, should be above reproach in that respect herself."

The good gentleman looked awfully puzzled, for how would he guess at the crime I had locked up in that box?

"Good-morning," says I, walking away; "the time may come when I shall feel a new exaltation, but just now—well, good-morning."

I went away meek and humble as a pussy cat. When I looked down at the box in my hand it seemed as if I was carrying a coffin.

Well, I buried my poor little pet in that identical box, with

4

the blue ribbon about its neck; but the poem I forwarded to *him* in Boston. I may be meek and humbly conscious of my own shortcomings, but the Grand Duke of all the Russias shall never go home with the idea that Vermont hasn't got poets as well as Boston, and that young ladies cannot put as much vim and likewise maple-sugar into their poetry as that smart fellow, Dr. Holmes, simmered down in his.

Just read mine and his, that's all!

I do think that nothing can equal the forwardness of some New York girls. Would you believe it, one stuck-up thing has just stolen my beautiful idea, and sent her card to the great Grand Duke tied round a bird's neck; but it was like stealing a fiddle and forgetting the fiddlestick. A card isn't poetry. There is no accounting for the vanity of some people; but the best proof of genius is imitation.

XV.

CHRISTMAS IN NEW YORK.

DEAR SISTERS:—Thanksgiving is the great Yankee jubilee of New England. Then every living thing makes itself happy, except the turkeys, and geese, and chickens. They, poor martyrs, have been scared into the middle of next week by the yells, and shrieks, and awful cackling of the whole army of winged creatures that sit in ten thousand ovens, with their legs tied, their wings twisted, and the gravy a-dripping down their sides and bosoms, like rain from the eaves of a house. Of course, for that day, every barn-yard in New England goes into mourning. The poor hen is afraid to cackle when she lays an egg, for fear of having a gun cracked at her. Even the fat hogs look melancholy in their pens, for a smell of roasting spare-ribs comes over them, and they seem to

ruminate mournfully on some means of saving their own ba-
con.

Of course, there must be some unhappiness even on a New
England Thanksgiving, or earth would forget itself and turn
into heaven all at once. Besides, who thinks of the scared
goblers, when he has a plump turkey roasted brown as a berry,
scenting the whole house with richness? I for one could not
bring myself to the foul contemplation—excuse the wit—spon-
taneity is perhaps my fault.

Well, what Thanksgiving is to New England, Christmas-day
is to New York. Everybody goes to meeting in the morning,
and everybody takes dinner with everybody else after that.
For days before it comes the streets are full of covered wagons,
and men and boys, loaded down with bundles, crowd against
each other on every doorstep. In fact, half New York just
throws itself away in presents on the other half, which pitches
just as many back. Thus every street and house is a hubbub
of gifts and a blaze of light, from Christmas Eve till after
Christmas dinner.

Christmas Eve, dear sisters, belongs to the children. What
there is of 'em in these parts, and the jubilation they have, rich
and poor, black and white, is enough to warm the heart in
one's bosom. There is a gorgeous old Dutch ghost that they
think comes prowling over roofs and down chimneys in the
night, to bring them presents. This comical old fellow sets up
Christmas trees for the rich, and fills woollen stockings for the
poor, and makes himself a magnificent old humbug that every
child in the city worships and will believe in, though the little
misguided souls know at the bottom of their hearts that, somehow or another, this Santa Cláus and their own parents have a
mysterious understanding and private moneyed transactions,
that mix things terribly. Still, they really do believe in the old
fellow, just as you and I believe in dreams. It is the last
thing a little girl gives up, unless it is her dolls.

Speaking of dolls, I wish you could see the scrumptious little ladies that have been sold here this week. You and I were

awful proud if we could get a rag-baby, with drops of ink for
eyes, and its cheeks reddened with a little pokeberry juice;
but the dolls they sell here are such beauties!—yellow hair,
frizzed around the face like thistle-down; rosy cheeks, and eyes
that shut with such sweet laziness if you lay the little things
down. I declare, it's enough to make one long to be a child
again, to take one of these dainty creatures in your arms.

The Saturday before Christmas I went out with Cousin E. E.
Dempster, to buy presents. She came in her carriage, with the
driver and another chap in regimentals on the front seat, outside, and a great white bear-skin inside that just swallowed us
up to the waist, as if we had settled down in a snow-bank of
fur. Under that was a muff for your feet, and some contriv-
ance that must have been a foot-stove hid away, for it was as
warm as toast.

Well, sisters, such things may be extravagant, I know; but
they are nice, if it wasn't for one's conscience.

The carriage turned down Broadway, which is the street
where the most splendid stores are found. It really was worth
while to see how that driver—with his fur gloves that made
his hands look like a bear's claw—guided them horses in and
out, among the omnibus-stages, the carriages, and carts, that
just turned the street into Bedlam. It fairly made me catch
my breath to see how near the wheel would come to some
other wheel, and then just miss it. Every stage that went
lumbering by made me give a little scream, it came so near to
running us down. But Cousin E. E. sat there buried in the
white fur, as cosey as a goose on her nest. It aggravated me,
and I asked her if she wasn't afraid nor nothing.

"Oh no," says she, a-leaning back and half shutting her
eyes; "it is the coachman's business. I should discharge him
if anything happened."

"But you couldn't discharge him after you were mashed to
death under them great omnibus wheels," says I.

E. E. smiled. What a calm, lazy smile she has!

"No," says she; "but there would be a fuss, and my name

would get into the paper. Everything has its compensation, Cousin Frost."

Before I could answer, the carriage stopped in front of a large, high store, with great, tall windows, all one shiny sheet of glass on each side of the door, through which you could see lots on lots of silver and gold and precious stones, all in confusion, but, oh, how gorgeous !

"This is Ball, Black & Co.'s," says she, a-going up to the door, which seemed to open of itself, and in we went.

You have read the "Arabian Nights' Entertainment." I remember the time well, because we all got "kept in" after school for being caught at it. Well, that cave wasn't to be compared to what I saw in Messrs. Ball & Black's store. From floor to roof, all was one dazzle. Gold clocks, with silver horses tramping over 'em; colored men and women—reconstructed figures, I reckon; white stone women, a-standing, sitting down, scrouching themselves together, or riding lions a-horseback, bold as brass, filled one long room, like a regiment of military trainers. Then there were chandeliers of glass, in which no end of rainbows seemed to be tangled; dishes of sparkling glass, set in a frostwork of silver or gold, and—I may as well stop; no genius could give you an idea of the gorgeous things it was my privilege to see in those long rooms.

When we had wandered upstairs and downstairs again, Cousin E. E. stopped at one of the counters, and wanted to look at some rings. As for me I wanted to look at everything. What was one ring compared to whole stars, and bands, and clusters of shiny, white stones, that seemed to have been dug out of a rainbow—all mixed up with other stones, red as blood, green as spring grass, blue as the sky, and white as snow-crust. Why, sisters, that counter was just one bed of burning sunshine. It dazzled my eyes so that I can hardly remember anything distinct enough to describe it to you.

Well, Cousin E. E. bought her ring, which had a green stone set in it. I saw her hand a lot of money over the counter to pay for it, which riled my conscience a little; but I said nothing, the money being hers, not mine; still, how much good it might have done some missionary society.

Well, out of this store of gorgeousness we went, and got into the carriage again.

Cousin E. E. said she had bought so many things that this was about the last place she had to go to, and, as it was getting pretty near dark, I must go home with her and help fill up the Christmas tree. Cecilia would be dreadfully disappointed if it was not splendid, and they all thought so much of my taste.

I made no objections; why should I? Christmas Day in a boarding-house isn't full of ravishing promises, so I just snuggled down into the white fur, again, and let the fellow with bear-skin claws drive me where he had a mind to.

XVI.

THE NIGHT BEFORE CHRISTMAS.

OH, sisters! there is something touching and splendid in a Christmas tree. Just fancy one of our mountain spruces, towering almost to the ceiling of a room, green as when it was cut from the woods. Think of this tree, hung all over with little wax candles, bunches of pale-green and purple grapes, teinty red apples, golden horns and baskets chuck full of sugar things. Stuffed humming-birds, looking chipper as life. Butterflies, that seem to be flying through the green of the trees, and a whole camp-meeting of dolls sitting around the roots, and then tell me if the Christmas time of a New York child isn't like living among the people of a fairy book.

This was the sort of tree set up at Cousin Dempster's, Sunday night before this last Christmas day. Of course, we couldn't think of breaking the Sabbath, but the minute it was sundown, at it we went. Of course, we didn't want the little girl to know what we were a-doing; but the first we knew, in she hopped, as chipper as a humming-bird, and would keep interfering and changing things, in spite of all we could do.

At last, her mother got her dander up and told her to march right off to bed, just as a woman born in Vermont ought to order her own child; but the tantalizing thing just hitched up her shoulder, and said, " She wouldn't go, nor touch to the tree was for her own self. The house was her par's, and she'd do just as she'd a mind to in it."

With that, Cousin E. E. blazed into a passion, and took her child by the arm, with a jerk that sent her flying into the hall. Then I heard a screeching and a scrambling up the stairs, and it seemed to me a slap or two—I hope I wasn't mistaken about that—then a door slammed, and Cousin E. E. came downstairs like a house o' fire, with both eyes blazing, and one cheek red as flame. Could it be that the slap I heard was from the other side, or had it been a free fight?

" That girl will be the death of me," says she, walking about like a lion in its cage. " I never knew a worse child."

" I'm sure I never did," says I, with more than my usual spontaneiety, for I felt it.

" You never made a greater mistake," says E. E., fierce as a hen hawk. " It is because she has so much more brains—spirit—genius than any other children. A more splendid character never lived than my daughter Cecilia."

I said nothing; maybe it would have been just as well if I had held my tongue before.

" She is a favorite everywhere," E.E. went on, cooling down like a brick oven after the coals are hauled out.

I said nothing.

" Ahead of girls twice her age," E. E. went on. " She speaks French like a native."

" Is there anything more to put on? " says I.

" Yes," says she, " we will have the presents ready for the

morning. I meant to have some of Cecelia's friends here to-morrow night, but she wanted the tree to herself."

With this, E. E. brought an armful of boxes and things from the next room. The first thing she set up against the stem of the tree was a doll, dressed in a splendid silk ball-dress, with a long, sweeping train, and teinty rose-buds in her yellow curls. The blue eyes were natural as life, and her face was just lovely. Then she brought out a Saratoga trunk about as big as a foot-stool, which was crowded full of dolls' dresses, just such as a live young lady would be proud to wear.

"Isn't it beautiful?" says E. E.

"I should think so," says I; "how much did it cost?"

"A hundred and twenty-five dollars," says she. "I sent to Paris for it."

"A hundred and twenty-five dollars?" says I, lifting up both hands; "that would keep a poor family how long?"

"I don't know," says she, short as pie-crust, "but a poor family wouldn't amuse my Cecilia, and these will."

"Just so," says I; "what is this for?"

"Oh, that is her father's present—pink coral—hang it across one of the limbs," says she.

I hung the beads among the spruce leaves, and enjoyed the sight; they seemed like a string of rose-buds twisted in with the green.

"There now, we will finish in the morning," says E. E. "I wish Cecilia had invited her little friends; it will seem rather lonesome."

With this, Cousin E. E. gave a little sigh, and we went off to bed, telling me that I must be sure to get up in time for early service, which she wouldn't miss for anything.

XVII.

EARLY SERVICE.

EAR SISTERS:—Before daylight on Christmas morning, I went to early service at the highest church in New York city, which, after all, isn't anything to brag of in the way of steeple.

There is a brick meeting-house on Murray Hill that beats it all to nothing, for that has just the longest and pointedest steeple that I ever set eyes on. Still, everybody allows that the little Episcopal church I went to, Christmas morning, is the very highest in all America; and, though in my heart I don't believe it, having eyes in my head—there is no chance for me to take a measurement, and what can I say against the word of everybody else? Still, to you in confidence, for I don't want to get into a schismatic controversy, I dare take an oath that the brick church on Murray Hill is twice as high, to say nothing of the sharp-pointedness of the steeple and the hilly ground.

Cousin E. E. Dempster says she is high church from the crown of her head to the sole of her foot, which I didn't dispute, for she always had high notions. She gave me strict charge, when I went to bed, Christmas Eve night, not to sleep late, and be sure to be ready for an early start.

Well, I went to bed feeling as if I had got to start by some swift railway train every hour of the night, and must be ready for them all. It was Sunday night, you know, and I woke up twice with a start, before it was next week; got up, felt for the matches I had laid handy, and went to bed again, and dreamed that I was trying to get into a steamboat with two steeples, which put off, and left me freezing on the dock.

Like one of the wise virgins, I had brought a candle upstairs, and some matches, which was an improvement on their old lamps, I dare say; but I wasn't much afraid of the dark, and didn't keep it burning, only left everything ready.

4*

After that dream, I started up, struck a match, and found that I had been just fifteen minutes in getting that steam church under way. So I went on dreaming, starting up, and lighting matches all night, till at last I hadn't but one left, and with that I lighted the candle, and a gas-burner by the bureau, and began to dress myself.

Before I got through, Cousin E. E. was at the door, with her beehive bonnet on, and wrapped up in fur.

"Almost ready? I am so glad, for the day is just beginning to break, and I wouldn't have it broad light when we get there, for anything," says she. "Wrap up warm, for it has blown up awful cold in the night."

I did wrap up warm; put on a veil, and tied my mink-skin victorine, with three tails on each tab, close around my neck.

We went downstairs carefully, for only one burner was twinkling in the hall, and the whole house was dark and shivery.

"Come in here," says Cousin E. E., opening the dining-room door.

Under the glass globe, in which two or three chilly lights seemed longing to go out, the ghost of a table was spread, with a great deal of silver, and very little to eat.

"Just a cup of coffee and a mouthful of toast before we start," says E. E., sitting down behind a great silver urn in her furs and her beehive; "for my own part, I could do without that."

She poured me out a cup of coffee—it was half cold and awfully riley—and asked me to help myself to a piece of toast, which had black bars across it, as if it had been striped on a gridiron.

"Things are getting cold," says E. E., "they have been standing so long. The cook has been out an hour; but she knows I consider this my penance."

"Out where?" says I.

"Oh, to early service."

"An hour?" says I; "why I thought we were going to early service. It isn't daylight yet."

"I know," says Cousin E. E., with a sigh, "but her church is a little higher than ours."

"Higher," says I; "then there is some meeting-house a notch above yours?"

"Yes, cousin," says she, mournfully, "but we are creeping up. Every year brings us a step nearer."

"Just so," says I, wondering what she meant.

"By and by we shall have confession," says she.

"Oh," says I, "there isn't a meeting-house on Sprucehill that would take in a member till she had made a confession of religion."

Cousin E. E. shook her head, and observed that I didn't understand, which riled me a little, having been a member—well, no matter how long.

"Even now we have humiliation and penance."

I was trying to swallow a mouthful of the bitter toast and riley coffee, and couldn't in my heart contradict her.

"To that end we get up early, cast aside sleep, and, in all weather, go on foot to the altar. Each year the church is opened, and the candles lighted earlier and earlier, as souls more clearly see their way to the true faith."

"Just so," says I; "by and by they will be good enough to light up, and open the day before, I suppose."

The clock on the mantel-shelf struck. Cousin E. E. started up, and put both hands in her muff. I followed her out of the door, and into the street.

Well, sisters, if there is a desolate spot on earth, it can be found in the streets of a great city after the lights have been put out, and while the sky is gray. To pass by houses in which thousands and thousands are sleeping, is like wandering through the lonesomeness of a graveyard. The morning was awful cold; before we got to Lexington Avenue the veil was stiff on my face. I felt the tears a-freezing on my cheeks, and my teeth chattered so that I couldn't speak. When we reached St. Albans—that is the name of Cousin E. E.'s church—two such shivery mortals you never saw. I say, sisters, there wouldn't have been much use in warming us against a good fire in any place just then. I don't mean to be satirical or irreverent, but when you go to early service at the break of day, and in the depths of winter, I think ice-water and snow-drifts might make a solemn impression on the sinful heart.

XVIII.

HIGH CHURCH.

ST. ALBANS may be a High Church, though I couldn't see it; but it certainly isn't very sizeable; and as for coldness, the very curls on my head shivered as if they grew there.

Cold, yes; I should think that church was cold; but you never saw anything more beautiful than the picture it made when we went in. Right before us was a white altar—not a communion table like ours at home, but a little platform with steps to it, set thick with candles, and loaded down with wreaths of white flowers. I tell you, sisters, it seemed to me as if the angels must have been down overnight, and moulded those flowers out of the drifted snow, and breathed life into them, they looked so pure.

On each side of this altar was a great, large candle, five feet high, and thick as a young tree, burning with a slow, steady fire, and some of the smaller candles twinkled like stars among the flowers.

All overhead and down the walls of this little meeting-house were great wreaths of ground pine, ivy and hemlock, crowded with lights and sprinkled with flowers, and these flung shadows on the walls more lovely than the wreaths themselves.

I was chilled through and through, but I don't think it was that which brought all these solemn feelings into my mind, for the tears that had frozen on my cheeks ran freely now, and my eyes kept filling again. I'm sure I can't tell the reason, only that everything was so still and beautiful.

The pews in St. Albans have no cushions, and everybody can sit in them, only there is a placard on each, inviting the poor to sit down for nothing, but telling those that have money to give it, to support the church; which is just what our meeting-houses do, though they only chuck the plate at you, without a written warning.

Cousin E. E. and I sat down in one of the pews, and slid our knees to a board running along in front, to kneel on, and covered up our faces a minute or two; then we looked up, and there, close by the altar, stood the minister; but, oh, goodness! how he was dressed out. He had on, first, a black silk gown, with great bishop-sleeves, then a white linen dress, that I should think was a night-gown, only it was on a man, and it isn't many women who would like to lend such things to be used in meeting-time. Over that he wore a white satin cape.

Cousin E. E. pronounces it cope, but she does finefy her words so since she came to York.

On that was worked a cross, in gold and silk, like a Free Mason's apron in some respects. He held a book open in his hand. I could see that he was shaking with chilliness, and the words rattled like icicles from his lips. Close by him stood a boy, dressed in a red frock, with a white one over it.

I whispered and asked Cousin E. E. what his name was; she answered back—"Acolyte," which was a name I never heard before.

After a while the congregation began to move out of the pews, a few at a time, and crowd up to the minister. Then they knelt down before him, and he gave them bread and wine close to the altar, instead of having it handed about as they do in our Presbyterian meeting-houses. Cousin E. E. went up with the rest, and wanted me to go with her, but I could not bring myself to partake of the Lord's Supper from a man in his shirt-sleeves, and with a silk cape on ; so I shook my head and sat still, watching the altar.

After they had done coming up to him, the minister knelt down and prayed awhile; then he got up, and the boy in red shirt and white frock handed him a black hat, with four corners, which he put on his head; then he took something from' the altar and walked through a side door, still wearing his double-cocked hat. The boy followed him out, and then a man came round among the pews with a plate, in which Cousin E. E. dropped a gold piece with a ringing noise that made people look round. I followed up with five cents, and was astonished to see how little ring it had after the gold; nobody looked round at me.

It was broad daylight when we came out of that little meeting-house, and not quite so cold as it had been ; but still I was glad to keep my muff up to my face, and we walked toward home like a house afire.

"Well, how did you like the service ? " says Cousin E. E., as we shivered along—"impressive, isn't it ? "

"Very," says I; "only do tell me what it was all about. This getting up and sitting down and bowing at nothing is more than I can understand."

"Oh," says she, "I ought to remember you came from a Congregational part of the country."

"And Methodist—to say nothing of Baptists and Quakers," says I.

"Yes, I mean all that," says she; "but the church, as a church, is but little understood among you."

"Well, as you came from the same place, you ought to know," says I, rebuking her city airs in my most austere manner.

"Well, yes," says she; " but one doesn't hear much of the true church so far in the mountains. Even you seemed puzzled by a good many things this morning."

"Well, yes," says I—"the four-cornered cocked hat, for instance."

" The four-cornered cocked hat! " says she, stopping short on the sidewalk. "What do you mean? That was the barette."

" Oh," says I, " that is what they call it! Well, then, the four-cornered cocked barette—what does the minister wear that for? It isn't generally considered good manners for men to wear hats in meeting."

" Oh, there is a clerical reason I can't quite explain, but it is a part of the ceremony."

" Just so," says I—" and the night-gown."

" Surplice, you mean," says E. E.; " oh, that is worn everywhere, in High and Low Church alike."

" Well," says I, " there may be a reason for such things, but a respectable black coat is what I've been used to."

" Yes, I know," says she; " but some people prefer the surplice and cope."

" Now tell me," says I, " what on earth has a minister to do with a woman's satin *cape*, all crimlicued off with gold and silk work ? " I put an emphasis on the word cape, to rebuke her finefied way of pronouncing it.

" It is a part of the clerical paraphernalia, and gives richness to the vestments," says she. " But the altar—I felt sure that you would be pleased with that."

" Yes," says I; " the white flowers, the candles, and the evergreens were beautiful. But the red and white boy was too much for me; then his name—Acolyte—I never heard anything like it."

Just then we reached home, and shivered into the house to warm ourselves. Cousin Dempster was not up yet, and that child was sound asleep. It seemed to me as if we had been downstairs a week; but there was the Christmas tree, just loaded with presents; and there was the marble man and woman, looking cold as we were. And there we stood, hungry and shivering, for the help had all gone out to " early service," and forgot to heap coal on the furnace; and the end was, we just got

into our cold beds again, and shivered ourselves to sleep.   I
dreamed that a man, all in black and white, with a four-
cornered hat on—one tassel hanging over his eyes, and another
down his back—with something like a flash of fire about his
neck, was burying me ten thousand feet deep in a snow-drift,
and pounding me down with a candle as big round as my waist.
Then it seemed to me that I got out, somehow, and was trying
to warm my hands by the red frock of that boy, Acolyte, who
faded into nothing before my eyes, and left me sound asleep
as if I had never been to early service in my life.

XIX.

CHRISTMAS MORNING.

E had a good long sleep after early service, and were
all up bright as larks the next morning, wishing
each other a merry Christmas, and waiting for that
child to come down and see what Santa Claus had brought her.
By and by we heard her coming.   Mr. Dempster looked at his
wife and smiled, as much as to say, " Won't our presents surprise her!"· Cousin E. E. went to the door and opened it,
looking pleased, and so like her old self that I could have
kissed her.

At last Cecilia came in, sour as vinegar, with her hair half
combed, and her sash trailing.

" Why, this is what I saw last night," says she, crossly.

" Look at the foot of the tree!" says E. E., eagerly.

Cecilia looked, and saw the doll and the open trunk.   Her
lips drooped at the corners, her right shoulder lifted itself.

" A doll for me!   The idea!" says she.

Cousin E. E. turned away, I think, to hide the tears that
swelled to her eyes.   Mr. Dempster saw it, and says he :

"Cecilia, your mother spent a great deal of money for the doll—don't be ungrateful."

"Just as if I wanted her to do it. Baby things!"

"Well," says Cousin E. E., trying to brighten up her face, "there is your father's present."

Cecilia untwisted the string of coral, and looked at it.

"Coral is for babies! That is worse yet! I just wish there hadn't been any Christmas at all," says she, a-flinging the beads in a lovely pink heap on the floor. "There now—I'll just go up-stairs and stay there!"

"Wait a minute, my darling," says E. E.; "mother has got something else."

Cecilia turned back a step, but scorned to let her sullen face brighten, though her eyes grew eager when Cousin E. E. took a little paper box from one of the baskets, and opened it.

"See here!"

Cecilia edged up to her mother, saw the emerald ring, and snatched at it.

"I bought it for Cousin Phœmie," says E. E., a-looking sort of pleadingly at me; "but as you are so disappointed, I'm sure she won't care."

"Cousin Phœmie! The idea!" Cecilia muttered to herself, as she tried the ring, first on one finger, then on another. "Of course she don't want it—old as the hills!"

I did not say one word while that creature carried off the first Christmas present I ever had in my life; but it seemed as if I should choke. Isn't it hard that a spoiled child like that should have the power to destroy the happiness of three grown people? But she did it.

The Christmas dinner was enough to make your mouths water, from this distance—the noblest sort of a turkey, stuffed with oysters, and everything to match—but none of us had much appetite for it. You can judge what my feelings amounted to, when I have lived one whole month in a boarding-house and couldn't get up an appetite—no, not even for the whitest meat of the breast! Old as the hills, indeed!

XX.

ABOUT LIONS.

DEAR SISTERS:—Cousin E. E. had invited a lot of her friends to a stupendous dinner-party on Christmas Day, and she wanted me there for a lion, she said, though what on earth a great roaring lion had to do at a dinner-table I couldn't begin to think. The idea made me fidgety; but I didn't think it consistent with the dignity of our Society to ask questions, or let any one know that I didn't understand everything just as well as folks that have lived in York all their lives. Still I couldn't help trying to circumvent Cousin E. E. into telling me what I wanted to know in a way that some people might call femininely surreptitious.

"A lion!" says I. "Are such animals invited to a city dinner as a general thing?"

"Oh! not at all," says she; "the most difficult thing in the world to get hold of is a real, genuine lion; that is, one the whole world knows about, and wants to see."

"Why," says I, "if folks are so anxious about it, why don't they go up to the Rink and see Mr. Barnum's great monster animal. It don't cost much; besides, there are camels and monkeys, and lots and lots of things, thrown in."

Cousin Emily Elizabeth laughed till tears come into her eyes.

"Oh! Cousin Phœmie," says she, "you are so delightfully satirical."

"Do you think so?" says I, awfully puzzled.

"Yes," says she, "I do; but to me the eccentricities of genius are always interesting. To be an attractive lion one must say bright things, no matter how hard they cut."

"I wasn't aware," says I, "that lions were given to much talking."

"Oh!" says she, "that depends. There is your talkative lion, your learned lion, your silent lion—"

"That is the sort that I've always seen," says I; "now and then a growl, but nothing beyond that."

Cousin E. E. began to laugh again, till she had to hold one hand to her side.

"Oh! cousin, paws, paws," says she; "you just kill me with laughing."

"Yes," says I, "I don't deny that lions have paws, but it was speech we were talking about, and that I do deny."

Cousin E. E. just shrieked out laughing, though for the life of me I couldn't tell what it was all about.

"Now, don't you understand me—honest now—don't you?" says she.

"Why, of course I do; only nothing could be more ridiculous than the idea of a great, big, magnificent wild beast, with a swinging walk, and a tuft on the end of his tail, being showed off at a dinner-table. I for one shouldn't have a mite of appetite with such a creature prowling round."

"My dear, dear cousin, I'm speaking of human lions."

"Human lions! I always thought the creatures were awfully inhuman," says I; "nothing but a jackal can be worse."

"I mean great people—celebrated for something—bravery, literature, the arts, sciences," says she.

"Well, what of them?" says I.

"In society we sometimes call them lions."

"O—oh!" says I, drawing the word out to give myself time. "So you really thought I didn't understand. Why, of course. Dear me! cousin, how easy it is to cheat you!"

"Oh!" says she, "one must get up early to match you women of genius, I'm aware of that. What dry humor you have, now, looking so innocent and earnest, too!"

I smiled benignly upon Cousin E. E.; if she could find any humor in what we'd been a-talking about, it was more than I could. Lions! Where does the joke come in, when human beings are called such names as that? Wild beasts, indeed!

"How really modest you are!" says Cousin E. E. "Anybody else, who could write as you do, would have known that she was meant when I mentioned lions."

I dropped my eyes, and folded both hands.

"It will be the great feature of our party," says she. "Our friends will know that you are a blood relation, and that pleases Dempster; besides, you converse so beautifully, too."

"Do I?" says I, folding one hand over the other, and back again.

"And look so—so distinguished."

I drew my figure upright, and looked into the glass opposite. My cousin had chosen her words well; there was something imposing in the bend of that head. I say nothing; but she was right. Indeed, so far as I am concerned, she generally is.

Early in the morning I sent down for my pink silk dress. Cousin E. E. looked as if she was going to say something against it, at first; but, after a little, her face cleared up, and I heard her muttering:

"This is the third time. Nothing on earth but a woman of genius could stand that; but she has got enough to carry it off."

I said nothing, but thought of that bill, and just made a calculation of how much it would cost a woman to rig herself out if she went to many parties, and only wore a dress that cost five hundred dollars once.

Well, sisters, Christmas Day came, and we were up by daylight, for Cousin Emily Elizabeth is, as I have told you, a High Church woman and an Episcopalian. We haven't got any meeting-house of that denomination in our neighborhood, and I don't exactly know what high and low church means, without it is that one set hold to meeting-houses with a belfry, and the others stand up for a high steeple—a thing that I told Cousin E. E. we common people didn't aspire to; at which she laughed again, as if I had said something awfully witty.

Well, in another report I have given you an account of this daybreak meeting in the High Church, but just now I am taken up with the Christmas dinner.

Now don't calculate, because we eat dinner punctually at noon in Vermont, that people here do the same thing, because it is nothing of the sort. Poor working people do that in this city, and nobody else. The more genteel and the richer you are, the later you eat your meals. Most of the well-to-do merchants eat dinner at six. Men that have got above earning their own living dine later yet, and some have got so disgustingly genteel and rich, that I don't suppose they dine till next day.

Cousin Dempster attends to business yet, so he settled down on eight o'clock for his dinner, and a splendid affair it was.

When Cousin E. E. and I came rustling downstairs with a cataract of silk rolling after us, I just screamed right out. The sight of that table was so exhilarating, glass a-shining—silver dishes and things a-sparkling—flowers heaped up in flower-pots and twisted in wreaths around the glass globe overhead, which flashed, and sparkled, and glittered as if it had been frozen up with ten thousand icicles that flung back all the light without melting a drop. The silk curtains were all let down. The carpet looked like a flower-bed, and the whole room was a sight to behold.

Cousin E. E. shut the glass doors that looked as if a sharp frost had crept over 'em, and we sat down on the round sofa in the front room, ready for company, with nothing but those two marble folks to hear what we said.

But peace and quietness will never come to a house that has a fast child like Miss Dempster, as the creature calls herself, in it. We had hardly sat down and got our trains spread, when in she came, all in a fluff of white muslin, and a flutteration of red ribbons, with her hair a flowing down her back, crinkle, crinkle, and her—well—limbs just strained into silk stockings and kid boots laced down ever so far below her frock, and looking *so* impudent. Down she sat on the round sofa, and begun to swing her heels against the silk cushions.

" Why, daughter," says Cousin E. E., " what is the meaning of this ? "

The child laughed and flung back her head.

" It means," says she, "that I'm not to be cheated into staying upstairs when a Christmas dinner is on hand.   I'm ready for it, and I wish the company would come."

" But, my child, you are too young."

" If I'm too young, where do you find your old folks ? " says the saucy thing, shaking out her ribbons.

" Cousin E. E., I would not permit it," says I, for I couldn't help speaking to save my life.   " She isn't of an age to go into company." •

" Well, you are old enough, and a good deal to spare," says the impudent thing.   " No mistake about that ! "

I drew up the train of my pink silk dress, and walked across the room in a way that spoke my indignation, without words. When I turned to go back that creature was right behind me, with her head up, measúring off the carpet, step by step, with me.

Sisters, I confess it, the strangling of that child would have done me a world of good ; my fingers quivered to begin.   But she just burst out a-laughing, and, would you believe it ? her mother laughed too, but turned red as fire when I caught her at it. ·

Before anything more could be said, Cousin Dempster came in, and the door-bell kept up such a ringing, that we were in a flutteration till, one after another, the company came in ; ladies and gentlemen dressed up as if it had been a ball they were invited to.

XXI.

DINING IN THE DARK.

ISTERS, I'm afraid you would be taken aback by such dresses as filled Cousin Dempster's parlors that night. Such necks, such arms, no sleeves to speak of, nothing but a skimpy band across the shoulders; heads loaded down with braids and puffs, and great, long curls, which fell on those bare necks and covered them up into a little decency. Then the figures—mercy, how the dresses stood out behind; every lady seemed to be humpbacked below the waist. It takes time to get used to genteel society, I can tell you, and any amount of blushing has to be gone through.

Well, when we had all got together, Cousin Dempster came up to me and crooked his elbow. I put my hand on his arm. The glass doors opened as if of themselves, and into the dining-room we went. The other ladies and gentlemen all locked arms, and followed us in good order. Cousin Dempster whispered to me as I went in,

" The dinner is *given* to you, remember."

I said yes, I would remember. I hadn't even thought of paying for it, but I suppose he wanted to set my mind at rest on that point, which was kind, but unnecessary, as we never charge for meals in Vermont, except at taverns.

" They were all invited to meet you," says he, at which I just turned round and made a low curtsey to the whole lot of 'em, before I took my seat, which was at Cousin Dempster's right hand.

On the other side was a proper, pretty girl, with a neck like water-lilies, and cheeks like ever-blooming roses. She was a girl that laughed very low, when she did laugh, and looked at gentlemen sideways from under her eyelashes. One of those girls that speak as if ice cream would not melt in their mouths. An awful handsome young fellow came with her.

Well, we all stood up waiting for Cousin E. E. to sit down, which she did. Then the rest of us rustled into our places, and half a dozen waiters went circumventing round us with little oysters, shells and all, on plates, which they set down before each of us, with a teinty silver pitchfork to eat 'em with. Then they brought plates with a few spoonfuls of soup in them, which they cleared away the minute we laid down our spoons. After that, came plate after plate, and the waiters kept filling the glasses that stood before us—pink, green, yellow, and white—with cider that bubbled and sparkled, and made the blood come faster and warmer into my face every time I tasted it.

At first there hadn't been much talking; but now the ladies grew chipper, as so many canary birds, and the men followed suit.

Such soft, low laughing, and such sweet voices I never heard at one table in my life.

But while we were all enjoying ourselves so much, the lights in the glass balloon above us began to flash up and down, as if a high wind was rushing over them. Then all at once they quivered—winked furiously, as if they were joking with us— and went out, leaving us all in stone darkness.

Then the ladies shrieked faintly, or laughed; some of them jumped up, I among the rest, wondering if the Day of Judgment had come.

Cousin Dempster called out for the waiters to go and see what ailed the gas, and all was rustle and bustle and confusion.

Perhaps I moved from my seat and dropped into some other without knowing it. I can't be certain about that or anything else; but all at once I felt an arm around my waist, and while I was holding my breath, with astonishment, some one kissed me.

I gave a little scream, and pushed away that impudent arm with all my might.

The arm wore a coat-sleeve—I can take my oath to that—

and if I was used to such things I should say that there was a beard about the lips that touched my face.

Sisters, it seemed to me for a minute as if Cousin E. E. really had got a roaring lion in her dining-room.

While I sat there breathless and wondering if he would have the impudence to repeat that audacious conduct, a soft hand took hold of mine, and a sweet voice whispered in my ear:

"Forgive me, dearest, I did not mean to be rude."

I did not speak, but his penitence touched me with compassion. Softly I pressed the hand, in token of a relenting heart. How could I be hard on a man who meant no real harm, considering the temptation.

He whispered something more, but I could not hear distinctly; for just then a waiter came in with a candle in his hand. Says he, "The gas works are blown up, and all Murray Hill, and more too, is in total darkness."

Then there was a burst of voices; everybody laughed and everybody had something to say, which no one listened to.

"Bring candles," Cousin Dempster sung out.

"But the candlesticks—we have not got one in the house," says his wife.

Then everybody laughed, and Cousin Dempster laughed loudest of all.

"Find something," says he, "for we must have light."

The waiter, says he, "Yes, sir, we'll do our best," and out he went.

By and by he comes back, and all the rest of the waiters with him. Every one had a stone beer bottle in each hand, from which a tall white candle rose like a steeple to a church. There was not a smile on their faces.

City waiters are never expected to smile, but each man set his two bottles down on the table, and drew back.

Dempster burst out laughing; the rest burst out too; some giggled, some choked, some pealed out the fun that was in them like wedding bells.

Everybody laughed except me and an elegant young gentle-

5

man, with blue eyes and a soft beard, that sat next me. He
stared in my face, and I would have stared in his, only I
couldn't bring myself to look in his eyes.

Oh, sisters, it was dreadful! I had got into that young
girl's place and she was in mine, and a teinty bit of court-
plaster that I had put on the corner of my mouth, where the
skin had been a trifle rubbed, was sticking right on the plump-
est part of his under lip.

Oh, sisters! I thought that I should have died with shame.

He looked from me to the young lady, and she looked at
him. I looked first at one, then at the other, from under my
drooping lashes.

She smiled, she touched her lip with one finger; he touched
his, the mite of court-plaster stuck on his finger. Then she
began to laugh, and so did he; the chairs shook under them.
They made no noise, and the redness of their faces was lost
in the shadow cast by the beer-bottles to every one but
me.

Cousin Dempster was busy trying to crowd an extra candle
into one of the wine-bottles that had just been emptied,
while he sat before the chair I ought to have been sitting in.

"We must have a little more elegance at this end of the
table," says he.

"Wax candles and champagne bottles for this lady."

He stooped down, expecting me to answer him; when he
saw *her* face all glowing with blushes.

"Ah!" says he, laughing, "we have got a little mixed here,
Cousin Frost. It will never answer to come between man
and wife in this fashion, especially when they have been only
three weeks married. Supposing we change round again?"

I arose—she arose—we exchanged glances, then exchanged
seats.

The lights from these beer bottles were numerous, but not
brilliant. Under the shadows we concealed the emotions which
disturbed us.

He looked funnily penitent, whenever his eyes caught mine,

which was often, for somehow I could not keep looking on my plate all the time.

As for that young creature, she seemed to be brimming over with fun.

After a little, I began to feel myself smiling. It really was droll, but not so *very* unpleasant.

XXII.

NEW YEAR'S DAY.

DEAR SISTERS:—After all, this city of New York is a wonderful institution. Vermont has its specialties, such as maple-sugar, pine shingles, and education; but in such things as style, fashion, and general gentilities, I must say this great Empire City isn't to be sneezed at, even by a Green Mountainer. Of course we are ahead in religion, morality, decorum, and a kind of politics that consolidates all these things into great moral ideas—as rusticoats, greenings and Spitzenbergen apples are ground down into one barrel of such sweet cider as we used to steal through the bunghole with a straw. You will recollect the straws—a Down-east invention, which these degenerated Yorkers have stolen, and are now using unblushingly for mint-juleps, sherry-cobblers, and such awful drinks as New England has put her foot down against with a stamp that makes inebriating individuals shake in their boots. But New York won't put her foot down, and the encroachment upon our patent-right for straws is just winked at.

Dear me, how one thing does lead a person's mind into another! I took up my pen to write about New Year's Day in New York, and here I am, back in that old cider-mill behind our orchard, with heaps of red and yellow apples piled up in the grass, and the old blind horse moving round and round in

the mill-ring, dragging along that great wooden wheel, under
which we could hear the soft-gushing squelch of the apples,
while all the air smelt rich and fruity with them.

Do you remember the luscious juice dropping from the press,
and the full barrels lying about, with the sweetness beginning
to yeast through the bungholes? Then it was we pounced
down upon them with our straws, and it was these straws that
brought New Year's Day in New York and the old cider-mill
at home into my mind at once. Thus it is, my sisters, with us
children of genius; thought is born of thought, feeling springs
out of feeling, till creation and re-creation become spontaneosi-
ties.

Some people have said of Phœmie Frost that she lacks phil-
osophy and that transcendental essence which becomes the
highest female type in New England. If any such caviler
should reach our Society, have the moral courage to point out
that last paragraph, and see if the wretches have forgotten to
blush for themselves.

Christmas Day isn't anything very particular outside of the
Episcopal Church, in our parts. Somehow the Pilgrim Fathers
took a notion against it when they cut away from the old country, and built square meeting-houses all over New England.
But they set up the same thing under a new-fangled name.
Thanksgiving was just the same to them, and showed their independence; so they roasted and baked and stewed, and made
pumpkin-pies a specialty—because the cavaliers in England
couldn't get pumkins to compete with them—and went into
their meeting-houses to thank God that they had good crops,
instead of going down on their knees—which they didn't, because of standing up to pray—in solemn gratitude that the
blessed Lord was born upon earth.

Sisters, as a New England female, it would be against nature
to say that the Pilgrim Fathers wasn't right in sinking Christmas in Thanksgiving, and thanking God for full crops, because
the corn and potatoes were things they all could understand
and accept with universal thankfulness; but about the birth of

Christ, and its merciful object, no two sects that I ever heard of could agree, much less the Old Church and the New Covenanters.

There it is again; my pen is getting demoralized. Christmas has come and gone. What more have I got to say about it? Why, just nothing. Wise people accept the past and look forward.

Cousin Dempster insisted upon it, that I should come up and spend New Year's Day with them. Cousin E. E. was going to receive calls, and wanted some distinguished friend to help her entertain.

I went.

Early in the morning the empty carriage came down to my boarding-house, with those two regimental chaps on the out seat.

I was all ready, with my pink silk dress on, and my front hair all in one lovely friz; but I just let the carriage wait that the boarders and people, with their faces against the window opposite, might have a good chance to look at it. Then I walked down the stairs with queenly slowness; the long skirt of my dress came a-rustling after, with a rich sound that must have penetrated to the boarding-house parlor, for the door was just a trifle open as I went by, and three faces, I could swear to, were peeping out as if they had never seen a long-trailed, pink silk dress before. Then I heard a scuttling toward the window, and, while I stood on the upper step, gathering up the back cataract of my dress, those same faces flattened themselves plump against the glass.

Of course I did not hurry myself on that account, but took an observation up and down the street while I tightened the buttons of my glove, though one of the regimental chaps was a-standing there and holding the door wide open.

"Why shouldn't I give the poor things just this one glimpse of the fashionable life to which genius has lifted me," says I to myself.

Influenced by this idea, I paused, perhaps, half a minute,

with my foot on the iron step, and asked the regimental chap,
with the air of a queen giving directions, if it was very cold?
and if Mrs. Dempster was quite well, that morning?

He bowed when he answered both these questions, with the
greatest respect; which was satisfactory, as the people on both
sides must have seen him do it.

Then I stepped gracefully into the carriage and sat down,
buried to my knees in billows of pink silk. Over that I drew
the robe of white fur, and waved my hand, as much as to say:
I am seated; you can close the door. Which he did.

One thing is curious about the streets of New York on New
Year's Day. Not a woman or girl is to be seen on the sidewalks.

The garden of Eden, before Adam went into the spare-rib
business, wouldn't have been more completely given up to the
desolation of manhood, unrefined by sweet female influence.

But every man that I saw, going up or down, looked
bright and smiling, as if he expected to find an Eve of his
own before the day was over, and I shouldn't wonder if a
good many of them did.

XXIII.

THE NEW YEAR'S RECEPTION.

COUSIN E. E. DEMPSTER was all ready, and standing
as large as life in one end of her long parlor, when I
went in. The first sight of that room made me start
back and scream right out. I had left daylight outside, but
found night there. The blinds were shut close to every window. Over them fell a snow-storm of white lace, and over that
a cataract of silk that seemed to have been dyed in wine, its
redness was so rich and wavy.

Tho two great glass balloons were just running over with brightness that scattered itself everywhere—on the chairs, tho cushions, fhe carpet, and a great round sofa which stood, like a giant cheese, in the middle of the room, all covered with silk, and with a tall flower-pot standing up from the centre, running over with flowers, and vines, and things.

This queer sofa, that seemed to have burst out into blossom for the occasion, was a New Year's present, Cousin E. E. said, and quite a surprise. "Then there is another," says she, a-pointing towards a marble man, dressed in a grape leaf, that seemed to have been firing something at the stone girl, and was watching to see if it had hit. "Of course you have seen the Apollo before?"

I looked at the stone fellow sideways, then dropped my eyes.

"I—I don't know," says I; "maybe I should know him better if he had his clothes on."

"Look again. You must have seen him," says she.

"No," says I, a-turning my head away; "I—I'd rather not till he goes out and fixes himself up a little."

Cousin E. E. laughed till her face was red. While she was tittering like a chirping bird, that little creature Cecilia came tripping into the room, with a blue silk dress, ruffled over with white lace, just reaching to her knees, her yellow hair a-rippling over that, clear down behind, and a wreath of pink roses on her head. She looked at me from top to toe, gave her head a toss, and went up to her mother with the air of an injured princess.

"That old pink silk again ! What did you let let her wear it for? New Year's Day, too. The idea ! "

I heard every word of it, for the stuck-up thing didn't trouble herself to speak low. My face had been hot enough before, but it burned like fire now, and my bosom heaved till itstormed against my dress and almost burst it.

"Hush ! " said Cousin E. E., looking scared; " she will hear."

"Well, let her. As if I cared! The idea!"

I stepped forward, with my finger lifted, and my dress sweeping. It must have been an imposing sight, for E. E. raised both hands, imploringly, and says she, " Cecilia, come and see your father's present."

" Oh, isn't it gorgeous? " sang out the child, clasping her hands, and turning her back square on me while she went up to the stone fellow. "Such a splendid mate for Venus! "

" Yes, I should think so," says I sarcastically; "only Miss Venus does seem ashamed of herself; but the fellow is bold as brass."

The girl's lip curled like an opening rose-bud; she gave a nipping laugh, and I just heard " old fogy " break through it so saucily that my blood riled.

" Did you apply that to me? " says I, a-lifting my finger.

"No, no, nothing of the kind," says Cousin E. E., catching her breath. "You quite misunderstand Cecilia. Dear me, that is a carriage; people are beginning to call. Cecilia, my love, do try and make yourself agreeable."

"Just as much as to say that I could be anything else," says the aggravating creature, a-hitching up her shoulders.

Sure enough, some one was coming, and no three canary birds in a cage ever fluttered into their places quicker than we did. Cousin E. E. seated herself in a great cosey chair, all cushions, spread out her dress on the floor, and leaned a little sideways as if she was sitting to Brady for a picture. I gave my pink silk a wide swoop, and let it settle down on the carpet in ridges; then I leaned my elbow on the silk cushions of the great round sofa, and drooped my head a little as if breathing the scent of so many flowers had made me a trifle faint. That child ran to the glass, shook out her lace ruffles, and stepped back again to admire—well, her limbs—just as if she had been a stone girl, and was in love with herself. I swan to man she made me sick and faint, if the flowers didn't.

There was a noise in the hall-way, and I caught a peep at a handsome young fellow prinking himself in the great looking-glass set in the hat-stand. Then he came in, tripping along with his hand held out to Cousin E. E., who went forward with her train following after, took his lilac glove in her hand, smiled up in his face, and said how glad she was to see him.

Before he could answer, that forward child came up and held out *her* hand. She, too, was delighted; wondered he hadn't been there lately. Indeed, she began to think he was never coming again.

The young fellow did seem to be taken aback a minute, for the forward creature had just cut her mother out; but he soon began to talk and laugh with her as chipper as could be, and only stopped to give me a nip of a bow when Cousin E. E. introduced him.

Well, my opinion is I gave him as good as he sent; but short measure at that; for I just lifted my head as if taking a sniff at the flowers, and that was all. If that young man thought I was brought up in the woods to be scared by owls, he found out his mistake. He was standing with his back towards me when I heard E. E. say, in one of those whispers that cut to the ear keener than a scream :

"It is Miss Phœmie Frost, the celebrated writer."

"What," says he, "Miss Frost, the person on whom the Grand Duke levelled his eye-glass at the opera three times, and who was prevented opening the ball with him by the machinations of the committee ? "

"The same," says Cousin E. E.

Before she could put in another word, that young gentleman had wheeled round in his patent leather boots, and was making me a bow that went so near the floor that his lilac gloves fell below his knees. Then he rose slowly, like a jack-knife that opens hard, and stood there a-smiling in my face as if I had just treated him to a quart of maple molasses fresh from the kettle.

"Miss Frost," says he, " I'm happy to make your acquaintance ; your writings have been my delight—in fact, a household word in our family—for years."

5*

"Years?" says I.

"That is, ever since you began to honor the world with the emanations of your genius," says he, with an open wave of both hands.

I bowed. I half rose from that round sofa. I knew by the soft, quivering sensation that smiles were creeping to my lips, and giving them a lovely redness.

" Sir," says I, "you are complimentary. I am but a young beginner in the paths of literature—a timid worker in the great harvest field of thought."

He smiled; he moved the billowy folds of my dress with infinite reverence, and seated himself timidly beside me. Then he talked books to me—broken and fragmentary, but exquisite. He could understand why the Grand Duke was so anxious to get back to New York. That poetry of mine must have lifted him right off from his feet. What a lovely talent poetry was!

I sat upright, but looked downward, hiding the pleasure in my eyes by my drooping lashes. Faithful, heart and soul, to one noble being, I refused to look into the admiring eyes of another. His insidious praises of my genius made no impression. The image of a man six feet two, with a sky-blue scarf across his princely bosom, stood at the portal of my heart, and the young gentleman with curled hair and that light-colored mustache sighed, and sighed in vain.

That forward little creature, Cecilia, saved me from temptation. Up she came, with her frock and her hair all in a flutter.

" You haven't seen our new statue," says she, a-pulling at his hand.

The young gentleman arose from my side with a look that went to my heart. As he stood before that pre-Adamite stone man, I got one good, long look at his face. As true as I live, he had found out some of Cousin E. E.'s ways of making herself beautiful! for his eyes had shadows under them, and his cheeks were like roses. Now, sisters, did you ever? Only think of a Green Mountain fellow doing that!

But now another lot of men came in, dressed up to kill. Some had yellow kid gloves on, some lilac, and some gray. Their patent-leather boots shone like looking-glasses, and some of 'em tipped along as if they were treading over eggs and didn't mean to break 'em. Cousin E. E. introduced them all, and I had to rise, and bow, and make long, sweeping curtsies till my back ached, and my poor mouth felt dry with trying to look unconscious when so many of 'em told me I was a household word in their families.

When the first lot of 'em were going out, Cousin E. E. just put back the red curtains at one end of the room, and behind 'em was a table all set off with silver, and glass, and flowers, and great, tall dishes crowded full of fruit and mottoes, all standing under the hot sunshine of one of those glass balloons, a-glittering and a-flashing like a house afire.

I couldn't help giving a little scream, it was all so rich and beautiful—with two colored waiters in white gloves, ready to help everybody.

Cousin E. E. stood at one end of the table—for it was a stand-up meal—and asked her visitors to take birds, and oysters, and terrapin. What the dickens is terrapin? Have you any idea, sisters? I ate some, and it had a stewy sort of taste, as if it had been kind of burnt in cooking.

Well, one took one thing, and one another. Then each fellow wiped his mustaches, and the waiters came round with cider bottles, loaded over and chained up with silver, and the cider hissed and bubbled and sparkled as they poured it out into the glasses, that started narrow at the bottom, but spread out into dishes at the top, giving a chance for little whirlpools to the cider—which *was* cider, I can tell you; it had vim enough in it to make your eyes snap.

When the glasses were full we all took them up. The gentlemen muttered "Compliments of the season," and we answered "Compliments of the season" Cecilia and all—who just had the impudence to stand on tip-toe, and knock her glass against that of the fellow with lilac gloves and curly hair. Then we all drank and sipped, and, as that party went off, another came in—stream after stream—till night. It was the same thing over and over again, till ten o'clock at night, when Mr. Dempster came home, looking awfully tired out; then we just gave up. Sisters, this has been the hardest and most confusing day that I have known in New York. It seems as if my joints never would get limber again. But then I had a real good time, though the cider did begin to get into my head towards night. It couldn't have been made out of Vermont apples, I feel certain—they haven't got so much dizziness in 'em.

XXIV.

MIGNON: A NIGHT AT THE GRAND OPERA.

SISTERS, we went to the opera—that is, dear sisters in the cause, the Grand Duke and I were there; both of us seated on red cushions, and so near that we could exchange glances through our eye-glasses, which draw a beloved object close to you. They are a great invention which has not yet reached that portion of the country where prayer-meetings take the place of operas.

I felt in my bones that he would meet me there; and when Cousin Emily Elizabeth sent me word that she had got a loge—which means a little square pen in the gallery, cushioned off like a first-class pew—and wanted me to go with her to hear the great primer-donner, I just got that dress out again, and set the frizzing-pins to work, and did myself up so scrumptiously that I don't believe that a creature on Sprucehill would have known me. Don't say this is extravagant, and flying in the face of Providence. If He don't want silk dresses worn by the elect, what on earth does He make silk-worms and mulberry-leaves for? That is a question that we'll have debated over in the Society some day. Until then, oblige me by not saying, openly, that I'm a free-thinker, because I'm nothing of the sort. Not that my taste, since coming to the opera, has not got a notch above Greenbank or Old Hundred, in the way of music; I am free to own that it has.

Well, Cousin Emily Elizabeth had sent word that I mustn't wear a bonnet, or think of such a thing; and she sent me down a fur mantle, made of white kitten-skins, I reckon, with little black tails dropping all over it—just the tips, which needn't have hurt the black kittens much, if it *was* all day to the white ones. So, when I come down, holding up my long skirts with one hand, and folding this fur across my innocent bosom, she just screamed out from the carriage that I looked gorgeous enough to turn the great Grand Duke's head, which I felt to be true—for women are not given to praising each other for nothing, anyhow.

The opera-house in New York would take in our biggest meeting-house, and leave room for a wide strip of carpeting all round it. It has got three galleries, and ever so many places, that look like pulpits and deacon's seats, all cushioned and curtained off beautifully.

We went up to the first gallery, and got into Cousin Dempster's loge-pew, which was just big enough for four people. This was fortunate, for our skirts and fur mantles took up every mite of room that Cousin D. did not want; but he put up with it beautifully, and just scrouched down behind us, with his head rising above our shoulders, which would have been rather uncovered if it had not been for the fur, which tickled mine a little; but I bore it with fortitude. You who know me will understand that.

The opera-house was crowded full; every pew was crammed, and the benches down below couldn't be seen, the people were so thick. The pew loges were running over with handsome girls, and old ladies that tried their best to look like girls, and couldn't, not having the country freshness that some people bring with them from the mountains.

But the three pulpits on the second gallery were empty yet—all empty, and gorgeously red, waiting for *him.*

At last, a great green curtain that hung just beyond this sacred place rolled up. The lights in a great glittering balloon, all hung with ropes of shiny glass beads which fell down from the centre of the roof, blazed up, and when I dropped my head from looking at it, all the other end of the room was crowded with a gang of the queerest-looking people—men, women, children, and dogs—that ever you did see. That was the opera, Cousin E. E. said; though how an opera could have a house and a cart in it, beat me.

Well, sisters, I give up. Roll every singing-school in Vermont into one crowd, and they couldn't begin to burst out like that; men, women, and girls, just went in for a splendid time, and they had it. First, a pew full of fiddlers, drummers, tromboners, and bas-violers, let themselves out in a storm of music that made the ten millions of beads on the glass balloons tremble like hailstones. Then the whole gang lifted up their voices, and the music rolled out just as I reckon the water does at Niagara Falls. Such a general training of music was enough to wake the dead out of a New England grave, where they sleep sound, I guess, if they do anywhere.

By and by they rose up, and began to wander about, making their funny little white dogs play, and some of the girls began to dance about. It was a travelling-show, you see, and some of the upper-crust people came out of the house I spoke of, and listened. One was a lady, dressed out to kill in a striped skirt, black velvet, and yellow silk; another yellow skirt bunched over that, and then a blue dress puffed above both, and her hair just splendid. I tell you she was a dasher!

But the people were all busy unloading the cart; they took out bundles and baskets and things. Finally a girl, that had been lying asleep on the load, jumped down, with her shoulders hitched up, and looking cross as fire at everybody that came near her. She was barefooted and bareheaded, and had nothing but an under night-gown and petticoat on, which seemed to aggravate her, for she looked scowling enough at the handsome young lady, and would not double-shuffle worth a cent, though all the men and women were trying to make her.

The moment she jumped off from the cart, the folks in the seats just ran crazy, and began clapping their hands and stamping their feet like a house afire; I never saw people act so in my life. It was enough to frighten the poor thing half to death. Instead of that, it seemed to tickle her mightily, for she came forward, with her bare feet, and made a little mincing bow, and almost laughed.

Then the strangest thing happened. First one, and then another, of the show-people, instead of reasoning with the wilful creature, just went to waving their arms and singing at her. I declare it was enough to have made a minister laugh when she turned, and began to sing back at them, sometimes spiteful, and then, again, with tears melting through her voice. An old man in gray clothes, that looked crazy as a coot, sung at her, sort of hoarse, and mournfully. Then a young fellow, in a green coat and high boots, dropped into the affair, and he sung at her. Then the handsome lady in blue and yellow burst out and sang at her too, filling the whole opera-house with music. By watching and listening, I found out this much. This girl was an orphan, picked up by the band of players, that made her dance and sing for her keeping. The fellow with the green coat and boots felt sorry for her, and bought her up, short gown and all, from the tribe of players. Then she put on the dress of a pretty boy, and waited on the handsome woman in yellow, who was one of them actress-women, and dead in love with the young fellow in boots. He was awfully in love with the actress woman too, which just aggravated that girl-boy out of her seven senses, poor thing! When she happened to watch them together, you should have seen her fling down her cap, and kick it about. There was some human nature in that, but singing love out before folks beats me. I couldn't bring myself to anything of the kind—not if the Grand Duke were standing before me with his arms out, shouting Old Hundred.

Goodness gracious! that girl-boy had taken up my thoughts, so that I didn't know when the Grand Duke came into his pulpit loge. But there he was, standing up, and looking right toward me, so pleasant.

I threw back my fur mantle a trifle, and taking Cousin E. E.'s fan, waved it gracefully, hoping thus to cool off the blushes that bathed my cheeks with a rosiness that I feared might not harmonize with the tints already there.

Still he looked my way earnestly, and with the fire of admiration in his blue eyes. A young thing sitting in the loge-pew behind me began to turn away her head and hide behind her fan, as if she had anything to do with it. The conceit of some people is astonishing!

Cousin E. E.'s little spy-glass lay in her lap. I took it up; I held it to my eyes, and devoured him with one burning glance. His heart seemed leaping to mine through the glass. I knew it. I felt it. Indeed he won't be the first of his noble race that has lost heart and soul to a country girl.

The Prince sat down, and when there was a lull in the music, clapped his hands with joy. Oh, my sisters! it is something to have given such supreme pleasure to the Grand Ducal soul.

He looked at the play; I looked too. Souls in sympathy have but one thought. I pitied that poor girl-boy with all my heart—my own happiness made me compassionate. How she suffered when that woman with the yellow skirts and the young fellow in boots were singing love to each other! Once she got wild, and dressed herself in a pink silk, and—well, she made one of those toilets that Cousin E. E. understands so well. I was sorry to see her exposing one or two little things that should be a secret with the sex. But she did, and the yellow lady caught her at it, and sung awfully provoking things at her.

Well, she just tore off the dress, scattered the lace trimmings about, put on her old duds, and ran away.

Then the house got on fire; the whole swarm of people come

out helter-skelter, singing to the flames that didn't mind the music more than if it had been buckets full of water. Firemen came running with ladders that nobody climbed, and pails of water, that the firemen carried round and round, in and out, like crazy creatures. I am sure I saw one fellow, with a white pail, pitch through the same window into the red-hot flames fifty times. The poor girl-boy, being desperate, just pitched in, determined to burn herself, while the woman in yellow and the man in boots looked on.

This went right to the cruel man's heart; he jumped in after her, carried her away from the devouring flames, and fell in love with her like a man. Of course, being a decent kind of a fellow, he couldn't keep on singing out his love to both girls at once with enthusiasm, and began to neglect the yellow girl in a way that brought tears into her voice whenever she came pleading to him under the window—which she did, not having the pride of all the Frost family in her veins.

Of course this did no good; men never come back to women that whine. The girl—for she had given up boys' clothes —had got him safe; he didn't care a chestnut-burr for all the other's singing, but took to the little vagabondess with all his heart and soul.

Now something else happened. The old man in gray got his mind again and turned out to be Mignon's father (have I told you that was her name?). He was a rich old fellow, with a house furnished with gilt chairs, and everything sumptuous— so, of course, the fellow in boots stuck to her more than ever.

I don't know what became of the woman in yellow, but as for this other girl, she came out first best in every respect; especially at the end, when ever so many flowers and baskets and things were just poured down upon her. For my part, I thought the yellow girl ought to have had full half of these things, for I liked her quite as well, if not better than the vagabondess.

Well, the green curtain went down for good, and the whole congregation got up to go out.

"How do you like Nilsson?" says Cousin E. E., as she was
fastening her fur mantle.

"Nilsson!" says I, "I haven't seen her yet."

"Why, yes you have—she just came out."

"What!—that girl-boy?"

"Yes, Mignon."

"You don't say so," says I. "Who then was the girl in
yellow?"

"Oh! she is Duval."

"Well, I like her at any rate, poor thing; it was a shame
to treat her so."

That moment I felt that the great Grand Duke was gone.
Not one more glance. It was hard!

XXV.

THE BLACK CROOK.

SISTERS :—Since my intimacy with Imperial Royalty,
Cousin Emily Elizabeth Dempster has been as proud
as a peacock of our relationship, and speaks about the
Court of all the Russias as if she expected to have an ice-palace
built on the Neva for her, every winter, for the rest of her life.
This may be natural—I dare say it is ; but I'm afraid that Russia
—being an awful despotism—wouldn't stand too many of one's
relations crowding into the Imperial corn-crib, that being a free-
born institution peculiar to high moral ideas which my great
Grand Duke did not stay in Boston long enough to imbibe.

Still, being a relation and born under the star-spangled banner, why shouldn't she have her own little hopes? I ask myself this and resolve to do my best for her. Being a first cousin
she has her rights.

This morning E. E. sent down a little straw-colored letter

with a picture on the envelop just where it seals, and asked me to go with her and Dempster to see "The Black Crook," which she wrote was a spectacle worth looking at. They had got seats at Niblo's to see it after ever so much trouble, and were sure that I would be delighted.

Delighted! What about! I never hankered much for eye-glass or spectacles. I wish cousin E. E. would be a little more particular about her spelling—that sometimes makes goose-pimples creep all over me—but a spectacle, singular, spelt with an "a," gives one just a tantalizing sense of growing old, more provoking than saying the thing right out. I can't see any more sense in one spectacle than in half a pair of scissors, but maybe she can. At any rate I don't mean to go gadding down to Mr. Niblo's theatre just to see that.

But the "Black Crook," I'm beat to know what that has to do with spectacles or eye-glasses. I have read what our minister calls pastoral poetry, and almost always find it divided off into hill-side lots, where some stuck-up young creature in the farming line, is tending sheep, with a long crook-necked stick in her hand, with which she

> Just trains the little bleating lambs,
> "With fleece as white as snow,"
> And points out with her crooked stick
> Just where they ought to go.

Excuse poetry, but, like a pent-up spring, it will break forth; nor must you suspect me of plagiarism. Remark—the second line has honest quotation-marks, which is doing full justice to Mary who owned the particular lamb which has become immortal from its whiteness and exceptional training.

But all this does not bring us any nearer to what this Black Crook means. I have been studying this matter over. Of course a crook is a crook. Put the neck of a winter squash on the end of a bean pole, and you have it.

But the Black Crook. Black? Ah, why didn't I think of that before? From the name, I suppose it is some reconstruction instrument for hooking-up taxes and bonds, left behind here in New York by some run-away Southern governor.

Well, now, I *should* like to see that—anything left behind by one of those fellows must be a curiosity.

Yes, I made up my mind to accept Cousin E. E. D.'s invitation. The theatre would be something new anyhow, and it is the duty of my mission to see all things and hold fast to that which is good.

Well, just before dark, I got out that pink silk dress and the two long braids, and shut myself in with the looking-glass over my bureau, which is always reflecting, but says nothing, or one might be afraid to trust it on some occasions.

I was almost ready, when Cousin Emily E. come in so suddenly that I hopped up from my chair, and gave a scary scream. The face in the glass turned all sorts of colors, and seemed to scream too, and looked half-frightened to death. Cousin E. E. laughed, and shut the door. Holding up both hands, says she:

" What, in that dress ! My dear cousin, it is to a theatre we are going."

" Well, I reckon your letter told me that," says I, a-spreading out the skirt of my dress along the floor.

" But we do not dress like that for a theatre," says she, a-looking down at her black silk dress, which was all fluttered over with narrow ruffles. " No trains, dear Cousin Frost, no lace—a plain walking-dress and bonnet—nothing more ? "

I looked at the shiny waves of pink silk lying around my feet, and at that face in the glass, and was just ready to burst out a-crying. It was too bad.

" You thought this just the thing when we went to hear that Miss Nilsson sing," says I, looking mournfully at that face in the glass, which was almost crying.

" Yes ; but that was the opera—this only a theatre. You see the difference," says she.

" No, I don't," says I.

" Well, you will," says she. " It's the fashion. You, who write about fashionable life so beautifully, ought to know that."

"Just as if I didn't," says I; and the fire flashed into my eyes while I took off my pink dress; and put on my alpaca, which has got a new overskirt trimmed with flutings.

"There," says I, flinging the pink silk down on the bed, "will that suit?"

"Beautifully," says she. "Now get your shawl and bonnet."

Which I did.

The carriage held four of us this time, for Cousin E. E. had brought that little girl of hers, who sat huddled up in the back seat. When her mother told her to change places, "The idea," says she, giving her head a fling, and eying me like an angry poodle-dog; then she flounced down in the front seat, so huffish and sulky, that her father said, in a milk-and-waterish way:

"My darling, don't be naughty."

And his wife told him not to interfere between her and her child. She knew how to bring up a young lady, and he mustn't attempt to break her spirit; at which the heap of sulks in the corner muttered that it wasn't in him to do it.

There isn't so very much difference between the Opera House and Mr. Niblo's theatre; only, one is piled up sky-high with cushioned galleries; and the theatre is considerably out-of-doors, especially in the lower story. We sat right in front, for Cousin E. E. said that the "Crook" could be seen best from there. I said nothing, but waited. Some people love to ask questions, but I would rather find out things for myself—it's a saving to one's feelings in the long run.

Well, the theatre was jammed full of people, mostly with shawls, and cloaks, and bonnets on. Cousin E. E. was right. What is genteel in one place is vulgar in another—that is fashion.

That child insisted on trying all the seats, to see which she liked best; but we got settled at last, and just then up went the picture-curtain with a rush. I screamed right out, for the very first sight took away my breath. Oh! sisters, I wish you could have seen it. Such trees, such loads of flowers, such clusters and streams of light! Oh my! if Eve ever had a paradise like that, she was just the greatest goose that ever lived to be turned out of it for the sake of one little knotty apple. I've no patience with her!

While I was looking at this beautiful world, another scream burst from my lips, for, all in a moment, it was alive with women, so lovely, so graceful, so full of life, that they almost took away one's breath. At first, they all came whirling in, as figures do in a dream; but, after a minute, I just felt like sinking through the floor. Why, sisters, they might just as well have been dressed in flowers! In short, dress a full-grown girl in a double poppy, with fringed edges, and you have an idea of what I couldn't look at. I felt my cheeks glow with fire; my fingers tingled with shame. It seemed to me that every man in the house was looking straight into my eyes, to see how I bore it. I lifted my eyes, and cast one frightened look around me, ready to jump up and run from the first face turned to mine. Then I just covered my face with my open fan.

There wasn't a face turned my way. Every soul—men, women, and children—were looking at those girls, who whirled, and moved, and tangled themselves up in some sort of a wild, wicked dance, that must have been the work of Old Nick himself, for nothing less could have made me look on. My whole heart rose right up against those beautiful creatures, but somehow they seemed to hold me to my seat. Really, sisters, you have no idea how very enticing a woman can be who puffs a lot of gauze around her waist, throws a wreath of flowers over her shoulders, and dances like a whirlwind.

At first, I just covered my face with my fan, for I could not bring myself up to a straightforward look. Then, somehow, my fingers would get apart, and I found myself peeping through the slats just as shamed as could be, but yet I could not help peeping.

Mercy on me, what a whirl and rush of light! What a

flashing of gold; what a crowd of women dressed in nothing, and a little gauze thrown in—it made my head whirl like a top.

I can't tell you just when my hand dropped into my lap, but before I knew it my eyes were fixed on that great whirling picture, and my sense of shame was lost in a storm of music. All these glittering women were standing in rows, regular as the pickets on a door-yard fence, while one girl, with a wreath of green leaves and red berries on her head, was whirling on one toe round and round, till she seemed to be a dozen girls whizzing round in a cloud of white muslin.

By and by all the crowd of girls joined in and began dodging about among the trees and flowers, like—well I must say it, —like runaway angels determined to have a good time of it. Then a man, covered to his knees with silver scales like a fish, came in, and he had a dance with the girl in leaves and red berries. Such a dance—they backed, they advanced, they snapped their fingers at each other, they flung up their heels, they locked arms backwards, then broke apart, and began the most lively double-shuffle at each other that ever I dreamed of. It fairly took away my breath to see them.

"That is a splendid can-can," says that child, taking the little spy-glass from her mother's lap, and levelling it at the dancers. "Don't you think so, Miss Phœmie?"

I gave her a look; it was all I could spare just then, for some new people had come into the picture. A great tall fellow, with body supporters like bean poles, had come in with a lovely creature, who was considered a queen among the girls. Just as I was looking, he seemed to stretch himself out like a piece of india-rubber, and lifting one foot, swung it over her head without touching a curl.

So this was the "Black Crook," not that I saw anything like a crook, but the burning pictures more than made up for that, and the dancing was, well—stupendous.

Every once in a while a curtain would fall and shut out the pictures. Every time it was drawn up something more splendid than anything that had gone before came out. One picture was all in a veil of fog, through which the men and women roved like beautiful ghosts. In another, some of the cunning-est little dogs you ever saw danced, and begged, and acted a play for themselves, just like human creatures. At last came a great fiery picture, all gold and glare, and flowers planted in fire, with trees that seemed to be dropping golden fruit, in which all the crowd of beautiful girls were lying on banks and under trees, and perched like splendid birds up in the air. Then the curtain came down with a thud, smothering up the fire, and hiding everything. The storm of music broke off with a crash, and the crowd began to shout and yell, and stamp their feet till the whole building shook.

Sisters, this is all I can tell you about the "Black Crook." It is splendid, and wonderfully enticing; but you might as well expect me to give you a clear idea of a burning city. It is just one picture of gorgeous confusion and confused gorgeous-ness.

XXVI.

LIVING APART.

DEAR SISTERS:—There has been great tumult and trouble in New York since I wrote my last report. Something that relates to the honor of Vermont has thrilled the public mind to a fearful extent. A smart, genial, warm-hearted, dashing person, by the name of Fisk—Mr. James Fisk—born and brought up in our State, has been shot in the largest tavern in the city, where he died, I greatly fear, without a realizing sense that he was so soon to be called before his Maker.

Many of you, my sisters, can remember this man—a great, handsome, good-natured-looking fellow, with sunshiny eyes.

and a mustache that curled up like a pair of horns on each side of a mouth that always seemed ready to laugh at something. There wasn't a man that ever came to Sprucehill that everybody was so sure to remember. His great wagon, painted off like a circus, with four horses a-drawing it through the village, with a splash-dash noise of whips and wheels and hoofs, was enough to make the money spring right out of one's pocket. Mercy on me! Didn't he make the dry-goods fly! Everybody bought something of him, and I must say that everybody liked him. In the peddling line he was a sort of P. T. Barnum, only he didn't know how to stick to his trade as Barnum has. He drove his four horses; he made money like everything; he outgrew Brattleborough, which was his native place, and soon got above peddling, his native business.

The next step towards his exaltation and ruin was that he left Vermont, a man who will do that of his own accord is sure to run wild. Well, he left his native State. and set up at the Hub of the Universe, which every one knows is Boston, where he began his education as a financier and a millionaire.

Boston is a great city. I should like to hear any one dare to deny that; but, then, people here say that, in the way of financing, the Hub knows how to save, and skimp, and deposit, and get twice her share of offices out of the President of the United States; but, outside of that, she is nowhere, compared to New York. She has no idea of turning a sharp stock corner, couldn't get up a Black Friday to save her life; in fact, is only good at an old-fashioned tea-party. This is what Cousin Dempster says about Boston, and he ought to know, being a first-class broker in Wall Street, and New England born.

Well, of course, it wasn't long before Mr. Fisk outgrew the Hub, which hadn't room for all the spokes which he wanted to carry to his wheel, and off he comes to New York, gets into the Erie Railroad, and, goodness knows how he did it! but before people knew who he was, he went smashing and crashing up that road, prowled through Wall Street like a roaring

6

lion, or bear, or some other such animals as gore and claw each other in that neighborhood.

Well, after he had sent a good many brokers sky-high with his horns, and knocked others down with his paws, for he tackled in with both, he goes kiting off to sea by way of the Sound.

While people were wondering what he would do next, he had gone to work and fitted up great palatial steamboats, and invited the President to travel in them, which the President did, not dreaming that he was expected to build up a cattle-pen or a bear-garden in exchange for a little hospitality.

Well, it's hard satisfying a Vermonter when he once breaks loose from his native mountains. After gobbling up railroads and putting steamboats afloat, Mr. Fisk just swung back into Wall Street one day, and upset things generally in less time than any man ever did before. No shootist ever brought down more birds at a shot, than he left men in that street rich in the morning, and ruined at night. Cousin Dempster says it was awful.

Mr. Fisk didn't care, but wheeled out of the street just as he used to drive his pedler's wagon, with hoofs a-rattling and whips a-cracking, riding over ruined men everywhere in his track.

Besides all this, Mr. Fisk had a great, grand, overpowering Opera House, and carried on a theatre, in which women danced, like Black-crookers, and sang like—well, I can't tell what they did sing like, not having a comparison handy—but it was awfully interesting, Cousin Dempster said; and I believe him, for E. E. says he used to go to that Opera House alone so often, that she began to be afraid that he was getting into some business with Mr. Fisk that must be transacted in the evening—a thing she didn't like, the man being considered so overpoweringly fascinating.

I don't know whether Mr. Fisk belonged to the Woman's Righters or not, but there was a good deal of talk about him, such as would have compelled any religious society in Vermont to get up an investigation and some extra prayer-meetings, which he wouldn't have liked, being mostly given contrary-wise. But the one thing he hadn't done was to join a church, and, you see, nobody in particular had a right to call him to account but his wife, and she didn't.

Some people were mean enough to hint that his system of married life wasn't just the thing for a couple brought up in the purifying atmosphere of a Vermont village, and went so far as to turn up their noses because he lived about the Opera House and she in Boston, close to the very heart of the Hub, as if any woman could get further away from original sin than that.

But these slanderers knew as well as could be, that Mr. Fisk had a free pass on the telegraph and steam communication with his wife every day. Besides, didn't the newspapers give his most private actions to an admiring public, every few hours, and couldn't she read how blameless and self-sacrificing his life was.

Besides being a great financier and seafaring man, our Vermont pedler took up social life as a specialty, and distinguished himself among the high fashionables. The moral ideas that he had brought from Down East, were just as dashing as his Wall-street corners. He still kept the telegraph wires quivering with conjugal messages, and when he took domestic ease and the fresh salt air on the Jersey sea-coast, at Long Branch, in a high-swung carriage, with four seats, and stable help in trainer's clothes, wasn't his wife at another watering-place, called Newport, with a high-swinging carriage of her own, all cushioned off with silk, and with her gold-mounted harness rattling over six horses, just as black and shiny as his?

If that isn't conjugal sympathy, such as goes down among the upper crust of New York, I don't know what is.

Just the same number of horses, just the same swing in her carriage, just the same people—no, I am a little out there. She had relations in the seats, and he hadn't always.

But then, what is all that compared to a great many fash-

ionable, married folks in New York,—so extravagantly fond
of each other, that they make the Atlantic Ocean for a con-
necting link, year after year, and correspond tenderly in bills
of exchange.

Our poor, dead pedler from Vermont wasn't the only man
in New York who lived and loved by steam and telegraph.

XXVII.

MORE ABOUT FISK.

WHEN the New England mind, which is a little apt to
be troubled about the marriage relations of its emi-
grants, asks you about my report, you can say that
this New England couple were only following the upper-crust
fashion with married people in our great cities, where men and
their wives find the Atlantic Ocean more convenient than a
divorce court. Being imbued with morality from the Hub,
they only set an example of easy distances.

It takes a good, solid foundation of religion for even a born
Vermonter to stand against a sudden rush of money. This
man seemed to start fair. He began his life with *us*. Next
he went to Boston, the very spring and fountain of high moral
ideas, where every law has a higher law to nullify it. He left
his better half in the salubrious atmosphere, where she per-
formed her domestic duties alone, while he was toiling down
Erie railroad stock, and promulgating sweet sounds from the
Grand Opera House. Bound together in conjugal sympathy, by
ever-vibrating telegraph wires, what could have been more satisfactory and highly fashionable than these hymeneal relations?

This is what Cousin Dempster has been saying to me with a
queer smile on his lips, and something that seems almost sarcastic in his voice.

Says he, " If this way of life is persisted in, and is held respectable in social circles, who has a right to find fault when sin and sorrow spring out of it? Who among the thousands who abandon honorable homes for personal pleasures shall dare to condemn him ?

" Look over the list of outgoing steamers any month in the year, and see how large a proportion of husbands and wives travel together. Society, so slanderous in other things, is wickedly tolerant here, and makes a thousand excuses for the separation of married people.

" Children must·be educated. Just as if a free-born American boy or girl can't learn all he or she is capable of knowing in his own native land! Just as if any woman, who loves her husband and means to be a good mother, would listen for a moment to the idea of taking her family into foreign parts while her husband is tied down to business at home.

" Married people, who love each other, live together—temptations are serpent-like, but they seldom creep upon a hearthstone kept warm by domestic affection.

" Parents who are willing to live apart for the sake of their children, and call it a sacrifice to duty, may not know that they are hypocrites, but other people know it. Scandal thrives upon such things, and where scandal thrives domestic happiness perishes.

" The marriage relations are the soul of our social life ; relax them, take away one grain of their holiness, and you blast the blossom from which wholesome fruit can spring. When love and truth dies out of marriage, its vitality is gone. God forgive the men and the women who dare to hold the most beautiful tie that links soul to soul, as a wisp of flax, to be rent or burned at the will of our most evil passions.

" Can any human being make laws for himself and trample under foot those which have been for ages laid down by society, without meeting, sooner or later, with rebuke, and perhaps, ruin? Evil passions arouse evil passions. The profligacy and power of gold is sometimes most dangerous in a generous nature. In the hot sunshine of overwhelming good fortune, fiery passions are sure to thrive and tend to a poisonous growth. War is the mother of licentiousness. How much that men should avoid, and women shudder at, has sprung out of the civil war, which ebbs and flows even yet on the borders of our land! In that war men learned to be daring in other things than brave deeds, and women learned to be shameless, and glory in free speech, free actions, and free laws of their own devising.

"These thoughts are forced from me by the violent death of a man who had the brain and the heart to be an honor to our State, whose capacity and cordial good-nature might have gained him the love of better men than he ever knew in his brief and fiery career, and who had the brain to accomplish great things in the future."

I listened with breathless attention to what Cousin Dempster said. He spoke with feeling. I didn't think there was so much in the man. He got up from his chair and began to walk the room.

"I cannot dwell upon this man's wildly brilliant career," says he, "without a feeling of melancholy. Here existed the capacities of a great man, perfect health, wonderful energy, struggling aspirations toward the right—which he might hereafter have reached—generous. impulses running wild, strong affections, and overweaning ambition, all turbulent ostentations almost barbaric, and all hurled into nothingness by the blow of one bitter enemy.

"As he had lived, so they carried him to his grave, arrayed gorgeously in his coffin, lying in high state, not by the sacred altar of a church, but in the Grand Opera House, which had so long been the centre of his magnificence. Buried in flowers snow-white, as if gathered for the tomb of a vestal, glittering with gold, with clouds of perfume floating over him—in all the pomp of a monarch he was taken from New York, and carried for a last resting-place to Vermont.

"I wish it had been otherwise. Living as he did, dying as

he did, with the ruin of so many lives involved in his fate, that last journey should have been taken in simplicity and quietness. The lesson his death conveys is too solemn for display, too mournful for anything but stillness. The elements of a great man left Vermont only a few years ago; New York has sent back the ruins. Let them rest in peace."

Sisters, I did not think it possible that Cousin Dempster could get so fearfully earnest; his conversation has filled me with thoughts too solemn for careless utterance. In this man's death I hear a cry for merciful consideration—a solemn warning—a protest against the headlong speed with which this generation is trampling respectability under foot. This man's death is a subject of gossip now, when it should be a subject of mournful regret.

I do not speak here of the man who killed him, or the cause of his death. One is a subject that no lady would care to discuss. The other is in the hands of the law, which should be a sanctuary for the accused. The evidence has been heard thoroughly, and a jury has decided on it, merciful or not, its verdict is final.

But for Cousin Dempster, I should not have made this death the subject of a report, but some things that he has said startled me. Is it true that the alienation and separation of married people has become so easy and so fashionable? Can a husband and wife live apart months, years, and still keep up a pretence or the reality of affection, and be honored as respectable? I, for one, have no patience with such things. To me, marriage is a beautiful institution.

Do not smile, sisters; I am not thinking of the great Grand Duke now. In fact I am not thinking of myself at all. Cousin Dempster's earnestness has impressed me with apprehension and melancholy; he places this subject before me in a new light.

The man who is dead was in the full vigor of his life. The poor wept for him; he was good to them, and they believed that he had a kind heart. Sometimes that heart went back to the prayers of his mother. Had time been given him, something

tender and good might have found a noble growth in his nature.
We do not yet know, and never shall know, what he might have
been.

XXVIII.

SIIE WOULD GO.

DEAR SISTERS:—I have had a glorious and a refreshing season. I have felt, in the depths of my
soul, that the eyes. of all Vermont were on me in a
reflective way. As the moon is sometimes permitted to shine
before the sun goes down, I have added the light of my little
feminine luminary to the flood of public homage that sur-
rounds the greatest and best man that our State ever gave to
the world.

Saturday night, February third, was Horace Greeley's birthday. A gentleman up-town, who thinks the world of that
smartest\of good men, just made a house-warming on the occasion, and invited so many artists and poets, and editors and
statesmen, and people that Providence had labelled as something particular, that it is a wonder the roof wasn't blown off
with the yeasting of so much genius.

Of course the beauty and talent of old Vermont, wherever
it could be found, was hunted up, and invited with unusual
enthusiasm. Where beauty and talent could be found united
in one person—modesty forbids me to point out an instance—
of course an especial compliment was paid. My invitation had
a picture of the man, whose birthday we went to celebrate, in
the middle of the writing—a real good likeness, that I mean
to put in a locket and wear round my neck in honor of this
self-made man and of my own native State, which may have
double cause to glorify herself when the sixty-first birthday of
another person just standing in front of the Temple of Fame,

with her foot on the threshold, shall come round. I say nothing, but in the female line Vermont has laid up oceans of
future glory for herself.

Well, the day came. Once more I drew forth my pink silk
dress, and ironed out the flounces; one of them got a little
scorched, but I looped up the spot with a bow and a bunch of
roses, and found the scorch an artistic improvement. I twisted
my hair in corkscrews over night, and slept with my eyes wide
open, contented as a kitten, though the pull was tremendous.
I frizzed up the other woman's hair, for which I had paid ten
dollars in the Sixth Avenue, and made ready for the occasion
over night in a general way.

Of course Cousin Dempster and his wife were invited, being
my cousins, and so saturated with the family genius, that
people are constantly expecting it to break out, which it hasn't
yet, except in a general way. But Cousin D. made lots of
money in the war, and money is thought almost as much of as
talent by some people. Still, between ourselves, I don't think
they would have been invited if they hadn't come from Sprucehill; which is taking a literary position next to the Hub since
our Society has begun to publish my humble reports.

Well, just at nine o'clock, if you had been in front of my
boarding-house you might have seen a splendid carriage standing at the door, and that coachman, in his fur collar and cuffs,
sitting high up on the driver's seat, and scrouching his head
down while a storm of sleet and snow beat over him.

If you had looked toward the house, three or four eager
and curious faces might have been seen flat against every front
window as a certain dignified and queenly person came slowly
down the steps, with a white opera-cloak folded over her magnificent person, and a pink silk long train bunched up under
it, lining-side out.

The moment that carriage-door shut with an aristocratic
bang you might have seen those faces turn from the window
and look at each other—then noses turned up at sympathiz-
ing noses, giving out audible sniffs of that envy which the

6*

wonderful endowments of some persons are apt to engender in the inferior female mind.

But if you had looked into that carriage you would have seen it packed comfortably as a robin's nest in blossom time. There was my pink dress floating round me in rosy billows; there was Cousin E. E.'s corn-colored moiré antique swelling like a balloon on her side; and there was Cousin Dempster rising like a black exclamation point up from one corner, and *that child* drumming her blue kid-boots against the seat in another corner, and snarling because a gust of sleet came in with me before the fellow outside could shut the door.

When I saw her, my blood riled in a minute.

"Why, Cousin Dempster," says I, "children were not invited."

"Children, indeed!" says the child, giving her head a fling: "I suppose Cousin Frost thinks that nothing but old maids can be young ladies—the idea!"

"Daughter!" almost shrieked Cousin Emily E., a-catching her breath, and giving a frightened look over my way.

"My child, how can you be so rude?" says Cousin Dempster, stamping down among the fur robes, and mashing my foot under the sole of his boot.

I said nothing, but sat in dignified silence, wishing those two persons to feel that it was impossible the creature could mean me, but I trembled all over with righteous indignation, and wondered why that Bible benefactor, King Herod, had limited himself to boys, when he had such a glorious chance to sweep creatures like that out of existence in the female line. Oh! if I had been a Bible potentate!

"She was so anxious to go, being born in Vermont," says Cousin Emily Elizabeth; "it seems as if she knew Mr. Greeley."

"Reads the *Tribune* every day," chimes in Cousin Dempster, giving me a pleading look.

"I'll thank you to take the heel of your boot off my foot,

if you have held it there long enough," says I, with the firmness of a martyr and the dignity of an empress.

This wilted the whole party into silence, and we drove on, with the hail pelting against the windows, and lowering clouds inside.

All at once we got into a long line of carriages, and moved on as if we were going to a funeral instead of a birthday. Then the carriage stopped, the door was flung open, and we stepped under a long tent that stretched from the front door down a flight of stone steps and across the sidewalk. A carpet ran down the steps to the carriage, and we walked up that into the house; then through a hall, and upstairs, where we took off our cloaks and titivated up a little in a room half full of ladies, and blocked up with cloaks and things. I let down Cousin E. E.'s dress, and she let down mine; then we shook each other out, took an observation of each other from head to foot, tightened the buttons of our gloves, and went into the hall.

There stood Cousin Dempster, with his white gloves on, and a white cravat with lace edges around his neck, looking *so* gentlemanly. We went downstairs Indian file, for a stream of people were going down on one side all crimlicued off most gorgeously; and another stream was going up, with cloaks and hoods on, so there was no locking arms till we got into the lower hall. Then we just tackled in. I took one arm, E. E. took the other, and *that creature* followed after, looking like an infantile Black Crook in her short muslin skirts and bunched-up sash.

XXIX.

MR. GREELEY'S BIRTHDAY PARTY.

THE parlors were large and light, and crowded full. Just beyond the door I saw a man standing, with both hands at work, shaking out welcomes to his friends, as a chestnut bough rattles down nuts after a rousing frost.

There he stood—the honored son of our dear old State—looking benign as Mr. Benjamin Franklin, and sweet-tempered as if he had fed on native maple-sugar all his life. I looked eagerly for his " old white coat," but he had on a bran-new black one ; his hair, long and snow-white, fell down almost to his shoulders, that were rather broad than otherwise, which is needful considering the burdens that have been piled on them. I really think any stranger, going in there, would have known that this man owned a birthday by his face, it was so radiant with good-nature.

By and by we hustled our way to the door. A man that stood there whispered something to Cousin Dempster, who whispered back. Then the man sung out—

" Mr. and Mrs. Dempster—Miss Phœmie Frost ! "

Mercy on me, wasn't there a fluttering when that name rang through the crowd, as if blown by the trumpet of Fame. I felt myself blushing from head to foot, my heart rose into my mouth. I clung with feminine reliance on my cousin's arm, and, thus supported, prepared to endure the hundreds of admiring eyes bent upon me.

Mr. Greeley came forward. The moment he heard that name he seized the two whitely gloved hands that I held out to him.

" Miss Frost, of Vermont," says he.

I pressed his hands. I could not speak. A little address, full of poetry, that I had been thinking over in my mind, melted into chaos. I could only murmur something about birthdays and long lives. Then some new people crowded me away, and I felt myself alone long enough to take a look at the rooms. They were gorgeous with pictures and flowers; radiant with gas, which fell like August sunshine through a thicket of vines, and flowers woven in among the burners in the chandelier, and dropping down half way to the floor.

The marble slabs under the looking-glass at each end of the rooms were matted over with flowers, and from the top streamed down long feathery vines which ended in little bunches of red roses that swung loose before the glass, and left another vine there. Over the doors and windows these vines and flowers trailed themselves everywhere. Some beautiful pictures were on the walls. The centre one was of Greeley himself—just like him—bland and serene, smiling down upon the crowd as if he longed to shake hands over again.

This picture was just crowned with a mat of white flowers, in which the year our Greeley was born, and the present year, were woven with bright red flowers. Down each side the feathery vines trailed and quivered. I tell you, sisters, it was beautiful.

Before I could take in a full view, people had found out where I stood, and came crowding round me so close that I had to take in a reef of my pink silk dress, and they kept Cousin Dempster busy as a bee introducing them. So many people had read my writings, so many people had been dying to see me, it was enough to bring blushes to my cheeks and tears to my eyes. This, said I, is fame—and all Vermont shall hear of it, not for my sake, but in behalf of the Society.

The rooms had been full of music all the time, but now the toot horns and fiddles stopped, and I heard the tones of a pianoforte from the further end of the room, then a voice struck in—loud, clear, ringing. We pressed forward, people made way for us, and we got into the ring.

A young lady was standing by the pianoforte, singing " Auld Lang Syne." Greeley stood by her, holding her bouquet in his hand. How smiling, how satisfied he looked as the heart-stirring old song rang over him! Close by stood his only sister, Mrs. Cleveland, a fair and real handsome woman, dressed in blue sllk, with a white lace shawl a-shimmering over it. She looked happy as a blue jay on an apple-tree bough, and made everybody welcome over again when Mr. Greeley had done it once—just as a kind, warm-hearted woman ought to stand by a brother she is proud of, and looks like.

Near by were her two daughters, just the nicest girls you ever saw. One of 'em in a pink satin dress with lace over it, and the other in blue satin with lace—just lovely!

When the lady who did " Auld Lang Syne " went away from the pianoforte, every lady in the room began to clap hands, they seemed to be so glad that Mr. Greeley had found time to have a birthday. Then Miss Cleveland, in the blue dress, sat down, looking sweet and modest as a white dove; and she sang, too, real sweet; and then the people began to clap hands again. It seemed as if music just set them off into tantrums of delight because our great white-headed Vermonter had ever been born.

I joined in with a vim; for if there is anybody I like and am proud of, it is the man who was standing there smiling among his friends, with that great, lovely bunch of flowers in his hands, and a little one in the button-hole of his coat.

The wife and two daughters of our statesman and friend were over in England, so that his family connections didn't spread as if he had been President of the United States. But then he had a great many honest friends, and that made up for it considerably. There stood Mr. and Mrs. A. J. Johnson, who had carpeted their stone steps, set up a tent over their hospitable door, and turned their parlors into a blooming garden, just to show the respect they had for him; and they did it beautifully, making his friends theirs. At any rate, I can answer for one; for any person who does honor to a Vermont man who has glorified his State, can count on the faithful friendship of Phœmie Frost during his natural life.

At eleven o'clock, exactly, we all crowded around Mr. Greeley, and shook hands with him over again. Then we shook hands with Mrs. Johnson, who looked sweet, and was nice as nice could be; and with Mr. Johnson, and so on. After that, we all flocked out, with cloaks and hoods on, feeling that an evening like that was a refreshing season which will not be forgotten by some of us, so long as we live.

One thing I forgot to mention—and I do it now, with tears in my eyes. In the front parlor, on a line with Mr. Greeley's picture, was one that made the heart ache in my bosom, and which will bring tears into your eyes, one and all, I know. It was the picture of Alice Cary. You have read her poetry; you know how good she was from that poetry; but I have learned some things about her here, that, as a Society, you should hear about. But I respect her memory so much that it must be in a report by itself. She was a great friend of Mr. Greeley's, and her shadow seemed to smile on him as it hung upon the wall.

XXX.

LEAP YEAR.

DO you know that this is Leap Year? Do you begin to feel the glorious flood of liberty which it lets in upon the female women of this country? As a society and as individuals, let us press forward to the mark of the prize—I beg pardon.

This is not exactly a religious subject, though it does relate to the hymeneal altar, at which we have never yet been permitted to worship—a lasting and burning shame, which I, for one, begin to feel more deeply every day of my life.

True, my own prospects are brightening and glorifying, but circumstances have brought them, for the present, to a dead halt. But for the burst of golden sunshine let into my sad destiny by this opening Leap Year, I should be growing pale with suspense—for you know the great Grand Duke, though courteous and devotional, did not speak out in a perfectly satisfactory manner. I knew he meant it; for no robin's nest in laying time was ever so full of warm and brooding love as those blue eyes of his. But a cruel fate took him hence before the thrilling word was spoken, and left me trembling with doubt, pining in loneliness.

I know the reason of this now ; there is not a doubt that he has been anxious, like myself, but imperial royalty has its impediments. My Prince must bow to the exactions of a lofty station. I took up a paper the other day, and read something that made the heart leap in my bosom as a trout jumps after a fly. The Emperor has heard of the great Grand Duke's admiration. All Russia has heard of it and me. It is even reported that he has married a lovely and talented female, without waiting for the Emperor to say yes or no. The description answers, you will perceive. I felt myself blush, like a rose in the sunset, when I read it. "Lovely and talented." Sisters, there can be no doubt about it !

I felt my cheeks burn and my heart broaden with a sense of coming exaltation. Why should the Emperor refuse ? Are we not all queens in this country, and is not a woman of genius an empress among queens ?

I'm afraid the Emperor of all the Russias does not yet comprehend the great social system of our country, where the fact of being a woman has infinite nobility in itself—to which peculiar privileges are attached; for instance, the privilege of carrying pistols and shooting down men in hallways and street cars in a promiscuous fashion.

As I have said—to be a woman in America is to be everything. That is why I think it unreasonable that Imperial nobility should be forbidden to match itself here. Once we had aristocracy of money, but since the war, when people became rich in no time by selling shoddy and things, that has levelled down like a sand heap. But one aristocracy is left now, and that is the aristocracy of mind. Genius is the nobility of the mind. Now as long as the Prince unites himself with that, what has any one, even his august father, to say against it?

But there is no doubt I have given the Imperial heart some anxiety. *His* manner was so impressive; his spy-glass was levelled at my countenance so often, that it is not to be wondered at if the violence of his passionate admiration did get about and fly on the wings of the wind to his Imperial home. There it was sure to make an excitement. American ladies have married lords and marquises in England, counts and princes in other countries, and make first-rate lordesses and marchionesses and princesses too. In fact, just as good as the born nobility, and better too; but up to this time it is left to a lovely woman of genius to exalt America into the region of imperial highness. Money—for your lords, etc., etc., etc., generally want that with American beauty and grace—money has done its utmost. Now genius comes in, and modesty crowns itself.

I am satisfied that the great Grand Duke is only waiting, from a feeling of doubt and modesty. My heart compassionates him. Up to the first of January, I could do no more. Female propriety forbade it, but now—now all is changed. Modesty is disenthralled.

It is Leap Year. St. Valentine's Day approaches. The windows of every book-store are a-blazing with valentines, burning with love, eloquent of the tender passions, pictorial and poetical.

The Queen of England offered herself to Prince Albert. It must have been a touching scene. How modestly she suggested the flame that was kindled in her youthful heart, and still lies smouldering in the ashes of that good man's grave. I don't think she waited for Leap Year—but I will. No one shall say that Phœmie Frost has forgotten what is due to her sex.

St. Valentine's Day emancipates the womanly heart. I have bought a valentine, white satin, surrounded by a frost work

of silver lace, sprinkled with gold stars. On the satin is a little boy with wings, hiding behind a rose-bush, firing arrows
through it from a bow which he lifts up roguishly. These arrows are aimed at an Imperial figure mounted on a wild horse,
and running down a buffalo—a unique and beautifully suggestive idea. This was the poem which gushed with spontaneosity from my disenthralled mind:

> Come back, come back, from the buffalo raid !
>   Here is fairer game for you ;
> At thy feet the lovingest heart is laid
>   That ever a Grand Duke knew.
> A lady rich in womanly pride,
>   Whose soul clings unto thine,
> Is ready to be an Imperial bride—
>   Kneel with thee at Hymen's shrine.
> Come back, come back, or thy haughty sire
>   Will command, and all is lost ;
> But he cannot extinguish this holy fire
>   In the bosom of ———

Sisters, I ask you now, isn't this a gem? It isn't just the
thing to put your name to a valentine, they tell me, but this is
something deeper and more poetic than such things usually
are. It means mischief, as Cousin Dempster says. It is a
proposal, buried in roses and veiled in sweet and modest verse,
such as a lady might almost send at any time with a few
blushes. It will reach him out in that vast wilderness of dead
grass, where he has been deluded off by Mr. Sheridan, and has
risked his precious life in a terrific manner, shooting great,
monstrous buffaloes, which are animals, they tell me, something
like an overgrown ox, only the hair is longer, and they are kind
of hunched-up about the upper end of the back, just as if the
last city fashions among ladies had got to be the rage out there.
Imagine my feelings, sisters, when I heard that the Grand
Duke was off with that fellow and a squad of wild Indians, all
in war-paint and tomahawks, hunting these terrific creatures.
It almost made me feel like a widow. There he was, brought

up so tenderly, eating broiled buffalo hump, and drinking champagne and things out in the open lots, as big as all out-doors, and sleeping in a tent. Think of it! With his own right hand he shot down twenty-five of these humpbacked monsters, and means to carry their skins home with him to Russia. I suppose Mr. Philip Sheridan will be for studying the military tactics of Russia from St. Petersburg to Siberia as soon as the great Grand Duke gets back, for he isn't the sort of fellow, folks tell me, to give up a chance like that. Gover-nor Palmer, of Illinois, has, at any rate, given him leave of absence from the Chicago fires, and there isn't anything much to keep him from hunting in Siberia if he wants to.

Well, I got my valentine all ready; directed it to the Grand Duke in a delicate, ladylike way, and took it with my own hands down to the post-office.

"Be very careful of this," says I to a young man who stood at the post-office window, "and see that it goes straight to his Royal Highness; I want it to reach him the first thing in the morning on Valentine's Day."

He looked at the address, and muttered to himself:

"For His Royal Highness the Grand Duke of all the Rus-sias: care of Philip Sheridan and a wild Indian whose name a refined lady could not bring herself to pronounce; Buffalo Plains, America."

"My dear madame," says he, all at once, "this is no address at all; it would never reach the Grand Duke."

I caught my breath.

"Not reach him?" says I.

"No," says he; "the Grand Duke has gone beyond the reach of the mails."

"Goodness gracious!" says I; "but no matter about that, if he hasn't got out of the reach of the females."

"But he has."

My heart sank in my bosom like a soggy apple-dumpling.

"What—all females?" says I. "Won't that reach him, any-way? it is important—very. Great destinies depend upon it."

"I can put it in," says he; "but ten chances to one it will get into the dead-letter office."

My heart grew heavier and heavier, but what could I do?

"Put it in," says I; "live or die, it must go!"

He took my valentine and pitched it off into a heap of letters, just as if it had been a dead leaf. It fairly made me faint to see it handled so; but the fellow turned his back on me, and I went away heart-sick.

One comfort I had in all this—if my valentine could not reach him, that of no other female could; and my offer is sure to be first, though I shouldn't wonder if that girl who sent him her card tied round a canary bird's neck might try. She's forward enough, anyway.

Then, there is another comfort—Valentine's Day don't cover the whole Leap Year, and there are other men than the great Grand Duke in the world. We females have a whole twelve-months to try our luck in. Of course any of us would aim high the first months; but after that, the game will grow smaller and wilder, as a general thing, and our chances less.

For my part, I mean to be up and doing. One disappointment isn't going to break my heart; I've had too many for that; but if human energy and human genius can avail anything against an adverse destiny, my signature will be changed before this year closes.

XXXI.

A MAN THAT WOULDN'T TAKE MONEY.

COUSIN DEMPSTER is real good to me; no mistake about that. A day or two ago, he says to his wife, says he:

"Supposing we take Cousin Phœmie down to an oyster lunch at Fulton Market. That is one of the lions of the city."

I fairly hopped up from my chair when he said this, just as cool and easy as if he had been talking of rabbits lapping milk. What on earth had I to do with city lions, and such animals? Wild beasts like these are in no part of my mission, now are they?

Cousin E. E. saw the scare in my eyes, and smiled.

"I know it seems strange to people from outside," says she; "and it really is a dirty place; but somehow ladies and gentlemen have made it the rage."

"Do the creatures rage fiercely?" says I.

Cousin E. E. looked puzzled a minnte, then she answered:

"Oh," says she, "fashion takes queer twists sometimes; in this case it really is unaccountable. The people crowding into those wooden dens—and the eating done there is wonderful."

"Eating!" says I, feeling my eyes grow big as saucers. "Eating! Do they feed before folks, then?"

"Oh, yes; every lady goes; you never saw anything like it. Such Rockaways and other bivalves are to be found nowhere else."

"Rockaways and bivalves!" thinks I to myself; "what kind of animals are they? Never heard of bivalves before in my whole life, but the other puts me in mind of old Grandma Frost's splint-bottomed rocking-chair. No need of saying rock-away to her, for she was always on the teater. But she's dead now, and the last time I ever saw her Boston rocker it was away back of the chimney, at the old homestead, scrouged in between the stones and the clapboards, with one rocker torn off and an arm broken. I couldn't help asking Cousin E. E. if she remembered that chair.

"Oh, yes," says she; "somebody hustled it off into the garret the moment she'd done with it. I saw it there a year after the funeral, with the patchwork cushion of red and blue cloth moth-eaten and gray with dust."

Now, my father owned the old homestead while he lived, and I took this as a slur on our branch of the Frost family. This riled me internally, but I couldn't contradict her, and felt myself blushing hotly, rather ashamed of the Frost family.   But the truth is, as a race, we are none of us given to much antiquity.   No female of our family was ever known to get over forty-nine in her own person, though many of them have lived to a wonderful old age.   This was curious, but a fact.   Such unaccountable things do sometimes run in families.   But these are facts that I sometimes choke down—I did it now.

" We were talking of something else, and got on to chairs," says I.

" No uncommon thing," says Cousin Dempster, laughing.

I laughed too, but that child turned up her sniffy nose, and, looking at her father, said :

" The idea ! " which wilted him down at once.

" But these bivalves and Rockaways—what do they do with them ? "

" Why, eat them, of course."

" Eat them ?   How ? "

" Raw."

" Mercy on me !   Raw ? "

" Well, Cousin E. E., it shan't be said that you are related to a coward.   I'll go down to see these city lions; but when ? "

" Well, to-day," says Cousin Dempster.   " Just come down to the office about noon, and I'll go with you."

" Just so," says I, feeling a little shivery.

" Would you like to go, darling ? " says he speaking to his little girl, as if half afraid.

" Me, papa, down to that horrid place all meat and butter, and fish and things ?   The idea ! "

I was so grateful to the stuck-up thing, that I'm afraid Cousin E. E. saw it in my eyes, for she sort of clouded over and said :

" That, after all, she didn't think she cared to go, but that needn't keep Cousin Phœmie at home.   Mr. Dempster would take her."

" Well, just as you please," says he, a-taking his hat, " I'm at your service—singly or in groups.   Good-morning."

Well, in the afternoon, I asked Cousin E. E., in a kind of natural way, if she meant to go to that feed. But that child called out:

"No, no, mamma, don't go; I won't be left alone."

So Cousin E. E. said she had a bad headache, and thought she wouldn't go, but that needn't keep me.

Now, sisters, I wasn't brought up in the woods to be scared by owls, as we say in our parts—and if that little upstart thought she would keep me at home by domineering over her mother, she soon found out her mistake, for in less than two minutes a young lady, of about my size, came downstairs, with her beehive bonnet on, a satchel in one hand and an umbrella in the other.

"You will find the way easy enough," says Cousin E. E. "The cars take you close to the office, and you will get splendid oysters at the market."

Oysters! the very word made my mouth water, for if there is a thing on earth that I deliciously adore, it is oysters—such as you get here in York.

"Oysters!" says I, "why didn't you tell me that before?"

"We did," says she; "of course we did!"

I was too polite to contradict her; but I'll take my Bible oath that not one word about shell-fish of any kind had been mentioned that morning—nothing but a great city lion, Rocka-ways, bivalves, and animals like them. Still I said nothing, but went out encouraged by the idea that I was to have something to eat as well as the lion.

It was afternoon, and the street-car wasn't overfull, so I took a seat in one corner and began to think over a piece of poetry that I have got into my mind, which shortened the way to Dempster's office wonderfully. In less than no time I seemed to get there, but he had just stepped out. One of the clerks said that he thought he had gone to the market for lunch.

Oh, mercy! I felt as if my oysters were all out to sea again. I was too late.

"Which is the way to the market?" says I.

"I will show you," says he—which he did—walking by my side till I got in sight of a long, low, broad-spreading building that seemed all roof, and stone floors opening everywhere right into the street.

"Now," says the young gentleman, "you won't help finding your way, for there is Mr. Dempster himself."

He lifted his hat and bowed so politely that I felt impressed with a desire to reward him. Taking out my pocket-book, I handed him a ten-cent stamp, with a grateful and most benevolent smile on my countenance. I am sure of that from the glow I felt. He blushed—he seemed to choke—he stepped back and put on his hat with a jerk, but he didn't reach out his hand with the grateful spontaneosity I expected. His modesty touched me.

"Take it," says I, "it is no more than you deserve."

"Excuse me," says he; and his face was as red as a fireman's jacket.

"Good-afternoon;" and as true as you live he went off without taking the money. I never saw anything like it.

XXXII.

A DEMOCRATIC LUNCH.

S soon as I could recover from the surprise any New England woman would feel at a thing like this, I saw Cousin Dempster coming toward me.

"Come, hurry up," says he. "You were so late, I thought perhaps you had misunderstood, and come directly here. This way; be careful where you step; Fulton market is not the neatest place on earth."

I was careful, and lifting the skirt of my alpaca dress between my thumb and finger, gave a nipping jump, and cleared a gutter that ran between Cousin D. and myself. Then we walked into the market, with a whole crowd of other people, and trained along between baskets and square wooden pens heaped up with oranges, and things called bananas—gold-colored, and bunched-up like sausages, but awful good to eat. Potatoes, apples, books, peanuts, chestnuts, pies, cakes, and no end of things, were heaped on high benches on each side of us wherever we turned, till at last we passed through an encampment of empty meat-stands, and from that into a wooden lane with open rooms on one hand, and piles on piles of oysters on each side the door.

Every one of these rooms had a great rousing fire burning and roaring before it, and a lot of men diving in amongst the oysters, with sharp knives in their hands.

"Let us go in here," says Cousin Dempster, turning toward one of the rooms that looked cheerful and neat as a pink. The floor was sprinkled with white sand, and the tables had marble tops, white as tombstones, but more cheerful by half. As we went in, a man by the door called out, "Tuw stews!" Then again, "One roast—one raw on half-shell!"

Another man began firing pots and pans at the heap of blazing coals before him the moment this fellow stopped for breath. All this made me so hungry that I really felt as if I couldn't wait; but I kind of started back when I saw ever so many gentlemen and ladies in the room, sitting by the tables and feeding deliciously. Some of the men had their hats on, which did not strike me as over-genteel. But, after this one halt, I entered with dignity, placed my satchel in a corner, and took an upright position on one of the wooden chairs. Cousin Dempster sat down, too. He took his hat off, which I felt as complimentary, and a touch of the aristocratic.

"Now, what shall we have?" says he.

"A stew," says I, with a feeling of thanksgiving in my mouth.

Cousin D. said something in a low voice to the young man, who went to the door, and called out;

7

"One roast! one stew—Saddlerock!"

I started up and caught that young man by the arm, a-feeling as if I had got hold of a cannibal. Saddlerocks, indeed!

"Young man," says I, "you have mistaken your party; we didn't ask for stewed grindstones—only oysters."

He looked at me, at first, wild as a night-hawk, and seemed as if he wanted to run away.

"Don't be scared," says I; "no harm is intended; it is an oyster stew that we want—nothing more. I'm not fond of hard meat. If you don't know how to cook them—which is natural, being a man—I can tell you. Now be particular—put in half milk, a considerable chunk of butter, not too much pepper, and just let them come to a boil—no more. I do hate oysters stewed to death. You understand?" says I, counting over the ingredients on my fingers—"now go and do your duty."

"Yes'm," says he, and goes right to the door, and sings out: "One stew!—one roast!" so loud that it made me jump. Then he came back into the room, while I retired, with dignity, to my seat by the table.

It seemed to me that Cousin Dempster didn't quite like what I had done, for his face was red as fire when I sat down again, and I heard him mutter something about the eccentricities of genius. Indeed, I'm afraid a profane word came with it, though I pretended not to hear.

By and by, in came the waiter-man, with two plates of cabbage cut fine, and chucked a vinegar cruet down before me; then he clapped salt and pepper before Cousin D., with a plate of little crackers. Then he went away again, and came back with two plates full of great, pussy oysters, steaming hot, and so appetizing, that a hungry person might have made a luscious meal on the steam.

Oh, Sisters! you never will know what good eating is till you've been down to the Fulton Market, and feasted on oysters there; you can't get 'em first-rate in any other place. Try it, and you'll find 'em weak as weakness compared to these. Hot, plump, delicious! The very memory of them is enough to keep a reasonable person from being hungry a week. Talk of Delmonico's! I never was there; but if it beats this room in the Fulton Market in the way of shell-fish, I'll give up all my chances this Leap Year.

Well, when we'd done eating, two pewter mugs were set on the table, and Cousin Dempster handed one to me. I've heard of these mugs as belonging to bar-rooms and over intimate with ale and beer—things that I wouldn't touch for anything on earth, maple-sap being my native drink—so I pushed the cup away, really ashamed of Cousin D.; but he pushed it back a-kind of laughing, and says he :

" Just taste it."

" Beer ? " says I. " Never."

Cousin D. lifted his mug to his lip, and drank as if it tasted good. I was awful thirsty, and this was tantalizing.

" Try it," says he, fixing his bright eyes on me. " How do you know it is beer till you've tasted it ? "

" Just so," says I ; " I didn't think of that ? "

I took up the mug, and sipped a cautious sip. Beer, indeed! That pewter cup was brimming over with champagne-cider, that flashed and sparkled up to my lips like kisses let loose. Then I bent my head to Cousin Dempster, and just nodded.

Never think you have drank champagne-cider till you've taken it flashing from a pewter mug, after oysters, in Fulton Market; till then, Sisters, you will never know how thoroughly good-natured and full of fun a lone female can become. Some people might think champagne-cider like maple-sap with a sparkle in it, for the color is just the same; but it is considerably livelier, and a good deal more so, especially when one drinks it out of a pewter cup, and hasn't any way of measuring.

Bold ! I should think I was, after that. Bold as brass.

" Come," says I, taking up my satchel, " I'm ready to see that city lion, the Rockaways, and the bivalves fed. They have no terrors for me now. I've got over that. Where is their dens, or cages, and how often do they feed ?

Cousin Dempster set down his pewter mug, and just stared at me with all his eyes.

"What is it? What do you mean?" says he.

"What! the lion, to be sure! Didn't you say that I would see one of the city lions when I came to Fulton Market?"

That man must have been possessed. He leaned back in his chair, he stooped forward, his face turned red, and, oh! my how he did laugh!

"What possesses you, Cousin D.," says I, riling up.

"Oh, nothing," says he, wiping the tears from his eyes, and trying to stop laughing, though he couldn't; "only—only this isn't a menagerie, but a market. Did you really think there were wild beasts on exhibition? It was the market we meant."

Then I remembered that E. E. had called me a lion once. Now it was the market, and there wasn't a sign of the wild beast in either case. There *he* sat laughing till he cried, because I couldn't understand that ladies and markets were not wild animals. Says I to myself, "I'll make you laugh out of the other side of your mouth,"—so I turned to him as cool as a cucumber:

"What on earth are you te-he-ing about? I only want to walk around the market and see what's going on. Isn't that what we came for?"

Cousin D. stopped laughing, and began to look sheepish enough.

"Is that it?" says he.

"What else?" says I. "You didn't think I expected this great, big, low-roofed market to have paws and growl, did you," says I. "I would growl if the city were to set me down in the mud of this pestiferous place. So you thought I really meant it. Well, the easy way in which some men are taken in is astonishing. They never can understand metaphor," says I. "But the bivalves and Rockaways. What of them?" says I.

"Swallowed them," says he. Sisters, the dizziness in my stomach was awful.

XXXIII.

DEMPSTER PROPOSES A TRIP.

EAR SISTERS:—I have been in Washington. The great city of a great nation. I have seen the Capitol in all its splendid magnificence, its pictures, its marbled floor, its fruit tables, and its underground eating-rooms. I have seen the White House, and have had a bird's-eye view of the President of these United States.

I will tell you how it happened. I was getting anxious and down in the mouth; my valentine had been given to the winds of heaven—no, *they* would have carried it safely through ten thousand herds of buffalo cattle—but it had been given to the mails, and they are *so* uncertain, spell the word which way you will. Day after day I waited and watched, and sent down to the post-office to be sure there was no mistake in that department; but nothing came of it; no answer reached me. I became peaked and down-hearted, so much so, dear sisters, that Cousin Dempster got anxious about me, and one day asked me, in the kindest manner, if I would like to run on to Washington with him.

" Run on to Washington," says I; " how far is it, cousin ? "

" Why," says he, " about two hundred and thirty miles, I should say."

" Two hundred and thirty miles," says I, almost screaming. " Why, Cousin D., I couldn't do it to save my life."

" Oh ! " says he, " it isn't a very tedious ride."

" Ride," says I. " Why, didn't you ask me just now to run on with you ? How can I do both ? "

Cousin D. laughed, and began to rock up and down till he almost bent double; though what it was about I couldn't begin to tell.

" Well," says he, " just get your trunk or carpet-bag packed, and I'll call for you in the morning. Emily Elizabeth can't leave home just now, and it will be a great pleasure to me if I can have you along."

" If you'd just as lief," says I, " I'll speak to Cousin E. E. about it; under present circumstances, a young girl like me can't be too particular. I'm told that a good many married men have got a habit of travelling toward Washington in what seems like a single state, and it's wonderful how many of them have unprotected females put under their charge—sometimes, both ways. If E. E. has no objection, I'll be on hand bright and early."

Dempster kept on laughing, and I went upstairs wondering what had set him off so, but when I asked Cousin E. E. if she had any objection to my travelling to Washington with her husband, she began to laugh too, as if it was the best sort of a joke that a York lady should be expected to care about her husband's travelling off with other feminine women.

" Why," says she, a-wiping the fun and tears from her eyes with a lace handkerchief, " what do you think I care! We don't keep our husbands shut up in band-boxes here in the great metropolis.'

" No," says I to myself, " nor do you get much chance to shut 'em up at home, according to my thinking."

" Besides," says she, with comicality in her eyes, looking at me from head to foot: " I should never think of being jealous of you, Cousin Phœmie."

Here, that child looked up from a novel she was a-reading.

" The idea," says she, which was exasperating; especially as Cousin E. E. kept laughing.

" That is as much as to say you don't think I'm good-looking enough to be afraid of," says I, feeling as if a cold frost was creeping over my face. "Thank you."

Cousin E. E. started up from her lounge, which is a cushioned bench rounded off at one end, and a high-backed easy-chair at the other; and says she :

" I didn't mean that, cousin; there is no one for whom I have so much respect. It was on account of your high religious principle and beautiful morality that I was so willing to trust you with my husband."

"With papa. The idea!" chimed in that child, giving her head a toss. "They'll think it's his mother."

"My daughter!" shrieked E. E., holding up both her hands, and falling back into the scoop of her couch.

"Oh, let her speak!" says I, feeling the goose pimples a-creeping up my arms. "I'm used to forward children. In our parts they slap them with a slipper, if nothing else is handy."

"A slipper; the idea!" snapped that child.

I didn't seem to mind her, but went on talking to her mother.

"But here, in York, the most careful mothers wear button boots, and keep special help to put them on and off, so the poor little wretches have no check on their impudence."

"Mamma," snapped the creature, "I won't stand this; I won't stay in the same room with that hateful old maid. I hope she will go to Washington and be smashed up in ten thousand railroads. That's the idea!"

With this the spiteful thing walked out of the room with her head thrown back, and her nose in the air.

"Let her go," says E. E., sinking back on her couch as red as fire. "The child has got her share of the old Frost temper. Now let us talk about Washington. Do you mean to go *incog.?*"

"Incog! Oh, no," says I, beginning to cool down. "We mean to go in the railroad cars."

Another glow of fun came into Cousin E. E.'s eyes—she really is a good-natured creature; some people might have got mad about what I said to that child, but she didn't seem to care, for the laugh all came back to her eyes.

"Of course," says she, "but do you mean to go in your own character?"

"Why," says I, "don't people take their characters with them when they go to Washington?"

"They sometimes leave them there," says she, laughing, "but this is what I mean; if I were you I'd take this trip quietly, and look about a little without letting people know how great a genius they had among them. By and by we will all go and take the city by storm."

"Just so," says I, delighted with the plan, which has a touch of diplomacy in it—and I am anxious to study diplomacy under the circumstances, you know; "creep before you walk—that is what you mean."

"Just pass as Miss Frost—nothing more—and make your own observations," says E. E.

"I will," says I. "It's a good idea. I don't think the people in Washington were over polite to my great Grand Duke, and I mean to pay them off, some day."

"That's settled," says E. E. "Now you have no more than time to get ready."

XXXIV.

IN WASHINGTON.

 HURRIED back to my boarding-house, packed up that pink silk dress and things, put on my alpaca dress, tied a thick brown veil over my beehive, and packed my satchel till it rounded out like an apple dumpling.

We started that night. Cousin D. wanted me to go into a long car where people slept, he said; but I saw a good many men with carpet-bags going in there, which looked strange, and though I have great faith in the integrity of Cousin Dempster, a young lady in my peculiar circumstances cannot be too particular; I declined to go into that curtained, long car, and sat up in a high-backed chair all night, wide awake as a whip-poor-will, for Cousin Dempster was on the next seat sleeping like a mole, and his head more than once came down so close to my shoulder that it made me shudder for fear that people might not know that he was my cousin's husband, and snap up my character before I got to Washington.

Well, at last we got out of that train, I stood with both feet in the heart of the nation, and a great, flat, straggling heart it is.

"There it is—there is the Capitol," says Cousin Dempster. "Look how beautifully the sunshine bathes the dome and the white marble walls."

I looked upward—there, rising up over a lot of tall trees and long, green embankments, rose a great building, white as snow, and large as all out-doors. The sun was just up, and had set all its windows on fire, and a great, stout woman perched on the top of a thing they call the dome—which is like a mammoth wash-bowl turned wrong side up—looked as if she was tired out with carrying so much on her head, and longed to jump down and have a good time with the other bronze-colored girls that show themselves off, just like white folks inside the building.

Well, later that day, 1 went right up to that heap of marble, which in its length and breadth and depth filled my soul with pride and patriotic glory. I really don't believe there is another building like it on the face of the earth. Freedom, honesty, and greatness *ought* to preside there.

Why, sisters, there are whole rooms here of clouded marble, ceiling, floor, walls—everything polished like the agate stone in your brooch, and I do think that the hottest sun can hardly force a beam of warmth through.

Down in the great wandering cellars you come upon staircases of beautiful marble, fenced in with railings of iron and gold and brass all melted together and called bronze, up which deer, as big as young lambs, are jumping, and branches of trees are twisted. There are ever so many of these staircases, and they cost one hundred thousand dollars apiece. Think of that! and mostly where it is so dark that you can't but just see them.

"I hadn't only one day and night to look about in, so I went

7*

up there before Congress got to work, as I wanted to see things without having people know that I was there. But by and by a lot of men came swarming in, and I felt like making myself scarce.

I went back to the hotel and got a little sleep.

It was dinner time, and near candle-light when I woke up; and when we got through dinner, Cousin D. told me to hurry up, and we would take a look at the White House.

"Shall I get out my pink silk?" says I. "Does the President expect me?"

"Oh, no," says he; "no one is aware that we are here. We will drive to the White House, see all that is to be seen, and start home bright and early to-morrow morning."

"Then the alpaca will do," says I.

"Of course," says he; "anything."

I wasn't sorry. This travelling all night is apt to take the ambition out of the most energetic character. The difference between pink silk and alpaca was nothing to me now.

Well, in an hour after, the carriage we rode in stopped under a great square roof, set on marble pillars, which spreads out from the steps of the White House to keep people sheltered from the storm and sun when they get out of the carriages. It was dark now, and two great street-lamps were in brilliant combustion each side of the steps.

Between us, sisters, that White House that we hear so much about is no great shakes of a building. Compared to the Capitol, it is just nowhere.

Cousin D. rang the knob, which was silver, and a man opened the door.

"We should like to see the House," says Cousin D.

"Certainly," says the man. "Walk in."

We did walk into a large room, with a few chairs and two or three pictures in it; nothing particular, I can tell you.

"This way," says the man.

We went that way, into a great room, long and wide as a meeting-house, choke full of long windows, and with three awful large glass balloons, blazing with lights, a-hanging from the roof.

The carpet was thick and soft as a sandy shore, and had its colors all trampled in together, as if some one had stamped down the leaves of a maple camp into the grass as they fell last year.

" The chairs and sofas and looking-glasses were bought when General Washington was President," says the man.

" Mercy on me ! you don't say so," says I. " They look rather skimpy for these times, don't they ? " says I; but then his way of buying things and spending money was a little skimpy compared to the way Presidents spend money now; but, of course, we grow more deserving as we grow older. " Now, those red silk curtains that almost hide the lace ones, did they belong to Washington ? "

"Them ? Oh, no; we change them every four years."

" Then they go out with the President," says I.

" We don't think that he will go out yet awhile," says the man, looking a little wrathy.

" Well, I hope he won't, for great men are scarce in these times," says I, wanting to mollify him. He said nothing, and I followed him through a door into a smaller room, so full of green that it seemed like stepping out of a blazing sun into a fern hollow. The walls were green; the carpet was green as meadow grass; the sofas and chairs were cushioned with green satin. The glass balloon seemed to have a sea-green tinge in it, though it was blazing like a bonfire.

Not a soul was in the room, and we went on to the next which was long, rounded off at the ends like a lemon, and blue as the sky. Down the tall windows came curtains of blue silk, sweeping over white lace. The chairs seemed framed in solid gold ; their cushions were blue silk.

" This is the celebrated blue room," says the man.

" I've heard about it," says I.

" And this," says he, " is the red room. The President has given a dinner-party to General Sickles this evening, and they are now at the table. Would you like to look in ? "

Before I could answer, we were standing in the red room, and looking through at a table crowded round with gentlemen and ladies, dressed like queens and princes, some of them looking handsome as angels.

"That is General Sickles," says he, "a-sitting by Mr. Grant."

I looked in, but could only see a face, not over young, turned towards a lady who was listening to him, as if every word he dropped was a ripe cherry. She had a good, honest face, and I liked her.

"That is Mrs. Sickles, sitting by the President," says the man.

"What, that girl! you don't say so. Why, he might be her father."

It was the truth—a young, black-eyed thing, rather pretty and childish, sat there by General Grant—I knew it was Grant by his features—talking to him as if he had been her brother. Her dress was high up in the neck, but most of the ladies there wore them so low that I felt like turning my eyes away; but Cousin D. says that low-necked dresses always rage as a chronic epidemic in Washington, so I mustn't be surprised.

"That is General Sheridan," says the man.

"That little cast-iron image, General Sheridan!" says I, a-starting back. "The fellow that cured a whole tribe of Indian women of small-pox with bayonets and bullets! I don't want to see anything more! Just let us go away, cousin; I haven't been vaccinated, and he might break out again."

"Hush! hush! he isn't dangerous," says Cousin D.

"Dangerous!" says I, "just ask the Governor of Illinois. Wasn't it General Sheridan who dragged off the Grand Duke among the Indians and buffaloes? I tell you again I won't stay another minute in the house with that man!"

Sisters, I kept my word. We departed at once.

XXXV.

GETTING INFORMATION.

Y DEAR SISTERS: —I made what people here call a flying visit to Washington, which means, I suppose, that the railroad cars go about as swift as a bird flies, which they do, if one is allowed to choose the bird—a white bantam, for instance, with clipped wings. Well, I really don't know much about the speed, only I was awful tired when we got out of the cars at Jersey City, and we had the lonesomest drive home just before daylight that two tired mortals ever undertook. The whole city was still as a graveyard, and put one in mind of those cities over the sea, dug out of the ashes in which they have been buried hundreds on hundreds of years.

To me, sisters, nothing is more dreary than a great city shut up and full of sleeping people. Only think of it! half a million of human beings all lying in darkness, unconscious of both happiness or misery, just as if sleeping in their tombs, only that the first glow of sunshine brings them to life again. Did you ever think of it?

Now, in the country the stillness is not so mournful—there is a sense of out-door freedom there. The leaves stir with life on the trees. The brooks murmur and gurgle and laugh by night as they do by day. The birds flutter now and then, and the winds whistle and whisper, filling the night with a stir of life. But here—here in a great city, a ghost-like policeman, or a poor straggling wretch who has no home but the street, is all that you see. Indeed, coming home before daybreak isn't a thing I hanker to do over again.

Well, after pulling at the bell-knob till I'm afraid Cousin Dempster swore internally, we got into the house, and had a good long sleep before breakfast.

"I'm so glad you've come," says Cousin E. E., "for the Liederkranz comes off to-night, and I was afraid we should lose it. Of course you'll go, Cousin Frost?"

"Well," says I, "perhaps I can tell better when I know what the thing is. It's a crabbled sort of a word, that might belong to an aligator or kangaroo ; and I don't care overmuch for wild-beast shows, any way." Cousin E. E. laughed.

"Well," says she, "in some sense you are right. There will be a show of wild animals such as never roamed in field or forest, but none of them are dangerous ; at any rate, in that form."

"Are they in a circus, and is there a clown with a chalky face and red patches ? " says I.

"The circus ! " says she, a-holding up both hands. "Why, it is to be in the Academy of Music, and the first people in the city are going."

"To see them feed ? " says I.

"Well, that may be a part of it, but the principal thing is the parade."

"But where do they feed the animals—not in the boxes with red velvet cushions, I calculate ? "

"Oh, how funny you are ! Of course not ; the supper is set out in Nilsson Hall, and is served *à la carte*."

"What ! " says I ; "do they bring in fodder by the cartload for the creatures ? Now, really, Cousin E. E., there is nothing astonishing about that to a person born and bred in the country. You and I have ridden on a load of hay, piled up so high that we had to bend down our heads to keep from bumping them against the top of the barn door, when the hay went in to be put on the mow ; so we need not see the same thing meached over here in York."

"Dear me ! " said my cousin ; " you are just the brightest and stupidest woman——"

"Young lady, if you please," says I.

"Well, young lady—that I ever set eyes on—can't you comprehend that it is a ball we are speaking of ? "

"A ball ? " says I ; " then what did you call it a Liederkranz for ? "

"The Liederkranz ball. It's a German word."

"But I don't speak Dutch. How should I, not being an old settler of York Island," says I.

"Well, never mind that. The Liederkranz is a masked ball."

"A masked ball! Now what do you mean? I've heard of masked batteries, but they went out with the war."

"There it is again; you won't take time to understand," says Cousin E. E., a-lifting both her hands in the air. "This is a ball where people go in character."

I arose at once, burning with indignation.

"Cousin E. E.," says I, "do you mean to insult me? What have you seen in my conduct to lead you into supposing that I would go to any ball that was out of character?"

"Do sit down," says she.

"Not in this house," says I. "It isn't my own dignity alone that I have got to maintain, but the whole Society of Infinite Progress is represented in my humble person."

"But you are mistaken. Was ever anything so absurd! Do speak to her, Mr. Dempster. You know how far it is from my mind to give offence to Cousin Phœmie."

Cousin Dempster, who had been rubbing his hands and enjoying himself mightily, now smoothed down his face, and spoke.

"A masked ball, Cousin Phœmie, is an entertainment, you understand."

"Just so," says I.

"In which each person takes some character not his own."

"All slanderers, are they?" says I.

"No, no; they assume a character."

"Oh!" says I, a-drawing out a long breath; "make believe have one?"

"They dress the character, and act it."

"Well?" says I, completely beat out.

"Some dress themselves up as beasts and birds."

"What?"

" And some as tame animals."

" You don't say so ! "

" The ladies put masks on their faces."

" Masks ! now what are they ? "

" Pieces of silk, or gold and silver cloth, with holes for the eyes, and a fringe over the mouth. Then over the dress they put on a great circular cloak, with a hood to it, and loose sleeves that hide the shape, so that a man don't know his own, wife."

" Oh, it's a hide-and-seek ball; but ain't some of the ladies in danger of losing themselves," says I.

Cousin Dempster laughed, and his wife turned red as fire.

" People who lose themselves at the Liederkranz, generally get found out in the end," says he.

" But I must hurry down town. Will you go ? Everybody will be there. It is the place to meet a prince in disguise."

As Dempster uttered these words, my heart gave a great, wild bound, and my breath stopped. What if *he* were to be at the ball in disguise, seeking a safe and private interview.

" Yes, yes, I will go," says I, " but I don't know either ! The mask and cloak ! "

" Never mind about them," says E. E. ; " I have a couple ready, feeling sure that you would go."

" Then it is settled," says Dempster, snatching up his hat. " I will be on hand. So good-morning ! "

XXXVI.

THE LIEDERKRANZ BALL.

EAR SISTERS :—That night about ten o'clock, three of the funniest-looking people you ever set eyes on might have been seen creeping—like black, and pink, and yellow ghosts—down Cousin Dempster's front steps.

I had on a long yellow cloak, trimmed with black velvet, that just swept down to my feet and covered them up. Then over my face was a black velvet mask, with gold fringe, that swept down to my bosom like an old man's beard, and over that my hood was pulled so close that not a lock of my hair could be seen.

Cousin E. E. wore a pink cloak, trimmed with white swan's-down, and her mask shone like silver.

Dear sisters, you wouldn't have known me from the Queen of Sheba.

Dempster was black all over—mask, cloak, and boots. It seemed as if half a dozen funerals had been rolled into one, and hung on him.

Well, we crowded into the carriage and drove off. It seemed as if we never should get untangled from the drove of carriages that swarmed around the Academy of Music, and when we got in, and found ourselves struggling with the crowd, we almost wished ourselves back again.

I looked around everywhere, as I went, for that tall and princely form ; but the crowd was so thick, and the dresses so queer, that it seemed next to impossible to find out anything or know anybody. The lights from the great glass balloons poured down rainbows on the crowd, that moved and chatted and laughed till the noise was confusing as the dresses.

"Step back, step back !" says Cousin Dempster, all at once, "the procession is coming."

We did step back, and tried our best to see the procession ;

but the floor was pretty much on a level, and, though I stood
on tiptoe, all that I could see was, now and then, the head of
an eagle, or a bear, or a giraffe, rising above the crowd, while
the music rang out in thunders of sweet sounds, and the people
swarmed in and out of the little square pews in the galleries,
like bees hiving on a hot summer day.

Of course, I knew well enough that all this moving circus
was make-believe, and that every wild animal had a man in him,
just as every man has the shadow of some animal in his nature.
But I couldn't help stepping back and shuddering a little, when
a great big lumbering elephant rolled by, with his trunk curled
up in the air, and almost trod on me.

"Oh, mercy, !" says I, with a little scream. "He's enough
to frighten one out of a year's growth!"

"Don't be terrified," says a voice behind me, and I felt an
arm a-stealing around my waist; "I am here to protect you."

I looked up. My heart stopped beating. The stranger was
tall, majestic, and the eyes that shone through his mask were
blue as robin's eggs. He had on a black cloak, and the mask
covered his whole face; but how could I mistake the princely
bend of that head, the breadth of those majestic shoulders.

He drew me back from the crowd. I forgot Cousin Dempster, E. E., and everything else, in the ecstacy of that sweet
surprise.

"You have forgotten the roses," he whispered, with a look
of loving reproach.

I felt for the bouquet Cousin Dempster had given me—it was
gone.

"I must have dropped them as I got out of the carriage,"
says I. "But when did you come?" I added, in a whisper,
tremulous with bliss.

"Oh, I came an hour ago, and in the usual way," was his
sweet answer; "but, not seeing the flowers, I doubted."

"Ah! how I prayed that you would grow weary of that
miserable buffalo hunt, and return!" says I.

He seemed just a little puzzled, but at last broke out:

"Oh, it's all a grotesque farce. Why should wise men turn themselves into wild animals, if it is only in sport? I never enjoy such parties for themselves."

" I am glad to hear you say that," says I; "and more glad that you have left off hunting with Phil Sheridan; he might have led you into some Indian camp filled with Modocs, who would have shot you for sport."

" Sheridan," says he. " Oh, he doesn't stay in one place long enough to do much harm."

" Exactly," says I ; " but he works quickly. Still, you are here, safe and sound; why should we waste time over him ? "

"True enough," says he; " so take my arm, and let us promenade."

I took his arm, and clasping both hands over it after a fashion I have seen prevalent among young girls when they walk out with their lovers by moonlight, moved proudly through that throng—very proudly—for I knew that long cloak covered imperial greatness that would have astonished that assembly, had they known as much as I fondly suspected.

" Tell me," says I, in a soft whisper, " did you receive a valentine ? "

" Did I receive a valentine ? " says he. " Why do you ask ? "

" Ah ! " says I, " do not question me."

" But I must. Tell me something about it."

" It was original. It was poetry," says I.

" Poetry—and yours! How can you doubt its effect ? "

" I do not doubt. Are you not by my side ? " I whispered.

He drew my hand under his loose sleeve, and pressed it tenderly—so tenderly, that I did not know when the handkerchief it held escaped from my grasp to his; but, directly after, I saw him thrust something white into his bosom. It was my very best handkerchief, embroidered with my name; but I said nothing—how could I ?

We walked on. The crowd swarmed and hummed like bees in a clover-field. Now and then a great gray eagle flapped by, or a bear prowled along; but, after all, it was a clumsy make-believe, and didn't scare anybody much.

By and by a lady came along dressed just like me—yellow and black all over.   She stared at me, and I stared at her—just my height—just my air—modest, but queenly.   There was a trifling difference—she wore a bunch of red roses on her bosom.

After staring at me awhile, she drew softly round to the other side, and it seemed as if she was saying something to *him.* I can't tell you what happened next; for just then four great big gilt candlesticks walked into the middle of the room, and began to dance, in a way that fairly took me off my feet.   It really was too funny.   The style in which they hopped up and down, crossed over, and stalked about, was enough to make a priest laugh.

"Isn't it awful queer !" says I, a-turning to the man who had come so far to tell me of his love.

He was gone.   I stood there alone in the crowd, my limbs shook, my heart sunk like lead.   How had I lost him ?

Wild with a sense of widowhood, I wandered to and fro over that ball-room.   Many people spoke to me ; some gentlemen in disguise wanted to walk with me; but I evaded them all. Some I answered ; to some I gave nothing but sighs.   At last I felt tears stealing down under my mask, my strength gave way, I sat down on a cushioned bench in a fit of despondency. The cup of bliss had sparkled at my lips, and been dashed aside.

What did I care for the men and women who were whirling, talking, and dancing around me !

"Cousin, are you almost ready to go home ?"

It was Cousin Dempster who spoke; he had been searching for me high and low, and was shocked to find me sitting there alone.   I said nothing, but, like that Spartan boy, gathered the yellow waves of my cloak over the vulture that knawed at my poor heart, and followed my cousin out of the crowd—still looking eagerly for that one noble figure, but looking in vain.

XXXVII.

HOW DID THE PAPERS KNOW?

EAR SISTERS:—Would you believe it? Cousin Dempster had hardly got down to his business after the ball, when a telegram—I think that is the name of the thing that he said came flying over the wires—called him to Washington again. Cousin E. E. made up her mind to go with him this time, and nothing would satisfy her but that I must join in and cut a dash with them. After the strange way in which that majestic man in the black cloak had gone off with the yellowhammer of a female, I had felt so down in the mouth that nothing seemed to pacify me. If it really was the great Grand Duke, his conduct was just abominable. I wouldn't have believed it of him; taking off a lady's handkerchief in his bosom, and that the best one she had in the world, and not bringing it back again. Such conduct may be imperial, but it isn't polite, that I must say, though it wrings my heart to find fault with him. If he had brought it back the next day, of course it would have been different; but he didn't, and there I sat and sat, waiting like patience on a—on a stone wall, smiling, but wanting to cry all the time.

"It'll do you good, and cheer you up," says Cousin E. E.

"Maybe it will," says I, drawing a heavy breath, "but I don't seem to expect much. February is gone, and no answer to—"

I bit my tongue, and cut off what it was going to say about that valentine, for that was a secret breathed only to you, as a Society, in the strictest confidence.

"This time," says Cousin E. E., "there shall be no secrecy. The whole world shall know that the rising genius of the age is with us. The day we start, all the morning papers will announce that Mr. and Mrs. Dempster, of ———, have gone to Washington, accompanied by that celebrated authoress, Miss

Phœmie Frost, who cannot fail to meet with every attention from the statesmen and high fashion of the Capital."

"But how are the papers going to know?" says I.

E. E. laughed.

"Oh, Dempster will manage that; he's hand-and-glove with ever so many city editors," says she.

"Oh!" says I.

"There are some things that even genius itself don't know how to manage," says E. E., nodding her head, and smiling slyly; "but they can be done. As soon as we get to Washington, all the papers there will catch fire from New York, and the Senate will get up another committee, and vote you a seat in the diplomatic gallery by ballot. We'll break right into the Japanese furore, and carry off the palm," says she, kindling up like a heap of pine shavings when a match touches it.

, I began to feel the proud Frosty blood melting in my bosom.

"The woman who writes is more than equal to the man who votes," says she.

"There is no comparison," says I. "Women are women and men are men—nobody thinks of comparing rose-bushes and oak-trees—one makes timber and the other perfume; we shelter the roses, and let the oaks battle for themselves. So it ought to be with men and women—"

Cousin E. E. cut me short.

"That is beautifully expressed," says she, "but save it for one of your reports or literary conversations; my head is full of Washington."

"And my heart is full of sadness," says I, beginning to droop again.

"Nonsense, you will be happy as a bird when we once get a-going," says she.

Cousin E. E. isn't a woman of great depth, but she knows a thing or two about fashionable life.

The York papers *did* announce to the world that a distinguished party had gone on to the seat of government, and, singular enough, it was done exactly in E. E.'s own words—a circumstance that rather puzzled me. What was more—the very day we got to Washington all the papers there did the same thing, which set us at the top of the heap at once.

I hadn't the least idea of interfering with the Japanese that came to us from California, and in that way seem to be turning the world the other side about from what it used to be; but when genius takes the bit between its teeth, it's apt to scatter things right and left. I suppose it was the newspapers did it, but I hadn't been a day at the hotel when a letter come to us from the President's mansion, which invited us to come to the White House and see the Japanese presentation—in full dress.

I declare I felt myself blushing all over when I read that. Did any one suppose that we were a-coming to meet those outside potentates half dressed? Some of them, perhaps, unmarried men.

"The idea!" as that child would say. I showed the card to Cousin E. E., who seemed to think it all right, so I said nothing, though the whole thing had riled me so it seemed as if I never should stop blushing.

"What does it mean," says I.

"We must go, Dick or Lottie," says she.

"Go—how?" says I. "Haven't they got horses and carriages in this great city, that we must go in an outlandish thing like that?"

Here E. E. broke into one of her aggravating titters; but when I gave her a look she choked off, and says she:

"It means low necks and short sleeves."

"Low necks and short sleeves! Why didn't they say so, then? What has any Dick or Lottie got to do with it? But it's no use; I won't wear anything of the kind. Those who want to have a shoulder-strap for a sleeve, and their dresses too short at one end and too long at the other, can; I won't—there!"

"Oh! you are privileged; genius always is," says E. E.

"That is, genius is privileged to be decent in Washington. Well, I'm glad of that," says I. "Some young ladies may

like to go about with bare arms and shoulders—let them.
I wont!"

XXXVIII.

RECEPTION OF THE JAPANESE.

WELL, SISTERS, that afternoon the distinguished party mentioned in the papers got out of a carriage, under that square roof in front of the White House steps, and walked with slow, stately steps into the ante-room, that I told you of. One of them—a tall, imperial-looking person—was robed in a flowing pink silk, just a little open at the throat, where it was finished off with white lace with a snow-flake figure on it. A long curl fell down this lady's left shoulder, and there was a good deal of frizzing about the lofty forehead, and any amount of puffs back of that.

The other lady—who naturally kept a little in the background—wore white satin, cut to order about the neck and shoulders, and a lot of white stones on her bosom and in her hair, that shone like fire in a dark night.

The man at the door seemed to know us, for he said, "If it's Miss P. Frost and her friends, walk this way."

We did walk that way, and drew up in that lemon-shaped room, which is so blue and white that you seem to think yourself in the clouds when you go in. Right in the centre of the room is a great big round ring of seats, cushioned all over with blue silk; and right up from the middle of it rose a splendid flower-pot, crowded full of flowers—white, pink, and all sorts of colors—with great long green leaves a-streaming over the edges, and broad, white lilies, that seemed cut out of ragged snow, a-spreading themselves among the green leaves.

A hive of ladies, all in long-trained dresses, and necks according to order, were sitting or standing or moving across the room, looking as proud and grand as peacocks on a sunshiny day. Among them was the President's wife—a real nice, sociable lady—who looked just as she ought to in a black velvet, long-trained dress. In fact, of all the women in that room, I liked her the best, she is so sweet and kind in her manners. The minute we came in she turned round and gave us a warm, honest smile, which was about the only downright honest thing I've seen in Washington, as yet.

" Miss Frost," says she, " I'm delighted to see you and your relations. My friend Senator Edmunds has told me about you ! "

"Thank you," says I. " No one need want a better recommendation than he can give. We think the world of him in our State."

" I'm glad to hear that," says she. " We think a great deal of him too; in fact, Vermont honors herself in the Senate. But you are looking at the flowers; they are all Japanese, in honor of the Embassy."

" You don't say so," says I; "did the Japanese bring the flowers along with them from Japan ? "

She laughed a sweet, good-natured little laugh, and says she:

" Oh, no; we raise them in the hot-houses."

Just then there was a bustle in the ante-room, and I saw a slow line of queer-looking little folks filing along toward the east room. Mrs. Grant had turned to talk to Cousin E. E., and I just slid out into the green-room, and stood inside the door to see what all the fuss was about.

Standing against the great window, nearly opposite to me, I saw the President of these United States, with a lot of men around him in black clothes, and farther on stood another lot with their coats all covered over with gold and stars of precious stones a-hanging one after another on their bosoms, and some wore swords, and some didn't; but I tell you there was such a blaze of colors and flash of gold that it seemed to light up the great long room like sunshine, which was convenient, for there wasn't enough in the sky that day to light a family to bed.

8

While I was wondering what all this magnificence and glory meant, Cousin Dempster happened to see me, and came up to the door.

"What on earth does all that signify in a free country," says I. "It looks like a circus. Do they mean to ride in there? I don't see no horses; and it seems to me their hoofs will spoil the carpet when they come in. Are the Japanese people fond of horses?"

"I don't know about that; the President is," whispers Cousin Dempster. "But never you mind that; he keeps 'em in his stables, and they're not likely to come here."

"Then these fellows in the gold coats will only do rough-and-tumble, I suppose," says I.

"Hush!" says Cousin D., looking round to be sure that no one heard me. "The rough-and-tumble has been pretty much done up in the Senate this winter."

"Oh!" says I.

"There will be a good deal of it in Philadelphia and Cincinnati, and all over the country, I'm afraid, for I don't think General Grant cares much about that sort of gymnastics."

"Jim what?" says I.

"Turning over and over from one side to the other!" says he.

"I think he's right," says I. "A circus can't be much without horses and hoops, and that fellow with the painted face; but why don't the show begin, such as it is? What do they stand there for, looking lonesome as a cider-press in winter?"

"My dear cousin," says he, looking at me sort of pitiful, "do remember it is the ambassadors of all Europe, to say nothing of South America, that you are speaking of."

"Ambassadors," says I; "so you call them by that name here, do you?"

"They represent governments, kings, and queens."

"I've seen that done in the theatre beautifully. You remember when we went to see 'Julius Cæsar,' who wanted to be King of Rome; but I didn't know as they ever did such high-mightiness off on horseback, or through a hoop," says I.

"But, Phœmie, these men are genuine. For instance, that gentleman with so much red and gold about him represents Queen Victoria."

"What, in such clothes—hat, coat, and all the rest? I don't believe it," says I. "You won't impose upon me to that extent."

"Not her person," says he, a-getting out of patience, "but her Government."

<hr>

XXXIX.

THE JAPANESE.

WELL, sisters, that minute there was a commotion in the room. Those who had been leaning against the wall stood up, and the strange-looking men Cousin D. called ambassadors straightened up and fluttered a little, as peacocks spread their feathers when the sun breaks out.

Before I could speak, in came the highest cockalorum among the Japanese, which wasn't very high after all.

"Good gracious!" says I to Cousin D. "The man out there told me the ladies must all go into the blue room. Here I've been hiding behind the door, so as not to be seen, and the first Japanese stranger that comes in is a female woman! Goodness gracious! and so are all the rest!"

"No, no," says Cousin D., "it's a man—they're all men."

"With those Dolly Vardens on?" says I. "Do you think I was brought up in the woods, to take doves for night-hawks?"

"It's the Japanese fashion," says he.

"For men to dress in—well, skirts?"

"Certainly. Don't you see that the lower skirt is formed into loose trousers that two or three of 'em wear?"

I did look, and saw that the black silk underskirt some of these heathen Japanese wore was puckered up a little around the ankles, just enough to show off two peaked shoes, that must have been lovely wearing for a foot that was all great toe, but awkward for one that wasn't. In fact, I began to be awfully puzzled about the dress of the first one that came along, for above the skirt of purple silk was a Dolly Varden, all but the puffing out, of black silk, spotted over with white needlework. To top off all, this Japanee wore the funniest sort of a thing on the head, like a shiny black wash-bowl, with a hole in it, from which a stumpy black ball stuck up in the air—about the pertest-looking thing you ever saw. Around the edge was a white binding, all curlicued off with queer black figures, and a lot of stiff black stuff streamed down from behind, like a crow's tail.

This dress was tied round the waist with a silk scarf, and to that hung a long, black sword, sideways, with the point sticking out behind, furious as could be.

Only two of the Japanese were dressed in these frocks, figured off with white, with purple—well—skirts, under. Three others had thin purple—well—skirts, puckered up into baggy trousers, which showed off their peaked, hawk-bill shoes beautifully. These five high Japanese came marching one after another—Indian file—looking as solemn as eight-day clocks. Then came five more with black Dolly's, bound with purple, and with purple figures worked on the backs, and the underskirts puckered up into trousers. Every one of them had swords, and they all marched straight up to the President with them dangling by their sides.

"There, do you see that," whispered Cousin Dempster. "Are you satisfied now? Women do not, as a general thing, wear swords."

"They may be strong-minded," says I.

Before Cousin Dempster had time to speak, the little Japanee that they called Iwakura had got right before the President. There he made a low bow, and, as if jerked by the same string, the whole row, one behind the other, bowed to each other's backs. Then Mr. Fish, a tall, fine-looking gentleman, they called Secretary of State, came forward and introduced the head Japanee to the President. Then came another bow, and another, and another, till the whole ten got into a row near the President. Then General Grant and Japanee Iwakura made beautiful speeches at each other. Then there came more bows—low, slow, and delightfully graceful—and then I gathered up the skirt of my pink silk and fled, like a bird, into the blue room, where the ladies were waiting like pigeons anxious for corn.

After all, I think those Japanese must have been men. The ladies got into such a flutter as they came in, and took so much pains to make themselves agreeable, which it isn't likely they would have done if those scull caps and swords hadn't meant something masculine. Then there was more low bows, and we ladies swept back our trains, took steps and curtsied just as easy and graceful as they did, and Mrs. Grant talked a little with a Japanee. He told what she said to the others, and what she did say was just sweet and natural, which was a proof that she didn't consider the Japanese as strong-minded females in the least. So after we came out I told Cousin Dempster that I was satisfied that they were as great men as little fellows, five feet and under, could be, and I asked him, in confidence, if any of them were so unfortunate as to be unmarried?

XL.

THAT DIPLOMATIC STAG PARTY.

T is wonderful, dear sisters, how one thing grows out of another in this world. When it got about that I had been invited to help the Mrs. President to entertain the Japanese dignitaries, every lady in Washington that was going to give a party sent me and my Cousin Dempster an invite, till we began to think no more of square letters, with monographs on them, than you care for chestnut burrs when the nuts have dropped out.

But there was one of these documents that we rather jumped at, because it came from a man that was almost as good as born in Vermont. Maine is, after all, something of a New England State, and Mr. Brooks, member of Congress from New York, the man I spoke of, came from there, and had a seat in the Legislature of that State when he was only just of age. So we all rather took to him, as New England people will take to each other when they scatter off into other States, and do honor to the one they come from.

The minute his square document came, Cousin Dempster said at once that he would accept, and I, who had done honors with Mrs. President, made up my mind there, right on the nail, to do just as much for the Brooks family.

Well, I never took off my pink silk after we came from the White House, only bunched it up a little more behind when we went down to dinner, and after that screwed up my hair for a new friz, while I took a nap in the great puffy easy-chair that stood in my room; for this doing honors hour after hour is tiresome to the—well—ankles.

Having my dress on, I took something of a nap, and seemed to be dragged out of my sleep by the hair, when E. E. came to call me, which was, maybe, owing to the tightness of the crimping wires that caught on the cushion when I jumped up, and gave me an awful jerk. But I soon got over that, and gave my hair an extra frizzle before I went out, which was improving to my general appearance, and very relieving to the head.

Cousin E. E. had put on a span-new dress, observing, modestly, that a genius could appear in anything, but she hadn't the position which would stand wearing the same dress twice.

" For the sake of New England," says she, " I mean to do my best," which she did, in silk, like a ripe cherry, with wave over wave of black lace over it, and a bunch of white stones on her bosom, burning like a furnace when the light struck them.

Well, once again we packed ourselves into a carriage, and then, huddled up in waves of red silk, rolled off to Mr. Brooks's house, which isn't far from the President's homestead.

" There don't seem to be many here yet," says I, as we got out of the carriage, and went up the high steps, holding our dresses with both hands.

Before Cousin D. could answer, the door was opened, and the man inside waved his hand, which had a span-clean white glove on it, and told us to walk upstairs, which we did, dropping our dresses as we went, till they trailed half way down the steps in waves that the fellow with white gloves on must have thought sumptuous.

Two or three young ladies were in the dressing-room, and that was all. I shook out my dress before the glass, gave my hair an extra fluff, and went into the hall, where Cousin Dempster was standing.

" There don't seem to be many ladies here," says I; " in fact, none to speak of."

" Oh," says he, " they're not expected. You and my wife are exceptions."

" Just so," says I.

" This is a stag party," says he.

" A what ? "

"A stag party, where ladies sometimes manage to see and listen. You will have a chance from the back windows, I dare say; only sit low and keep still, the flags will conceal you."

"Oh! it's a stag party at the table, and crouching dears all around," says I, "is it?"

Cousin Dempster laughed till he nearly choked.

"That's capital," says he. "You are getting too bright for anything."

I couldn't quite make out what I'd said that set him off so, but I suppose he did, for he kept on laughing all the way downstairs, and the fun hadn't left his face when he introduced me to Mr. Brooks, who was in the room we entered, talking with some ladies that had come to look on and help his daughter to talk to the Japaneses, who don't understand a word of English.

Sisters, I really think we New England people ought to be proud of Mr. Brooks, for he's not only tall and large, and real handsome, but he's a self-made man, having worked out his own education by the hardest toil. He edited a daily paper before he was twenty years old; was a member of the Maine legislalature when he was twenty-three; and travelled all over Europe on foot before he was twenty-five. He has been in Congress, off and on, twelve years, besides travelling all round the world between whiles, which brought him hand-and-glove with the Japanese, the heathen Chinee, and all the other outlandish people that we send missionaries to, and convert a dozen or so once in fifty years.

Well, Mr. Brooks seemed real glad to see us, and was polite as could be; so was his daughter and all the other ladies, when they found out who it was they had among them. He'd been in Vermont, of course, before going round what was left of the world, and his praise of the Old Mountain State was something worth hearing. He asked about Sprucehill, and said that he had pleasant reminiscences of that place, having kept a school in one just like it in his vacations in college. Particularly he recollected a sugar camp where he used to drink maple sap, and eat sugar till it had been a sweet remembrance to him all his life.

While we were talking in this satisfactory manner, the fellow in gloves sung out a name that got so tangled up in his mouth that it set my teeth on edge. Then came another, and another that I didn't listen to; for that minute I saw a pair of peaked shoes coming through the door, and above them Mr. Iwakura, with that glazed punch-bowl on his head, and his black and purple dress hanging limp around him. He bowed low and softly. Mr. Brooks bowed back; then this Japanee turned to bow again and again, till I began to tremble for his neck, but he went through it all like a man; and when the whole lot had been bowed to, Mr. Brooks introduced them to me and the other ladies.

Mr. Iwakura seemed to remember that he'd seen me a-doing honors at the White House, for he bowed clear down till I thought his glazed punch-bowl would fall off, and his black veil stuck right out straight; but he rose again as if his joints had been oiled, and said something that sounded soft as cream, and sweet as maple-sugar, but what it all meant goodness only knows.

Then another heathen Japanee stepped forward, and says he:

"The Embassador wishes to say he is delighted to see a lady author, who is an honor to her country."

Here I laid one hand on my heart, and bent my head a little, not exactly knowing what else to do; and I said, with what I hope was becoming modesty:

"Oh! your Highness—is it Highness—Excellency, or High Cockolorum?" I whispered to the lady who stood next me.

"Excellency," whispered she back again.

"Oh, your High Excellency," says I; for, being by nature a conservative, I took what seemed best out of each. "You are too complimentary."

With that I made him a curtsey that over-matched his bow, for there was more of it a good deal, on account of his smallness, and my height, in which we were both a little peculiar.

The Embassador looked as if he hadn't time to answer; for he was busy bowing to the other ladies, and the rest of the

8*

Japanese all came up, and there was such a slow bending time among 'em that it was ten minutes before there was anything else done. Then we got a little mixed, and seemed to be ladies altogether, only those who were going in to dinner seemed to carry their own punch-bowls on their heads; as for dresses and so on, we were pretty much alike, and the master of the house in his black coat, and so forth, seemed the only man among us.

By and by Mr. Iwakura come back to where I was standing, and the young man came with him to do up the talking.

"I have never before seen a lady that wrote books," says he, in the sweetest manner; which the other repeated in English that wasn't half so musical.

There was an inward struggle in my mind; the compliment was sweet, and I longed to keep it; but truth is truth. My foot is on the threshold; I have looked into the Temple of Fame, but am not yet what I hope to be; but the truth is, I haven't written any books, *as* books, yet. It wounded me to say so, but truth is a jewel that I have resolved shall shine, like a railroad man's diamond, in my bosom, forever.

"Your High Excellency," says I, with brave self-control, "my humble efforts have not yet been bound in covers, but they will soon increase to that extent. Have you no female authors in that Japanee country of yours?"

When the young man expounded these questions to Mr. Iwakura, the eyes of his High Excellency began to sparkle from one sharp corner to the other, and he smiled blandly—

"Oh yes! we have ladies who write in Japan; but not lines of wisdom, like yourself; they write poems."

"Love poems?" says I.

"Mostly," says he; and his little eyes lighted up from corner to corner—"love poems, home poems, and such things as ladies understand by heart."

"The Japanese language is so sweet," says I, "the ladies cannot be very strong-minded that write it."

"Strong-minded—what is that?" says he.

"Manly, strong; sometimes fierce," says I.

"His Highness does not quite comprehend," says the young man.

"Then I must illustrate," says I. "For instance, if an American woman were to dress as near like a man as—well, I beg pardon—as his High Excellency and his friends dress like women, we should call them high-minded."

"But do they? Shall we see any ladies like that?"

"You will no doubt see females like that," says I, with dignity.

XLI.

THE DINNER.

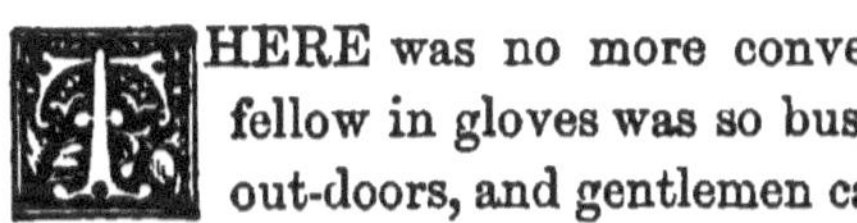HERE was no more conversing just then, for the tall fellow in gloves was so busy, opening and shutting the out-doors, and gentlemen came pouring in so thick and fast that we all had to attend to them. I was sorry for this, as the conversation was taking a turn that would have been of interest to us as a Society. I was just going to ask about the marriage relations among the Japanese, and intended to enter into a delicate investigation regarding the present company. But a smart, handsome, bright-looking gentleman came in, dressed up to the nines; and before I could say another word to Mr. Iwakura, this gentleman was bowing to me, and I was making my best curtsey to him. I was just delighted, for he looks a soldier, every inch of him, standing up straight as an arrow, but bowing so graceful and easy.

Then others came pouring in, and we ladies were busy as bees doing the honors.

There was no end of generals that bowed to me that night. There was General Farnsworth, from Illinois State, about the tallest and most manly gentleman among them. The long, sweeping beard that fell over his bosom was something splendid.   If that man wasn't born in New England, he ought to have been—that's all.

But I haven't room nor time, in a short report, to give particulars about a hundred or so gentlemen.   They were all men that you've heard of over and over again, for in his invitations Mr. Brooks had just skimmed the cream off from Congress, and it was something beautiful to see it pour itself through the parlors into the great dining-room, built on purpose for "that night only."

It didn't take long for the parlors to empty themselves into that room when a whisper went round that dinner was ready. In less than five minutes after, another fellow in white gloves came sliding into the room, and spoke low to Mr. Brooks,—we ladies were left alone, looking at one another, like babes in the woods.

A cat may look on a king, and ladies do sometimes look in upon stag parties.   Well, I got a little restless, and began to wonder how the cat got a good look, and how I could get a peep at the feeding stags.

While the rest were talking, I slid off to one of the back windows, which opened upon the great banqueting hall—you have seen that term in novels—and, hid under a cataract of stars and stripes, I saw and heard all that was going on, and a splendiferous sight it was.

The great hall was hung every which way with flags.   They rolled over the ceiling in waves, fell down the wall in festoons and curtains, striped, starred, mooned, crossed, tangled in gas lamps, looped up with flowers.

Rings of gaslights dropped half way down from the roof, and from them baskets of flowers swung over the great, long tables that were just one glitter of silver and glass, flowers and fruit, at which a hundred or more gentlemen were seated.

Great candlesticks, spreading out with branches of gold and snow-white candles, stood half way down each table, and rising up above them were tall pyramids of flowers, crowded in with pineapples, grapes, pears, oranges, and sugar things enough to feed all the children in Washington for a month. Smaller flower-pots, crowded in with fruit, were scattered every once in a while along the tables.

Back of Mr. Brooks's chair was a banner with a lot of lions rampaging over it, and a harp worked in one corner of it. Over that was another banner, with a full moon and a baby moon blazing away on it, and all around them was a whole hail-storm of stars that seemed to catch fire from the gas, and burn of themselves.

The whole room was light as morning, and gorgeous as a sunset. Sisters, believe me, the way those men were enjoying themselves was enough to make a genuine woman grind her teeth. The popping of corks as they flew from the bottles was loud and swift as the guns fired on a Down East training day, and the gurgle of wine as it foamed into the glasses was mellow and constant as the flow of that brook through the hemlock back of our old school-house.

Then the talking, the laughing, the hail-good-fellow way in which everything was done, just aggravated me out of a year's growth.

By and by Mr. Brooks got up and made a speech, welcoming the Japanee guests and praising Japan beautifully. Then he asked General Farnsworth to do the same thing over again, which he did in the most splendid way.

Then Mr. Iwakura got up and poured out a soft, slow flood of words, that seemed sweet as new cider, with which the whole company was charmed almost to death, though there wasn't a soul that knew what it was all about, any more than I did.

Then Mr. Iwakura sat down and gathered his purple frock over his knees, satisfied that he had done his duty, whether the rest understood it or not.

Then they all drank wine till there was no let up to that sound of militia firing and of running brooks, except when somebody was melting soft-solder over somebody else, which they tell me, here in Washington, is the high privilege of a stag party.

My opinion is that they are ashamed to compliment each other so broadly when ladies are by, knowing that no crowd of females could be brought to the pitch of glorifying each other after that fashion, or would stand it to hear so much flattery wasted on a lot of men when they were by.

XLII.

IN THE BASEMENT OF THE CAPITOL.

WELL, sisters, that chunky woman on the top of the great iron wash-bowl, that some giant seems to have turned upside down on the roof of the Capitol, has more to do than any other female I'm acquainted with, if she can keep the flock of men they call Congress in any kind of order. No wonder she has the look of the kitchen about her, and seem to be carrying a bundle of soiled clothes on her head for a wash in the clouds! for, of all the sloppy places I ever heard of, this great marble building seems to be the beatomest. Congressmen seem to be always getting out dirty clothes here, beside whitewashing every now and then, raking each other over the coals, and doing all sorts of kitchen and garden work.

Cousin Dempster told me all this before I went up to see exactly what Congress was, and it certainly upset me, you may just believe. That great building, which might be cut up into half a dozen palaces for kings to live in, turned into a wash-house and national laundry! The very thought made me creep all over.

I always like to investigate matters from the foundation, so the first thing I did was to go into the basement story of the building, and see what the kitchen arrangements amounted to. Of course Cousin D. could be of no use to me, and Cousin E. E. declined the subterranean raid, as she nippingly called it, which ended in my going into the underground department alone.

Well, the first thing that struck me was the duskiness of the place ; it was like travelling through a sunset that had no color in it. · The whole building seemed to have put on a gray mantle and gone to sleep. I went upstairs and downstairs, travelled over miles of stone floors, and through forests of great stone posts that looked strong enough to have a world built atop of them. Once in a while I caught sight of a man scooting along in the dusk before me like a black ghost; and once I heard noises like the rush of a steamboat down below me, and began to suspect that the wash-house and lime-slacking department was lower down yet. I opened two or three doors, and looked into a good many dark and deserted rooms piled up with books and crowded full of all sorts of things. Once or twice I saw the head of a man popping up between piles of books, but no sign of washing, as yet.

Well, I wandered on and on, till at last I came to a great kitchen that looked lively enough. Lots of men were moving about, fires were burning. and there was a lovely scent of roast chickens and boiled garden-sass—I beg pardon, vegetables. I would have gone in and asked some questions about the wash-tubs, but not a female woman was to be seen—and I hope I know what is due to my sex too well for any attempt to draw the attention of men in the service of their country by the presence of attractions that—well, I was going to say that the charm of high female society might have seemed a little out of place so low down in that stone wilderness. So I took a new turn, and came out in a grand eating department, crowded full of tables, where ever so many gentlemen and ladies were eating, talking, laughing, and drinking bottled cider till their eyes sparkled.

I went into the room with that quiet dignity which some people have said was the greatest charm of your missionary, and spreading out my skirts a little, sat down by one of the tables. A very genteel young man came up to me that minute, as hospitable as could be, and asked with a bow what I would please to have.

"Oh, almost anything that isn't too much trouble," says I.

Says he, "There is everything on the cart."

He pronounced "cart" with a drawl that riled me, for, if there is anything I hate, it is the stuck-up way some people have of twistifying common words: but I didn't want to rebuke the fellow too much, and answered in the bland and Christian way you have so often praised, my dear sisters, that I did not wish to stay long enough for them to unload a cart, but if he had just as lief as not, would take some baked pork and beans—that is, if there was any handy.

The fellow shook his head.

"No pork and beans!" says I; "do you call this national house-keeping?"

That brought the fellow up to a sense of duty in no time. He snatched up a little thin book that lay on the table, read it a minute, and then went off. By and by he came back with a dish in his hand, on which were a few beans, all brown and crisped to death, with a skimpy slice of pork lying across the top.

I took the dish in my hands, and examined it up and down, right and left, with an air that must have cut that fellow to the soul, if he had one.

"You call that pork and beans?" says I, a-lifting my forefinger, and almost shaking it at him. "Why, young man, it looks more like a handful of gravel-stones."

The young man spread his hands a little, and looked so confused that I began to feel sorry for him.

"Never mind," says I; "no doubt you have had the awful misfortune of being born out of New England, and that is punishment enough. It is the fault of our Congressmen if the great New England mystery of baked beans has not been explained and elucidated in the national kitchen," says I, "most people do degenerate so when they once get out of the pure mountain air. But then our statesmen may consider this a woman's mission. Perhaps it is. There was a time when females understood such things, but we have got to hankering after offices and votes and rostrums, till such things have become nostrums—excuse the rhyme, if you don't happen to be a poetical young man," says I; "it isn't extraordinary that such things are neglected, and that the great New English dish introduced by the Pilgrim Fathers has degenerated into this."

Here I pointed sarcastically at thepebble-stones, and, with killing irony, asked him to send me something to eat.

He took up the dish, and seemed glad to go—no wonder, my words had cut him to the soul. By and by he came back, and handed me that thin book which hadn't half a dozen leaves in it, and, says he:

"Will madam make her choice?"

I opened the book, and tried to see what it was all about; but there was nothing to read. A lot of English words twisted out of all shape and meaning, with some figures cut up in short rows, were scattered over the pages as if they had been shook out of a pepper-box. The only thing I could make out that seemed to have a sensible meaning, was—beef. This I read out loud—glad to find one good wholesome word to light on.

"Roast beef," says the fellow, and away he went.

There was no use trying to get anything like reading out of that ghost of a book; so I sat still and looked on, wondering what brought so many ladies into the Capitol, as they are not considered Congressmen yet.

XLIII.

PHŒMIE DINES WITH A SENATOR.

EAR SISTERS: I had moved my chair back a little, for it seemed rather lonesome sitting there with nothing but a table-cloth spread before me, and a castor on it, when a gentleman came in and sat down on the other side of the table, just as if I hadn't been there.

He took up the skimpy book, and began to read, as if he understood every word of it—figures and all. By and by a young fellow came up to him. They whispered together a minute, and the gentleman kept pointing at the book.

Just then, the young man that I had been so sociable with, came up with some dishes in his hand, which he set down on the table, then spread his hands a little, as much as to say, politely: "Set to, ma'am, and help yourself;" which I did.

Sisters, the national kitchens want renovating. There is female missionary work here enough to keep half our Society busy for a year. That beef was never roasted by a fire. I'll take my oath of that. It never swung on an iron skewer, inside of a tin oven before a hickory-wood fire, since it was a born calf. There's no cheating me in such things. Why, this beef had a taste of chickens, and oysters, and baked pork about it, so strong that you couldn't at first tell which it was, or if its birthplace was a barn-yard, a hen-coop, or the salt sea ocean.

Yes, there *is* mission work in these subterranean kitchens. Still, if members of Congress know how to wash and whitewash so well, they might take the cooking in hand too. Perhaps they have, though.

When men try a hand at woman's work, or women take up the business of men, it's apt to mix things up till you don't know which is which. I rather think the members have been down here, while the women were lecturing on politics upstairs. It looks like it, in both places.

Well, I didn't want to find too much fault. Human nature could not stand the pork and beans, but I tried my best to put up with the beef, and make believe it was delicious.

.Just as I took up my knife the other young fellow came to the table, and set some dishes down before the gentleman. Then he took a knife and hacked away at a long-necked bottle till he got the cork loose, and let the whole affair, foaming and sparkling, into a glass. The sight fairly made my eyes sparkle, for I was awful thirsty, and the rich gurgle made me more so.

"Sir," says I, a-holding out my glass to the young man, "if that's Vermont cider, and I seem to feel as if it is, I'll thank you for a glass."

The gentleman looked up quickly; turned to the young man with a funny sort of a smile, and nodded his head, just as if it was anything to him.

I'm not quite certain about it, but if that foaming stuff was cider, it must have been made from russet apples, for it brightened me up all over till every drop of blood in me seemed to sparkle.

"It would be near about impossible to drink that through a straw, it bubbles so," says I, feeling it my duty to be sociable, and make the gentleman feel quite at home at the national .table. "I think the cider is about the only thing that don't degenerate when it leaves New England."

"The cider," says he, opening his eyes wide.

"Yes," says I, holding out my glass again, "that keeps its own vim, and a little more so. Take another glass yourself, sir!"

I thought as I was first at the table, and a lady, that he would expect a little extra attention, and gave it with my usual bland politeness.

He smiled, and his eyes began to sparkle under the gold glasses he wore.

"Certainly," says he, "you are very kind; from Vermont I think you said."

“ Just so,” says I.   “ Sprucehill.   Let me help you to a little of this roast beef, if I may call it so.”

“ Thank you,” says he, and that funny smile crinkled his lips again, “ I am well served.”

It struck me as rather singular, that he, being a gentleman, didn’t offer me any of the dishes on his side of the table; but he didn’t, and, as a gentle rebuke, I said to the young man who stood behind him :

“ Please to pass some of those dishes this way ! ”

The fellow blushed and hesitated, and looked at the gentleman in gold spectacles, who blushed a little, too, but said to the young fellow:

“ Certainly ; why don’t you pass them over to the lady ? ”

There was something in a dish that looked a little like mashed potatoes.   I helped myself with a spoon, and tasted it.

“ What is this ? ” says I.   “ Your potatoes taste awful cheesey.”

“ It is not potatoes, but calf’s brains au gratin,” says he.

“ Calf’s brains, a grating,” says I ; “ calf’s brains, and I eating them.   Young man, I’ll have you investigated for this ! Calf’s brains, indeed ! do you think I’m a cannibal. Take the heathenish dish out of my sight.”

The gentleman laughed, and says he:

“ I will relieve you of it.”

Then he drew it over his way and began to eat.

I declare, sisters, I couldn’t bear to see that man finishing up the dish as if he liked it. He seemed to have brains enough of his own, without wanting to rob a spring calf of what little belongs to it.   But he finished the dish and got up to go, making me a real polite bow as he went away from the table.

When he was gone I beckoned to the young man.

“ Is that man from the Sandwich Islands, or where ? ” says I.

“ That gentleman ! Oh, he’s a Senator from the West,” says he. “ The whitewashing committee hate him like poison.   He gives them enough to do, I can tell you.   Awful in that direction.”

"You don't say so," says I. "Is that the man who has raised the price of lime and whiting to such an extent?"

" That's the very man."

" Dear me! and he eats brains—cheesey at that. I never saw anything like it."

" Oh, that is a very popular dish, ma'am.

" With Congressmen?"

" Yes, ma'am, with Congressmen."

" Especially?"

" Especially."

" I shouldn't wonder," says I.

When I hitched my chair back, and took up my satchel, the man put a bit of stiff paper in my hands, with some figures on it. I thanked him and went out, feeling a little lighter than I had done, on account of the cider. The young man followed me a step or two, and seemed as if he wanted to say something; but that was a familiarity I had no idea of encouraging; so I passed on, determined to find the other kitchen departments, and set up a private investigation of my own. But at the foot of a flight of stairs, all made of spotted marble, I met Cousin Dempster, who was looking for me.

" Oh, here you are at last! Where on earth have you been?"

" In the kitchen and dining-room, so far," says I.

" Kitchen—dining-room!" says he. " Oh! you have been into the restaurant—not alone, I hope."

" Oh, yes," says I; " there was plenty of company; but the cooking is enough to try a person."

" Why, did you order refreshments?"

" Refreshments were offered to me," says I, " and I accepted them, as a free-born American woman has a right to do at her country's table."

" What are you talking about?" says Cousin Dempster, almost angry. " What is that in your hand?"

" A bit of paper that the young man gave me as I came out," says I.

"But you should have given this up," says he, turning red.

"What for?" says I.

"Did you pay nothing?"

"Pay! of course not. Who ever thinks of paying anything to the Government?"

"You do not understand."

"What?"

"You have been into a restaurant," says he.

"That's more than I know of, never having been in one in my born days."

"And have come away with this!"

"Look a-here, Cousin Dempster," says I; "does this great nation keep a boarding-house, or a tavern, in its Capitol? That's what I want to know. Do you think I mean to insult the country I was born in?"

"It keeps a restaurant for the accommodation of members," says he, "and you've been in it. Just give me that check; the country don't feed its statesmen—at any rate, directly."

I gave him the square bit of paper, and, when he left me alone, just sat down on those marble steps and waited.

I don't wonder these investigating committees want to shirk their duties. I, being only a committee of one, and self-constituted, feel as if I'd had quite enough of exploring down-stairs. But what on earth Cousin Dempster is making such a fuss about, I have no idea. One would think there was something dreadful on that square piece of paper by the way he acted; but he's like everybody else, I suppose, when he gets to Washington, and can't make himself more than half understood on any subject.

XLIV.

MARBLE HALLS.

EAR SISTERS :—In my last report I gave you a dim account of the underground department of Congress. In fact, it was so dim down there, that I couldn't see anything clearly. I hope this report will have a little more brightness in it; but of that I am not at all certain, for a downright honest look at anything here in Washington is like snatching at a handful of fog.

After wandering over all that town of cellars and basements, in search of the whitewashing department and the washing-room, I came away without seeing a sign of them. It seems to me that the cooking and eating is all that one finds done openly here. About that, too, there is something that riles the New England blood in my veins. No wonder I couldn't make out half that those waiter chaps said to me.

There, in the great kitchen of the first nation on the face of the earth, free-born American citizens sit down contentedly and eat French dishes, with bull-frogs in them, I dare say, and eat them, too, on the European plan. The European plan ! as if the fine old fashion set by the Pilgrim Fathers was not good enough for their descendants! It's enough to cur-dle the blood in one's veins to see what our country is coming to, with a plan of broken-down old Europe in the very base-ment of our Capitol. Do our members of Congress remember the time when their fathers ate samp and milk on a table set against the wall, with one leaf spread? Sometimes the rich-est of them in our State got a little maple molasses with the samp, but oftener it was skim milk, and nothing else. But men were men in those days; I—that is, I have heard my mother say so—of course, I wasn't old enough to know exactly at what time samp and milk got out of fashion as a first-class domestic meal. I can't help but think, sisters, that the male sex began to degenerate while we were children, or we should never have been left in our native village to form a society, which seems destined to enlighten this generation, without increasing it.

Well, sisters, Cousin Dempster found me sitting on those hard, beautiful marble steps, thinking over these things in a saddening way. He insisted on it that I should leave off my subterraneous investigations, as he called my travels in the basement, and see Congress meet.

I declare, it's a Sabbath day's journey from one end of that great long marble building to the other. The marble stairs I had been resting on came up near the Senate chamber. Cousin Dempster said, "But perhaps we had better go over to the House first."

"Whose house?" says I, getting out of patience; "I thought we had come to see Congress."

"So we have," says he; "it will assemble in a few minutes, so we must hurry and get into the House."

"Why don't Congress assemble in this building?" says I.

"Of course it does, at the other end," says he.

"Then what on earth do you want to take me into any other house for? I want to see Congress! As for the houses in Washington, they are no great shakes, after all. New York wouldn't take the best of 'em as a gift."

"Cousin Phœmie," says Dempster, sort of impatient, "you are the most extraordinary combination of a woman I ever saw."

I stopped short and made him a curtsey to the ground—slow, graceful, and infinitely sarcastic. He seemed to feel it keenly.

"Judges, a little more competent than you are, have said as much before," I observed, scathing him through and through with my eyes.

"I mean no offence," says he, "but really you are the brightest, and—and stupidest woman!"

"Girl, if you please," says I.

"Well, girl. In some things a child could teach you; in others, you fairly dazzle the brightest of us."

"Thank you," says I; "just crown me with bitter-sweet, and have done with it. If there is anything that riles me more than another, it is a double and twisted compliment."

"There, there! do be reasonable, and hurry along," says Dempster, a-trying to shuffle out of the whole thing; "don't you see the members crowding into the House?"

"I haven't seen the house yet," says I, not half pacified.

"Of course not—how can you, till we get there?"

Cousin Dempster walked on, and, of course, I had to follow.

"Wait one minute," says I, "while I look at this great round picture overhead. What on earth is it all about? The women up there look mighty unsafe. Now, what room is this, with its roof in the sky, and its floor solid stone?"

"It is the rotunda," says he; "the national pictures are all around you, but we haven't time to look at them now—some other day."

I couldn't help looking back, for such a room I never saw in my born days. It was like a stone park roofed in so high up that the pictured women overhead seemed perched among the clouds. Over them the light came pouring like water down a cataract, filling the broad space below as if it had been all out of doors.

But I had no time to see more, for Cousin Dempster led me through a hallway and into another round room, except at one end, where a gallery ran straight across and then curved around the whole room, hooping it in like a horseshoe. In front of the straight gallery ran a row of stone pillars—tall, large, and shiny as glass—spotted, too, like the leopards in a show, and towering up like the pillars in Solomon's Temple, which the Queen of Sheba travelled so far to examine. The idea that she took all that trouble to get acquainted with Solomon, is just ridiculous. Why, it would have taken the hymeneal monarch a whole lifetime to have introduced her to his family in a decorous way. Besides, if he provided for his own

9

household out of the government, only think how busy he must have been in finding places for the relations of all his wives! No doubt he let the Queen of Sheba see his Temple, and left her to be entertained by two or three hundred of his wives. Not being a ladies' man, what more could he do?

Well, as Cousin Dempster says, I do sometimes let my pen run away with me; but when it turns toward the Scriptural history of my sex, I let it run.

XLV.

RANDOLPH ROGERS' BRONZE DOORS.

"ELL," says I to Cousin D., "what room do you call this?"

"Oh, this is the old House," says he.

The old house! Sisters, there are times when I think Dempster is beside himself. I did not deign to answer him, except with a look that would have stopped the sap running from a young maple in the brightest April day you ever saw. He didn't seem to mind it, though, but went on as if I hadn't pierced him with my eyes.

"These doors," says he, swinging back the half of a door that seemed to be made of brass and gold and powdered green-stone pounded together, and cut into the most lovely pictures that you ever set eyes on—"these doors open to the new House. They are by Rogers, and cost thirty thousand dollars."

"Thirty thousand dollars for these two doors, Cousin Dempster! I have just been a-wondering if you were crazy, and now I know you are."

"Upon my word," says he, "that is just what they cost."

"What! thirty thousand dollars?"

"Thirty thousand dollars."

I bent forward, and looked at the door—close. It was sunk deep into squares, and each square had a picture of men and women that seemed to be busy at something.

" What is it all about? " says I.

" Every picture is taken from something connected with the history of our country," says he.

" You don't say so," says I. " Who did you say made them all? "

" Mr. Rogers, a sculptor from Ohio. One of the great geniuses of the age, and one of the finest fellows that ever breathed."

" Do you know him? " says I.

" Yes," says he. " I got acquainted with him in Florence, years ago, when Elizabeth and I went to Europe on our wedding trip. He was then a rising man, hard at work on the art that he has since done much to ennoble. I am glad to see his great genius embodied here, where it will live as long as the marble on the walls. The country has honored itself in this almost as much as it has disgraced itself in placing some of the vilest attempts that ever parodied art in conspicuous places here."

Cousin Dempster's face turned red as he spoke—red with shame, I could see.

" It is enough to make an American, who understands what real art is, ashamed of his country," says he.

" But what do they do it for? " says I.

" Because two-thirds of the members sent here do not know a picture from a handsaw! but impudence can persuade, and ignorance can vote. Why, I once heard a Member of Congress speak of the statues in the Vatican as coarse and clumsy compared with the attempts of a female woman who could not, out of her own talent, have moulded an apple-dumpling into roundness."

Cousin Dempster had got into dead earnest now. He knew what he was talking about, and I couldn't help feeling for him.

" Some day, Cousin Phœmie," says he, " I will take you

round and show you the abominations which have been set up
in this building—a disgrace both to the taste and integrity of
the nation.   You will understand the impudent pretension for
which our people have been taxed in order that the National
Capitol may be made a laughing-stock for foreigners, and those
Americans who are compelled to blush for what they cannot
help."

"Cousin Dempster," says I, "why don't the press take
these things up and expose them?"

"That is exactly what I want," says he.   "It is for that very
purpose I want you to go around among these distorted marbles
and things.   Your Reports may do some good."

"But I don't quite understand them myself," says I, blushing a little.

"Trust genius to discover genius," says he.   "You could
not fail to see faults or merits where they existed.   All the
arts are kindred.   Poetry, painting, sculpture, go hand-in-hand.
You understood the beauty that lies in these doors at a glance."

"One must be blind not to see that," says I.

"Of course; well, cousin, we will give a day to these things
before we go home; but now, hurry forward, or we shall be too
late to see the House open."

"Just as if there was a house in all Washington that wouldn't
open for us if we chose to knock or ring," I thought to myself,
but said nothing, for Dempster was walking off like a steam-
engine, and I followed down one long hall, and up another—all
paved with bright-colored stones—till it seemed as if I were
walking over a rock carpet.

XLVI.

WAS IT A MEETING-HOUSE?

EAR SISTERS:—At last we came to some wide marble stairs, with a twist in the middle, and they led us into another long hall with a stone carpet, out of which some doors covered with cloth were opening and shutting all the time for folks to go through.

Cousin Dempster swung one open for me, and I went into what looked like a meeting-house gallery, with long seats a-running all around it, cushioned off with red velvet, or something. Right over what seemed to be the pulpit, was a square gallery by itself, which I took for the singers' seats, but it was full of men—not a female among them—and they all seemed busy as bees laying out their music for use.

Cousin E. E. was sitting near this gallery. She beckoned to me, so I went in. I sat down by her and whispered:

"I didn't know we were coming to a meeting. Dempster never said a word about it."

"Hush!" says she. "The chaplain is going to pray."

I did hush, and saw the congregation come in and walk down the aisles and take their seats. Some brought books that seemed like Bibles under their arms; and all of them took off their hats, as was proper.

One thing struck me as peculiar: no ladies came into any place but the galleries, and up there they whispered and laughed in a way that made my blood run cold.

By and by a man came in, walked down the broad aisle, and went up into the pulpit.

Two or three men were sitting in the deacons' seat, which ran along below the pulpit, and they began to whisper together —a thing I didn't like in the deacons of a church.

The minister put his hands together beautifully. The congregation stood up, as good Presbyterians ought to do, and I stood up too, with my arms folded, and bending my head a little, while a solemn prayerfulness crept over me ; but the next minute I dropped both arms and opened both eyes wide.

The minister was coming down the pulpit stairs. The congregation sat down. The deacons each took up a pen—so did the singers, who hadn't sung a note yet.

"What *does* this mean?" I whispered to Cousin E. E.

"The prayer is over," says she.

"Over!" says I. "Why, the minister hadn't begun to tell the Lord what sinners we all are."

"Oh!" says she, almost laughing out in meeting, "that would be too heavy work for one man. Only think how much of it there is to represent in this place."

"Cousin," says I, "your levity in this sacred place shocks me."

"Sacred place," says she. "Oh, Phœmie, you will be the death of me."

"Have you no regard for your own soul?" says I, in an austere whisper that ought to have riled up the depths of her conscience.

"My soul, indeed!" says she, with her eyes and her lips all a-quivering with fun; "as if people ever thought of such things here."

I dropped into my seat—her sinful levity took away my breath.

The woman absolutely began to talk out loud, and didn't even stop when a man got up in the congregation and began to exhort. In the distress her conduct gave me I did not hear just what he said, but at last he held out a paper. A handsome little boy came up and carried it toward the pulpit and gave it to one of the deacons.

Up to this time I had thought the congregation Presbyterians, but the boy puzzled me. I remembered the little fellow in red at that High Church service, and thought perhaps the good old New England stand-by meeting had got some of these new-fangled additions to their board of deacons. The thought troubled me, but not so much as the conduct of that congregation. The ladies in the gallery behaved shamefully—I must say it. They whispered, they laughed, they flirted their fans and flirted with their lips and eyes. Sometimes they turned their backs on the congregation downstairs. They kept moving about from one seat to another. In fact, I cannot describe the actions of these females. The idea of piety never entered one of their heads—I am sure of that.

There must have been a good many notices and publishments to give out; more than I ever heard of in our meeting-house, for ever so many papers were sent up to the pulpit, where another minister sat now ready to begin his sermon.

I must own it, there was some confusion among the congregation in the body of the church. The members moved about more than was decorous, and there was whispering a-going on there as well.

In Vermont the minister would have rebuked his congregation—especially the flighty females around me.

I was saying this to Cousin E. E. when that man in the pulpit took up a little wooden hammer that lay on the desk before him, and struck it down with a force that hushed the whole congregation into decency at once.

I was glad of it, and in my innermost heart said " Amen ! "

By and by a man got up to exhort. He must have been brought up as a clerk in some thread-needle store, I should think, by the way he measured off his long, rolling sentences, that seemed to come through the bung-hole of an empty cider barrel; and his arms went spreading out with each sentence, as if he were measuring tape, and meant to give enough of it.

" Who is that ? " says I, whispering to Cousin E. E.

" That," says she, " is a gentleman from ———."

" No doubt he's a member," says I; " how earnest he seeks for protection ! "

" Of course he is a member or they wouldn't let him speak," whispers she.

" I know that," says I. " The Presbyterians don't allow

any but members to speak in their meeting, of course ; but it
seems to me they do a great deal more talking than praying
here, or singing either."

" Oh, I don't believe any one but the chaplain ever thinks
of praying here, and he cuts it short as pie-crust."

" Don't be irreverent," says I.

Cousin E. E. got up from her seat ; so did Dempster.

" Come," he said, " I am tired of hearing about salt."

" Especially if the salt has lost its savor," says I, hoping to
draw both their thoughts to the Scriptures, and get them in a
proper frame of mind for the occasion.

"The tax is what I want it to lose," says he, and I saw
by his manner that thoughts of humility and prayer were
far from him ; so, rather than join in this mockery of holy
things, I followed him out of that beautiful and sacred edifice,
softened, and, I hope, made better by the service in which my
soul had joined.

" Well," says Cousin Dempster, when we stood once more
on the stone carpet of the hall, " how did you like the House ? "

" What house ? " says I.

" The House of Representatives, to be sure," says he.

" When I have seen it, I can tell you better," says I.

" Oh, nonsense ! you have seen it," says he, " in full session,
too."

" Look a-here, cousin," says I; "all this morning you've
been talking about old houses and new houses, as if this heap
of marble was a green, with buildings all round it.   I've seen
the place you call a rotunda—halls, with scrumptious stone
carpets on them, and as fine a meeting-house as Solomon need
have wanted.   Now, if you want to show me that house where
the Representatives meet, do it, and no more parsonizing
about it."

" But, cousin, I do assure you, we have just come from it.
You have heard the members speaking."

" I have seen a meeting-house, and worshipped in it," says I.

" Are you really in earnest ? " says he.

"Would I, the member of a church, trifle on a sacred subject?" says I.

"Oh!" says Cousin Dempster, a-leaning his back against the marble wall—"oh! hold me, or I shall laugh myself to death."

I wish he had. There!

XLVII.

EASTER.

MY DEAR SISTERS:—Christmas isn't a New England institution, and High Churches are not indigenous to the Down East soil. The Pilgrim Fathers took a notion against that species of holidays, and their descendants were forbidden by law to make mince-pies and such like, in celebration of that particular day. In fact, Christmas was turned out of meeting, and Thanksgiving adopted in its place. As for High Churches, in the good old times there wasn't a steeple to be seen. The meeting-houses were spread out on the ground, roofed in like barns, and quartered off inside into square pews, like a cake of gingerbread. The only thing that looked like a steeple in those days was the minister, when he stood up to pray. Sometimes he leaned a trifle backward to let the congregation see that there was no chance that he would ever bow down to that old English Church, against which the dust from his feet had been shaken.

The deacons ranged in that long seat under the pulpit, with iron-clad faces and hearts, that had grown rocky in their uprightness, were such men as you don't meet often nowadays. They not only shook the dust from their feet against the Church of England, but scattered a good deal on the Quakers and other sects that crept in from the Old World, with an idea that they might have a sneaking notion of their own where trees were so thick and men so upright; but you and I know they found out their mistake.

Our blessed old forefathers sought Christian toleration for themselves when they came into the wilderness, not for anybody else. They knew exactly which was the shortest way to Heaven, and meant that other people should follow it straight up.

Having cast off the old Church of England, and sang Thanksgiving hymns on Plymouth Rock—which after all, sisters, wasn't much of a rock to brag of as to size—of course our forefathers weren't likely to drag any of the worn-out institutions along with them, so, as I have said, they dropped Christmas, set their faces against steeples, turned their altars into cherry-wood communion tables, clad their souls in iron, and New England was purified from the dross of the Old World.

This is why Christmas amounts to nothing among us.

New England has always been an independent part of the United States. The footprints of the Puritans are not quite worn out yet, and in turning our back on saints and such, we have nigh about forgotten that our part of the country had anything to be thankful for, except a fine grain harvest and abounding hay crop.

Well, not knowing much about Christmas, sisters, you will be glad to hear something about Easter, which comes at the end of Lent, and is a time of rejoicing in this city, I can tell you. Let me explain:

Lent is a wonderful still time among the church people who are given to fish and eggs, and morning service for weeks and weeks while it lasts. But the last three days are what I want to tell you about; for during the time when hard-boiled eggs are so much the fashion, Cousin E. E. and myself were in Washington, where people rest a little from parties, and eat a good many oysters in a serious way, but could no more get up a regular Easter jubilee than they could tell where the money goes to that ought to build up the Washington monument, but don't.

No; Cousin E. E., who keeps getting higher and higher in her church notions, was determined to spend her Easter at home.

"Easter! what does that mean?" I seem to hear you say. "Is it a woman, or was it named after one? Is it—"

Stop, sisters, that question is too much for me; I don't know. Wasn't there a handsome woman of the Jewish persuasion who put on her good clothes and came round the king, her husband, when her relations were all kept out of office, or something of that kind? Perhaps this Easter is named after her; but then it seems to me as if the names weren't just the same. Anyway, the three days they call Easter mean a solemn thing that we haven't thought enough of in our parts, up to this time.

It means those three days when our Lord lay in the tomb. The first day, sisters, is held in remembrance of a death that was meant to make men holy. That was suffered for you and me. It is called Good Friday, and a great many people in these parts hold it as the most solemn day of all the year. I think it is. My own heart bows itself in dumb reverence as the thought of all it means settles down upon me. I wonder that so many years of my life have gone by without giving the day a thought. Surely, sisters, Christ did not die for the Catholics and Episcopalians alone.

Well, sisters, I did not mean to preach or exhort out of season, but my heart has been touched, and out of its fulness I have spoken.

"Are we a-going to your High Church?" says I to Cousin E. E. when she came to my room Friday morning, and asked if I was ready.

"No," says she; "even that does not reach my ideas of what is due to the occasion. We will go still higher—to St. Stephen's."

"Catholic, isn't it?" says I.

"Yes," says she, with a sigh, "the Mother Church. You will, at least, be interested."

"I never was in a Catholic meeting-house," says I, "but to-day I feel like worshipping anywhere, cold as it is."

"Not so cold as our Lord's tomb," says she, shivering a little.

I, too, felt cold chills a-creeping over me.

"Come," she says, "it is time."

XLVIII.

A CHURCH HIGHER YET.

SISTERS, we never spoke a word all the way to St. Stephen's Church, which is not a mite higher, and not near so handsome as a good many other meeting-houses we had to pass. A crowd of people were going in, and we followed into the darkness; for the whole space was full of gloom, like a foggy sunset. Here and there lights shone out like stars in a cloud, just enough to make the gloom strike home. The church was shaped like a cross, and had more than one altar in it. That which stood at the head of the broad aisle had just lights enough around it to make its whiteness ghostly, and to tremble over a great picture back of it, where figures in some harrowing scene seemed to come and go in the foggy air.

Yes, the air was foggy and thick, with sweet-smelling smoke, that came from some brass lamps a couple of little boys were a swinging back and forth by chains linked to them; and there, standing right in front of the altar, was a man all draped out in black robes, and a white overdress, praying. Sisters, it was awful solemn; I couldn't but just keep from sobbing right out.

"Look!" says E. E.; "isn't the chapel of the Virgin beautiful?"

I did look; and there at my left stood an altar covered with flowers, and blazing with lights starting up like a crown of glory through the darkness.

"Why is that altar so bright, while all the rest of the meeting-house is almost dark?" I whispers to E. E.

"That is the chapel of the Virgin, and there lies the body of Christ."

"The body of Christ!" says I, with a start.

"Yes," says she, bowing her head. "You cannot see it, for the flowers cover it, as we strew them over the graves of those we love; but the holy body of our Lord is there, waiting for the resurrection."

"Waiting for the resurrection!" says I. "How can you say that, E. E., when our Lord was resurrected almost nineteen hundred years ago?"

"Oh!" says she, shaking her head and whispering, "that was so; but the body of Christ is there this minute, under the flowers."

"Cousin E. E., are you crazy? Do you believe that in earnest?"

"I do," says she a-folding her hands and dropping down her head.

"But how—how can it be?"

"I cannot explain, dear cousin; but it is so. It is, indeed."

"E. E., are you a Roman Catholic?—do they believe that?"

"Every one of 'em."

"And are you a Roman Catholic?"

"Not yet," says she; "you know well enough that I belong to the Episcopal Church; but my pilgrimage is not ended."

Cousin E. E. bent her head and spoke low. I felt the old Pilgrim blood rile in me; but just as I was a-going to speak again, a low, mournful noise went a-rolling through the meeting-ing-house, that chilled me down like ice-water. It came from behind the great white altar, which looked to me like a big tombstone with night-fog floating over it. Through the fog I saw two rows of wooden seats, with high backs; and in them sat men, all in black and white clothes, singing dismally. No --it wasn't singing, and it wasn't reading; but a long, rolling drawl, in which a few tones of music seemed buried and were pleading to get out. With this dreary sound, came the sobs and mournful shivers of the cold wind outside, which made my blood creep.

It was too much; I could not bear it. Tears came into my eyes like drops of ice; I felt preceding shivers creeping up my arms.

"Do let's go home—I feel dreadfully," says I, catching hold of Cousin E. E.'s dress.

"Wait," says she, "till they have done chanting the Psalms."

I couldn't help it; but sunk down on my knees, covered my face with both hands, and let that awful music roll over me. It seemed like a call to the Day of Judgment.

At last the sound died off; the wind outside took it up dolefully, and seemed to call us out into the cold air. We went, feeling like ghosts, and never spoke a word all the way home. How could we, with that awful feeling creeping over us?

XLIX.

EASTER SUNDAY.

DEAR SISTERS:—It seemed to me as if I never could go into that Catholic meeting-house again; but when Sunday came, E. E. got up so cherk and bright, that I couldn't say "No" when she wanted me to start with her to St. Stephen's meeting-house.

"You will hear no more crying and sobbing," says she, "everything will be bright and beautiful; no more penitential psalms; no more darkness. Christ has risen!"

My heart rose and swelled, like a frozen apple thrown into hot water, when I got into the meeting. It was raining like fury out of doors, but inside everything blazed with glory. The great white altar flashed and flamed with snow-white candles, bunched like stars in tall candlesticks, branched off with gold. Two great candles, as thick as your waist, burned like pillars of snow afire inside, on each side of the steps. Up amongst the golden candlesticks were two square Maltese crosses—like the cross we are used to, only one end is cut off short to match the others—all of white flowers, with just a little red at the tips, as if a few drops of innocent blood had stained them. Then there were beautiful half-moons made of milk-white flowers lying on beds of purple flowers, but there was no other color on that altar.

On an altar which I had not seen in the darkness, when I was there before, a lamb—as large as life, made out of flowers so white that it seemed as if they must have grown in heaven itself—stood among the lights that shone, like crowded stars, out from behind it. Across its shoulders this lamb carried a cross so blood-red, that it chilled me through and through.

Above this altar hung a great cross six feet high, which seemed to float in the air. It was made of gas-drops that quivered into each other, and struck out colors that the fire seemed to have drank up from the flowers, and turned into light that was glorious.

Over this cross floated a crown of fire, that seemed to tremble and shake with every gust of air, as if it had just floated down from heaven, and, meeting the cross, hovered over it.

I had but just time enough to see all this, when from the other side of the great altar, came a lot of boys, walking two and two, with white shoes on their feet, and white dresses— I should have called them frocks if it had been girls that wore them—all fastened with crimson buttons, and crimson silk scarfs were thrown across their shoulders. Then came a lot more, dressed in scarlet frocks and white shoes; and after them another class in white, with purple scarfs across their shoulders.

These boys—they were real handsome little fellows—stood themselves around the altar. Then came two men, all in black and white, and after them four others, dressed like kings and princes, all in scarlet and gold, and lace and precious stones. ·

These men knelt down on the steps of the altar. Then everybody in the meeting-house knelt too. After a few minutes they got up, and out from somewhere in the meeting-house, a low roar of music burst over us, and with it came a rush of voices singing out, "Lord, have mercy on us! Lord, have mercy on us."

Then there was a lull, and after that a whole torrent of gushing music, with an undertone of rolling sounds, and out of the noise came these words that seemed to catch up one's heart and fly away with it:

"Glory to God on high, peace and good-will to men!"

Oh, how this rush of sound rose and swelled, and glorified itself! It seemed as if you could see Christ rising from the sepulchre, and all the angels of heaven rejoicing over it.

Then came more music. I cannot tell you what it was like, only it made my heart stir and throb, as if it wanted to break loose and mount upwards, singing as it went.

At last a low voice sung, all alone, clear and high as a bird in the air. After that, deep, deep silence settled on the whole congregation, and everybody dropped down on their knees. Then one of the men in scarlet and gold went a step higher on the altar, and took from it a gold cup, which he held high up in one hand. Out of this cup he lifted a round thing that looked more like a cracker than anything else, and held it up between his thumb and finger. I was going to ask E. E. what it was all about, but she was bending forward, with her face almost on the floor, and everybody around us was taking an extra kneel, which I did not understand. Everything kept still, the congregation bent close to the floor, and everybody seemed to be thinking to themselves for as much as ten minutes. Then the whole congregation lifted its head. The boys in red and white frocks swung the brass lamps, which sent clouds of sweet, white smoke up amongst the flowers, and out came another burst of music, louder, sweeter, and more triumphant than anything I had heard yet. It just carried me right off from my feet.

After this, one of the crimson and gold men on the altar turned round, and spread out his arms. Two others caught hold of his dress, and held it out on each side, and dropped it again. The boys in white and scarlet and purple made themselves into double lines, and walked out of the door they came in by. The leading scarlet and gold man took the gold cup in his hands, and followed after, and the other men in their sparkling dresses—with those two in black and white—walked beside and behind him while he carried it out.

There was a little stir in the congregation after this, but by and by the man who had stood on the steps of the altar and carried out the cup, came back in another dress, and went up into a little cubby-house of a pulpit, where he preached a beautiful sermon, which I didn't understand a word of, and then Easter was over in that church.

When we got out of church I felt like a bird with its wings spread out wide. It was raining like Jehu, but I didn't care for that; the music, the flowers, the bursts of light had made me feel like another creature. Even the stormy sky looked splendid. But when we got home, I began to think over what I had seen and heard, and as soon as Cousin E. E. seemed to feel like talking, I put a few questions to her.

"Cousin," says I, "who were the men that came out there, all glistening with gold and things, and stood on the steps of the altar?"

"Them? Why, they were the priests."

"Oh! And the one who held that cup in his hand—wasn't he something a little more particular than the rest?"

"He was the arch-priest."

"You don't say so! But what was that round thing he lifted out of the cup?"

“ That ?   Why, Phœmie, that was the Host ! ”

“ There was a host of people on the floor, of course ; but I mean the little thing he held up between his thumb and finger ? ”

“ That ? ” says Cousin E. E., a-lifting up both hands, as if I’d done something dreadful.   “ That is the holy wafer.”

“ The what, Cousin E. E. ? ”

“ The body of our Saviour.”

“ Oh, cousin, how can you ? ” says I, a-feeling myself grow cold all over.

“ It is so, Phœmie.   As yet you may not understand the mystery, but in time you will see it.”

I couldn’t answer her, she was in such solemn earnest ; but then and there I made up my mind that we should have to talk over that matter in earnest before long, for I felt the Pilgrim blood riling up in my bosom.

“ Do Episcopalians believe that ? ” says I.

“ Those that take a high stand do,” says she.

“ Well,” says I, “ we won’t talk that over just now.   But whose boys were those that swung the lamps and stood round the altar ? ”

“ Oh, those were the acolytes.”

“ Any relations to the boys we saw at morning service ? ” says I.

“ Oh, they are all the same.”

“ Mercy on me ! ” says I ; “ what a large family of boys—and so near of an age, too ! ”

E. E. lifted her head and gave me the ghost of a smile—that was all.   I believe she felt that talking was a sin just then, and I felt a little that way myself.

“ That music was splendid,” says I, “ and the flowers.   I don’t think I ever was in any meeting-house that seemed so close to heaven.   But then I always had a hankering after such things.   And why not ?   If God gives us music and flowers, light and sweet odors, can it be wrong to render them back to him? Cousin, I never knew what power there was in such things till now."

"Phœmie," says she—and a queer smile came over her face—"I shouldn't wonder if you go back, at last, a High Church woman. Then what would the Society say?"

I felt myself turning red—as if I, Phœmie Frost, could change in the religion of my forefathers!

"No," says I; "there I am firm as a rock; but with firmness, I hope, cousin, that I join toleration. It seems to me that our Pilgrim Fathers made a mistake when they expected all mankind to think with them, and another mistake when they put aside the holiest and most solemnly beautiful days of all the year—those upon which our blessed Lord was born, suffered, and ascended into heaven.

L.

THAT MAN WITH THE LANTERN.

DEAR SISTERS:—I am back in Washington. So is Cousin E. E. and Dempster, who has got a case before Congress; and when a man has that he just makes up his mind to take permanent lodgings in a sleeping-car, and make his home by daytime in a railroad section.

You never saw anything like the hurry in which such men live. As for the married ones, their wives scarcely see them at all unless they catch 'em flying with a railroad ticket in one hand, and a carpet-bag, swelled out like an apple-dumpling, in the other.

To us women this kind of life is tantalizing—very.

When Cousin D. came up from Wall Street, all in a fume, and says he: "Come, ladies, if you've a mind to go to Washington, just pack up and get your things," we both

rushed into the street like crazy creatures, and came back
with our pockets crammed, and our hands full of hair-
pins, bits of ribbon, lengths of lace, and so on. These we
huddled into our trunks the last thing, drew a deep breath, and
said we're ready, half scared to death with fear that D. might cut
short the hour he has been kind enough to give us, and start
off alone—a thing he was just as like to do as not, being a man.

It's astonishing how much can really be done in an hour.
When our time was up we had five minutes to spare, and sat
with our satchels in our laps, waiting for Cousin D.

This time, being with E. E., I just said nothing, but let
things drift, which, after all, is about the easiest way to get
along. Instead of going in among the easy-chairs, as we did
before, they took me into the sleeping-car, which is a great long
affair, with what we call bunks, in our parts, made lengthwise
on each side, with a narrow hall running between. The bunks
had curtains, and looked ship-shape when they were once made
up; but it was funny enough to see great tall men spreading
sheets and patting down pillows for female women to sleep on.

Cousin E. E. and I had a little mahogany pen, with two
bunks in it, which is considered extra genteel, and we went to
bed, first one and then the other, not having room enough for
more than one to undress at a time. When our clothes were
hung up, and we inside the bunks, the pen was choke full,
and off we rattled, with a jounce now and then that made you
catch your breath. It was like sleeping in a cradle, with some
great hard-footed nurse rocking you in a broken trot.

I had just begun to get to sleep, when what do you think
happened?

The door was pushed open, and a man looked in. I started
up, riled to the depths of my woman's soul. Never before,
since I was a nursing baby, had any man looked on my face
after it was laid on my pillow.

What did the creature mean?

I scrouched down in the bunk, pulling the sheet over my
head, and peeped through an opening, half scared to death.

That man had a lantern in his hand, a dark lantern, with the fire all on one side. It glared into my bed like a wicked eye.

"What, oh, what *do* you want?" says I. "Remember, we are two innocent females that seem to be unprotected, but we have a gentleman outside—a strong, tall, powerful man. Advance another step and I scream."

The man opened his mouth to speak; his one-eyed lantern glared upon me; he smiled as if overflowing with good intentions.

"Go away," says I, speaking in a tone of command from under the bedclothes, "or if it is my purse you want, take it; but take that evil eye from my countenance."

The man took the little pocket-book from my trembling hand; he opened it with cold-blooded slowness, took out a long strip of printed paper Cousin Dempster had told me to take care of, and tore it in two before my face. Then he put one of the pieces back, while I lay shaking and being shook till the teeth chattered in my head.

"Spare me," says I, with the plaintive wail of a heroine. "Take all I have, pocket-book and all, but, oh, spare me; spare me!"

He held my pocket-book towards me. I shivered, I shrunk; my hand crept forth like a poor timid mouse, and darted back again.

The man—this stealthy railway burglar—seemed touched with compassion. My helpless innocence had evidently made an impression even on his hardened nature; he laid the pocket-book gently on the pillow, and modestly turned his one-eyed lantern away, pitying my confusion, and feeling, as any man with a heart in his bosom must, that I was scared out of a week's growth.

I breathed again. My heart swelled with thankfulness that a great danger was passed. I pushed back the blankets, and looked out while a timid shudder crept over me.

The man was there yet, stooping down to Cousin E. E.'s bunk. I heard paper rustle. Had he spared me to rob her?

Why didn't she scream? Why didn't she command the creature to leave her presence?

Robbery was nothing, but that cool way of breaking in upon two sleeping females had the ferocity of a wild beast in it. Was he killing my cousin—smothering her with pillows so that she could not scream out? The thought drove me frantic. My arms were goose-pimpled like a grater.

"Why don't you order him out? Why don't you scream for Dempster?" says I, feeling a thrill of hysterics creeping over me. "If you don't, I must.

"All right," says the burglarious wretch, giving us the dark side of his lantern, and slamming the door. Then all was mournfully still. I half rose and leaned over my bunk, pale, breathless.

"Oh, cousin! speak to me if you are alive," I pleaded.

"What is it; what is the matter, Phœmie?" says a sleepy voice from below.

"Ah, thank Heaven, you are alive!" I cried, a-clasping my hands in a sweet ecstasy of gratitude. "Did he attempt to strangle you?"

"He. Who?"

"Why, that man. That prowling monster, with the one-eyed lantern!"

"Oh, he only wanted my ticket; he meant no harm," says she, more than half asleep.

I drew back into my bunk, and let her go to sleep. Ignorance *is* bliss. She felt safe, and I left her. Why should I disturb her innocent rest with the knowledge that a railroad she trusted in was infested through and through with brigandation. If she knew the truth, I was certain that E. E. would never be coaxed or reasoned into travelling again, so I determined to keep a still tongue, and never mention this attempt at burglary again to any human creature.

I have made up my mind to one thing, though. Phœmie Frost will never travel again without a pistol under her pillow. What good object can any man have in smashing into the midnight dreams of two innocent females, and wanting to examine their pocket-books? I tremble to think what the feelings of the great Grand Duke would be if he had heard of the terrible danger I have been in.

Of course I never closed my eyes again till the long train of cars crept like a great trailing snake into the depot at Washington.

LI.

MRS. GRANT'S RECEPTION.

SISTERS, Washington is splendid just now. In New York the winter seems to have frozen up all the sap in the trees; not a bud on the limbs, not a tinge of green even on the willows, which are the trees of all others that give out their greenness first in the spring, and keep it latest in the fall. The trees that grow in the Park were brown and naked when we left the city.

Here the buds are a-swelling. The willow-trees are feathered over with leaves as soft and pale as the down on a gosling's breast. The beech-trees are covered over with soft, downy buds, that float on the air like full-grown caterpillars. Even the ragged old button-balls are shooting out leaves like sixty, and the young trees at the Smithsonian Institution, and the old ones below the Capitol of the nation, are bursting into greenness, while the grass seems to spring up fresh in your path as you walk along.

I declare it is a satisfactisn to breathe the air which is kissing so many buds and flowers open; and I feel sort of guilty in doing it, when I know that the hollows around Sprucehill are choked up with dead leaves, if not with drifted snow, and it will be weeks yet before the maple-sap will take to running.

Nature is an institution that I hope I shall always be fond

of and appreciate; but men and women are, after all, the noblest work of a beneficent Creator, and, from the delicate greenness and the soft airs of spring, I turn to them.

At two o'clock, yesterday, Mrs. President Grant had a grand reception at the White House. There hasn't been the ghost of one while Lent kept people down to a fish diet and morning meetings; but now, when the flowers of Easter-Sunday have all withered up, people begin to visit one another again, and this grand reception at the White House sort of opens the way and sets the fashions a-going once more.

Well, when the time came, Cousin E. E. and I were on hand. My pink silk dress was a little rumpled; but I shook it out and smoothed it down.

Cousin E. E. came out like a princess, in pale lilac-colored silk, with a whole snow-storm of lace crinkling over it. I declare, sisters, she looked fresh and sweet as the first lilac that blows! I was really proud to introduce her as my relation.

Cousin Dempster, having a claim, had to go to the Capitol; so E. E. and I went together—no gentlemen being absolutely necessary to a daytime reception, you know.

Well, we got out of the carriage as light and chipper as two birds. The driver held out his arm to keep our dresses from touching the wheel, as they streamed out after us; and I must say Vermont didn't suffer much as to ladies when we walked, with the slow dignity befitting persons with the eye of a State upon them, into the blue room, where Mrs. President Grant recepted. Well, I reckon the ladies were two to one against the men in that blue room, and it just looked lovely!

In the centre of the room stood the round, blue silk sofa, I have told you about, cut up into seats, and rising to a point in the middle, as if a silk funnel had been turned bottom-side up there. On the nozzle end of this point a great white flower-pot stood, a-running over with pink and white flowers, rising in great clusters one above another, till they brightened the whole room with a glow like early morning.

In front of this ring sofa the Mrs. President stood, looking just as smiling and sweet as a bank of roses. She had on a pink dress—no, not exactly what we call pink—but the color was soft and rosy as a cloud; snowflaky lace floated around her arms, and shaded her neck, which was plump, and white, and pretty as any girl's. She hadn't a sign of a flower, or anything on her head; but the soft, crinkly hair curled down to her forehead sweetly, and she seemed almost like a young girl. Everybody there said that they never had seen her look so handsome.

Well, there she stood, with a nice little lady on one side, helping her recept; and she did it sweetly, which was likely, she being the wife of Senator Morton, of Indiana, one of General Grant's biggest sort of guns. You have heard of Senator Morton, of course. He was a first-rate fellow during the war, when he just buckled to and raised a half a million of dollars on his own account for the Government, which was grand in itself, and accounts for the way the people in Indiana almost worship him.

Well, this lady was his wife. She looked young, and was dressed nicely—not just like a girl, but as if she had her husband's dignity to take care of, as well as her own good looks.

When we got to the door of this room, a gentleman came up, and, after making a bow, wanted us to tell our names. Cousin E. E. answered:

"Mrs. Dempster, of New York, and Miss Phœmie Frost, of Vermont."

He didn't seem to hear distinctly, but bent his head; and says he:

"Miss, did you say?"

I flushed rosy-red, and my eyelids drooped, for I was thinking of the Grand Duke.

"At present," says I.

Then the gentleman called out so loud that everybody could hear him:

"Mrs. Dempster—Miss Phœmie Frost."

10

I say, sisters, did you ever see a cage full of canary-birds flutter when a cat was looking through the wires? If you have, that can give you some idea of the buzz, hum, and rustle that was going on when we came up to the front of that round sofa, and gave Mrs. Grant and Mrs. Morton one of those sliding curtsies that set off a long-trailed dress so well.

Mrs. President Grant smiled sweetly, and held our her hand. I took that hand, I pressed it kindly—for I like that woman, whom poverty could not daunt, and sudden prosperity could not spoil. She's a good, motherly, nice woman, and my heart warmed to her as I took her hand in mine.

"Miss Frost, I am delighted to see you back in Washington," says she; "especially as the weather promises to be so pleasant."

"In some places we are apt to forget the weather, finding everything bright and pleasant without regard to it," says I.

When I spoke, the ladies around crowded up to listen, and looked at each other, smiling. One or two gentlemen came up, too, and when I bowed my head and walked on, giving common people a chance, one of them came up to me, and says he:

"Miss Frost, I think I have the pleasure of claiming you as a constituent," says he.

"A what?" says I.

"A constituent," says he, a-smiling softly.

"No," says I; "I don't remember being connected with any family of that name."

"But you are from Vermont?"

"I am proud to say 'Yes,'" says I, a-bowing my best, in honor of the old State.

"Then I have some claim on your acquaintance," says he. "My name is ——."

I reached out my hand. The fire flashed into my eyes. "Our United States Senator?" says I.

"I believe the people have given me that honor," says he.

"And honored themselves in the doing of it," says I.

I declare the man blushed, showing that high parts and extraordinary knowledge haven't made him conceited. But I hadn't said a word more than the truth. Vermont, of all the States of the Union, I do think, has done herself credit in her choice of Senators. There isn't in all the Senate a man that either of 'em cannot hold his own with, and I don't believe a rough or ungentlemanly word or action has ever been on record against either of them."

Before he could answer, a gentleman came and spoke low to him. Then he said, with a pleased look:

" This is Mr. ———, our other Senator, Miss Frost, who is, I am sure, as glad to welcome you here as I am."

I turned, and saw a tall, spare man, with the kindest, mildest, and most speaking face I ever set eyes on. His voice, too, when he spoke, was just benign. I gave him my hand. If I looked half as glad as I felt, he must have seen the warmest sort of a welcome in my eyes. I felt honored by an introduction to these men. Not because they happened to be my own Senators, but because they are men of heart and brains, capable of understanding what the people want, and both honest and strong enough to maintain what they understand. I write this without hesitation, knowing that there isn't a society or household in Vermont that will not agree with my way of thinking about them.

I don't think much of beauty in a man, but there's no dreadful harm in being good-looking, and in that respect our Senators pull about an even yoke with each other, and can't be overmatched by many States in the Union.

Well, we walked about the room, and had a good deal to say concerning the Old Mountain State, while the crowd went in and out down the east room, through the parlors, and into a great, long greenhouse, blazing out with flowers that grew so thick and smelled so sweet that I longed to stay there forever. But by the time I was ready to leave, the company had thinned off, and Cousin E. E. was waiting for me, a little out of sorts, for somehow I had lost her in the crowd ; but she soon came to,

and when I told her our Senators were going to call on us at
the hotel, she chirked up.   After all, Cousin E. E. *is* a good-
hearted creature as ever lived.

LII.

REPRESENTATIVE WOMEN.

DEAR SISTERS :—My ambitious longings are satisfied.
I have stood before the Mrs. President of these United
States, and in that august situation sustained the honor
and dignity of our Society in a manner that I hope will meet
with your united and individual sanction.   Mrs. Grant has
had a great many ladies of one kind and another standing by
her side as honored guests of the nation, but I do think the literary strata of the Union has never been fully represented before.
I do not say this vaingloriously—far be it from me to claim
anything on my own merits—but when the reputation of our
Society is concerned, I am ready to stand up among the best,
and hold my own even in the national White House.

That I have done according to the best of my abilities, and,
I trust, to the satisfaction of the Society, but I claim no credit
for it.   Any of us young girls can bow and smile, and give out
words that melt into a vain man's heart like lumps of maple-sugar,
and that is about all that is expected from the female women
who perform Society in Washington, and real pretty, smart
women most of them are; but after all, they are only acci-
dental females, and get there just because their husbands happen to be elected to a place, and wouldn't even be heard of
if some smart man hadn't given them his name—more than as
like as not—before he knew himself how much it was worth.

Now you will understand, sisters, that no man, though he
should happen to be smart as a steel trap, and pleasant as a

willow whistle, can give extra brains or sweet manners to a wife who hasn't got 'em in her own right. So there is a chance that some short comings in the female line are not very uncommon.

The senators and judges and cabinet people are, as a general thing, the picked men of the nation, but they choose their own wives, and some of them haven't half so much taste in the fine arts, to which many of this generation of women belong, as they have knowledge about politics. Still, these ladies are what they call representative women, and, nationally considered, are the cream on cream of American society. That is a fact, too, as far as they represent their own husbands. By marrying great men, or those who are merely fortunate, they are only lifted more clearly into the public view, where their virtues and their faults are held up for general examination. Still, it is wonderful how popular some of them get to be, and how soon they learn the duties of their places.

Sometimes a first-rate woman happens to marry a first-rate man, and takes her place by his side naturally. A good many such women have earned a place for themselves in society quite equal to any their husbands have been chosen to hold by the people.

Mrs. Madison, Mrs. Polk and Miss Lane were among these, and, as a perfect lady, well known for years and years in Washington, Mrs. Crittendon, the widow of Senator Crittendon—formerly Mrs. Ashley—is always mentioned side by side with her husband, and stood quite as high among women as he did among men. In my opinion, there is a senator's wife from Minnesota that can hold her own with the handsomest and highest of those that have gone before; but as she is extra modest too, I give no names.

Then there is another, I will say it, who has done honor to her position and credit to her husband, and that is Mrs. Ulysses Grant. She is just a good, honest, motherly woman, pleasant to look at and pleasant to speak to. She acts out what she pretends to, and pretends to be just what she is. If this woman hasn't pulled an even yoke with her husband, both in the war and after the war, no female of my acquaintance ever did. It's of no use talking, I like that woman.

But I am a-going at a rate that wants pulling up, so I tighten the bridle and take a new turn.

What I began to write about was, a reception at Mr. Horatio King's, which always takes off the first skimming of cream from Washington society.

Mr. King is a New England man, and was born and brought up in Maine, which lifts him almost to a level with us of Vermont.

In fact, in the way of statesmen and authors, I am bound to say that Maine pulls an even yoke with the Green Mountain State. So far as authors are concerned, I'm afraid she goes a little ahead of us.

The city of Portland was just a nest of authors before they took wing and settled down in other places.

John Neal, one of the most splendid men and brilliant writers that ever put an American pen to paper, was born there, and has spent most of his life in his native place.

N. P. Willis was born in Portland; so was Sebe Smith, who called himself Jack Downing in his letters.

Longfellow's family was rooted in that town long before he honored it by being born.

James Brooks, who was for years a pillar of strength in Congress, and who started the first newspaper correspondence ever thought of, in the *Portland Advertiser*, which he edited before he was twenty years old, was a native of Portland, which city he represented in the legislature, then travelled all over Europe on foot, and settled down in New York before he was twenty-six. After this he spent twelve or fifteen years in Congress—earned a place, second to no man there, as a statesman, travelled over Europe three times, visited Egypt and the Holy Land, and finished his travels by a trip round the world, taken between the sessions of Congress. Beside this, he never ceased to be the leading editor of the New York *Ex-*

press, and his book about Japan, China, and so on, which Mr. Appleton, of New York, has published, is one of the best books of travel extant.

Beside all these, Mr. King made his first literary start in Portland, where, as a young man, he edited a weekly paper. But he has lived most of his after-life in Washington, generally holding a high position there. During a portion of Mr. Buchanan's administration, he was Postmaster-General of these United States, and at all times he has been considered a man worth knowing.

LIII.

A LITERARY PARTY.

DEAR SISTERS :—Of course I, being a young girl of New England, felt myself at home in Mrs. King's house the minute I entered it. There is something in the air of a dwelling like that, pure and breezy, like the morning winds on the Green Mountains. I felt myself growing frank and cheerful as I got into the hall. The parlors were crowded full—three of them—with people that one liked to look at, and longed to know; for every face had an idea in it, and, beyond that, a good many were right down beautiful.

But beauty by itself isn't enough to get an invitation here, and good clothes count for just nothing, though there was plenty of them, and I didn't feel as if my pink silk was too much. Something a little more austere, in the velvet or alpaca line, might have been more appropriate to the occasion. Still, there was a rosy brightness about my silk that had a tendency to give a glow of youthful thoughtlessness to intelligence, and combine an idea of high fashion with genius.

Mr. King, and his daughter, a proper, pretty stylish lady,

stood near the door when I went in, with the train of my dress streaming back into the hall, and some natural rose-geranium leaves circling my brow in a way that was calculated to remind an observing person of Miss Corinne when she was crowned in the Capitol at Rome.

Mr. King come forward to meet me with his hand held out. He is a thin, spare man, with the sweetest and kindest look in his face that you ever saw. I had intended to just touch his hand, and make a sweeping salute, half bow, half curtsey, that would take in the whole admiring crowd; but his frank, smiling welcome just took me right off from my feet, and I gave his hand a good, hearty New England shake that made him feel to home in a minute.

Mr. King led me into the parlor, and gave me a soft seat among the cushions of a sofa in the middle room, just as Solomon must have waited on the Queen of Sheba. Then, feeling that the eyes of more States than Vermont were upon me, I spread out my skirts, leaned one arm on the sofa cushion, and settled myself just as Mr. Brady had done it when I sat to him for a picture; thus adding an artistic feature to the fashionable and intellectual embodiment of my first appearance. . Thus, with downcast eyes and a modest demeanor, which must have been attractive, I waited for the literary programme that lay before us.

It commenced beautifully. Mr. King took his place under the chandelier of the middle room, and welcomed his friends with a very poetic and touching little speech, which ended in a farewell which almost brought tears into my eyes. This was his last reunion for the year, and he seemed to feel the breaking-up a good deal, and his kind voice shook when he mentioned the possibility that death might carry off some of the friends who had brightened his home, before they all met again.

When Mr. King sat down there was dumb silence for a little while; for the whole crowd seemed to feel all he had been saying, deep in their hearts. But this soon changed into smiles and a soft rustle of dresses, for a nice elderly gentleman got up and made a delightful speech, full of cheerfulness and nice friendly feeling, which brightened the whole crowd up like spring winds in a flower-garden.

After this, another pleasant gentleman arose with a written poem in his hand, which he read under the gaslight, filling the whole room with the sound of his friendly voice.

The poem was written to Mr. King. It was full of sweet thoughts and grateful thanks for all he had done to make his friends happy. But he blushed like a girl, for its praises seemed to take him by surprise, and, like all men of real talent, he is modest as can be.

The lady who wrote this sweet poem was Mrs. Neeley, who has been writing to the Washington papers ever so long, in a way, too, that any woman might be proud of. She sat directly behind the gentleman who read her poem, and looked real nice in her crimson velvet dress.

After this a lady got up and read something mournful about three curls of hair that a man had taken from his wife's head— golden when she was a child, brown when she was a bride, and snow-white when she lay dead.

There was a sort of sob went through all the rooms when this poem died out. Then, after a little, every lady began to cheer up and laugh; for the same lady was reading a poem, half Dutch, half English, about a dog howling, which was so funny that I almost forgot my dignity as the representative of your Society, and near about clapped my hands—a thing I should have regretted to the day of my death.

This dog poem set everybody into a state of high gleefulness and some music struck up in the front room, which could be heard a little now and then above the hum and rush of conversation that set in with the crowd, where artists, authors, and statesmen, and scientifics mingled in, and chatted promiscuously, saying such bright and wise and witty things, that they fairly made my eyes snap. I cut in, too.

What is the use of being the emissary of a literary, scientific, and moral institution, if one can't hold up her end of the

10*

yoke in conversation? I did my best, sisters. An artist stood near me; I talked with him about pictures till, I do believe, he thought that I had been born in Rome, and cradled with Michael Angelo—an old fellow, that both painted and made marble men in Italy years ago. Then I had something to say about flowers to an agricultural bureau scientific, and about the chemistry of something to a savant or savan, or a word like that, of the Smithsonian Institution. I tell you, sisters, it was sharp work; but I flatter myself you were not in any way disgraced.

By and by I was introduced to the Chief Justice of the Court of Claims—about as smart a lawyer, and clear headed a judge, as can be found in these parts, I can tell you. He was not long ago United States Senator from Missouri, and has left his mark among the statesmen there; but his genius lay as much in expounding the laws as in making them. He has written some capital law-books, too, and could mate with any judge, statesman, or author that came across his track. His wife joined in a little now and then, as only a right down sensible and handsome woman could. It does one's heart good to see a great man and most lovely woman mated so for once.

That was just what I did in Mr. King's parlors, and, when we stopped talking, it struck me that the gentleman knew a great deal more of literature than your missionary has yet learned of statesmanship or law. In fact, an evening in Mr. King's parlors does teach one humility, and I begin to discover that a person may be capable of writing poetry, and making a fair report, without being able to teach science to a professor, jurisprudence—I hope I have got the word right—to a judge, or high statesmanship to a senator. In fact, in the present state of society, it seems to me that the best of us have got to live and learn—live and learn.

LIV.

DRESSING FOR A PARTY.

Y DEAR SISTERS:—You have no idea how many kinds of parties there are in Washington. Some are called receptions, because they take place in the day-time, in houses where every mite of sunshine is shut out, and the gas set to blazing as if it were midnight. That is, night isn't turned into day here one bit oftener than day is turned into night.

Then there are ladies' lunch parties, where the daylight is allowed to shine in; and picnics, where one gets a little too much of it, besides being tired to death, and nothing to show for it.

Besides these, there are political parties, where men get up entertainments that are called caucuses, which no lady is allowed to join in. Besides dinners and breakfasts, and so on, without end, which makes life in this city just one rush and tumult—to say nothing of Congress, which is just that, and a good deal more so.

Last week, Cousin E. E. and I had so many invitations that we didn't know what to do with them. We should have had to go out to three breakfasts, two dinners, and six parties a night, if we had attempted to do more than read them all. For since Mr. King's literary reunion, the popularity of your missionary has increased like a rolling snowball, and her invitations came by the peck and half bushel.

Well, out of this heap, there was one or two places that I felt like honoring with my presence. So E. E. and I sat down and wrote a little note—all ladies write *little* notes nowadays —and relieved the intense anxiety of the people who had invited us, by saying, in the most polite way, that we would come.

This act of kindness had its reward in the feeling that we

had relieved more than one anxious host, and given certainty
of a brilliant success to parties that must necessarily have been
in doubt until certain of our coming. With my usual modesty,
I say "our," wishing to give E. E. her little chance, you know.

The invitation we resolved to honor was from one of the foreign ministers. Of course I expected that there would be a
good many religious people there, and, as I hadn't mingled
much with persons who were over pious for some time, I an-
ticipated a refreshing season; for a foreign minister must have
a noble missionary spirit, and, no doubt, came to Washington
on purpose to reform the members of Congress, which is a work
of Christian mercy, if ever there was one.

For this reason, my spiritual nature was aroused, and I was
burning with desire to help in the noble cause, and let foreign
nations know that we had women in this country that could be
at once brilliant and devout, celebrated and conscientious; in
fact, women who could gracefully combine two characters,
hitherto supposed to be opposite.

Yes, I was resolved to go to this ministerial reunion. Had
I not been at Mr. King's literary gathering, which lifted me,
as it were, out of a frivolous, fashionable life into the purely
intellectual, and now, should I refuse to bathe my soul in the
purer element of high Christian fervor? No, a thousand
times no !

On a religious occasion like this, I felt that a modest dress
—simple black alpaca, for instance, with a pink bow at the
neck—would be about the thing; but Cousin E. E. got almost
huffy about it.

"Why," says she, "at the Foreign Minister's a full toilet is
expected, always. It is but proper respect."

"Cousin," says I, "no one can have more respect for the
ministerial functions than I have; no one ever attended meeting more faithfully. Am I not a missionary myself? Do you
think I would or could fall short of the mark of the prize of
the high calling? If alpaca isn't the thing, I am open to reason and pink silk."

"That will do," says she, a-brightening up, "looped up with black velvet and bows, and *décolletté.*"

"Dic o' nonsense?" says I, riling a little.

"Well, low neck and short sleeves," says she.

"At a meeting of ministers?" says I. "Cousin E. E., are you crazy?"

"Well, do as you please," says she, "only I tell you it will be expected. I intend to be very low, with a strap for a sleeve, and all my jewels."

"I shall be content with the jewels of the soul," says I, with an austere rebuke in my voice; for if there is anything that riles me up more than another, it is flashy dressing where one's mind should be given up to solemn thoughts. "Cousin E. E., there are times when levity of dress and lightness of speech are to be excused, but this isn't one of them. Put a bridle on your tongue, and something more than a strap over your shoulder."

E. E. colored up, and gave her head a toss.

"Phœmie," says she, "you are past finding out. Do as you please, and just let me do as I please."

I lifted my forefinger in gentle warning; for, with all her fashionable crotchets, E. E. is a good soul as ever lived, and I don't want to be hard on her, feeling that great minds should be forbearing, especially in religious matters. So we parted good friends, and I went into my room to get ready for the solemn occasion.

I took out my pink silk dress—for the alpaca was a little rusty—and laid it out on the bed. Then I ripped some black velvet ribbon from another old dress, and tied it up into bows that looked scrumptious as new. After that I brushed my hair out straight, and braided it in an austere fashion appropriate to the occasion. Not a friz or a curl was to be seen; for this once I threw aside the other woman's hair, and was from head to foot myself again.

"Neat, yet genteel," says I to myself, when my dress was on and the black bows in place. "Nothing flash or frivolous, though everything refinedly elegant. No minister, be he ever so strict a disciplinarian, can find fault with me. I suppose the critics of all the religious papers will be there. Well, let them draw my portrait; I am ready for the ordeal."

With these high thoughts in my mind I went downstairs; but the sight of my cousin made me step back with both hands thrown up. She was just on fire with jewelry and precious stones. They flamed out on her neck, twinkled in her ears, and shot fiery arrows through her hair. Her cheeks were rosy red, and her eyes had shadows about them that had come since she went down to dinner. Perhaps she had taken a nap in a dark room, though. The dress she wore was soft and white and floating, like a cloud in the sky; and there was black lace mixed with it, and roses tangled up with that. I declare to you, sisters, if that woman had been going to a worldly party, she couldn't have been titivated off more than she was. It riled me to look at her.

Advice scorned isn't to be offered again. I said nothing, but let E. E. go on in her frivolous career.

LV.

FOREIGN MINISTERS.

DEAR SISTERS:—We entered the carriage, where Dempster took the front seat, just buried up in his wife's dress, and sat there like an exclamation-point gone astray. As for me, I sat upright and thoughtful, resolved to do my duty in spite of their shortcomings.

We reached a large brick house; before it a line of carriages kept moving like a city funeral, only people were all the time a-getting out and walking under a long tent that sloped down from the front door.

"There will be a full Conference," says I, in my heart, for I was too much riled up by E. E.'s dress for any observation to her.

One thing struck me as peculiar. None of the ladies wore their bonnets, and a good many had white cloaks on, huddled up around them as if they had been going to a party.

If I hadn't known the house belonged to foreign ministers, I really should have thought from the look of things that we had lost our way, and got into somebody's common reception. As it was I got out of the carriage, and went up the steps with my bonnet on, and holding up the train of my pink silk, feeling that so much appendage was out of place.

A colored person in white gloves opened the door, and waving his hand like a Grand Duke—oh, how that word goes to my heart—said:

"Front door, second story."

Another time I should have known that this meant that I could take off my things there. But now I felt almost certain that the ministers were holding a prayer-meeting, or conference, or something in "the front room, second story," so I went upstairs with a slow and solemn tread, feeling that the rustle of my pink silk was almost sacrilege.

I went into the room and looked around. It was full of women, wonderfully dressed women, all in low necks and short sleeves, and white shoes—laughing, giggling women, who looked over each others naked shoulders into a great broad looking-glass crowded full of faces that couldn't seem to admire themselves enough.

I stopped at the door. I scarcely breathed. What could all those rosy-cheeked, bare-armed ladies be doing in that house?

I asked this question, of course, of Cousin Dempster, who came into the hall a-pulling his white gloves on.

"Dempster," says I, in a low voice, "what does this mean? Where are the ministers?"

"Oh, they are in the back room. You didn't expect them to be turned in with the ladies, did you?"

" Well," says I, " it is customary in our State now, though it was not formerly, when the men sat on one side at prayer-meetings, and the girls on the other, but I didn't think that notion had got to foreign parts."

I don't think Dempster heard me clearly, for that minute his wife came out of the room, blazing like the whole milky-way of stars.

" Why, Phœmie," says she, a-holding up both the white kid gloves she had just buttoned on, " you don't mean to go down with that bonnet on ? "

" I should think you would be ashamed to go into a con-ference or a prayer-meeting with it off," says I, severely.

E. E. stared at Dempster, and he stared at her. Then he hitched up his shoulders, and she gave her hands a little toss in the air.

I didn't seem to notice their antics, but went with them downstairs, where I heard the sound of music, which didn't strike me as so sacred as it ought to be. Besides, there was a buzz and a hum like a hive of bees swarming, which was puzzling.

When we went into the great, long room, that seemed run-ning over with light, the crowded state of the congregation astonished me. There wasn't seats enough for one quarter of the worshippers.

Sisters, I was the only one present who had studied the sacred decencies of a bonnet and shawl. The rest were dressed—well, they weren't dressed at all about the arms and shoulders, which shocked me dreadfully ; the mere presence of a lot of ministers ought to have made women more decorous.

Would you believe it, the people round the doors stared at me as if they had never seen a beehive bonnet, with feathers floating over it, before.

Some people might have felt shocked at so many eyes turned on them, but I was in the straight and narrow path of duty, and their looks passed by me like the idle wind. If they didn't understand the solemnity of the occasion, I did.

"There is the Minister," says Dempster, "let us pay our respects."

"Why," says I, "there don't seem to be either a reading desk or pulpit here!"

I don't think Dempster heard me, for he began to edge our way through the crowd, till we got clear into the room, which was so full of flowers and lights and music that I began to think the foreign ministers were keeping up Easter-Sunday yet.

A gentleman was standing near the door with some ladies around him. Dempster took us straight up to him.

"Your Excellency," says he, "Miss Frost. Miss Phœmie Frost, of Vermont."

I didn't think that exactly a proper place to be introducing people in, and measured off my bow accordingly, and passed on without troubling myself about the ladies around him, who seemed to wonder at it. As if I wanted to know them!

When we got into the crowd again, I whispered to Dempster:

"Do tell me where the foreign ministers are!"

"The Ministers! Why you have just been presented to the very highest of them," says Dempster.

"What, that man," says I, "with precious stones a-twinkling on his shirt-bosom, and a bit of red ribbon in his buttonhole, who seems to have cut up his words with a chopping knife? You couldn't make me believe that, Dempster!"

"But it is, upon my honor, Phœmie; and those gentlemen standing around him are all Ministers, or persons sent out with them. Almost every civilized nation is represented here to-night."

I looked around at the persons Dempster pointed out—some were young, some old, some you could understand, others you couldn't; most of them were talking and laughing with the ladies around them. I didn't see a downright serious face in the whole crowd.

"Them ministers!" I said, scorning Dempster's attempt to deceive me.

" Every one of them is a Minister now, or means to be."

" Dempster, I don't believe you."

" Well, ask some one else whom you can believe," says he, a-turning red.   " Here is Miss ——, she can tell you."

I didn't hear the name clear, but Dempster introduced me to a young lady that had just sat down by me.

" Are those men who are chatting and laughing so, really ministers ? " says I to her.

" Most of them are; the rest are connected with the Legation," says she.   " Elegant, don't you think so ? "

Before I could ask her what newfangled society had been got up under the name of Legation, a young gentleman with a round gold glass screwed into one eye, came out from the hive of ministers, and walked toward us, moving along slow and lazy, as if walking were too much for him.

The girl was all in a flutter when she saw him a-coming our way.   She looked at me as if I had a seat that she wanted for some one else, but I didn't move; and after shaking out her dress as a cross hen flutters its feathers, she pretended to look the other way, as if she didn't care a mite whether the young minister came up or not.

Oh, the airs some of these school-girls put on is disgusting.

The young divinity student came up with a sort of half-dancing step.

" Miss," says he, a-bowing and chewing up his words as if he'd a piece of sweet flag-root in his mouth, " delighted to—aw—aw—have the honor of seeing you here—am, indeed."

She bowed, she prismed up her mouth, waved her fan a trifle, and says she—

" Of course you ought to have expected me.   I am a little exclusive, but always make a point of coming here."

The young—no, he wasn't over young, but did his best to look so.   Well, this foreign student just turned his glass on me, his impudent little eye stared right through at my bonnet. Then he looked at that finefied girl, and they both smiled at each other.

This riled me.

Then a couple of young ladies crowded by us, laughing a little. The divinity student turned his glass—eye and all—upon them, then he turned to the young creature by my side, and says he, curling up his wisp of a mustache:

"Now, really, miss, what is the reason all the American young ladies have the manners of chambermaids?"

I felt my Yankee heart spring straight up into my New England mouth; but the foreign snipe wasn't speaking to me, so I sat still and listened for what that young creature would say.

"The manners of chambermaids!" says she, "did you mean that?"

"Really—yes—I think they have, you know."

"Well, I will not contradict you, for you generally are right," says she, as meek as Moses—yes, Moses in the bulrushes, "but not quite all, I hope."

The mean thing couldn't keep from trying to wring a compliment for herself out of this insult to the general American female.

The fellow had sense enough to see what she wanted, and he gave it to her.

"Aw—aw—of course there are a few lovely exceptions, you know," says he, a-bowing so low that his eye-glass dropped out of his poor little eye that looked like a green gooseberry without it. "I speak of American women, generally, as having the manners of chambermaids."

I couldn't hold in one minute more. No coffee-grounds, twice soaked, ever riled up like my temper.

"If *you* find American ladies acting like chambermaids," says I, "it's because they feel compelled to adapt themselves to the company they are in."

Here I bent my head with a low, dignified bow, and waved my fan with a calm but decided motion.

That little humbug of a young lady looked half scared to death. The divinity student ground his glass into his eye, looked at me from head to foot, and says he:

" Aw, aw ! " and walked away.

The girl looked after him as if she wanted to cry, but just then a great whirl of music burst from the next room, and I thought the meeting was about to organize, when a tall fellow, with his mustache quirled up like an ox-horn, came tetering up to the young female by my side.

" May I have the honor ? " says he.

The girl turned her head sideways, and rolled up her eyes like a pullet drinking.

" It is a quadrille, Count," says she, " and I never join in one."

" A quadrille, pardonne ! You are right. When you daunce —if you daunce—why, of course, you daunce a round daunce."

The fellow flung out his white hands, making a little dive forward with each word; then he saw my face, which must have spoken volumes, and slacked off his antics. I don't think he liked the cut of my smile, for, crooking up his elbow, he leaned forward, and says he:

" May I be honored with a promenade ? "

She took his arm, and the two fluttered off into the crowd, which was pouring off into a large room beyond the one we were in.

" The meeting is going to commence now in good earnest," I thought. " I'll try and get a seat where I can hear."

Cousin Dempster and E. E. came up, and I joined in. The lecture-room was long, and lighted up beautifully. Right in front of the door was the singers' gallery, hung round with red cloth, and over that hung great wreaths of flowers, but I saw neither pulpit nor reading-desk.

"Where will the minister be ?" I whispered to Cousin Dempster.

" Oh, he will open the ball."

" Open the ball ! What *do* you mean ? " says I. " A minister dancing ! I won't believe it."

" Why, they all do," says he, innocent as a lamb. " No better dancers in Washington."

Sisters, what *do* you think of that? Was I to blame when I insisted on leaving that house at once? Would you have had me sit by and witness this degradation? "No," says I to Cousin Dempster, "I won't stay. If ministers of the Gospel will do such things, I, as a New England woman—girl I mean —would be committing a sin to look on."

"But you do not understand. They are Foreign Ministers. sent here by other nations, which they represent."

"So much the worse—how dare they set such examples? " says I.

"Ambassadors! can't you understand? "

"Of course I understand. All ministers are ambassadors from the Lord; but I never heard of their dancing, except that Shaking Quakers do now and then, which is a part of their religion, and they are only elders, anyhow."

"But there is no religion in these things! "

"I should rather think not," says I, a-walking resolutely toward the door. "Now it's of no use explaining and apologizing to me. Dancing ministers ain't of my sort. I'm going right straight home."

Sisters, I went.

LVI.

GOOD CLOTHES.

DEAR SISTERS:—I told you in my last Report that there were three or four invitations that I had made up my mind to accept, for I have got so now, that it is my privilege to pick and choose who I will honor and who I will not.

Well, the person I distinguished this time was just one of the handsomest and nicest ladies that you ever sot eyes on. Everybody that knows her says that. No bird pluming itself on an apple-tree limb full of blossoms was ever more graceful; no church member could be more kind-hearted. She is just a sumptuous young woman who worshipped a true-hearted, high-minded father with all her might and honored him in all her acts. It is a great pity she wasn't born in Vermont, but that cannot be helped now. I wish it could.

Of course I felt it a privilege to represent your Society before a lady like this; for it seems to me as if she were born to be an ornament to this great nation. I say this because I really think she is good as good can be. Miss Kate Chase, though she did marry a United States Senator, will always be best known to the country as Chief Justice Chase's daughter, and a compliment to her is a compliment to him, which I, as a distinguished wom—I beg pardon, young girl—could pay, and still preserve that reputation for correct deportment which, I am proud to say, follows me wherever I go.

Well, not wanting to keep Mrs. Sprague in suspense, and feeling that she might be pining for my autograph to lie uppermost in the great dish, all gold and stone pictures, which she keeps full of letters and cards and things, I wrote her a sweet little letter, in my finest hand, with a green and red " P. F." twisted together on the straw-colored envelope, saying that I would come.

After that I felt calm and content, knowing how much happiness I had given.

Cousin Dempster and E. E. had an invite too. I really hope they have sense enough to know the source from which all these attentions come, but sometimes I doubt it. Still, they do look up to me.

The night came, and found me ready. E. E. had told me that when Mrs. Sprague gave a party, her guests almost always came out in span-new dresses. Her entertainments were *the* entertainments of the season. Nobody had yet been able to come up to her, let them try ever so much, and people dressed accordingly.

Of course I wasn't going to be behindhand on a fashionable occasion like that, where a certain person was sure to be an object of special admiration and envious criticism, so I went to work at once, and turned my pink silk wrong side out with my own hands.

Then I took an hour or so of solitary shopping, and had the things I bought carried straight into my own room, for I had given out that I had a sick headache, and wanted to sleep—a fib so delicate, that it seemed almost conscientious, besides being worth forgiving on account of its originality.

Well, I worked away like everything, determined to show the world, for my own private enjoyment, that genius wasn't limited to writing, but would sometimes break out in silks and laces and flowers, with astonishing effects. So my heart rose, and my fingers flew.

That headache of mine lasted three days, without intermission. During this season of affliction, my meals were brought up on a hotel tray, and I took care to order them myself—the toast and tea, which cousin sent up at first, not being quite satisfactory as a persistent diet.

At last my dress was ready. E. E. said *she* had ordered hers from Worth, ever so long ago, expecting that something super-elegant might turn up, like Mrs. Sprague's party. I didn't ask who Worth was, not thinking a masculine mantua-maker worth inquiring about; but I kept a close mouth about my own toilet—that word needs explaining, sisters. With us it means a half-moon table, curtained down, and ruffled over with spotted muslin, and set under a looking-glass. But here it means your whole dress—frock, boots, everything that you wear from top to toe. This is why the word " toilet " comes in so naturally in my Report. But understand, it does *not* mean a table—quite the contrary.

You should have seen me when I came out of my room that evening. Up to this I had been harmonious in my dress, but newness was the thing here, so I had studied the grandly poetical harmony of contrasts. My aim had been something poetical and striking.

My pink silk had turned beautifully. It looked good as new, if not more so; the fresh lining hunched it out behind, till a good-sized baby could have sat on it, as such little fellows billow themselves among the clouds in an old picture. Contrast, I have told you, was my idea—novelty my object. Pink and white roses I had worn, black velvet, too, and natural geranium-leaves, which are given to wilting fearfully; so I cast these things all aside, and looped up my dress with pond lilies, of a rich orange color.

Sisters, the effect was wonderful. The broad green leaves on the pink ground, the yellow flowers clustering amongst them. The lilies of red gold entwining my head was a picture in itself—to say nothing of the tall and elegant young person who, as I may write, carried off the dress.

You should have seen Cousin E. E. when I swept into the room, where she stood ready, my pink silk rustling, my golden lilies on the high quiver, my hair crinkled in front, curled behind, and looped up with those yellow flowers. Sisters, her surprise was really a tribute.

I did not deign to ask her how she liked my dress. The look that followed her first surprise was clouded with the envy she did not dare to speak. I was seized with a desire to punish such malice, and swept up and down the room, looking back on my train, as a peacock spreads his tail-feathers in the sun.

E. E. looked ready to burst. She saw that her own dress was nowhere, and resented it in angry silence. So I kept on walking slowly up and down, in order to bring her into a reasonable state of mind, which Christian exertion, I am sorry to say, failed.

Dempster came in, and he, too, was struck dumb with admiring surprise. He looked at me, then at E. E., but said nothing. Still the comparison must have been humiliating to a man who really does take some pride in his wife.

LVII.

THE PARTY OF THE SEASON.

DEAR SISTERS:—The carriage was full to over-flowment; E. E. and I filled it with the sumptuosity of our garments. Dempster was nowhere. Now and then the carriage jolted his head into sight—that was all.

Mrs. Sprague lives in a great, square corner-house that looks rich and respectable—two things that do not always come together in these days, when people creep into society, and build themselves up there on the property that should belong to the Government. It has some wide, jutting windows, and plenty of room inside.

The hall-way was crowded full of ladies, and so was the stairs. Some were going up, and some were coming down. The first in shawls and cloaks, the others with their arms and necks uncovered, or with just a shadow of lace on them, nothing more.

The great square chamber that we went into was as full as a bee-hive. Silks swept and rustled against each other like oak-leaves when the wind shakes them. The great looking-glasses were full also—you saw a crowd of handsome faces coming and going in them all the time. Each glass was like a picture always changing.

The bed was covered over with cloaks and shawls, but you could see that the bedstead was beautifully carved, and the pillow-cases were ruffled all round and edged with lace. On a table near the door was a case of shiny black wood, curlicued with gold, and lined with velvet. In it was a lot of gold things, essence bottles, knives, scissors with gold handles, and glass cases with gold lids. It lay open, and anybody could use the things that wanted to; I didn't, but had a good look while E. E. was titivating in the crowd before the glass.

My dress must have carried out the grand idea in my mind

when I made it, for all the ladies stopped, and gave me a good, long look before they went out, and I could see smiles of approbation dancing about their mouths.   My triumph commenced, sisters, even in the dressing-room.

Dempster was waiting for us, and we followed him downstairs into the largest and handsomest room I've seen in Washington City.

It was just afire with lights.   The great curving window was crowded full of flowers; every table in the room blazed out with them.   Two folding-doors, like those we have in a Vermont meeting-house, opened into another great room, just as rainbowish with light, and smelling just as sweet with flowers—I never saw anything like it.

A crowd went in with us, and we had to wait till they let us go up to Judge Chase and Mrs. Sprague, who stood in the front room.

Goodness gracious, what a female woman that is ! •No willow tree was ever half so graceful, and, as for manners, the nicest woman I ever saw is nowhere to her.   Her dress—well, I really cannot say that it didn't pull an even yoke with mine —at any rate the contrast between us was striking, nothing could have been more so.   But I can say, without vanity, the crowd as it came in stopped to look at mine quite as much as it did at hers.   Original taste, you know, sisters, is everything; then literary genius united with taste isn't easily matched.   Still, Mrs. Sprague's dress was well worth noticing.

" What did she wear ? " I hear you say.

Sisters, your wishes are laws to me.

This lady, for she *is* a lady, every inch of her, as I have said, was a complete contrast to your missionary.   Her dress had three colors; blue satin in front, wreathed across with a wreath of rosebuds and leaves over each flounce.   Running up each side were other wreaths, fastening down the edges of a long train of white silk, that was fastened in a wide box-plait at the back of the neck, and swept away to the carpet, where it fell and floated like a snow-drift scattered over with roses, for they were done in needle work all over the white robe, and seemed to grow there. The dress was cut square about the neck, and filled in with lace. She had half-sleeves, too, a thing I was glad to see, for some of the stuck-up persons who came there with no sleeves, and their dresses cut short about the neck, might have taken it for a rebuke. Thank goodness, I didn't.

Mrs. Sprague wore some jewelry. A wreath of blue stones with white ones that shone like rain-drops in the sunshine, was fastened in her hair, and hung quivering in her ears. She had gold bands, full of fiery stones, on her arms, and some gold thing fell down to her bosom, set with something that looked to me like half-ripe cherries. Pink coral, E. E. said it was.

There now, you have Mrs. Sprague's dress, and you have mine. I say nothing. Certainly hers was handsome. I am not the person to draw comparisons, but, from the notice given to mine, I had no reason to be dissatisfied.

Chief Justice Chase stood by his daughter, and shook hands with me in the most friendly manner—he was quite impressed, I can assure you. He was large and tall—in fact, grand in his appearance. His smile was enough to make any one long to know more of him. It reminded me a little of the great Grand Duke's, which made my heart beat a little sadly.

We moved into the crowd. There I saw a lot of those foreign ministers. One of them bowed to me. I gave him a dignified bend of the head. This messing-up of divinity and parties goes against my ideas of propriety.

A Vermont minister would be turned out of his pulpit if he ventured to show himself in a worldly gathering like that.

" What are you so dignified about, Cousin Phœmie ? " says Dempster. " Didn't you see the minister bowing to us ? "

" Yes," says I, " but I don't mean to encourage backsliding and worldly amusements in Christian leaders. They have no business here."

"But they are not particularly Christians," says he.

"I should think not," says I; "and the Churches that sent them here ought to know how they are going on."

"But the Churches did not send that gentleman. It was the Queen."

"Exactly," said I; "and isn't she the head of the Church. No, no, cousin, you can't make excuses for them."

"But their mission is political," says he.

"Of course," says I. Church and State—I understood."

A whole lot of candles, white as snow, were burning over the wide doors. That opened into another long room where a great picture, worked with a needle, years and years ago, hung on the wall, and crowds of people were moving about. Then came a storm of music, and I saw one of the ministers tetering off with a lady as if he were going to dance again.

"I declare I won't look on," says I to Dempster; "take me somewhere else."

He did take me into a little room full of books, and there—standing round a table on which a great giant of a china bowl stood, filled to the brim with punch, on which slices of lemon floated temptingly—we found some more of them ministers, each one with a full glass in his hand.

Sisters, I stood there like a monument, and saw them drink that punch with my own eyes—more than one glass apiece, too. Ministers, indeed !

While we stood watching them in one door, they went out by another, and then Dempster took us in.

E. E. sat down on a sofa ; so did I. Dempster went up to the great bowl, and began to dip out the punch with a big silver ladle as if it had been soup. He filled two glasses. A slice of lemon floated on each one ; they looked deliciously cool, and I was thirsty. Sisters, I took that glass, and I drank of the punch. After that I began to feel more charitable toward the foreign ministers. In fact, I rather think a sweeter and more benevolent feeling came over me in all respects, for a soft mistiness settled on the crowd, and the dancers were peculiarly mazy. I felt myself smiling blandly, and, in fact, glided into a state of dreamy enjoyment that was pleasant.

The music stopped; the dancers locked arms, and moved toward an open door through which a fresh flood of light was pouring. We followed into a great tent, hung all round with damask linen. Two long tables, loaded down with great vases full of fruit and flowers; steeples, and towers, and baskets, made out of candy, and running over with sugar things; peaches, and grapes, and all sorts of fruit, natural as life, but candy to the core—all delicious and gorgeous and—well, I haven't language to express it; but the whole thing was sumptuous.

All down and around these two long tables great wreaths of flowers and leaves, half buried in moss, made a border of bloom, and over them the light came pouring, while the music sounded nearer and nearer, and the crowd poured in.

Really, sisters, I can say no more. That whole scene was more than I can describe. It just sent me home dizzy with bewilderment.

LVIII.

DOWN THE POTOMAC.

DEAR SISTERS:—The Father of our Country was a great man—no doubt on that subject. He conducted a war on small means and with few men, which gave us a country that will be a crowning glory of all ages, if we don't melt down and go to nothing under the hot sunshine of our own prosperity. He was a great man and a good boy, not because he cut down the cherry-tree and wouldn't lie about it, for good boys and great men are not made out of one action, but a harmonious character which produces many good actions.

Then again, I am not so certain that the action was what it is cracked up to be, anyway. In the first place, good little boys don't cut down their father's fruit-trees. Generally, they like to climb them a great deal better, especially when the cherries are ripe. I know that—being a girl, who could have borrowed a hatchet and made myself immortal by chopping instead of climbing to pick half-green cherries, which I did, and tore my frock, besides getting a pain in the—well, heart, which two things betrayed me just as the little hatchet betrayed George.

Now, when my mother asked me what the mischief I'd been about, I didn't think of saying I couldn't lie, because I could, and longed to do it; but I knew that New England women would find me out and give me double "jessie" if I piled a whopper on top of the green cherries and torn frock, so I told her I didn't know, being conservative—took my whipping like a man and a trooper, scorning to cover up two sins under one pious truth.

I didn't follow George Washington's example, for two reasons. First, I had never heard of the hatchet; and again, the story don't wash to a degree that is expected of high-priced morality. When the youthful boy, Father of our Country, said he *couldn't* lie, he was a-doing it that very minute. What boy ever lived that couldn't lie? Lying is born in 'em, and they take to it as naturally as a kitten laps milk.

The fellow that wrote that story was a' botch. Why didn't he make little George say, " Father, I won't tell a lie; so there —I cut down the cherry-tree with my little hatchet."

There would have been something heroic and above-board about that—a struggle against temptation foreshadowed, and a brave determination to stand up to the rack, fodder or no fodder, worthy of a boy that meant to be father of the man, who in his turn was the father of his country, thus doing up all his paternity in a wholesale way. But to say he couldn't was so sneakingly good that I don't believe it of him. In fact, I don't believe one word of the story.

Put that down on the records of your Society.

Of course, one never thinks of George Washington, that a nice boy, showing a hatchet, does not come in as the first picture.

The reason I happened to think of it was an invitation to go in a Government steamboat down to Mount Vernon, Washington's old homestead, and see the tomb where he was buried.

Of course I wanted to go. When the President of these United States gets out a Government steamboat on purpose to carry a distinguished New England female down to the tomb of her country's forefathers, it's an honor she's bound to accept.

I did accept it with enthusiasm, and at once invited Cousin Dempster and E. E. to go with me, for it always gives me pleasure to act as a sun to their moon.

The Japanese were invited to join me on the boat, and as many as two hundred other people were allowed to go down, which I was rather glad of—they being amongst the best—and my nature being social, as you know.

Well, between nine and ten in the morning, we drove up to the Navy Yard—a place where the Government builds the ships that are always being altered, and mended, and made worse than they were before. It's like a village on the water, is this Navy Yard, with a high wall around it, and a gate big enough for our carriage to go through, which it did, taking us down to the water in fine style.

"Do you want to go on board the 'Tallapoosa'?" says a man on the wharf.

"The 'Tallapoosa'!" says I to Dempster. "What outlandish thing is that?"

"The steamboat," says he.

"Well, why don't they call it a steamboat?" says I; "such airs!"

With that, I jumped out of the carriage, taking a neat dancing step as I touched the ground, and spread my parasol.

Just then another carriage drove up, choke full of little dark men.

"It is the Japanese," says Dempster.

"The Japanese!   How can you say so?" says I.   "Where
are their punch-bowl hats and stiff veils?"

"Oh," says Dempster, "they have given those things up,
and dress just as we do now."

"Dear me!" says I, a-looking into the carriage from under
a slope of my parasol.   "How funny they look with stove-
pipe hats, and boots, too—oh my!"

The Japanese were getting out of their carriage, but they
seemed as if afraid of straining too hard on their clothes, and
stepped on the ground as if it was paved with eggs.

Bang!

"Oh, goodness gracious!"

It was I that screamed out these words, and I hopped up at
least half a yard from the ground, for somewhere, close by, a
great gun went off—roaring over the water, like thunder.

"What does that mean?   Does anybody want to murder
us?" says I, shaking like a poplar-leaf.

"No, no," says he, "they are only saluting us."

"Saluting *me?*" says I.   "How dare they?   Of course
they knew I should jump and scream.   So loud, too!   No
young girl would stand it."

With that, I lifted my parasol, and walked across the plank
on to the deck of that steamboat, and sat down.

Them Japanese came after, and sat down close to me.   Mr.
Iwakura looked at me, and I looked at him.   He smiled, and
I smiled.   This Japanee knows how to smile with his eyes, and
that's more than a good many other men can do.

Then I felt it my duty to talk a little, as these Japanese had
been invited on my account; so, thinking that he would expect
something original from me, I said:

"I think we shall have a pleasant day, Mr. Iwakura."

"Yes," says he, in real cunning English, looking as if he
appreciated my little speech.

"I really hope," says I, "that you and your friends will feel
quite at home."

He said "Yes," again, and smiled.

Thát smile was catching.

"I wonder if Mr. I. left a wife behind to languish for that peculiar expression?   If not—"

I checked these roving thoughts as incompatible with former ideas.

The steamboat was puffing and blowing, and giving a scream now and then.   It began to tremble—it veered and made a slow plunge down the river.   The decks were crowded with ladies and gentlemen—all smiling happy—that seeming to be overjoyed to have the pleasure of coming with me.

The Potomac River is just lovely.   All the trees along its banks were budding and feathering out with greenness.   We passed by a town.   Then a great round heap of stone walls, that they called the Fort.   The grass was green around it, and some soldiers came out on the walls to look at us as we swept by.

It was pleasant; I felt the occasion to be something like that on which that Egyptian woman went down the River Nile in a row boat; so I lowered my parasol as we passed the Fort.

At last the steamboat made a dead stop in the river.   We were right opposite Mount Vernon.   I looked at the sacred old place from the water.   It was lovely in itself, standing there on a high knoll, carpeted with soft spring grass, and with tall trees a-bending over it.   The sunshine lay on the water and the shore, but that old house was a good deal in shadow, and all the more pleasant for that.

Some smaller boats came up to the steamboat.   We got into them and went ashore.

11*

LIX.

MOUNT VERNON.

OUNT VERNON had looked lonesome enough till now; but when we all landed it was like a picture. We wandered about; we broke up into little crowds, and the whole place was alive with happy people.

Mr. Iwakura and the rest of the Japanese walked slowly up the road. Dempster, E. E., and I went with them till we came to a tomb dug into the bank, with an iron fence before it.

Iwakura took off his stove-pipe hat and held it, just as if he had been at a funeral. The rest did the same, looking sad and touchingly solemn.

I dropped my parasol low, to hide the tears that came gushing up to my eyes, without warning. Cousin E. E. began to sob.

I turned away, longing to creep off into some dark corner, and have a good cry all by myself.

A good many of the people had gone up to the old homestead which is spread out low on the ground, and has a stoop with pillars running all along the front. From this stoop you can see the bend of the river and the blue of its water through the trees. There was a well near by that put me in mind of home; a lot of girls were drinking from the bucket, and chirruping together like birds around a spring.

I didn't like the sound just then, and went into the hall-way of the old homestead. There was nothing worth while in it but a great, big, heavy key, covered with rust, and big enough to knock a man down with.

"This," says a gentleman, a-standing close by me, "is the key of the Bastille."

I jumped back.

"What!" says I—"that old prison in Paris, where men were buried alive, without trial?"

"The same," says he. "Lafayette gave it to General Washington."

I felt myself shuddering, but said nothing. The subject struck me dumb. We went upstairs into the chamber where Washington died. It was not over large, and low in the joints ; but the windows looked out on the trees and the river, which took away some of its gloominess. Nothing but a bedstead, with high, spindling posts, was there.

" Did he die on that ? " says I to a gentleman near me.

" No," says he, " but on a bedstead just like it."

I turned away. What business had a sham bedstead in that room ? The idea of it riled up something besides sympathy in my bosom. I had rather see bare walls than a bedstead *like* the one he died on. Why don't they take it down ?

We went into the parlor. It isn't over-large, and looks cheery. An old, coffin-shaped piano was there, with broken wires ; some old china plates and dishes were piled together. That was about all.

I couldn't stand it. The tomb had sunshine about it, and wasn't half so gloomy. The hall-door was open, and I went out. A little way from the house was Washington's flower-garden, where a few jonquills and crocuses were spotting the earth with yellow. Near that was a large brick house, long and low, crowded full of plants which had flowers on them.

This wasn't Washington's greenhouse, but a bran new one, which looked like a spring bonnet worn with a ten-year old dress. This riled me too. It seemed to me that the old homestead should be kept just as Washington left it. Newfangled improvements are an aggravation.

Before I came away from Washington there was a good deal of talk about the lady who lives here and takes charge, but I couldn't for the life of me find out anything that seemed extravagant or wrong about her. The truth is, the ladies of this country have spent years collecting money to buy Mount Vernon, and make it a place sacred to the nation, but they failed in obtaining a fund large enough to maintain it with honor.

The society give this lady no remunerative salary, and nothing but a pure missionary spirit could keep her in that dull and mournful place. If she raises money enough to keep the homestead in repair, it is all any one ought to ask, and all the nation wants. But for my part, I scorn this quiddling way of making money. There is a meanness about it that disgraces the nation.

The thing that should be done is this: put the whole concern into the hands of Congress. It ought to belong to the nation. Washington was not the saviour of a lot of women only, but of the whole country. Let the country have possession of his old home, and appropriate all the money needed to keep it in perfect order, as Washington left it. If the women of America raised money enough to buy the estate for no better purpose than to peddle out a sight of Washington's tomb for twenty-five cents a sight, and keep flowers to sell, they have sent their patriotism to a mighty small retail market.

Well, in the afternoon we all went on board the steamboat again, and had a good time running up and down the river, which is just one of the things I should like to do every day; for the day was bright enough to keep one out-doors forever, if it would only have lasted so long.

When we had got out of sight of Mount Vernon, a band of music came on deck, and played like anything, while we went down into the cabin, one party at a time, and ate dinner, which tasted delicious, I can tell you—to say nothing of the bottled cider, and such like, that kept the corks a-flying about like bullets.

It is wonderful what smartness that cider gives to a person. It sparkles through one like the first spring sap in a maple-tree.

When I went on deck again, my limbs felt springy as a steel trap, and I couldn't help dancing along, for a band of fiddlers and toot-horns was a-pouring out music, that, joined to the cider, was enough to make one want to dance with her own grandfather.

They did dance, sisters—I own it, with shame and contrition. I joined in with the other young girls, and flatter myself they know by this time what a genuine Virginia reel is.

Forgive me, I know it wasn't just the thing for a church member to do, especially while returning from that tomb; but bottled cider and fiddlers must be a stronger power in the hands of the Evil One than anything I have tried yet; and more church members, and ever so much older persons than me, just made that deck shake with their dancing, half the way up that beautiful river.

Still, my head aches this morning, and I have a sort of backsliding feeling. The truth is, Tombs and Virginia reels don't seem to gibe in together.

LX.

MR. GREELEY'S NOMINATION.

EAR SISTERS:—What do you think of the dear old Mountain State now? Have you reason to be proud of her, or have you not? Do you understand what she has done lately in the way of literature—in the female line, I mean—and now, only think of it, the next President of the United States is expected from that sacred and hilly soil.

I know that Vermont will be almost tickled to death about this. It will be a crown of glory to her mountains, and a song of rejoicing in her valleys. The sap in her maple-trees will start earlier, run brighter, and sugar off more gloriously than it has ever done before. Up to this time, Vermont has never had her share of honors at the national Capitol, but now her time has come.

I am so glad I went to Mr. Greeley's birthday party, and I haven't a doubt that a great many other persons feel pretty much as I do about it. When I shook hands with him there, and saw him standing in the midst of his friends, with his kind face looking smooth and enticing as a sweet baked apple, I little thought it might be the next President of these United States that was enjoying himself over a birthday. But things do get tangled and untangled dreadfully in this world of ours —don't they? and the most uncertain thing on this side of sundown is any man's destiny. The most certain thing is the popularity of success. It seems to me now as if I think considerable more of this great Vermonter than I did last week, but what has he done to make me?—that's what I should like to know. He's just the same man ; has just as many faults— no great new supply of virtues. In fact, what has he done this week more than he did last, that I should feel a sort of honor and glory in being his friend?

I have been putting these questions to myself, and the answer makes me feel a little meachen. I am the missionary of one of the most august bodies that can be found in this or any other country. I represent a body of blameless, heroic ladies, whose glory it is to be above prejudice, and capable of self-judgment—ladies that are ladies, and wish to set an example of Christian womanliness to their own sex and the rest of mankind, feeling that " the eyes of all Vermont are upon them."

I am all this, yet I feel the humiliation of thinking all the better of a man because a great hullabaloo of other men have declared before the world that they want him for President of these United States. This is weak, but natural—natural, but awfully weak. Why should we let crowds of men we never saw judge for us? But then, how are we to judge for ourselves?

After all, this self-government is a difficult thing to carry out. What man really does govern himself?—either through his brain, or heart, some one else governs him. He gives himself up by the wholesale to a crowd, or by retail to his own family.

In the parlor of our hotel last night there was nothing but confusion and commotion. I went down there with Cousin E. E., for we all felt the glory that had settled down on us in a reflected way, and longed to enjoy it before folks. So down we went, trying to look as if nothing was the matter, but feeling the smiles quivering and playing about our lips like ladybugs about an open rose.

The parlors were full. Everybody had something to say. Some were smiling, some looked ready to cry, and others looked grim as gunlocks; but most of the faces we saw were beaming like a harvest moon.

As for me, I felt—yes, as the poet says, "I felt—I felt like a morning star."

"Well, Miss Frost, how do you like it?" says a little mite of a woman, with pink ribbons spreading out on her bosom. "What do you think of the nomination?"

"Think?" says I. "Why, this is what I think—the sun will rise and set on the top of the Green Mountains like a crown of glory, after this."

"Will Vermont go for him?" says another, cutting in.

"Will the mountains stand on their old rocky base?" says I. "What a question!"

"Then you think it will?"

"Think! I know it will. When did that glorious old State neglect one of her own sons?"

"But it's so strange!" snivelled the little woman.

"Strange!" says I; "what is strange?"

"Why, that Mr. Greeley should be nominated."

"Well," says I, with cutting irony, "do you think it strange that the people of this country should choose an honest man once in a while? ain't we always ready to reward merit? Haven't we done it in the military way with General Grant? Haven't we a right to go into a new field? First the sword, now the pen."

"Oh! not that; but—but—"

"Well, but what?"

"He's so—so peculiar."

"Yes, he is," says I, "if integrity, simple good faith, and sound sense is peculiar—and I begin to think it is."

"Do you know him, Miss Frost?"

I drew myself up, and that feeling I have spoken of came over me. It was a temptation, and—well, I and Mrs. Eve are a little alike in our feminine weaknesses; I'm glad I have Bible support in the disposition to fib a little that comes over me.

"Do I know him?" said I. "Yes, intimately."

"Ah!" says she.

"You can judge how intimately," says I, smitten with compunction, and craw-fishing down into a deceiving truth, "when I tell you that I was an honored guest at his birthday party."

"You don't say so!" says she.

I didn't feel bound to remind her that I had said so, and only drew myself up a trifle, and waved my fan back and forth with a dignified movement.

"And you really think well of him? But, then, he is an editor, and authors always have a sort of affinity for gentlemen of the press," says a pert young creature, twisting her head on one side, and coming up to me.

"I think well of him," says I, "because he is a man that has worked his way up in the world by the hardest; studied wisdom from the type he was setting, when he had no time for books; worked like a Trojan to support himself days, then sat up half the night to improve his mind. Mr. Greeley is in all respects a self-made man. This nomination is but the proper and natural crown of a busy life like his; of integrity like his, and of wisdom like his."

"You talk earnestly," says a gentleman, coming up into the little crowd that grew thick around me.

"Because I feel earnestly," says I, a-doubling up my fan, and laying down the law with it. "I don't pretend to know a great deal about politics, but I do know something about the history of my country, and it has never been better governed than when self-made men have ruled over it; but here is something more—the editor of a great daily journal is gathering up knowledge and wisdom every day of his life. He has opportunities for watching events and judging of actions that prepare his own mind for the exercise of power when it comes. "Why," says I, warming up, "the greatest statesmen that you have are editors and self-made men. The fact is, men who have worked their own way in the world, haven't time to be rogues, and very seldom are even grasping. It is your lazy fellow, who lives by the cunning that he calls wits, who is not to be trusted. For my part, as two candidates have to be in the field to have a good run, I am glad that those Cincinnati folks had the sense to take a man right out of the bosom of the people to govern the people. Brought up so close to the public heart, he'll know how it beats. Having been a working man, he'll know how to feel for toilers like himself, just as General Grant now feels for the soldiers."

"You talk like a book," says the young lady, a-twisting her head the other way.

"I didn't know till you told me, miss, that books did talk," says I, opening my fan again.

"Oh, yes, they do," says she, giggling.

"Bound to talk, I suppose," says I, a-smiling in my usual bland way.

They all laughed at this, but the girl looked around as if she wondered what it was all about.

I just made a little inclination of the head, and went on:

"We were speaking of self-made men, I think," says I; "such men have drifted away from New England, like shooting stars. Wherever they may shine, New England is proud of them, and claims them as her own; for this reason; and because I love my country, I am glad Horace Greeley is on the highway to be its next President. With him and Grant running neck to neck, I shan't care much which beats."

LXI.

WOMEN AND THINGS.

EAR SISTERS:—I wish you could have seen that stuck-up thing, with all the color taken out of her hair, perking herself up for an argument with me. All the people in the room had crowded round us, which set her all in a flutter.

"Oh, pray excuse me," says she, a-shaking her curls, "we are broaching into politics, and I assure you," says she, a-primming herself up, "I know nothing about such subjects."

"Why," says I, "you speak as if ignorance were something to be proud of."

"I—I do not pretend to know anything of politics, at any rate," says she, a-coloring up with inward madness.

"Indeed, what is politics," says I. "The history of the present? Why should the most refined lady on earth be ignorant of one period of history more than another?"

"Politics are things going on at the present time, and no real lady is expected to take interest in them," says she.

"What is the present time? The breath we are drawing— nothing more. That very breath has now gone into the past, which is history. All the rest is guess-work and prophecy," says I.

"Dear me, how strong-minded you are," says she, giving her curls a toss; "I suppose you would be splendidly eloquent on Woman's Rights too."

"No," said I, "all my life I have had more rights than I have known how to use, so I leave that question to persons who have no better field of ambition. Mine happens to be of a different kind. I want to make women wise, good, generous, faithful to duties that come down to them from their mothers. I want to improve women, miss, not turn them into contemptible men."

"By talking politics?" says she, as saucy as a sour apple; "what is the good of that if you don't go in for voting?"

"What is the good of any knowledge which may be turned into blessings by woman's influence?" says I, blandly.

"Then you believe that women ought to have influence in politics," says she.

"I think that women should have influence everywhere," said I, "but only as women. We are governed through the heart, and those finer portions of the intellect that people call taste. Men plant the grain and timber of every-day life with their strong hands, which God made for that very purpose. We women fill in the hollows and crevices and swelling banks with flowers and ferns and delicate shade-trees, which make the vigorous work of their strong hands beautiful."

Sisters, I said this to that stuck-up girl because I wanted to express an opinion on this subject—first, because it was my opinion, and again, because I know that it is yours, going as you do for it in a spirit of feminine spontaneosity. I don't want the nature of our Society misunderstood. We are not Woman's Righters, nor Woman's Wrongers, but straight out women, wanting nothing better on this earth than to be just as God made us, with a full, free, and generous development of all the femininities that belong to the sex.

For my part, I don't want to be a man; his work is too rough and hard for me. His thoughts have too heavy and coarse a grain. His clothes wouldn't fit me any better than his thoughts and duties.

We being women, according to a beneficent God's intention, have got enough to occupy a whole life in the same path that our good old New England mothers trod. We don't want to get out of that path into any other, and we don't mean to entice the children that are growing up amongst us into an idea that pure-thinking, hard-working womanliness isn't the highest and best destiny that God has yet given to his creatures.

I have no patience with women who scorn their own sex so much that they would rather turn into weak, meddlesome men than work, study, bring up children, and live as high-souled, loving women should. As for voting and all that, it's just turning gold into brass, and getting nothing but the baser metal for change.

Why, influence is a thousand times sweeter and more certain than legal power, and that is given to every woman who loves and is beloved.

As for my part, I should be ashamed if I couldn't persuade ever so many men to do any right thing I wanted. Shouldn't I be a fool to swap off that influence for the rights that only one man owns for himself?

If women want power, let them be sweet, good, and persuasive, wise enough to have their opinions command respect, and bright enough to enforce them pleasantly. That is the way to move nations, if the mind of woman ever can do it. At any rate, it is the way to govern families and make them respectable in the next generation; and out of families nations are made.

"Have you ever noticed one thing?" says I to the people about me. "Whenever women get dissatisfied with themselves and hanker after the rights of men, the very foundations of life seem to be breaking up all around us. Marriage ties fall into ashes like fire in hatcheled flax, morals are burned up, families torn to pieces, and society falls into revolt against law and religion. When women begin to hanker after votes, they hanker after divorces too, and, while they want unlimited power with men, throw away the noblest of all power over men—that of honest respect and a sacred consciousness of protecting."

If women will break thoough all the delicate safeguards and childlike purity which keeps them so much above men, that they are aspired after and worshipped, let them take the consequences. To be hustled in conventions, hissed off from platforms, and received with hidden sneers by three-fourths of mankind, doesn't seem to me half so pleasant and respectable as the friendship of one's neighbors, and the love of one's own family; but, if they like it better, I haven't the least mite of an objection. Only such things force an honest woman into awful bad company once in a while, and it sometimes happens that ambition leads them to shake hands with persons that sweet charity itself could never persuade the best of them to touch with a ten-foot pole.

"Don't think," says I, "that I go against female progress, or would stop its infinite capabilities—far from it. There are questions mixed up with this subject that ought to have our warmest sympathy and most ardent help. Female labor is one of them, and in that lies the greatest moral question of these times.

"When a woman finds herself doing the work nature carved out for her, with a man crowding her out, doing no more, yet getting double pay, only because he happens to be a man, it is a burning shame and disgrace to both sexes. If that injustice can't be swept away by fair means, I go in for trying any that a female woman can handle without bringing herself down to a level with the males who seem to be as sick of being men as some of our sex are of being women.

"Still, it seems to me that the best way of doing this is by such appeals for justice as have brought the women of New York State more freedom than they know what to do with. At this day there is no legal slavery for any woman in the great Empire State. The fact is, the women there have got their feet on the necks of the men. But this don't satisfy them, and they are all the time crying out for more, as the Scripture says, like the leeches—which is a passage of Scripture that I never have quite understood, because leeches in our day suck your *blood* without asking, and I never yet heard of one who went farther than a bite in the way of crying out.

"Excuse me," says I, drawing breath, "if I sometimes digress, and turn down a Scripture path in search of scientific truth or illustration. I was saying that a woman in New York State is to all intents and purposes master of herself—herself and husband too. If she has money when a poor fellow marries her, it is all her own to do with as she has a mind to,

just as much as if she had never been married at all. But he
has to support her, anyway, keep up the house, pay all the
bills, settle her debts, if she is mean enough to make them,
and she can be hoarding up her own money all the time, while
he has no more right to touch a cent of it than the man in the
moon.

"More than this; when he dies, she comes in for a full third
of his real estate for life, and has half his personal property,
to sell, give away, or do with as she pleases. If *she* dies, he
cannot touch a red cent. Then, again, she can sell all the real
estate that belongs to her, without so much as asking his advice,
but he cannot sell an acre or a wood-shed, and give a clear title,
without her written name to the deed. Then, again, if he
earns money, the law makes him support her; if she earns
money, he has no right to a cent of it.

"Poor, downtrodden creatures are these women of New
York State—don't you think so," says I. "Is it a wonder
they get dissatisfied with their hardships, and hanker after more
power, more freedom, and less work? When marriage is so
profitable, is it strange that some of them want a great deal of
it, and go through the divorce courts three or four times with
a rush, picking up scraps of alimony and leaving scraps of
reputation along the way.

"If it wasn't that I mean to stand by my own sex through
thick and thin, I should say that the laws lean a trifle over on
the woman's side in York State; but, being a woman, I keep a
lively thinking, while the other poor, downtrodden souls rush
to the women's rights meetings, and wring their hands in
desperation over the wrongs I have just explained."

"But what has this to do with your Society?" says Cousin
E. E.

"Everything. We are in for Infinite Progress. We want
women to be all that God intended them to be—the full companions and helpmates of men. We want them to cultivate all
the Christian and kindly virtues, not only because they make
women lovely and beloved, but because men are humanized,

softened, and made better by such help and such companionship. When men seek peace, rest, the inspirations of prayer,
they turn at once to us for tender guidance and sympathy.
Would they do that if we elbowed them at the polls, or held
knock-down arguments at the primary elections? No, no!
If we can soften human misery, strengthen weakness, make
women wiser and men better, it is all that the best woman
among us can ask."

Sisters, I had got too much in earnest. I felt the blood
come like a dash of wine into my face. It seemed to me as if
I were on a platform, lecturing, and the thought covered me
with confusion, like a crimson garment. I bent my head
slightly, and went away dreadfully ashamed of myself.

LXII.

A TRIP TO ANNAPOLIS.

DEAR SISTERS:—Another of those pleasant excursional entertainments which this nation gives to genius
in the female line has been offered to me, and I accepted. For my part, I think the country ought to be encouraged in giving these little testimonials to her favored
children. She hasn't done much of that in former years, but
has practised a good deal more on foreigners than she has ever
thought of doing where home-made writers are concerned.

Them Japanee potentials always seem to go along when an
entertainment is got up for me, and, if that didn't rather mix
things up, I should be glad of it; for Mr. Iwakura is just
splendid in his black coat and stovepipe hat, and talks beautifully with his little black eyes; I feel it in my bones he has not
left a heathenish impediment behind, or anything that ought to

stand between him and a wife who might carry fresh missionary spirit into his benighted land.

Of course, all the other Japanees were on hand, and seemed
to feel proud and chipper, as if the party had been made for
them instead of me; but I didn't mind that a bit. Even if
they did think so, what harm? There is so much happiness
in delusions, that I wouldn't rob those nice-looking heathens
of one for the world.

Besides the Japanees, a very distinguished party had been
invited to go with me, and I couldn't help but feel the whole
thing a triumph.

There was Postmaster-General Creswell, with a head of hair
and a beard that warmed you, it was so silky and bright.
There was his wife, too, a real pretty creature, with manners
as sweet as her face; and Mrs. Fish, almost a mate for a lady
I will not name for queenliness; and Governor Cook with his
wife. Besides these, there were lots of young people, and old
people, and middle-aged people, filling car after car, till we had
a whole train all to ourselves. The party was large, but so is
a genuine New England heart, and I managed to make them
all welcome in an off-handed, queenly way, which I hope was
understood. It certainly was by Mr. Iwakura, who lifted his
stovepipe hat and bowed like a native Vermonter before he
sat down.

Sisters, I do think there is a meaning in that—a Japanee isn't
likely to study the elegancies of our manners for nothing.
Still, I wish he wasn't a heathen. The Greek Church of
Russia sat heavy on my conscience, but a heathen! I shall
have to meet all this politeness with the icy chill of Christian
reserve, unless—the thing is possible, for, to love, all things
are so—that heathen should adopt our religion with the stove-
pipe hat.

There was a thing that troubled me a good deal before I
came away from the hotel that morning. I have been told
that Mr. Grant and our Vermont statesman have got up a
little spirit of rivalry about being President—a thing I never

dreamed of, they seemed such good friends, and, till now, I thought Mr. Grant had kind of half invited his old friend to take the chair. But it isn't so by any manner of means, and I'm afraid there may be some little dispute about it in the end, which will be unpleasant to those who like them both.

Now, sisters, here comes in the benefit of being a female, which is great in such perplexing cases. Female women are not expected to be consistent, and they're not expected to take sides for any great length of time. They can just climb any fence that comes handy, and sit on it with the dignity of hen turkeys at sundown if they have a mind to, and no one has a right to scare them up. But, considering myself as an exceptional female, whose duty it is to have ideas, I scorn the fence, and come right up to the crib, corn or no corn.

It is a duty I owe to the State, and from that I shall never turn aside. Besides—I own it boldly—in this case duty and a hilarious state of pleasure unite and make me jubilant as a Fourth of July salute. I like Greeley because he is first-rate as an author, an editor, and a man. I admire Grant as a brave soldier and as a man too, but then, the old State! I don't care who knows it—from this day out, white is my color.

But, feeling this in my very bones, how could I accept the great national compliment of a special train filled with admiring friends from the Government, which is General Grant?

I spoke of this to Cousin Dempster, and, says he:

"This makes no difference in the world. Take all you can from the Government. That is high patriotism."

I shook my head.

"Cousin," says I, "it kind of seems to me that this special train is a sort of a trap. How can I, a free-born Vermonter—national in some respects, and brimming over with first-class patriotism, but Vermont to the back-bone—first and foremost, lead off a party like this, one car choke full of Mr. Grant's cabinet people. Now, if Mr. Greeley and Mr. Grant should rile up against each other—which I hope they won't—don't you see that I am in an awful mixed position?—the National

12

Government on one side with that stupendous soldier at the head, and that great white-hatted Vermonter on the other? "

" That is, you want to be neutral," says Dempster.

" Well, yes—kind of neutral," says I, "and a little for both."

" Not exactly on the fence, but cautious," says he; " keep your boat in harbor till the tide rises and the wind blows, then hoist sail and catch up with the old craft that has been tugging on in shallow water? "

" No," says I, feeling the old Puritan blood beginning to boil up. " That may answer for some people, but not for me. An idea has just struck me; a woman's political ideas should be suggested, not proclaimed."

Without speaking another word, I put on my things, went right down to Pennsylvania Avenue, and bought a soft white hat, a little broad in the brim, which I turned up on one side. Then I went into a milliner's store, carrying it in my hand, and made a woman curl a long white feather over the crown, which gave the whole affair a touch of the beehive, stamping it with beautiful femininity.

With this hat on my head, and a double-breasted white jacket over my black alpaca, I took my honored place in the cars that day.

Of course I sat in the cabinet car, feeling myself the sole representative of Vermont in that august company. The ladies looked at me sidewise when I came in; some of the cabinet men half winked at each other and tried to smile. But that white hat was no laughing matter, and they wilted down before it.

LXIII.

AMONG THE CADETS.

DEAR SISTERS:—The train started, and there I sat in my glory till we got to Annapolis, just the sleepiest town, crowded full of the oldest houses and the slowest people that I ever saw in my born days. Some colored persons were dawdling around the depot, and a few lazy white folks passing down the street, stopped to look at us as we got out of the cars. Especially my white hat and double-breasted jacket seemed to take them.

Once I heard something that sounded like the beginning of a cheer, but the voices were so lazy that they couldn't carry it out, so it muttered itself to death, and that was the end of it.

Twenty of the Japanees were with me when I alighted from the car and spread my white parasol, which hovered like a dove over us, for I made it flutter beautifully as we passed along.

The cabinet people followed after, and just as we were forming to go down street, like a military training, my white hat and feather leading them on, a gentleman came up to us and began to shake hands all round. He was a tall, genteel sort of a person, with light hair and a beard soft and silky as corn tassels; but all under his eyes, blue powder marks were scattered, as if he'd spent half his life firing off Fourth of July powder salutes, and had burst up on some of them.

While I was wondering who it could be, Mr. Robeson, who has some dealings with navy yards and shipping, come up to where I stood, and says he :

" Miss Frost, allow me to present Commodore Worden, the gentleman who distinguished himself on the first Monitor."

Sisters, that minute the powder marks on Worden's handsome face were glorified in my eyes. I reached out my hands. I pressed his, my beaming eyes covered him with particular admiration. Feeling as if I were the colonel of that company, I longed to lift my white hat and give him a military salute. What I did say was significant.

"Worden," says I, "when certain events come about—I say nothing, but this hat and jacket are typical of what I mean—when these great and luminous events fill the hemisphere your glorious bravery on that iron flat-boat shall have its full record. I will myself send your picture to the great Grand Duke of all the Russias, and if there is a higher notch in the public shipping than you have, I know nothing of the friend whose colors I wear if anybody stands before you. I have seen the picture of your Monitor. To my eye it looks like a flat-iron, with the handle in the water; but it did good work, and so did you. Grant knows it. My own immortal statesman will appreciate it."

Commodore Worden bowed, and smiled, and squoze my hand so long that I began to feel anxious about my white gloves. But he dropped it at last, and we all moved on, my white feather waving in front, just like that which King Henry of Navarre wore in battles. Only mine was a peaceful emblem, dyed in the milk of human kindness, and curled up in the sunshine of prosperity.

We marched through dull streets and round deserted corners, cutting in and out every which way till we came to a large gate, which shut the Navy Yard out from the rest of mankind.

Then we filed through into a beautiful meadow, with the grass cut short, sprinkled over with trees, and cut into footpaths. Part of it was bounded by water, the rest by rows of handsome houses and great buildings that looked like factories shut up for want of work.

The minute I and Mr. Iwakura walked through the gate, bang! went a cannon; bang, bang, bang! seventeen times.

"What on earth is that?" says I, turning to Dempster, who was just behind me.

"It is a salute for us," says he.

"Us!" says I, with accents of disdain that put him in his place at once.

"For you, then," says he, smiling in a way I didn't like, for, having no envy in my own disposition, I cannot endure it in others.

Mr. Iwakura and I walked on slowly. He looked at me and smiled as the guns kept going off, till I counted seventeen; then they stopped and I was glad of it, for I remembered that our meeting-house bell tolls once for every year, when a person dies, and I felt a little anxious about the number of guns they might pile on to live folks. But they stopped short at seventeen, which is an age no girl need be ashamed to own, and which showed how young some persons can look in spite of hard literary toil.

Well, first we went into Commodore Worden's house, where Mr. Iwakura and I were introduced to Mrs. Worden and some other ladies. Then the rest came in for a little notice, and we filed off into the grounds again, where there was a general training of boys in blue jackets, with buttons and things, all armed with guns, which they handled like old militia men. Sometimes, when they poked their guns right at us, I kind of got behind Mr. Iwakura, who, being small, wasn't much of a shelter, but better than nothing. In fact, I was rather glad when this part of the fun died out.

After this, we went into one of the big houses where the blue boys live, and a whole lot of little, make-believe ships were shown to us, and two Japanee boys told Mr. I. how they were worked—which would have been interesting, only we didn't know a word of that language, nor much about the baby-house of ships, and didn't listen to what was said in English.

Then the boys in blue and buttons went into the meadow again, and got out a lot of small cannon, and banged, and ran in lines and squads down to the river, as if they were awful mad with the water and meant to dam it—dam it up, I wish you to understand, for even indirect profanity isn't in my nature.

After this, we all went down to a great, lumbering old ship, which is all the home these blue boys have the first year they come to the Annapolis school, which, being a sailor institution, gives them a taste for creeping into holes and sleeping on a yard or two of rope swung to the ship's beams—which may be pleasant fun, but doesn't look like it.

Sisters, it was getting along in the day, and, though in a certain sense spiritualized by genius, I was hungry. Mr. Iwakura, too, had a pitiful look in his black eyes; but a storm of music called us from hankering thoughts, and we all streamed, at a faster double-quick than the boys could show, into the great dining-room of one of the big houses. A splendid table was set out there, which we gathered round like a half-starved regiment on training-day. Then began such a practice in cider bottles, flying corks, and cider foaming and fizzing into glasses, as beat all the cannon and howitzer blazings of the day—for that ended in something, and the rest didn't.

It is astonishing what effect eating and drinking has on the feet; I could hardly keep from dancing all the way from that dining-hall to the other building, which is kept especially for dancing. Well, we did dance, for the music just took one right into the midst of it, want to or not. Besides, we hadn't been to a tomb, and nobody had been killed, so we just went in for it. My alpaca dress isn't over long, and I wasn't afraid of showing my feet when there was no train to tangle them up. We danced with our bonnets and hats on—we ladies, I mean—and the way my white feather rose and fell and fluttered over the rest was enough to wake up the American heart in every bosom present.

LXIV.

AMERICAN AUTHORS.

DEAR SISTERS :—You have heard of Mr. Shakespeare, a writer of old England. who died, years and years ago, in a little country place in England. He was celebrated for several things besides writing. Going to sleep under trees is one of them; shooting deer that belonged to somebody else—who took him up and made an awful time about it before a justice of the peace, who fined him, or something—is another. Then, again, he married an elderly girl, and forgot to live with her ever so long. While she stayed at home, he went up to London, and wrote plays and played them before her Majesty Queen Elizabeth, who ought to have reminded him of his married elderly girl, being her own royal self of that class, only not married. There is no reason to think she did have much influence in that direction though, for that particular queen was more celebrated for keeping husbands away from their wives .than bringing them cosily together.

The truth is, from the very first—when she got up a series of romping platonics with Lord Seymour, her step-mother's husband, to her last, gray-headed old flirtation with the young Essex—her taste ran against the practical idea of husbands living with their own wives. That non-matrimonial creature may have tried her power on Shakespeare—who knows ?

Sisters, there is one part of this man's life and character that may shock your religious feelings. *He wrote plays ; he acted plays too ;* and that female queen encouraged him in it. Now, ever since I went to see the " Black Crook," I scorn myself for ever having one mite of charity for such things, and I haven't the conscience to say one word in their favor to you, as a Society. Still, this Mr. Shakespeare did write some things

that might nave sounded tolerably well in a lecture or a sermon
that wasn't too strictly doctrinal.

Last night I was talking with a lawyer from away "Out West,"
who spoke real kindly about Mr. Shakespeare's writings, and
seemed to think if he had put off being born until now, and settled
"Out West," where he could have given him a hint now and
then, he might have made a first-rate literary man. "Even as
it is," says he, "I do my best to make him popular, for he wrote
some very readable things—very readable, indeed. For instance, not long since, in an exciting slander case, I quoted
these lines, with a burning eloquence that lifted the judge right
off from his bench :

> " 'He,' says I, ' that steals my purse, steals stuff ;
>   'Twas something, t'aint nothing, t'was mine,
>   'Tis hisen, and has been slave to thousands ;
>   But he that hooketh from me my good name,
>   Grabs that which don't do him no good,
>   But makes me feel very bad indeed.' "

"Is that the genuine old English that Mr. Shakespeare wrote
in ? " says I.

"Oh, that is the beauty of it," says he. "Shakspeare was
no doubt a very respectable writer, but perfection is the watch-
word of modern progress. Of course one doesn't introduce a
quotation of his without all the modern improvements. Shakespeare—"

"*Mr.* Shakspeare," says I, determined to keep up the dignity of authorship with my last breath.

"Well, Mr. Shakspeare would have made a very superior
writer if he had lived in this country and been fostered by an
American Congress."

"An American Congress," says I. "What on earth did
that ever do for writers ? "

"Why, don't it publish books for the members to give away.
Isn't that encouraging literature ? "

I said nothing, never having read one of the books in my
life, and never having seen any one that had.

" Then," says he, " hasn't every man that can write the life of a President of these United States before his election, been made an ambassador, or counsel, or something ? Didn't Pierce send Hawthorne to Liverpool, not because of his transcendant genius, but for the reason that he had written a paltry life of himself? "

" *Mr.* Hawthorne," says I, with expressive emphasis.

" And didn't General Grant send Colonel Badeau to London, after his life was taken by that young man ? "

" I give in," says I ; " the literature of this country has been fostered beautifully. Hawthorne was rewarded for degrading the finest genius this country has ever known, by writing a commonplace life of a ordinary man ; and Adam Badeau was made a colonel, and is now figuring in London, because all the talent he ever had was crowded into such a book. Yes, I give in. But one thing is to be relied on, each of the Presidents struggling to rule over this country next, has brains enough to write his own life. Grant has written his out with a sword, and Greeley can handle his own pen. He won't have any debts of that kind to pay off, and I'm awfully mistaken if the authors of this country won't stand almost as high with him as corporals in the army do now. In his time bayonets will be stacked, and pens have their day. During the next four years I shouldn't wonder if Mr. Shakspeare might have a little chance if he were alive."

" That puts me in mind," says the Western gentleman, " that a statue of Shakspeare is going to be unveiled in the New York Central Park to-morrow."

" To-morrow ? " says I ; " then I'm off to New York to see it done. By and by, when we have put all the British authors in marble, some one born in. America may get a chance."

" But Shakespeare belongs to the world," says Cousin Dempster, who was sitting near me.

" All men or women of genius belong to the world," says I, " just as far as the world knows them ; but the country in which a great man or woman was born, and has lived and writ-

12*

ten, is the place where he should be first honored. Have we done anything of that kind yet?   I'm not saying one word against Mr. Shakespeare; his monument ought to be in the most beautiful spot we have; but let the next statue be that of some first-class American. Mr. Shakespeare belongs to us as much as he did to England, because when he lived England was our country, and he belongs to us now. But since then we have cut loose from the Old World, and built up a powerful nation, where great authors, both men and women, have worked out their own birthright of genius, with no help but the power God has given them—worked it out, too, with not half the recognition that our Government and our people, to their shame be it spoken, have given to coarser and weaker intellects from over the sea."

"Why, Phœmie," says Cousin Dempster, "don't get so excited; do you know that you are talking like a book?"

"It must be an English book if any American takes much notice of it," says I; "but rile me up on this subject, and I don't know or care how I talk. In our part of the country we are Americans to the backbone, and we mean to keep so."

"Well, but this statue of Shakespeare was first thought of by the actors who have been living over his plays years and years —Booth, Wallack, Wheatley, and your dead and gone Halleck, set it a-going.

"What Shakespeare did for theatres, theatre people know how to acknowledge. They have some spirit; but what author ever comes forward and asks a place for his fellow-author? How can they expect the country to be generous to them when they do nothing for each other?"

It kind of took me down when Cousin Dempster said this, and not having anything to observe, I said nothing, but got right up, and says I:

"If we mean to start for New York, it's time to be getting ready."

LXV.

THE STATUE OF SHAKESPEARE.

ELL, sisters, we got to New York in time, and went right up to Central Park, which was just one garden of flowers, all in full bloom. The trees, too, were of a bright, lovely green, and the little lakes blue as a baby's eye, sparkled and rippled wherever the sun shone and the wind swept over them. A wide green circle, with lots of trees shading it, and great heaps of bushes heavy with pink and white flowers everywhere around it, was just alive with men and women. They were all in their Sunday go-to-meeting best, some on the grass, some in carriages, and all chatting, laughing, and enjoying themselves mightily, but crowding toward one spot.

Under these trees, where the grass was greenest, and the flowers brightest, there was a sort of pyramid, covered over with star-spangled banners of bright silk. Sweeping round that, like a ring cut in two, were platforms with rows on rows of seats, built against flag-poles, from which ever so many flags were a-streaming out on the wind. These seats were crammed and crowded full of people. The centre platform was roofed in, and just running over with men holding fiddles, drums, twisted horns, trumpets, great puffy bass viols, and everything else that could turn music into thunder, and thunder back into music.

There was an inside circle nearer to the pyramid, and our tickets took us there, among the greatest people of the country, which was an honor I felt in behalf of the society. This was the penetralia, which, I suppose, from the first syllable, was got up especially for authors. I took my seat in that honored place, and, spreading my white parasol, looked about me, feeling the exaltation of my position in a modest way, but willing that others should make their little mark even if I was there.

Well, the first thing that came was a crash that made me hop right up, and near about break my parasol. No wonder; for more than a hundred men were just flooding the air with music, that rose and fell and fluttered till the trees and bushes shook under it. I do believe the sweetness and the thundering outbursts would have inspired me to break into some good old tune myself, if there hadn't been so much rustling and talking and flirting all around me. As it was, there arose a clatter of confusing sounds that gave one's nerves a jerky feeling that I for one haven't got over yet. I do wonder why city people have no better manners. I should just as soon think of speaking out in meeting, as of chattering when others wanted to listen to music.

Well, after a hard tussle between the people and the music, the people came out first-best—more shame to 'em. Then a gentleman they call Judge Daly—a real nice-looking person— got out and reached out his arms toward the pyramid, wrapped up in flags.

The minute he did this all the people began to stamp and clap their hands, and fling out their handkerchiefs as if they had gone crazy. The more he tried to speak, the more they stamped and clapped and shouted; and he kept a-bowing real graceful, till by and by they stopped and let him speak.

Then he went right on and told them all about the statue, which ought to have been done and put up on the day that Mr. Shakespeare was three hundred years old, only the statue wasn't ready then, but that was of no account, when we considered how beautiful the whole thing was, and what an honor it would be to American art. Judge Daly was all alive with this idea, and spoke splendidly. When he had done, I just laid down my parasol, and clapped my hands till a pair of three-button gloves gave out. Sisters, that one clap cost me just three dollars and fifty cents.

When Judge Daly sat down, a gentleman walked up to the pyramid, and stood by it looking awful pale and anxious, as if the thousands and thousands of eyes bent on him had drawn all the blood from his body. He was a fine, handsome-looking man, and somehow I took a shine to him at first sight.

All at once his face flushed up, and I saw that he held the end of a rope in his hand. While I was a-looking and wondering, he gave the rope a jerk, and down come those silk flags, all in a wild flutter, and there stood Mr. Shakespeare as if he'd just stopped to rest a minute after walking, and had been struck with an idea which he was thinking over. His head was just a little bent, and he held a book up against his bosom, with his finger between the leaves.

Mr. Shakespeare must have been a proper handsome man about two hundred and seventy-five years ago. No wonder that elderly young lady fell in love with him. I could have done it myself, not because I am elderly, far from it, but because he was—well, I suppose because he was Shakespeare, and awful handsome at that.

Queen Elizabeth must have given him the suit of clothes he wears; for when I said his trousers were too puffy and short for my liking, and his cloak nothing to speak of in the way of a covering, a gentleman near me said the dress was Elizabethan.

This rather set me against the memory of Mr. S. He ought to have died rather than take anything from that cruel, hard-hearted old—I was going to say old maid, but refrain, not wishing to be hard on her, cruel as she was.

Oh, mercy, what a shout that was. It seemed as if every heart in that great crowd had burst out in a glow of admiration. Mine just fluttered like a night hawk. I stood up and whirled the white parasol over my head; more than that, I split the other glove, and was glad of it.

That Mr. Ward had been working eight years on the statue he had just uncovered, and our enthusiasm was his best reward. There he stood face to face with the people, who were to give him pain or cruel disappointment. I felt for him. No wonder his face turned white and then red as fire. Years of labor for one hour of triumph. He deserved all the praise he got, and that was stupendous.

The statue was now all uncovered, and the sunshine lay upon it. Sisters, it is beautiful; but one thing troubles me— the color.   Was Mr. Shakespeare of that complexion, or has the great man been darkened out of regard to the Fifteenth Amendment and Mr. Sumner? When a man is statued in bronze, does he always turn out a mulatto? I don't like the idea—it's carrying the Civil Rights Bill too far.

Judge Daly had made a present of this statue to the park, in his speech. Now Mr. Stebbins, the President of the Park Commissioners, came forward and thanked him for it in the nicest way. He was just the man to do it, though he is a broker and banker; for he cares quite as much for art as he does for gold. Wherever he finds genius, this man spends his money like dew upon it. It was he that gave Miss Kellogg her first start in music, and a good many other strugglers have secretly been helped by him when they felt almost like giving up. For my part, I honor and glorify such men. .

The next thing I saw was a grand-looking old man, with a long, white beard falling over his bosom, and soft, white hair floating about his head. I held my breath when this man arose, and while the crowd yelled and shouted and made the ground tremble under me, I looked at him with my heart in my eyes. What Shakespeare was to England, this old man is to America—the best part of the land that gave him birth. He made a long speech, a beautiful speech. I have read his poems, so have you; but the poetry of his spoken words, of his voice and looks, is grander than written language, and nothing that I can write will give you the least idea of it.

For my part, I hope that the next statue set up in the park will be that of William Cullen Bryant. What is the reason that we should wait till a man is dead before we give back something for the genius with which he has honored his country? The readers that may come up three hundred years from now owe him no more than we do. What are we waiting for, then? When Mr. Bryant sat down, there was another earth- quake of applause, which had but just time to stop, when it burst out again for Edwin Booth. The best actor, and one of the handsomest men you ever saw, came forward and read a long piece of poetry, which just made the blood stir like wine in your veins. There was a double gust of genius in this poem; because the poet Stoddard wrote it, and then Booth gave it the fire of his soul and the music of his voice, which seemed to float and whisper around the statue long after the crowd had scattered itself over the park.

LXVI.

RACING DRESSES.

DEAR SISTERS:—Don't be startled; don't hold up your hands in holy astonishment when I tell you that I—Phœmie Frost—your moral and—I say it meekly —religious missionary, have been to a horse-race. I am shocked myself now, in the cool of the morning, not exactly because I went, but from what happened after I got there.

Have I done wrong? Can a missionary, without knowledge, do her duty? If she knows nothing of sin, how can she warn against sin?

Then, again, is the running of swift horses sinful?

Sisters, I am troubled. The more one knows, the more one is perplexed and put about. It is so easy to condemn things by the wholesale that you know nothing about. One can speak so positive about them, for total ignorance admits of no argument, and is entirely above all evidence. That is why ignorant stubbornness is so self-satisfied and comfortable.

After all, I begin to think that "ignorance is bliss." Is there anything on this earth more snoozily comfortable than a litter of white pigs revelling with their mother in a mud-puddle—say in August? What do these contented animals care for the mud that soils their whiteness, with the pink skin shining through—rosy pigs, as one may call the kind I am speaking of. Think of them muzzling about in the rily water, free as air; then turn to your learned pig, chained to a master by the forced action of its own intellect—poor thing! obliged to play cards with its fore-foot, teach geography, and cipher out numbers like a schoolmaster—and then say if ignorance isn't bliss! Look in the little black eyes of the animal, and see the sad and hungry look that knowledge has brought to him!

To know is to want—to want is to suffer.

Where was I? Speaking about horses, naturally I wandered off down to other grades of animals—the laziest, largest, best-natured creatures of all—but, as you may observe with propriety, not suggestive of horse-races, which I admit and apologize for.

Well, right or wrong, I have been to the races at Jerome Park, which is a hollow among the hills, clear out of New York, and the other side of Harlem River. There, every spring and fall, the best horses owned about here are set a-going like wildfire, and the one that beats is thought the world of.

The park isn't much of a piece of woods, after all; a good-sized maple camp in Vermont has got twice as many trees, but then a good deal of it is turned out to grass. Then, again, a level turnpike curls in a ring all round one of the hills, and on the top of that is a kind of hotel, or long tavern, with a tremendous stoop stretched around it, where the upper-crust of fast horsedom crowd in to see the creatures run.

On the other hillside, right against the tavern, is a great long, open shed, with seats after seats sloping down from the inside, where the lower-crust of fast horsedom crowd in from the railroads, and so on. They have to pay for going in, but, for all that, haven't a right to go across to the upper side, which must be aggravating.

All the men that go to the upper-crust tavern wear a huge round thing with a ribbon fastened to their coats, and strut awfully under them, as if they were the crowning glory of all creation. Maybe they are; I don't know, not being highly educated in horsiness.

Well, Cousin Dempster has one of these medals, which he hitched to the lappel of his coat that morning. Cousin E. E. had been fidgeting awfully all the week about a dress she was bent on wearing, and when it didn't come home from the dress-maker's till late the night before, I really thought she would take a fit right before us all. But the dress came at last, and then she wheeled right round the other way with joy.

"Such a dress!" says she. "There won't be anything to match it. All my own idea, too"

Here she tumbled a cataract of silk from a great paper box, and shook it out till it fluttered like the leaves on a young maple-tree.

"Isn't it superb?" says she; "peacock green and peacock blue intermingled like a poem, sloping folds up the front breadth two and two, bunching splendidly behind, frilled, flounced, corded, folded, trailing, and yet demi to a large extent. Cousin Frost, Cousin Frost! did you ever see anything so original, so—so—"

"Scrumptious," says I, a-helping her out, "peacock green and peacock blue; if we only had the half-moons on the train now."

She looked at me earnestly; her soul had taken in the thought, and it burned in her eyes.

"Oh, why didn't I think of that?" says she.

I smiled. It takes genius to understand the fine irony of genius. Cousin E. E. is bright, but the subtle originality of a new thought isn't in her. That usually does in a family what this Government is trying so hard for—centralizes itself in one person.

It is not difficult to say where this supreme essence condenses itself in our family. Still, I do not object to other members making their little mark, and if E. E. can make hers in the peacock line, why not?

To my fancy, that dress was a nation sight too much. It was all in a flutter, silk heaped on silk. E. E. tried it on, and fairly waded in silk when she walked. There was neither elegance nor simplicity in it, nothing but a sickening idea of extravagance and money.

E. E. looked like a peacock, walked like a peacock, and seemed to feel like one. She took a little mite of a bonnet from a box that came just after the dress, and put it on. It was shaped like the small end of a loaf of sugar, with a pink rose and a bunch of green and blue feathers on the top, beehivy in height, but brigandish in shape, slightly pastoral, and a little military.

"Isn't it stylish?" says she, setting it on the top of her curls and puffs, with such an air.

"Original," says I, "but you know which is *my* color."

E. E. laughed till the feathers shook on her head.

"Oh!" says she, "Dempster and I are prudent. After the middle of July perhaps we may—"

"Till then," says I, "you'll sit on the fence peacock fashion."

We had more words, for E. E. is nobody's fool; but just then Cecilia came in, and I made myself scarce.

XLVII.

THE FIRST HORSE-RACE.

WELL, we started for the races in high feather. Cousin D. had just got his open carriage cushioned off beautifully. His horses had rosettes on their heads, and little looking-glasses about as big as a dollar flashing between their ears.

Cousin E. E. wore the peacock dress and the brigandish hat.

The parasol had a red coral handle, and, to own the truth, no horse on the race-ground looked faster than she did.

I followed her modestly. My pink silk seemed to grow brighter when it settled down against her green and blue; my white hat was looped up on one side with a white cockade, and the white feather streamed out banner fashion. With me all was simplicity, patriotism, and whiteness—pure as the distinguished individual of whom they were a delicate typification.

The drive up to that race-ground was just too lovely for anything. The horses fairly flew. The wind just shook the white fringe on my parasol, and kept my emblematical feather dancing after my hat. Cousin Dempster drove, and that girl Cecilia sat high up on the front seat by him, with her short dress ruffled and pinked about the bottom like a full-blown poppy; her—well, ankles visible to the knees, and all her hair floating out loose and crinkly. I say nothing, but ask you, as females of experience, what kind of a woman will that stuck-up child make, in the long run?

The race ground was gay as a general training when we got there. It had rained lately; the trees and grass were green as green could be, and thousands of red-birds, yellow-hammers, blue-jays, and golden-robins, seemed to have settled down around the long tavern, the hill-side, and under the old trees. I declare, the sight was beautiful.

Cousin D. had to show his badge and thing at the gate; then we drove up to the long tavern with a dash, hopped gracefully out of the carriage, and walked right in among the great crowd of gentlemen and ladies chatting, laughing, and moving about the long stoop.

Sisters, I do try to be humble, but it is awful hard work. When I went into that crowd, with my pink silk trailing and that white feather all afloat, the whole congregation seemed to break into groups and hush up, just to look at me. I didn't pretend to notice this delicate ovation, but walked slowly forward, and with a becoming blush on my cheek, while E. E. and that child kept bowing and shaking hands with everybody they met.

After I had seated myself in one of the great splint-bottomed chairs that stood in dozens on the stoop, the crowd felt at liberty to go on again—and it did. A flock of birds couldn't have twittered and tittered and flitted more joyaceously than the females crowded together on that stoop.

But I soon had something else to look at. Down in front of the hotel a lot of horses were prancing to and fro, up and down, breaking into a run here, wheeling round, going back, standing still, and generally cutting about in a promiscuous manner, as if they were dying to have a dance in the street.

Sisters, in all your born days, you never saw anything like those horses ! Slender, smooth as glass, with eyes like balls of fire, they just took the shine off from everything in the horse line that I ever set eyes on. But the animals were nothing compared to the funny-looking creatures that rode them. A circus was nothing to them—neither is a theatre. Some of them were dressed in red, some in yellow, some in blue; one had on purple—all fitting just as tight as the skin to a rabbit's back. Each one had a boy's cap on his head; and, in fact, they all looked like boys out on a spree. There was a place just above the long tavern where most of these fellows always took their horses after a little run and blow—that was a little, cubby house, built up high from the ground, in which some men stood like captains on a steamboat.

By and by there was a stir among the horses and a hustle among the men.

" They're going to start! they're going to start! " says everybody to everybody else. A flag on the little house seemed to break down. Then off the whole lot flew like a flock of wild birds. The flying horses rushed along the road, beating time on the hard ground, and fairly taking the breath from one's lips.

I gave a little scream, and jumped up. The whole crowd

rushed forward, and seemed as if it would pour itself over the railing of the long stoop.

" Where have they gone ? " says I.   " What has become of 'em ? "

" Here they come—here they come," shouted the whole crowd, answering me all at once.

And they did come skimming along the road like wildfire—flash—flash—now two horses abreast—now one ahead—now another—then a sudden pull up, and the brown horse had won. Now it seemed to me as if the whole squad came up pretty much at the same time, but the whole crowd fell to clapping hands over the brown horse.   I clapped too, and swung out my handkerchief as well as the rest ; for when a multitude go into a thing like that it just sets one wild.

Then the flag took another fall, and off went another squad of horses, and around the hill they went out of sight.   Then came a stormy sound of hoofs, and another streak of lightning dash in which a chestnut-colored horse showed his head first, and then came another rolling thunder-clap from the crowd, and " Joe Daniels has beat," ran from lip to lip, as if " Joe Daniels " had been up for the Presidential election and got all the votes.

Then the people cooled down, and, after a long wait, there was another rush, as if a whole training band had broke loose. We had hardly time to draw a deep breath, when they all came sweeping round in front of the long tavern, two of 'em just a little ahead, running so even and so fast, that I really believed that both of them beat the other, till the crowd began to clap and shout Alarm, which frightened me, for I thought something dreadful had happened ; but Dempster hushed me up, saying it was the name of the horse that had won the race, and he was glad of it, for his friend Travers was one of the warmest-hearted, kindest fellows in the world, and ought to have a horse win every day of his life.   This friendly little speech set me clapping my hands, both for the horse Alarm, his orange-colored rider, and the jolly-hearted man who owns him.

There was a great commotion after this. The whole crowd was in a wild whirl of excitement. All the ladies were talking about gloves and pools, and gentleman riders, while the gentlemen talked fast, looked eager, and were restless as caged birds. Something was going to happen now, I was sure of that.

"Do tell me what is the matter," says I to a gentleman that cousin had just introduced to me, "everybody is so excited."

"Yes," says he, "all on the keyvive."

What queer names they do have for horses. Alarm had just come in ahead, and now Keyvive.

"What kind of a horse is the Keyvive?" says I.

He didn't seem to hear·me. No wonder, for that very minute five horses, with such nice-looking fellows on their backs, took a start, like a flock of wild deer, and went up the road so swift that before I could see them they were gone.

"It is the hurdle-race," says the same gentleman, "splendid—splendid; what a leap!"

His eyes were bright as stars; they fairly danced in his head.

I sprang up, for a great wind seemed to be rushing around the hill. Then I gave a scream, for some wicked person had built a fence right across the road, and those five horses were galloping like mad right toward it.

"Oh, stop them—stop them—for mercy's sake!" says I, a-clasping my hands, and pleading wildly to every one around. "They'll be killed—they don't see that awful fence."

While I was screaming, the whole five horses came, one after another, sailed right over the fence, dived down like hen-hawks after a chicken, and away toward another fence that choked up the road. Before I could shriek out, and warn them, over they came, like a whirlwind, without touching the fence or seeming to care—over, and away up the road, taking one's breath with them.

"Mercy on me! what a providential escape!" says I to the

gentleman; " what wicked wretch could have heaped up things in the road?   I do hope they'll be found out and sent to State's prison.   Why, it's just as bad as blocking up a train of cars. Such nice-looking riders, too! "

The gentleman looked a trifle puzzled, then he smiled a little funnily, and says he:

" Perhaps you do not understand that this is a 'hurdle-race.' "

" No," says I ; " they told me that it would be horse-racing —nothing worse than that."

" Well," says he, " it is nothing worse than that, only a little more dangerous, and to you ladies more interesting, because the riders are all gentlemen."

" What, those men in the caps, gentlemen—not circus-riders, nor nothing ? "

He laughed, and says he:

" I dare say no one of them has ever been in a circus since he left off tunics, but they have learned to hunt, and love these hard leaps."

" You don't mean to say that they skiver over such fences on purpose ? " says I.

" Indeed they do, and build them higher and broader every year."

" You don't say so," says I, feeling my eyes open wide.

" They love the peril, for that increases the excitement."

" What if some of them were to be flung head over heels ? "

" Oh, that has happened."

" Not to-day ? "

" Yes, but fortunately the man was not killed."

I felt myself a-growing pale.

" But they don't know of it. Everybody is laughing," says I.

" Yes, it is generally known, but that is a part of the excitement.   In a crowd like this, it is difficult to realize trouble or death."

" How strange! " says I, putting the handkerchief that I

had torn with hard shaking into my pocket, with a deeply penitent feeling.

"It is strange," says he; "but this is no place for deep feeling, or you would not see so many smiling faces around you, for a gentleman who owns some of the race-horses, and came up only a day or two ago to see them tried, is lying dead in his home now."

My heart sank. I felt tears crowding up to my eyes. Death in one place—all this gorgeous confusion and wild gayety here. A lonely widow, weeping bitter tears; all these gay fluttering young people reckless and happy, in spite of it.

I arose, and looked around me. No one seemed to feel this man's death. Never in my whole life had I been in such a whirlpool of gayety. There was not a sad or thoughtful face in the crowd. Yet many of the persons there had known the man who lay dead in the city. I had never heard of him till then, but no smiles came to my lips after that mournful knowledge reached me. In the midst of all this hilarious gayety I felt the shadow of human suffering creeping over me, and I rode home from the race-park in sad silence.

LXVIII.

OFF AGAIN.

DEAR SISTERS:—New York City is full of epidemical contagions. Horse-racing is one of them. Every spring and fall it rages fearfully, especially among the female women who wait for the races—dress up for the races, and come out with splendiferous spontaneosity, whenever the fast horses are ready to run.

I have been up to see the creatures rush once, and sent you my report, which, owing to verdancy of mind caught from the

Green Mountains, was only skim milk to which I now pour in cream with a liberal hand. To own the truth, it takes more than one visit before a regular New England young lady can understand the inns and outs of a horse-race.

Now, I dare say you think it a sort of agricultural fair for animals—for the horsey kind meant to show off their beauty, try their speed, and encourage farmers to go in for improvement.

Exactly, and a good deal more so. Why, sisters, it's gambling—just gambling, open handed and above board, in which the upper-crust female women of New York take a hand with the men, and glory in it. But I mean to tell you all about it in the regular way, and shall do it as I go along.

You never saw such a crowd of carriages, wagons, buggies, and queer horse machines as crowded along the road when we got within three or four miles of the race-course. When we come to the long bridge that runs across the Harlem River, there were two lines of carriages stretching before and behind us, just as far as we could see, horses that tossed their heads and champed their bits, and shone like satin under harnesses mounted with gold and silver, with little looking-glasses flying in and out over their heads, and hoofs that struck the ground like the feet of a Vermont girl when she dances from the heart.

All these carriages were filled as if they were on the way to a high jubilation, choke full of ladies, with parasols hovering over them like wild birds taking wing, and great clouds of silk, lace gauze, and shiny stuff a-billowing over the sides, till you could but just see the silk cushions they leaned against. Then, again, some were crowded over with gentlemen, mostly in white hats—which delighted me—some with cigars in their mouths—some not—but every one of them just boiling over with good-nature and fun.

This was the way we went. Cousin Dempster has made a good deal of money in Washington—contracting, or something —and he got a spick-span new open carriage for this high occasion—a carriage made soft as a bird's nest with brown satin cushions, and that glittered outside like a crow's back whenever the sun struck it.

We had a great big fellow, in new plum-colored clothes on the driver's seat, and another genteel youngster by his side—all plum-color and hat-band, like the coachman. Inside, there was Cousin E. E. with a pea-green dress on, all flounces and fringe, and overskirts piled up so high behind that she couldn't lean back, and your missionary, Miss Phœmie Frost, in her pink silk (turned again), and the white hat with plumes of snow, which bespoke at once her good taste and her most sacred political preferences, which would keep going on both sides all I could do.

There, in the front seat, with his back to the horses and his face to us, sat Dempster, looking out with envy and bitter feelings on the men in buggies, that were laughing like fun, and smoking like New England stone chimneys. At such times I do not think that Dempster appreciates all the sweet benefits of female society.

Last and least, I am sorry to say, was that child, Cecilia, with a pink parasol about as big as a good-sized toadstool, fluttering before her face, and all in a storm of flounces above her knees, with nothing but kid boots and silk stockings below.

I do wonder what possesses Dempster and E. E. to train that child along wherever they go! She is just the aggravation of my life.

Well, with our open carriage yeasting over with green, pink, white, and blue, which Dempster broke up with a lean streak of black, we rolled through the gate of the race-grounds and came up, with a magnificent sweep, to the back door of the club house, when E. E. and I gave a neat little jump, and tipped gracefully around the long stoop, right into the upper crust society of New York.

Sisters, it was like wading right into a flower-bed! Everybody there had on her good clothes—I may say, her bettermost clothes of all. Red, green, purple, blue, white, black—every color or shade of color to be found in the sky, in flowers, in fruit, or in water, rustled against each other. Sisters, it was gorgeous! But one thing struck me as peculiar—most of these female ladies had the loveliest pink color in their cheeks all the time. While my face was turning red and white, as I grew warm or comfortable, theirs kept one steady pink. Ladies with hair as yellow as gold had ink-black eyebrows and lashes—things we never see together in the country. I don't understand it. Well, we had but just got seats on the largest stoop when the people below us let off a squad of horses that seemed to fly; for the mud was soft as mush on the road, and their hoofs made no more noise than as if they had trod on velvet.

Just before these horses made their first dive, Dempster came up to us with a person who carried a white hat in his hand, and held it out as if he wanted something put into it. I thought that somebody had been cheating the poor fellow, for there was nothing but little, crumpled bits of paper in the hat. Of course I did not want to equal these treacherous people in meanness, so I took out my pocket-book and dropped a five-cent piece into the hat, smiling benignly on the good-looking suppliant as I did it. I really was ashamed of Cousin E. E.; for instead of giving the poor fellow a trifle of money, she just nipped up one of the crumpled bits of paper, and, opening it, called out, laughing like a girl:

"I've drawn the favorite! Oh, isn't that splendid!"

I declare I was mortified by such silly nonsense, and wanting to keep up the credit of the family, dropped another five-cent piece in the hat, and nodded toward E. E., as much as to say: "Never mind; I give it for her."

Instead of thanking me, the man stared and turned a trifle red, as if the gratitude that filled his heart were trying to burst through his face. It was a noble feeling, and I appreciated it by another kind nod and smile.

Then he held out the hat to "that child," and she, too, snatched up one of the papers and began to giggle over it. I declare you might have lighted a candle by my face, it burned so.

"Is there no end to such meanness?" thought I, and once more I opened my pocket-book.

"No matter, Phœmie, I'll attend to that," says Cousin Dempster, waving his hand at me.

Out came his pocket-book then, and he took from it a handful of greenback-bills, which he gave to the man, who laughed as if he were half-tickled to death, and well he might be, for Dempster was as extravagant as the female portion of his family had been mean.

"Here is the last number, and our pool is complete," says he, taking a bit of paper from the hat, and dropping it into my lap. "Don't trouble yourself, Phœmie, it's all right."

I did trouble myself, in spite of his smiling face. Charity is one thing, and ostentation is another. After my gift, which I must say was liberal enough, there was no need of such a display as Dempster made. No wonder the man looked pleased as he marched away, with the money in one hand, and that white hat in the other.

When the horses came rushing by again, and made a sharp halt just above the house, the man came up to us choke full of pleasure, and wanted to look at my paper. I thought he was taking liberties, but gave him the mite of paper, and drew back in my seat, in proper fashion.

"Your horse has won," says he; "Mid-day has the race by a length."

With that he laid a roll of bills in my lap, and went away, bowing low, till his white hat almost touched the floor.

"Mercy on me! what does this mean?" says I, a-taking up the money. "Is the man crazy?"

"It means that you have won the pool," said Dempster.

Before I could ask him what on earth he meant, Cousin D. was swept off by a crowd of ladies, and three sandy-haired horses were put upon the run. I could not tell one horse from another, they were so alike; but they all were long and lank, with hind legs that looked as if all their strength lay in that direction to a wonderful extent, and the way they threw them out was surprising.

About this time I saw a great many white hats flying about, and men had pocket-books in their hands, while ladies talked wildly about gloves and neckties, and clapped their hands when the horses rushed by, and the word "pool" was in everybody's mouth—in fact, it was Bedlam let loose.

LXIX.

THE STEEPLE-CHASE.

ISTERS :—This horse hurdling is something that just lifts you right off your feet. All that I had seen was nothing to what was to come. All along the winding road, and the lots each side, some men went to building fences, till every few yards were fenced in, and yet seven long-legged, long-bodied, and not over fleshy horses, with riders in white, in blue, in yellow, and striped brown and yellow, were ready for another start, which they made like a thunderburst.

On they came, flying and flashing through the lots, like a flock of birds, right up to the first fence. I sprang up—everybody sprang up, wild and anxious—I expected to see the whole grist of them pitch head-foremost against the rails, when up they all rose, and away they went straight over, and off like a shot to the next and the next, clearing one after another, before you could draw a deep breath. Across lots, down the road, in and out they went, jumping fences, now abreast, now in a swift line, till they came up all at once to a pond of water.

I screamed right out, and felt myself growing cold, for they were rushing toward it full split, and it was wider across than the mill-stream back of our school-house.

"Stop 'em, stop 'em! They'll be drowned, they'll be killed!"
I screamed out, just crazy with fear.

No one minded me ; the whole crowd was too busy watching
those wild riders to mind me if I had yelled like an engine
whistle. They came rushing up nearer—nearer, almost in a
line, as if some enemy were ahead, and the whole squad meant
to ride right through and trample everything down. They
were close by the water now, with a low fence that side. On
they rushed—a whole cloud of hoofs ploughed up through the
air, and those seven horses went shooting like sparrows over
the fence and across the water. Their hoofs struck fire from
the stone wall on the other side, and away they went, pell-mell,
their riders shooting out colors like a broken rainbow, and the
crowd cheering them on as if it had been a sham fight on training-day.

On they flew like a young whirlwind, though one bay horse
they called "Blind Tom" fell short. The rider, trying to
bring him up, was pitched over his head, at which the crowd
was hushed, but burst out again when Blind Tom left the
poor fellow behind, and dashed on with the other horses neck
and neck round the fields, leaping a fence or two, before the
poor stunned rider could roll over and pick himself up.

Oh, it was too droll—that plucky horse, dashing along with
the rest, shooting over the fences, up to time, and acting like a
soldier charging under command. I could just have gone down
and kissed the splendid creature, and the whole crowd—thousands and thousands—set up shout after shout that you could
have heard almost on the Green Mountains.

Another horse came out first best on the second round, but
a couple of men, right behind me, insisted that Blind Tom
ought to have the money—what money I didn't understand—
but I agreed with the men, if there was anything that a horse
could accept, Blind Tom was the animal for the money.

Sisters, there don't seem much that is wrong about this.
You can't see any amount of deep iniquity in it, can you now?

I didn't discover anything poisonous to the moral character; but then we female women don't always see deep enough into great social and religious questions, and horse-racing is one.

What do you think the gloves and neckties meant? What hidden sin lay buried under the pools? What, after all, took that great multitude up to that beautiful hollow among the hills? Gambling, my dear; male and female gambling, nothing more, nothing less. The horses run for money. The jockeys ride for money. The men bet money, hats, gloves, hundreds, thousands, on this horse and that. Everybody gambles, and everybody likes it.

Sisters, that poor man's hat was a pool; there wasn't a drop of water in it; still it was a pool. The two five-cent pieces I threw into it were a dead loss to charity. The scraps of crumpled paper meant dollars. The heap of bills that I tucked away in my pocket-book, innocent as twenty lambs, was money that I had won gambling, ignorantly, innocently.

With Christianity at my heart, and gambling money in my pocket, I feel demoralized as a church member; yet I must confess it exhilated me as if I had been on the top of a high mountain, and was looking down with delicious dizziness. I a gambler, I a diver into pools no larger than a man's hat, but dangerous as the bottomless pit! I cannot realize it; and when realized, it seems to me as if I couldn't be properly penitent. That sort of thing doesn't seem so awful to me as it did before I got into it, in this pleasant, innocent, and sweetly promiscuous manner.

Is this "rolling sin like a sweet morsel under the tongue"? Am I getting faithless to the trust with which I set forth on this city mission?

This much I will say in my own behalf: horse-racing, if pernicious, is awfully pleasant, and horse-betting (gloves and neckties I mean) is—well—ditto.

Such a ride home as we had! Trees and grass, cool and green—no dust. The sun going down, and throwing red shadows across the fields. Carriages crowded full of smiling people, horses wild to pass each other and get home; yourself deliciously tired, with half a dozen swift horses chasing each other through your brain, and trampling down your conscience.

Well, sisters, I may have been wrong, but frankness is my peculiarity, and I should like to try it all over again, just once. Don't think hard of it, but I should.

LXX.

PREPARING FOR SEA.

EAR SISTERS:—With an aching head and bitter taste in my mouth, I take up my pen to write. Myself, and not myself, I sit here as if I had just come out of the upheaving of an earthquake. If I write anything of what happened yesterday, it must be sensational; for, of all sensations that ever riled up a human constitution, that I felt while out to sea beat all that I ever knew or heard of.

I have been out to a yacht race.

Horse-racing is a science not unknown, in its rudiments, to our rural population. You can remember when we took our first lessons, bareback, with a rope-halter looped around the horse's nose for a bridle. No—that was our second lesson; the first was on father's old grey horse, which was blind of one eye, and had a natural saddle curved into his back. Being a mite of a child, I sat in that hollow like a bird in its nest, hung on to the mane with one hand, and held a crooked stick before the eye that could see when I wanted the creature to turn. In this way I began my horse-alphabet. First, we waded through the plantains and burdocks, at a slow walk, with a stumble now and then, which set my little heart to quaking like a swampy bog trod upon. Then I grew venturesome, and the old grey warmed into a soft trot, which shook me up like anything, but was more exhilarating than the walk. With my bare feet pressed close to the animal's side and my fingers gripped into his mane, I began to rattle my stick timidly against his shoulder; at which he broke trot and racked himself off into a canter, which made my heart leap with every fall of his hoofs, and filled it with the courage of a trooper.

Didn't we wade through the burdocks and sweet ferns then! Didn't we ride round and round that pasture lot, without giving the dear old beast time for a bite of grass or a fair nip at the sweet ferns! Didn't my crooked stick rattle and my hair fly out in the wind! Didn't my mother scream after me, and my father rush out like a crazy man, with both arms spread out, and try to head Old Grey off! Of course he did. But the dear old horse didn't want to give up, and I didn't mean that he should; so he shied, and, of course, having nothing to hold him in by but the tuft of hair and the stick, he left father behind, and, I do believe, kicked up a trifle, just to show his independence.

That was my first lesson on horseback. On the second, my father insisted on haltering the creature, which gave me a pull at his head, and mane, too, which rather interfered with the use of my crooked stick, and bunched me up, till father called out to me to sit up straight—which I did, at last, going it with both hands on the halter, and the hair blowing about my face like a veil. That morning Old Grey and I jumped a brook a full yard wide, and cleared both banks beautifully.

After that I did a great deal of bareback riding, along the road and in the pasture lots, and could sit and ride like a trooper before I ever got into a side-saddle or knew what a curb-bit was.

Sisters, that is the way to learn things—begin at the beginning, and get a firm, steady seat before you attempt to cut a dash. The lady that can't sit her horse handsomely without regard to bit or stirrup, needn't set herself up as much of a rider—at any rate, in our part of the country.

So much for one kind of racing. Now for the water-course.

18*

We used to send little boats, dug out with a jack-knife, under paper sails, down that brook by the school-house, and see them swamped among the cowslips or capsized in the eddies, when we were in the A B C class. Some of us went far enough to sail down the mill stream in a canoe dug out of the trunk of some big tree. In fact, I have a remembrance of crossing a large river in a scow pushed forward with awful long poles. But beyond these rudimental experiences, ship-rowing is not indigenous to the Green Mountains, as a general thing, and I do not see how it can ever become a Vermont institution, yet awhile. Therefore I say, horse-racing you can understand, but ship-racing is really a novelty in the Mountains.

Now, a yacht, sisters, is nothing more or less than a baby schooner, which has two masts, or a sloop, that has one, built up slender and graceful, with a cock-pit, which is in the stern, and a cooking-room, which is in the bow, and all the other fixings which make it as much like a ship as a first-rate baby-house is like an old homestead.

Dempster has been to Washington, and got some contracts or something, and what does he do but come home one hot day when we were all just sweltering in white loose gowns, and says he:

"Girls, what do you say to going down to the Regatta?"

"The Regatta," says I, "what is that—anything cool?"

"Why, it is a race given by the Yacht Club," says he, "and of course it will be cool if we go out to sea."

"Well, I don't object to seeing, if that will make things cool," says I; "but how a club can race, except when it is in a policeman's hand, I can't begin to make out."

Cousin D. gave one of his long, hearty laughs, and says he:

"Now, really, Phœmie, don't you understand what a club is?"

I felt the blood rise up into my face.

"Don't I know what a club is?" says I. "Well, I should rather think so. There are hickory clubs, oak clubs, yellow pine knots, that answer pretty well, and locust clubs, but how a little ship can be turned into a club beats me ! "

" Oh, it isn't one ship that makes the club, but a good many," says he, " crack ships, too."

I just dropped the two hands I had been holding up, quite out of breath.

" So a good many ships make one club, do they ? " says I.

" Just so," says he. " When a lot of men join together for any particular thing, it is called a ' club.'   There is the Jockey Club, the Union Club, the Rural Club, the Union League Club, the Yacht Club."

" Oh, for mercy's sake, do stop before you club me to death," says I, clapping both hands to my ears.   " We have got timber enough in Vermont, but clubs of any kind are not in our line. Just tell me what you want of us, and we'll say Yes or No."

" Well, I want you to get into my new yacht, and go a little way out to sea," says he.

" To see what ? " says I.

" The Regatta."

" Can't you for once speak honest English ? " says I.

" Well, a Yacht Race," says he.

" That is, little ships running races," says I ; " but where ? "

" On the Atlantic Ocean," says he.

My spirit rose.   1 have seen the East River and the upper bay, and more than once have caught a view of the Long Island Sound from the car-windows, but a live ocean—a great, broad, heaving ocean, with waves roaring up thirty feet high, is an object we do not often get a chance to contemplate on the slopes of the Green Mountains.   Would I go and see that? Wouldn't I ? "

" Then you will go ? " says Cousin Dempster.

" Go ! " says I, " yes, if I have to walk afoot with snow-shoes on."

" Well, then, get your yachting clothes ready," says he.

" Pink silk ? " I suggested.

" Oh, no ; something that can stand the water," says he.

"Say black alpaca, with a white hat and plumes—principle and patriotism before anything else," says I.

"That will be lovely on the blue waves," says Cousin E. E. "I will wear a blue feather, and Cecilia shall turn up her Leghorn flat with an anchor."

"That's just the thing," says Cousin D., with maritime enthusiasm. "I have had the yacht painted white, and on her long white pennant you will find a name all Vermonters love particularly, and the world generally."

"What is her name?" we all said right out at once.

"The Vermonter," says he, straightening himself up proudly.

We all sprang to out feet, and clapped our hands with the wildest enthusiasm.

"I'm not afraid to dare the wildest storms on the ocean with that craft," says I.

"Nor I."

"Nor I."

Sisters, it was a spontaneous outburst of pure state patriotism—even that child Cecilia seemed to feel it—for ten minutes after she was busy as a bee, sewing a silver anchor on her Leghorn flat, and that day, for the first time, I kissed the child with spontaneosity.

LXXI.

YACHT-RACING.

ISTERS:—When you go to a yacht-race, the first step is peculiar. You get into a carriage or a car, and ride down to the docks. Then you steam off in a ferry-boat to Staten Island, get into a thing they call a yawl, which floats like a cockle-shell, and carries two or three people, and row off to one of the cunningest, prettiest, slenderest, most scrumptious little ships you ever set eyes on, sitting on the water like a white duck with its wings spread.

Some black-walnut steps fell down the side, over which I climbed, with my heart in my mouth, and jumped into a little pew, with a sofa running round it, and some light cross-legged chairs ready for visitors.

The sun was hot overhead and up from the water, so I just went down into the prettiest little cabin you ever saw, all finished off with shiny wood, like a lady's bedroom, and carpeted with sky-blue, with a pale touch of gray in it. Right by this were two lovely little bedrooms, all blue and cloud color, with snow-white beds and cloudy curtains. There were four beds in the cabin, too, built into the wall, and lots of silver things were shining on brackets and silver hooks.

A sofa, all cushioned with blue, ran down each side of the cabin, and on one of these I took my place while the rest came in.

Cousin D. had invited a dozen people to try his new yacht, and when they all came swarming in, it was cheerful as a bee-hive.

Some cramped themselves in the cockpit, some flung themselves on the long sofas of the cabin, some got under the sails, cosey as birds in a tree, two and two; but I always remarked that two men and two women somehow never got together; they were sure to split up one of each sort, just as they are apt to do on land.

Well, the yacht spread her sails, made a graceful dive and off she went, her canvas snapping and her colors flying. A whole squad of other vessels set sail too, and off we went like a flock of birds.

The water of the bay was blazing like quicksilver. Some white clouds cooled the sky a little, but everything around was sweltering with hotness. On we went, fleet and cheerful, sending up the water in sparkles, and flying toward the ocean, with green banks on each side of us, and that gloriously hot sun heating up the air like a furnace.

By and by we passed a couple of great stone forts, and came out into the ocean. Oh, what a broad blaze of sky and water—blue and silver everywhere, blue and silver!

On these waters, far out, lay a crimson ship, settled down like a mammoth red bird, and around that a crowd of little vessels, with their sails spread ready for flight. Ever so many steamboats, crowded with people, waited a little way off for the race to begin.

One of these steamboats had the President of these United States on board, and hung out its flag that all the world might know where to find him. We didn't try, but kept modestly down among the small craft.

By and by there was a fluttering among the yachts around the red ship; then a gun banged off, then another, and away the whole flock went, flying across the water in a white cloud.

After it went the steamboats, ploughing and snorting through the water, and after them a whole storm of sailing craft, all on the wing, each dashing up foam like fury.

Now the wind rose higher, and seemed to cool the air, while it spread out all the sails as they flew before it. This seemed to bring in a whole army of little waves from the great ocean, and, as true as you live, every wave had a white hat on.

I jumped up and fairly clapped my hands when I saw these waves trooping in, battalion after battalion, all tossing up their white hats and dancing forward, as if the winds were singing Yankee Doodle behind them.

Then the party in our yacht gave a shout.

"They are rounding the spit," says Cousin D. "Do look, Phœmie."

I did look, but saw nothing particular—who could? What would one spit be in a whole ocean of water.

Then came another shout.

"They have marked the boy."

"Goodness, gracious," says I, "is there a boy overboard? Do fling out a boat-hook or something!"

"Do not disturb yourself, Phœmie," said Cousin D. ; "that particular boy has been swimming in one spot these ten years."

"And alive yet?" says I, feeling my eyes widen like saucers.

"Just as live as he ever was," says he.

"You don't say so," says I. "Can we see him from here?"

"Yes; yonder!"

Cousin D. pointed toward something in the water, black, with a red cap on. There did not seem to be much danger of his sinking, for he kept his head high, and a good many boats were near enough to keep him up. I lost sight of him, and watched the vessels flying off again. But somehow, when they came in sight once more, my enthusiasm was all gone, and I began to feel limp and dreadfully discouraged. I haven't had such an uproar about my—well—heart, since the Grand Duke sailed, and that was very different, a sort of affectionate flutter, while this is beyond ex-pres-sion."

Sisters, at the end of the last sentence, my head fell into one of those blue cushions, and I have a dreamy feeling that waves with white hats on were bowing to me right and left.

I have lifted my head again. The yachts are coming in full split. As each comes up, the steamboats and vessels give a yell that makes the sea tremble, and scares all the birds in the neighborhood. One time they shriek—that is for the *Gracie*. Then there was a deep, long howl—that was for the *Jantha*. Then there was a yell, a shriek, and a howl, all together, which was for the *Vixen*.

What yacht beat, I don't pretend to know, but it comes to me as if in a hideous dream that it was the *Vixen*.

The next thing I have on my mind was, a table set out in the cabin, and the popping of corks from long bottles, with a sound that made me quiver all over. Then I recollect that some one was persecuting me with offers of something nice to eat, for which I shall loath them as long as I live.

Sisters, I did *not* see a single ocean wave thirty feet high—far from it—but those I did see were quite high enough. If you don't believe me, go to a yacht race, that's all.

LXXII.

MUSIC THAT IS MUSIC.

DEAR SISTERS:—I love music. My soul was brought up on Old Hundred, and refreshed from time to time with Yankee Doodle. The lively tones of a fiddle drove me wild with delight, in my foolish, school-girl days; and I cannot keep my feet still when one rattles of money-musk or the Opera Reel even now, when enthusiasm is delicately toned down into graceful ease.

The truth is, Nature is full of music, and we who live in a mountainous country know how much of it is to be found outside of instruments and the human voice. In fact, the sweetest music I ever heard has come to me through the woods—not from the birds, but the whispering leaves. Have you ever listened—with your heart—and learned, by the faintest sound, the different voices of the trees—the quick, soft rustle of the maple; the stronger sound of the oak-leaves; the weird, ghostly shiver of the pine-needles? I know little of music, if anything out of heaven can touch a human soul more tenderly than these sounds. Then the birds—what joyous or solemn music they can make! Have you never felt your heart leap to the singing of a robin among the branches of an apple-tree in full blossom, or shiver and grow sad at sunset, when the cry of a lonely whip-poor-will comes wailing through the dusk?

There is the music of trees in the spring, when their blossoms are sweet and their leaves are just unfolding—soft, cheerful, happy music, full of tenderness and love. Then there is the low, drowsy music of the summer-time, when bumble-bees and lady-bugs and humming-birds fill the warm air with greedy droning as they plunder the wild flowers of honey.

Did you never close your eyes, half go to sleep, and listen to them, with a lazy consciousness that you could rest and enjoy, while those little, busy creatures were singing at their work? I have, a thousand times.

Then comes the fall, when the hills are burnt over with red and gold and brown. How the full, rough-edged leaves strike together, with a sound of copper and brass—with a rustle and shiver that makes one think of military funerals. Then comes the swift, rustling sound of ripe nuts rattling from burs and husks; the coarse, bass voices of the crows among the naked stubble-lots; the mellow crash of corn-stalks, as the cattle tread them; the slow, liquid grinding of cider-mills, and the sharp sound of the hackle, where flax is broken for the spinning-wheel.

After this, comes stormy music—fierce, high winds, whistling sharp and shrill through the long, naked branches of the woods, which answer them back with moans and sighs and wild shrieks that make you shiver at night and hide yourself under the bed-clothes.

When I was a little girl, sisters, my heart rose and fell to music like this till I suffered terribly, sometimes, without speaking a word to any one—for these are feelings which one never does talk of—there is no language that I ever learned which will express them. But I have never heard any music that could reach my soul like that which God gives us in the blossom season—the summer, the fall of late fruit—and the bleak, hard winter, when the clash of ice against ice has a sound that no man or woman can reach.

This is my idea of music, and that is scattered far and given to all men alike. You can't gather it up and deal it out in great, thundering gushes. It isn't to be got for five dollars a ticket. In fact, the best and sweetest things we have are given to the poor and rich just alike—free, gratis, for nothing.

LXXIII.

HUBBISHNESS.

SISTERS:—The music I have just been writing about is not fashionable by any manner of means. Boston, the great central hub of all creation, can't bottle it up or engage it by the ton to astonish all creation with. She must have the manufactured article, and has sent all over the world to get it.

Every fiddler, flute-player, drummer, and curlecued hornman in Europe has been brought over here to thunder-out and roll-off billows of sound for people to pay for and wonder at.

We have a Niagara of waters that astonishes the world. Now the people of Boston are determined to give us, in a great, wild, conglomeration of voices, a full Niagara of sound.

I am New England all over, from the top of my beehive-bonnet to the sole of my gaiter, but—confidentially, among ourselves—don't you think Boston takes a little too much on herself? That narrow-streeted, up-hilly city isn't all six of the New England States by a long shot.

My opinion is that Boston is putting on airs, and I for one don't mean to put up with it. I hate stuck-up people, and I despise stuck-up towns.

Of course it is my duty to see all things in behalf of the Society, and to do my best to lay them before you. I cannot say that my ideas of Boston have not toned down considerably since I came to New York. Still New England is New England, and Boston is Boston, if she does now and then make a tremendous old goose of herself, and sometimes threatens to cackle the hub all to pieces.

Cousin Dempster hasn't much to do in summer-time, so he was on hand for the Great High Jubilee; and E. E. was just crazy to go; for she is what you call musical, and goes right off the handle whenever a fellow that can't speak English plays on the piano or sings to her in some language that she don't know a word of.

Well, we went, and found Boston just running over with people. Every house along the crooked streets had one or two flags a-streaming from the roof, or out of the windows—star-spangled banners tangled-up with red and yellow and all sorts of colors; some with eagles, some without, but making every street gorgeous, as if the Fourth of July had burst out before its time.

The Coliseum is a tremendous building, big enough to roof-in forty thousand people, and leave room for the whole swarm of drummers, toot-horners, piano-thrashers, blacksmiths, anvils, and swivel-guns, with a thousand people to blow, thrash, and blast them off, and twenty thousand singers behind, ready to pile in the thunder of their voices.

The Coliseum is grand, barny in its structure, and all out-doorish when you get into it; but there is a good deal to see before you do get into it. The streets were just jammed-up with people when we came in sight of the great building, which stands out in a bare piece of ground, without a tree near it, and the hottest sun you ever wilted under beating down on everything around it, till I felt as if approaching the mouth of a great New England brisk oven, heated to bake a thousand tons of beans in. The streets were blocked with people.

The little wooden bridges built over the railroads were creaking under the tramp of a never-ending crowd. The street cars were crowded like beehives till the horses could not move, and some of the cars broke down, choking up the track.

Female women, with red books in their hands, scrambled through the crowd. Little tents and shanties were scattered all about, everybody talked fast and loud—some in one language, some in another. It was like going into the Tower of Babel, with all the languages in full blast.

From one of the shanties we heard the sound of a loud, eager, wild voice, as of some fellow going to be hung, and wrestling for his life.

"What is that?" says I to Dempster. "What on earth are they doing in there?"

"Oh, it's a prayer-meeting," says he; "some man is wrestling with the Lord in behalf of sinful souls."

"Oh, that's it," says I, just disgusted: "Well, I hope he'll get through with his wrestling before we come this way again. To haul religion and force prayers into such a crowd as this, is making a farce of Christianity. We have churches for such things, and the calm of a holy Sabbath set aside for the service of God. Who has time to think of such things here?"

"Oh, it takes all sorts of men to make a world," says Dempster, pushing his way through the crowd, while E. E. and I followed, with that child a-dragging after us.

We went at the rate of three feet in as many minutes, and that wrestler's voice was wrangling over us all the time. If the angels caught one sentence, I'm sure they must have clapped their wings to their ears and left the hub to take care of itself.

LXXIV.

THUNDERS OF MUSIC.

WELL, at last we crowded and fought our way into the Coliseum, which was pretty well filled up when we got through the entrance.

It was a sight, I must say that. Before us was a whole mountain-side of benches, rising one above another till you could hardly see the end of them—benches, benches, benches—crowded down and running over with people, all in a state of bewildering commotion—humming, whispering, and rustling together like ten millions of bees in a mammoth hive.

You never saw so many female women together in your born days. Think of it, thousands and thousands with crimson books fluttering in their hands, as if each woman had caught a great red butterfly and was holding him out by the wings. All these female women were rigged out in gorgeous dresses, rustling, moving, and flaming with all sorts of colors, like a hillside covered with gorgeous flowers, broken up with a dash of blackness now and then, as if a thunder-cloud had settled down amongst them. These black patches were the musicians, the flower garden was the singers—almost all female women, with fans, and voices, and red books in motion.

Below were the people, crowded together by the acre, all jolly, smiling, and looking as if Boston were ready to burst her tire and whirl on her own bare hub, with all her spokes a-whizzing.

Flags streamed and blazed on the walls, the roof, and around the pillars. All the stars in the skies seemed to have been torn down, scattered on a blue ground, and hung over that great building. It was a grand sight, I must say that—grand, but hubby.

It was the German day, Cousin Dempster said. England had had her turn, France had flared up, and now Germany was to splurge just as much as she was a mind to.

Well, Germany did splurge, but she began with a loud, deep, woe-begone rush of music, that seemed to roll out from a graveyard where everybody lay uneasy in his grave and was begging to get out. This ended off when the day closed with a dreary, low complaint, as if they had begged long enough and gave up. Now and then they broke in with a grand crash that made me start from my seat, and went off in a low wail, with a storm of music between.

Something lively followed the first moan. Then a lady got up and sang all alone by herself, and her voice went floating through that great barny place, full, loud, and clear, as if ten thousand nightingales—not that I ever saw or heard a nightingale in my life, but I persist in it—as if ten thousand nightingales had broken loose in a swamp of wild roses.

" Who on earth is that?" says I to E. E.

"Madame Puschka Leutner," says she, clasping her hands. "Isn't she delicious?"

. Then out E. E. drew her handkerchief and set it flying.

"I never heard anything like it, so strong, so sweet, so spreading," says I, flirting out my own handkerchief with enthusiasm. "The human voice is something worth while in the way of music after all."

It was no use saying more, for up jumped all the thousands of people in that great encampment, out went a swarm of white handkerchiefs, flocking together like a host of frightened sea-gulls, and the roar of the people went up like thunder.

Then a great band of men, mostly with yellow beards and rosy faces, got on their feet, and went at the fiddles, the twisted horns, the drums and things, like crazy creatures, and the way the music rose, and swelled, and thundered out was enough to drive one crazy.

Once more that great crowd burst in with yells and shouts, and a wild storm of praise. Then one of the yellow-haired men stood up alone with a wide-mouthed toot-horn, made of bright brass, in his hand. After looking around a minute, he just put the horn to his mouth, and blew a slow, long blow. Then he went at it tooth and nail, bringing out great round tones that seemed as if they never would grow faint or die away.

I have heard a great many toot-horns in my life; in fact, I have blown a tin one myself to call the men folks in to dinner; but never did I hear anything like that. It was what Cousin E. E. called wonderful—so-low.

I couldn't quite agree with her there, for to me it seemed wonderfully loud and riotous, but it was enough to make one in love with brass toot-horns forever.

By and by something happened that just took the starch out of my New England soul. There, in the midst of all those dashy singers, one hundred and fifty men and women of the colored persuasion rose up in a human thunder-cloud, and broke into that noble song of freedom, which is a glory to one

New England woman, and a glory to New England, for no better thing has been written since the " Star Spangled Banner : "

> " Mine eyes have seen the glory of the coming Lord." .

Oh, sisters! there mightn't have been the highest-priced music in those colored voices, but the words are enough to wake up a dead warrior; they went through and through me as the wind stirs a forest. It was something to hear those dusky-faced freedmen chanting the glory of their own emancipation—something better than music, I can tell you. But the thrill of the thing was all gone when twenty thousand white people, with drums, trumpets, fiddles, organs, everything and every creature that could make a noise, thundered in, and bore all the sentiment off in a wild whirlpool of thunder.

I do wish the white people would stop helping the colored population so much. They only drown them out and stifle them. Why couldn't the jubilant darkies be left to sing their own song, and rush on with old John Brown without being whirlpooled up in twenty thousand white voices. They could have stood their own without help, I reckon.

There was a little resting spell after the darkies sat down; then came a great heaving crash and storm of music. Everything from a jew's-harp to an organ was set a-going, and behind them thousands of women sent up their voices amid a crash of anvils, the thunder of guns, and the ringing of bells that plunged one headlong into a volcano of sound that was neither music, nor thunder, nor an earthquake, but altogether a stampede and whirlwind of noises that engulfed you, body and soul. Ring—crash-bang—thunder rolling, rolling—oceans in tumult—whirlwinds of sound—armies crashing together—the world at an end !

That was what it seemed like to me. Sisters, I haven't a nerve left in my body; my temples throb, my heart feels as if it had been blown up with brass horns. There is a drum beating in each temple. Oh, if I could only hear a robin sing, or a brook in full flow—anything soft, and low, and sweet—it would be a relief.

LXXV.

SARATOGA TRUNKS.

EAR SISTERS:—Do you know where Long Branch is? I reckon not, owing to its being a sandy slip, cut off from the edge of New Jersey, and not much of a place over two months in the year; it hasn't got into the geography books as a school item of importance, though, if a President or two more should settle in there, it might lift it a notch higher.

But in duty bound, I am here in pursuit of my great social mission, and can tell you, confidently, that Long Branch is a great watering-place, brim full, and running over with fashion once a year, when the hot sun drives all the upper-crust people out of New York, and everybody that is anybody feels the want of extra washing.

When I speak of watering-places, do not understand that I mean a tavern corner with some brook emptying itself into a huge wooden trough for horses to drink out of. Of course, that is our Vermont idea; with a willow-tree shading the trough. That, no doubt, gave the name here. But the two things are no more alike than trout streams are like the broad ocean.

I ask no questions, always finding it best to wait and watch, and learn for myself; but when Dempster asked me if I would like to go down to a watering-place in New Jersey, I asked him if there wasn't Croton Water enough in the pipes for all the horses they kept.

Dempster laughed, and said it was salt water he was thinking of, and asked, right on that, if I had got a bathing-dress?

"A bathing-dress," says I. "Goodness, gracious, no. When I bathe, as a general thing, I—that is—I take off—"

Here I broke off, and felt myself turning red. I declare, Cousin Dempster has a way of putting things upon you for explanation, which I, as a single lady, with expectations, of course, find embarrassing.

Just then, E. E. came in, all of a flurry about her trunks; she wanted more and must have 'em, she said. Seventeen Saratoga trunks, and a basket or two, were just nothing to what she needed. Dempster must go out and get half a dozen more. Why, her fluted skirts alone filled three trunks.

Dempster went. To own the truth, he is an obedient creature as ever wore coat and—well pocket-handkerchiefs. It wasn't long before a lot of trunks—big enough for country school-houses—were piled into the hall, and then Cousin E. E. began to revel. Her bed was crowded and loaded down with skirts, dresses, shawls, bonnets, round hats, broad flats, peaked caps. You never saw such heaps and mountains of clothes; such a litter of small things; such stacks of boots and shoes.

It really seemed as if she was fitting out an army of feminines. Even Cecilia was down on her knees packing, and E. E. was deep in a high trunk with her slippers half dropping from her feet as she punched things in and pressed them down. The help, black and white, kept running up and downstairs like hens with their necks wrung. Every few minutes there came a ring at the door, and paper-boxes and bundles were set down in the hall, and struggled upstairs when any of the help thought it worth while to bring them, which was once in about ten minutes, all morning.

I think Dempster made a cowardly attempt to get out of the way, but it was of no use. On such occasions men are wanted, especially when the bills come in, and E. E. knows her privileges.

14

LXXVI.

THE DOLLY VARDEN.

S I stood looking on, wondering if cousin really meant to turn the house inside out, and set up a village of trunks somewhere on the sea-shore, that hard-working creature lifted her face, and looked at me deploringly.

"Oh, Phœmie," says she; "are you packed? How cool you look."

"Packed," says I; "oh, yes; I always keep my pink silk folded."

"But your summer things, are they ready? Surely you'll have a Dolly?"

"No," says I; "its years since I have thought of a doll, and I haven't the least idea of going back to my play-house days."

"But I mean a dress," says she, lifting her head out of the trunk, and wiping the swe—well, perspiration from her face. "A Dolly Varden. Don't you understand?"

"A dress, and some Miss Dolly Varden, all at once! Now I can't think what dress you mean; and, as for that young person, I don't know her from a bag of sweet corn. How should I? Never having been introduced!" says I.

E. E. just sat back on the floor, and drew a deep breath.

"Oh, Phœmie," says she, "you are so stolid about some things. Why, it is only a dress I mean."

"Then what did you drag in that young person for?" says I.

"Because she gives her name to the dress."

"I'm sure the dress ought to be very much obliged to her. That is if she came by the name honestly," says I.

"And it's all the rage now. You must order one, Phœmie."

"What, the dress or the girl?" says I.

Cousin E. E. got out of patience, and sprung up red in the

face. Across the room she went, slopping along in her slippers, flung back the lid of the trunk that seemed to be overrunning with poppies, marigolds, and morning-glories, and, giving something a jerk, brought up a puffy, short gown of white muslin, blazed all over with great straggling flowers—the morning-glories, poppies, marigolds that I had seen bursting up from the trunk.

"There is a Dolly," says she, a-shaking out the puffy, short dress, as if it had been a banner.

"Not by a long shot," says I, laughing. "It may be a whopping big doll's dress; in fact, it looks like it, for what woman on earth would ever think of wearing that? Why, the flowers would set her on fire."

"This is for Cecilia," says she, "but I have one just like it, and mean to wear it if you've no objection?"

"Not the least in the world," says I. "It isn't my mission to stop peacocks from strutting and showing their half-moons if they want to."

E. E. laughed. She is a good-hearted creature, and I set store by her after all.

"I will try this on," says she. "They are all the rage, I tell you. Try one, Phœmie; your tall figure would set one off splendidly."

"Do you really think so?" says I, beginning to take a notion to the great bunches of flowers which did stand out from the white ground with scrumptious richness.

"I am sure of it. No one carries off a dress so well," says she, "and it will be expected of you. Distinguished persons are so criticised, you know."

I looked at the dress again; the flowers were natural as life; the muslin was wavy, and white as drifted snow.

"But the cost?" says I. "A burnt child dreads a blisterous contamination. That pink dress of mine is a scrumptious garment—palatial, as one might say, but costly. The value of twenty-five yards of silk is a load for any tender conscience."

"Oh, a Dolly doesn't take half as much," says E. E.; "besides short skirts are the style on the sea-shore. The expense really isn't very enormous. In fact, almost any one can afford a Dolly."

I yielded. Human nature is weak, and I had a letter yesterday from uncle Ben, saying that the hay and corn crops are promising. Besides, there is a sort of reason just now why I should be a little self-liberal in the way of dress. As Cousin E. E. says, people do expect something better than alpaca and calico of high genius—especially when the form is tall, and the figure commensurate to the genius.

"But have I time? That French dressmaker will want three weeks, at least."

Cousin E. E. saw by this that the austerity of my economical education was giving way; so she jumped up, flipped the slippers from her feet, and was soon buttoning her boots and tying her bonnet, ready for a start.

"Where are you a-going?" says I.

"Where they'll take your measure and send the Dolly home to-morrow morning, or down by express. Leave it to me, and you shall have something really beautiful."

"Let there be plenty of flowers," says I.

"Of course," says she, "bright, rich colors."

"Hollyhocks," says I, "are my favorites; dandelions and feather-edged poppies come next; then a vine of trumpet flowers tangling the bunches together, would look scrumptious."

' "I see you enter into the spirit of it," says she; "but have you got everything else?"

"Everything else? Of course I haven't. Who has, in fact? But my pink dress is turned wrong side out, and packed."

"Have you a flat?" says she.

"A flat! I? Not that I can call my own. Dempster has introduced half a dozen, but I don't claim them."

"Oh, I don't mean men, but a broad straw flat that answers for a bonnet and an umbrella."

"No," says I; "I have a Japanese thing that opens like a

toad-stool, and shuts like a policeman's club. Will that do? That Japanese embassador gave it to me, with such a tender look. I never open it that his smile does not fall upon me like sunshine in a shady place."

"That will be distinguished; take it, by all means. But you will want the straw flat, and a bathing-dress as well."

"Now, Cousin E. E., says I, "what do you mean?"

"Why, you mean to bathe, of course?"

"Cousin E. E., have you ever seen a Vermont lady—not to say a woman of genius—who did not bathe?" says I, with dignity.

"But you will go into the water?"

"To a certain extent," says I, "that has always been my habit."

"But the ocean—salt water?"

"Well," says I, "salt water is beyond me; but if that is the fashion down at Long Branch, I don't object to a trifle of salt."

"The bathing is delightful," says she. "At the turn of every tide you see parties in the water all along the shore."

"Parties in the water—*parties?*"

"Ladies and gentlemen."

"What!!"

"Children, too."

"Ladies and gentlemen bathing together! Cousin, you—well, if I were telling a story like that to a congregation of born idiots, they might believe me—that's all."

"But it is true."

"And you call this a civilized country!" says I, blazing with indignation. "Emily Elizabeth Dempster, do you mean to say that men and women—gentlemen and ladies—go down to the salt water and bathe together?"

"Indeed they do."

"I don't believe it! I won't believe it! If my great-grandmother were to rise from her grave and swear to it, I would tell her to go back again and hide her face. Somebody has been imposing on you, Cousin E. E."

"Believe it or not, it is the truth," says E. E. "Ask Dempster."

"Ask Dempster! Do you think I have lost every grain of modesty, that such an outrageous question should pass my lips?"

"Well, believe it or not, as you like," says she, "I haven't time to prove it; only it isn't worth while to scout at what every one does, and you are a little apt to do that, Phœmie."

"So, if I lived among hottentots, I mustn't object to rancid-oil on my hair—but I think I should, anyhow."

"Well, well; get on your bonnet, or the Dolly Varden will never be finished in time," says she, laughing.

I put on my beehive, and we both went right down town. On our way we saw a wire woman standing in a broad, glass window, with a dress on, that took the shine off from anything I had ever seen in the way of a dress.

"There is a Dolly," says E. E., "and really, now, I do believe it would fit you."

We went into the store, had the wire woman undressed, and her Dolly carried up-stairs, where I put it on, behind a red curtain, with a chatty female woman hooking it together, and buttoning it up in puffs and waves that made me stand out like a race-horse with a saddle on. The girl was French, with a touch of the Irish brogue—just enough to give richness to the language.

I asked her what was the reason of it, and she said in their establishment a great many of the upper-crust Irish came to trade, and she had caught just the least taste of a brogue in waiting on them—which was natural, and accounts for the accent so many of these French girls have, which I must own has puzzled me a little.

When my dress was on, E. E. and this French girl led me up to a great, tall looking-glass, and stood with their hands folded, while I took an observation. The French girl clasped her hands, and spoke first:

"Tra jolly," says she.

" No," says I, " that is not exactly my state of mind—com-posed I may be, but not jolly, by any manner of means."

" She means that the dress is beautiful," says E. E.

" Oh! " says I, " why didn't she say so then ? "

" Well, she did, in her way."

" Magnifique," says the girl, cutting the word off with a squeak.

" Why can't you open your mouth wide enough to say mag-nificent," says I, " if you like it so much; nipping off words with a bite isn't one thing or another."

" Oh, but it is, beside the dress, that figure," says she, a-spreading her hands.

After all, the girl did manage to express herself. I was sorry for not understanding her at first.

Before I could say this, Cousin E. E. got out of patience.

" Does the dress suit ? for we have no time to throw away," says she.

" Suit," says I, turning round and round with slow enjoy-ment of that queenly figure in the glass. " Of course it does. Why, cousin, it is superb; the bunching up is stupendous. Then the pattern—a whole flower garden in full bloom."

" Then it had better be sent home at once, for we must go early in the morning," says she, short as pie crust.

I paid for that Dolly Varden with satisfaction. It might have been dear—I think it was, but there were no extras, and I knew what I was about from the first. Besides it was a smashing affair, rain-bowish, beautifully puckered up, and blazing with flowers.

Well, we went into the street, and then Cousin E. E. began :

" One minute, Phœmie; I want some hair pins."

We went into the next door and got the hair pins, then out again. After walking about fifty feet she broke out once more :

" Dear me, I forgot the black ribbon."

In she darted through another door, and came out stuffing

a bit of twisted paper into her pocket.   Ten feet more and she turned square about:

"Some pins, Phœmie; I must get some pins."

So we kept darting in and out of doors till there wasn't another in the street, and went home with both our pockets stuffed full of pins, lace, gloves, combs, buttons, and a general assortment of other small things, all of which E. E. had forgotten till the last minute.

That night I left her plunged headforemost into a huge trunk, with a sloping roof, her feet just touching the ground, and complaining bitterly because Dempster was not at home to help press the things down.

LXXVII.

STARTING FOR LONG BRANCH.

ARLY the next morning a big wagon-load of trunks drove from the door.   Then a carriage came up ready to take us to the boat.   It was awful hot, and the air in that house was so close one could hardly breathe.   The parlors were all shut up.   The stone girl and that other fellow had white dresses on, and for once made a decent appearance. The chairs and sofas were all done up in linen, the blinds were shut, and the whole house looked like a church whose minister had been sent off on his travels at the expense of an adoring congregation.

E. E. and I stood in the hall, I with a satchel in my hand, she with a little brown affair buckled on one side of her waist.

That child was a-standing in the open door, watching the men pile the trunks on the wagon.

"Mamma," she called out, as the man drove away, "I'm sure they have left a trunk, for I counted, and there was only nineteen."

E. E. ran to the foot of the stairs.

"Dempster, Dempster!"

Down came Dempster, looking hot and worried.

E. E. called out:

"Do stop the wagon, something is left."

Dempster ran into the street, stopped the man, and stood in the hot sun counting over the trunks. His face was in a blaze when he came back.

"It's all right," says he, "twenty of them, full count. Come, get into the carriage."

E. E. moved forward a step or two, then halted.

"The basement door—is it bolted?"

Dempster dived down to the lower hall and up again, panting for breath.

"The scuttle," said E. E., pointing upwards.

Dempster rushed upstairs, banged away at the roof, and ran down again.

E. E. drew down her veil, and tightened her shawl.

"Oh, Dempster, have you locked the wine-cellar?"

Again Dempster made a rush into the depths of the earth, and came up again dripping with swe—well, perspiration.

"There, I think everything is safe now," he said, offering E. E. his arm.

She took it a moment, then dropped it suddenly.

"Dear me! Dempster, you haven't been near the stable, and I haven't a doubt it is wide open!"

Dempster said something between his teeth which I tried my best not to hear; then off he went down the pavement, looking as if he would give the world to knock some one down. By and by he came back, panting like a mad dog.

"Anything more!" says he, savage as a jack-knife, wiping his face with a white pocket-handkerchief.

"Yes, dear," says E. E.; "I'm afraid I left my parasol— just run up and see."

Dempster went, and came down with the parasol in his hand.

14*

She took it, and got into the carriage. I followed, and
"that child" dived in after me. Dempster had his foot on
the step, when E. E. broke out again:

"Oh, darling, what shall I do?—Snip has been left behind.
I think you will find her in the bath-room."

Dempster dashed the handkerchief across his face, ran up
the steps in desperate haste, and by and by came out with
E. E.'s little black dog in his arms.

E. E. reached out her arms, but Cecilia snatched it from her
father. That moment a policeman went by, and E. E. leaned
through the carriage window.

"Why, Dempster, you have forgotten to *see* the policeman."

Dempster followed the man, diving one hand down into his
pocket. I saw him draw out some money, which the man
took; then poor Dempster came back on a run, and plunged
into the carriage.

"Drive on—drive on, I say—or we'll be too late for the
Long Branch boat!"

. The man did drive on, but E. E. jerked the check-string.

"Oh, husband, do oblige me just this once—I have left my
longest back braid on the bureau!"

"No," says Dempster, "I'll be—"

I put my hand over Dempster's mouth.

"Dempster," says I, "if you ever want to be a Christian,
this is the place to begin in, for here patience can have its
perfect work."

My gentle rebuke had its effect. Dempster got out of the
carriage, and once more mounted those stone steps.

By and by he came back with a long braid of hair trailing
from his hand. Then he planted his foot on the carriage step
with decision, and says he: ·

"Drive on!" which the man did.

LXXVIII.

THAT HAIR-TRUNK.

EAR SISTERS:—We are here at Long Branch, bag and baggage—Cousin Dempster, E. E., myself, and that creature Cecilia, who is more trouble than the whole of us put together. We came down in—not on—the *Plymouth Rock*, which is nothing of the sort, but a steamboat, as long as all out-doors, with room enough for a camping·ground for the next generation on the decks, and rows of state-rooms that would line the main street of Sprucehill on both sides, and have some to let. There was a whole lot of fiddlers and horn-players on board that began to play the minute we came in sight—a compliment that I should feel more deeply if it hadn't become so common; but somehow wherever I go, those musical fellows start up, and grind and blow till one almost begins to wish for the privacy of an obscure position.

Fame is beautiful, and reputation is the glory of genius; but when they are sounded out by fiddles in broad daylight, and blasted over creation by wide-mouthed toot-horns, innate modesty shrinks within itself.

I really felt this way when a squad of music-grinders burst out in high jubilee the moment my foot touched the deck. It was a compliment, of course, but the sun was pouring down upon us, hot as a fiery furnace.

The express-men were smashing our twenty-two trunks on deck end foremost, caving one in every minute or two, and I felt too hot and anxious for reciprocity when the musicians struck up, for all the genius and ambition was just burned out of me.

When we got aboard, the thermometer was running up so fast that another hitch would have made it boil right over. Those glass things ought to be made longer at both ends.

I haven't a blinding faith in express-men since I saw three

of E. E.'s best Saratoga trunks stove in, so I let the music
storm on while I kept watch of my own hair-trunk, which
came down from my grandmother on the father's side, who fed
the calf that gave up the skin that covers that trunk only with
its innocent life. She fed it with skim-milk from her own
saucer, and set store by the trunk on that account up to the
day of her death. Then she willed it to me in a codicil, that
being more sacred than the original testament, she said, which
I cannot understand—all testaments, old or new, being first in
my estimation.

Well, of course, I kept watch of that trunk, and when I saw
a great broad footed Irishman take it from the wagon and pitch
it ten feet on deck, I just shut my parasol, clenched it in the
middle, and went up to him.

"How dare you pitch my property on end in that way?"
says I.

"I hain't touched none of your property," says he, a-wiping
his forehead with the cuff of his coat. "Never see a bit of it."

"That trunk is my property," says I, pointing toward it
with my parasol, which I still held belligerently by the middle.

"Well," says the fellow, eyeing the trunk sideways, "it
does look sort of peculiar, but still I reckon it's nothing more 'en
a trunk, after all—one of the hairy old stagers—but only a
trunk, anyhow!"

"Sir," says I, with emphatic dignity, for the honor of my
ancestors was concerned, "that is a traditional trunk—a testa-
mentary bequest from my grandmother—who was revolutionary
in her time."

"What," says the man—"what is that you say?"

Here a real nice-looking gentleman came up to where I stood,
and says he to the man:

"You should be more careful, the trunk is evidently an heir-
loom."

"You are very kind," says I, relenting into a bow; "it's
only a hair-trunk—grandmother's loom went to another branch
of the family."

" Well, anyway, I'll put the crather by itself, and bring it to yez safe, marum, never fear," says the Irishman; and with that he sat down on my blessed grandmother's trunk and wiped his face again. Then he waved his dirty hand and motioned that I should go away, which I did, and found E. E. spreading her skirts out wide on a settee, and looking as innocent as twenty lambs if any one seemed to turn anxiously toward the extra seat she was covering up for me.

I took the seat thankfully, spread my parasol, and tried to catch a mouthful of air, but there wasn't a breath stirring. The water in the harbor was smooth as a looking-glass. The sky was broad, blue, and so hot with sunshine that it blistered one's face to look up.

I put a blue veil around my beehive, and wilted down into my corner of the settee. Dempster stood by us blowing himself with a broad-brimmed hat, but not a breath of air he got.

" I'll run down and see how the thermometer is," says he. " Never—never did I swelter under such a stifler in my life."

Off he went, swinging his hat. In a few minutes he came back again, panting with the heat.

" It's a hundred," says he.

" What? " says I.

" The thermometer," says he.

" And is it that which makes things so hot ? "

" Of course," says he, " one hundred is as much as we can bear."

" Then, why on earth don't they get rid of some ? What is the use of piling-up things to this extent ? For my part I never will travel on boats that carry these red-hot thermometers again. It's as much as one's life is worth. Nitro-glycerine is nothing to it; that blows you right straight up, but these other things pile on the heat and never come to an end."

Congress ought to put a stop to such dangerous freights being piled-up in steamboats. It's enough to breed suicides on the water.

Dempster wanted to laugh, I could see that, but his face just puckered up a little, and it was all he could do in that line. So he took a camp-stool, pulled his new white hat over his eyes, and fell into a soggy sort of sleep. There he sat, kind of simmering, like a baked apple in the mouth of an oven, till the steamboat stopped on the end of a sand-bank, and gave a lazy snarl, as if it was glad to get rid of us.

After this they packed the whole cargo of live people in a line of cars, and sent them off sweltering through the sand with the engine roaring before them like a fiery dragon

---

LXXIX.

AT THE BRANCH.

Y AND BY, we came to Long Branch, where the engine gave another long whoop, and were turned out into the sunshine again among stages, wagons, carriages, and all sorts of wheeled creatures, all looking as if they had been in a whirlwind of red dust.

Cousin Dempster had sent his carriage ahead, and there his handsome bay horses stood sweating themselves black, and dropping foam into the dusty road. We got in, helter-skelter —no one cared which was first—and were driven toward the sea-shore.

When we got in sight of the water the horses made a sudden turn, and wheeled into a wide, dusty street, that runs right along the edge of the water. It was an awful grand sight, but the waves didn't seem to have strength enough to move, only gave out a lazy sob once in a while, as if they were tired of carrying so many loafing ships about that hadn't spirit enough to flap their own sails.

Long Branch is a real nice place after all; and just the broadest, coolest, and most scrumptious tavern in it is the Ocean

Hotel, which stands just back of the sea-shore, stretching its white wings widely, from the centre building a quarter of a mile, I do believe, each way. Before the house is a great green lawn, with walks and carriage roads cut through it that lead from the house to the high bank, against which the ocean keeps beating all the year round.

On each side the walks are great white marble flower-pots— vases they call them here—choke full and running over with flowers and vines, and great broad-leaved plants that looked cool and green, hot as it was.

" Oh," says Cousin E. E. " Isn't that beautiful? So fresh, so bright, it is like a moving garden."

So it was. All along those deep verandahs that run clear across the front of the hotel in double rows, were swinging baskets full of flowers and cool green leaves—hundreds of them— brightening the whole broad front of the hotel, and under them was a crowd of people—gentlemen, ladies, and children—reading, chatting, sleeping in the great easy willow chairs, or walking up and down on the soft grass.

Sisters, I know now exactly the way an Arab feels when he finds a bright spring—which they call an oasis—in the deserts of Sahara, and hears the leaves shiver and the waters murmur. This hotel looked cool, still, and refreshing like that. All the front was in shadow, before it lay the deep blue water. Inside was Mr. Leland, a potentate among hotel-keepers, ready to make us at home.

There it was again. Ovations will follow me. I had but just taken off my dusty clothes, bathed my face and hands with cold water, and stepped out on the verandah, when a storm of music burst out from a little summer-house on the grass. Wherever I go this sort of ovation follows me. Music and flowers seem to be my destiny. No matter where I roam, in all the steamboats and hotels they send storms of homage after me. Well, I am grateful, and I hope bear these honors with Christian meekness.

I have been riding all along the beach. The sun has gone

down and the ocean ripples to the softest and blandest wind I
ever felt. The vessels that move on it show signs of life now.
Their great white sails bend and strain with a look of power.
The day has been hot, but a cool wind comes off the water, and
you breathe once more.

Sisters, do not be led to suppose that the Ocean Hotel, large
and grand as it is, means all Long Branch. Why, there is a
mile of hotels and cottages running along the beach, all swarming over with people. As you ride up the street you pass dozens
and dozens of little summer-houses, full of young people looking out at the sea, which comes in with a slow rush and swell
now that leaves a lonesome feeling in the heart.

LXXX.

THE RACE-COURSE.

HERE is a race-ground three miles from here, where
everybody is going this morning, though the weather
is hot and the ocean is sound asleep, with great silver
scales of sunshine trembling over it.

New York has come down in crowds to Long Branch, and all
the hotels have emptied themselves on to the race-course. Three
miles of road are covered with moving carriages, wagons and
stages—one cloud of yellow dust rolls along the road without a
break. Every carriage is gay with brightly dressed ladies.
Thousands go up or down on the railroad, whose engine stops
and pours out clouds of black smoke close by the race track.
From the cars a stream of people flow on to the course, packing
themselves into the benches of the Grand Stand, or scattering
on the grass around it.

When we got into the enclosure fifteen thousand people were
waiting, some in the hot sun, others in the hot shade, all choked
with dust and sweltering with heat.

We were late. There was but one thing that we wanted to see: the race between Longfellow and Harry Bassett—two of the swiftest horses in the country.

If horses could gamble I should call these two beautiful creatures black-legs, and the gayest of gamboliers; but as they can't do it themselves men and women do it for them.

This time twenty-five thousand dollars was to go to the swiftest horse—twenty-five thousand dollars—enough to build a meeting-house. Doesn't it make you tremble in your shoes; but that isn't all. Everybody was betting with everybody else, just for the fun of betting.

I saw a little shaver there, ten years old, who boasted that he had won three pair of gloves from a little girl of eight.

The cream of that fifteen thousand skimmed itself off and consolidated in a handsome square building that they call the Club House. We went there, of course, and soon got seats among a crowd of upper-tenists on the roof, which took in a view of the whole race-ground.

One or two horses, with funny little fellows on their backs, were moving up and down before the Grand Stand, but no one seemed to care about them. Harry Bassett and Longfellow were all they wanted in the way of fast horses.

Sisters, don't fancy now that Longfellow is of a poetic, or even literary, turn of mind. Nor do I want you to think that his owner named him after our great New England poet because he was fired with admiration of his genius. Nothing of the kind. I don't suppose that "old Kentucky gentleman" ever read a line of Longfellow's poetry in his life—may be, though I hate to think so, he never heard of him—at any rate this great, long, swift, beautiful animal was named after himself, and nobody else. His body is long and slender, very long, and that is why the colt got his name. I wish it had been the other way, but it wasn't, and truth is truth. In fact, I'm afraid literature isn't appreciated on the race-course. It takes all the romance out of one to know that this grand young horse was named after his own body, and not after our great New Englander.

Never mind about the name now, Harry Bassett is coming down the road, and slackens his speed in front of the Grand Stand. A beautiful, beautiful animal, with limbs like a deer, and a coat smooth as satin, colored like a plump ripe chestnut. Fifteen thousand people clap their hands, stamp their feet, shout, cheer, and flutter out their handkerchiefs as the horse goes by.

Sisters, you never saw anything like it. A camp-meeting, where every man, woman, and child was just converted, might be a comparison, with drawbacks.

Harry Bassett took all this cool as a cucumber. It didn't disturb a hair on his glossy coat. The creature knew that he was being admired, and liked it—that was all. Down he came by the Grand Stand, past the Club House, where he got another ovation and another whirlwind of white handkerchiefs, and, wheeling round, walked back again and gave the other horse a chance.

Longfellow came next—a little larger, a little longer, and heavier in the limbs—a splendid horse; but he did not take my fancy as Harry Bassett did. From the first minute I wanted that chestnut beauty to beat; there was something about him, I can't tell what, but he suited me.

I was half put-out with Longfellow for being such a grand, powerful fellow. When he came opposite the Grand Stand, out flew the handkerchiefs and out rolled the thunder, just as it had when Bassett went by. Both the animals were so handsome that you couldn't help clapping your hands.

Bless you, the splendid creature didn't care a cent for it all. The crazy applause passed him like wind. He liked the fresh air, and gloried in a swift run, on his own hook; twenty-five thousand dollars were nothing to him. But he showed off his magnificient proportions and allowed the hot sunshine to stream over his brown coat with the most abominable indifference.

I insist upon it, Longfellow is a noble horse, but not so handsome or so lithe in his movement as Bassett. If these two creatures should ever come to Sprucehill, I know you will all stand by me in what I say—but then every one of you would be turned out of meeting if you only looked at a race-horse through a spy-glass.

Well, when the two handsome beasts had shown themselves off long enough, they drew up together and made ready for a start. A red flag was floating close by them. There was no noise now; not a man in all those benches clapped his hands. Instead of that, the whole crowd seemed afraid to breathe.

The red flag fell. The two horses started close together, and kept so once round the course; then that long-bodied fellow began to stretch himself a little ahead. They passed us like two arrows shot from one bow, Longfellow's head showing first. Once more they went round. Now a roll of wild, thundering noises followed them. Longfellow was ahead; you could see a gap of light between them. Beautiful Harry Bassett tried his best; but that long-bodied trooper just flew, and came out yards ahead.

I declare it riled me. I know that the chestnut beauty could have beaten if something hadn't been the matter with him. Poor fellow! he looked awfully down in the mouth when he was ridden up right into the whirlwind of noises that rejoiced over that other horse. It seemed to me as if he knew the pain and humiliation of defeat, just as well as if he had been human; I am sure he did. Still, sisters, I stand by Harry Bassett.

Oh, mercy, how hot it was coming home those three dusty miles! How tired and thankful I was when we got safely into the Ocean Hotel, with plenty of lemonade and ice-water, with a cool wind blowing up from the water.

Sisters, I sometimes think you do not quite appreciate all the sacrifices that I make for you. The great want of our society, has been a thorough knowledge of what is going on in the wide world outside of Vermont and the Hub. That deficiency I am determined to make up by extra mission duties in the direction of general human nature. In order to prove or condemn a thing, one must see it in all its features. If ignorance were goodness, the universe would be crowded with pious people. But it isn't any such thing; and your pioneers and missionaries who mean to teach, musn't be afraid to learn. Now, there is a good deal to be said about races, and if 'twere not for the betting—which is gambling, under another name— I should rather like it. A noble horse in full training is a brave sight; and, next to a noble man or woman, I, for one, am glad to see him put forward. There isn't a bit of harm in swift running; but then twenty-five thousand dollars lost and won between two horses, is a snare and a delusion that the noble beasts have nothing to do with. I do not like that, and am quite sure that you will make it a subject of particular denunciation. I hope you will. Not that such things have ever found a mite of countenance in Vermont; but horses are raised there, and that may lead to something dreadful. If a patch of ground level enough for a race-course can be found in the State, some of these New Yorkers will be for fencing it in; and the way they are progressing here, some ambitious fellow may be wanting to charter the Green Mountains for a hurdle, for horses all but fly in these parts.

Understand me—I am not blaming the animals—they are just splendid; but betting, especially among women, is my abomination. It is an open gate through which feminines slide into a habit of gambling. I don't like it, and the sooner our American feminine women know my opinion, the sooner they will be ready to turn back and consider what they are about.

LXXXI.

·CLIMBING SEA CLIFF.

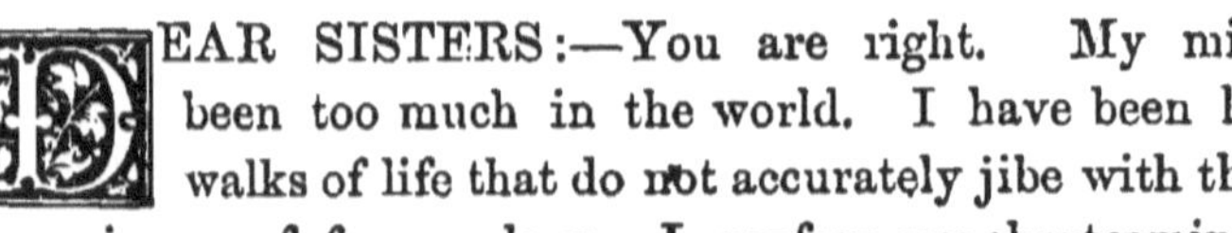

DEAR SISTERS:—You are right. My mind has been too much in the world. I have been led into walks of life that do not accurately jibe with the pious experiences of former days. I confess my shortcomings with humiliation, and am resolved on a season of mission duties in another direction than horse-races. They are exciting, and give one a high-stepping inclination. Still, my motive is good.

"Try all things, and hold fast to that which is good," is scriptural, but on some occasions may be temptations, especially when the thing that is good happens to be disagreeable, and the other is awfully enticing.

Any way, sisters, I am determined to do my duty in every walk of life, and the foremost duty this moment takes me far away from Long Branch, puts me on two steamboats and two short snatches of railroads, which land me at the foot of a great, sandy, high-sloping hill—some people call it a bluff— but which religious people of several denominations call " Sea Cliff Grove."

Now, Sea Cliff Grove is a sacred institution, lifted high up toward Heaven, and bathed in an especial odor of sanctity, conglomerated from ever so many different churches, and so centralized in a place that may, to the fanciful mind, be considered a city set on a hill.

Indeed, it is. If Jordan is a hard road to travel, Sea Cliff Grove is an awful hill to climb, even in a covered stage, with two long, thin horses dragging the blessed pilgrims upward with all their might.

Before we got clear up, there was now and then an encouraging glimpse of brightness from the dome of the tabernacle, covered over with tin, which blazed and sparkled and shone in the hot sunshine, till it set one's brain to sweltering. If it hadn't been for a cool fringe of trees running along the edge of the hill, it seemed to me as if the whole bluff must have burned up, and gone off in a blaze of glory. That dome, which looked like a great cone, roofed in with milk-pans set on edge, was the crowning glory of a new tabernacle—not the one built without hands, for it took a great many hands to build this great, rambling affair, besides the cottages and tents and long, open stoops, that look out on the sea from morning till night.

Among these tents and little houses and the great tabernacle, the man who drove us took his ten cents a-piece, and set us down, and wheeled about, singing "Old Hundred" to his horses, and swinging his whip with slow solemnity as he lumbered down hill again.

Then we started off afoot in search of Cousin Dempster's cottage, for he had sent on ahead, and hired one of the little cubby-houses for us to stay in till the religious season was over.

We found our cubby-house at last, but somebody else had got their nine points of the law out of it. So the man sent on beforehand had pitched a tent on the grass, which we went into like Indians just returned from a hunting-party—dusty, thirsty, and sort of wolfish for something to eat.

We took off our bonnets, and pinned them by the strings to the walls of the tent, which were of the best tow-cloth I ever saw out of Vermont. Then we shook ourselves, as hens do when they have been rolling in the dust, and pushed back our hair with both hands, which E. E. said was making a rural toilet worthy of the occasion. Then I, with the kindest intentions, shook out E. E.'s—full panier—and found it puckered-up with green burdock burs, which she had got on from the weeds on her way to the tent. These I picked off, one by one, while she was stamping her foot with a spirit that shocked me dreadfully in that sacred place, for all around us the people were singing and praying, and shouting "Hallelujah" and "Amen" and "Glory," in a way that made the pious teachings of my grandmother rile up within me. I looked upon the burdock burs as a judgment upon Mrs. Dempster, especially as I hadn't any puckerings in my dress to catch them in, and she had brought all her wordliness on her back.

LXXXII.

FIGHTING FOR TIIE BODY.

Y AND BY the shouts and noises hushed up a little, and there was a stampede, like a rush of cattle, in the grounds.

"Come," says Dempster, "or we shall get nothing to eat."

"Does that mean dinner?" says E. E., with a hungry look.

" Just that," says Dempster, " so look sharp ; for here it is every man for himself, and the——"

" Dempster ! " said I, stepping back with pious horror, " do you know where you are ? "

" Exactly ; bnt I know, too, that unless we look sharp, we shall feel flat when we get to the dining-hall and find everything swept off."

We took the hint. I lifted the skirt of my alpaca dress gently, between my thumb and forefinger, just enough to give an idea of the ankle without revealing it, and went out of the tent, imbued with the spirit of the place, but humiliated with worldly craving.

Sisters, if the denizens of this Sea Cliff are only half as earnest in their souls' salvation as they are in replenishing poor, frail human nature, there will be a glorious harvest of regeneration this holy season. The way they poured out of the tents, the houses, the long stoops, and through the bushes was fluttering and noisy as the flight of ten thousand chickens from a barn-yard. Still the crowd did not break all at once from the spiritual to the temporal wants of human nature. They kept on praying and singing in breaks and snatches clear up to the dining-hall, when the old earthly Evil One got uppermost, and each man seizing a knife and fork, went at the first dish he saw, and held on to it with one hand, while he did double express duty with the other.

Sisters, this crowd of sinners sanctified, and to be sanctified, was made up of about the hungriest mortals that I ever set eyes upon. The way those safety-seeking souls took care of their bodies was regenerating, I can tell you. For my part, after seeing every dish swept away from before me, with Christian fortitude becoming to the place, my carnal nature rose uppermost, and, seizing upon a plate of summer squash, I held on to it valiantly, while E. E. snatched a potatoe with its jacket on, from a flying dish, and Dempster wrestled with one of the saints for a plate of bread, as Jacob wrestled with the angels; only this saint was six feet high, wore a hood-brimmed straw hat, and carried off the plate of bread in his hands, after all.

I greatly fear Cousin Dempster didn't meet this test of a meek and lowly spirit with the fortitude of a martyr. In fact, I'm afraid he said something beside " Amen " between his grinding teeth, when that plate disappeared.

As for E. E. and myself, we got a spoon between us, and dined on the squash, generously giving up the potato to Dempster, with an admonition which did not seem to suit him much better than that stone-cold vegetable.

Well, when we had vegetated the inner man to this extent, and watched the swarm of hungry eaters devouring the food like a cloud of ravenous locusts, Cousin Dempster laid down his potato-peel on the table with mournful sadness, and said, plaintively :

" This is all we are likely to get; let us go."

" Wait," says I, " some one is going to return thanks."

" What, for two spoonfuls of squash and one hollow-hearted potato for three of us ?   Never ! " says Dempster.

Really, sisters, the spirit will have a tough job before it brings the proud nature of Cousin Dempster into a state of perfect sanctification. E. E. and I gave him a beautiful example, and looked as humbly grateful as two hungry female women could, over a double spoonful of watery squash; I fear he did not appreciate it though, for when a deep Amen rolled down the hall, after the thanks were given, he meanly growled out—well, a very peculiar word, that made my heart jump into my mouth. In any other place, I should write out boldly that Cousin Dempster—but in that out-door sanctuary—no, the secret of what he said shall go with me to my grave.

LXXXIII.

. LIONS AND LAMBS.

SISTERS:—The tabernacle under that tin roof will hold, well packed, six hundred anxious souls—each with a weak, human body attached. The seats are all cushioned with the softest pine, and have luxurious board backs. A stage rises grandly for the ministers of many churches who harmonize and fraternize like lions and lambs, each shepherding his own flock and drawing converts into his fold, wherever he can find a straggling sinner on his knees. The dining-room all at once emptied itself into the tabernacle; the ministers mounted the stage, and out in front came a man whose first words woke you up like the blast of a war trumpet.

A stout, smart, almost grand-looking man, who looked over the crowd as if he owned every man and woman in it, and meant to regenerate them in flocks, or turn them over to what-you-may-call-him at once. His dark face, broad forehead, and silver-gray hair looked strong, if not handsome. His light eyes gleamed out from behind a pair of gold spectacles, and when he got in earnest his heavy brows drew together and left deep lines between them which made him look stronger yet.

"Who is that?" I whispered to Cousin D.

"Inskip," says he, "the greatest gun amongst them."

"Dear me!" says I.

There was no time to say more, for that great gun was pouring a hot storm of eloquence into the crowd, and stirring it up as a north-easter lashes the hemlocks on our mountains. Sisters, the scene was wonderfully impressive. I felt the old revival spirit in all my bones. When he stopped a minute for the crowd to say Amen, the word rattled out like a discharge of guns on a training day.

By and by his discourse grew warmer and more startling. He just pitched headforemost into the cause, and stirred up that great congregation like a tornado. The Amens grew noisy, and were let off from lip to lip like fire-crackers on a Fourth of July. Then some one sang out " Hallelujah ! " and another " Glory, Glory, Glory ! " till the whole congregation broke into a young earthquake. Some started up, some rocked on their seats, and half a dozen fell to the ground, trembling, praying, and shouting " Hallelujah."

There was a mixture of all sorts of people in the crowd, which made it yeast over like a baking of bread when the rising is lively. When one got a-going the rest set in. Half the crowd were crying and the other half clapping hands.

Then Mr. Inskip rested a little, and a real handsome young gentleman stood up and sung beautifully. When he got through, the crowd joined in, every man, woman, and child singing on his own hook, which was noisy, and might have been harmonious if half of them had settled on the same tune, which they did, but cut across each other and sung out " Glory," when they forgot everything else, which made the music a little uneven.

Of course when a crowd like that gets a-going in a full blast of eloquence, stirring up consciences, and dancing and thrilling along the nerves, there is sure to be a whirlwind of magnetism heaving souls against each other till they cry out with the shock.

I looked around; the crowd was all in commotion; every face burned with excitement of some kind, for under that man's voice human nature was stirred, aroused, lashed into a fury of wild enthusiasm. Female women grew pale, and trembled on the hard seats ; men wilted down into childish softness ; children cried and shouted.

Before the stage was an open space, left free for sinners under conviction to come up and beseech the thrice-regenerated ministers to exhort and pray for them. Into this space those mostly stricken in the crowd, came like sheep looking for a shelter, some sobbing, some praying, some half sullen, as if the man's eloquent pleading for souls had forced, rather than persuaded them into that "Pen of the Penitents." But with each new convert, Brother Inskip broke forth in a new place, and the crowd shouted "Glory!" "Amen!" "Hallelujah!" till you could not hear yourself think.

The enthusiasm was catching. I felt it blaze and tremble over me from the crown of my head to the sole of my foot, and when a young minister joined in, and poured the notes of a beautiful hymn on the tumult, my heart fairly swelled with the glory of it.

I looked around for my cousins.

There was Dempster, with the eyes fairly dancing in his head, clapping his hands like an overgrown boy, though he did drop them when he met my look, and turned his head away, half ashamed of his own feelings.

I looked around for E. E., who sat with her mouth half open, while sobs came through her trembling lips.

"Oh, cousin, cousin, what shall I do? Have I really been regenerated, or has the Lord sent me here this day to be made a new creature?"

I did not answer her ; there was no chance for free thought or cool reason in a crowd like that. In fact, I began to feel like a vile sinner, myself, and as if being unregenerated was the duty of every female woman every time a camp-meeting offered a good opportunity. Seeing E. E. crying there as if her heart were breaking up, and both men and women wild with joy or grief all around me, I just caved in, pulled out my handkerchief, and sobbed with them, though what on earth we were all crying about I couldn't have told to save my life.

The truth was, the more some women cried the more others shouted; and when the meeting was over, everybody told everybody else what a refreshing time they had experienced under Brother Inskip's preaching, which was true as the Gospel, if tears refresh the soul as rain does the earth.

LXXXIV.

EXPERIENCES.

AFTER the preaching was done, the crowd broke up into sections and had a half-dozen prayer-meetings and spontaneous love-feasts, where men and women, and sometimes little children, got up and told all the strangers within hearing how wicked they had been—with tears, and sobs, and groans, that made one's heart ache. Still one and all of them seemed to enjoy their own depravity and put themselves down as such horrible sinners, that any amount of praying could not have dug them out of the degradation into which they dived headforemost and seemed to revel in, for a thousand years at least.

Everybody told his experience.

Among the rest, a young man from the Hub, slim as a beanpole and fiery as a race-horse, prayed and shouted, and sung, and blazed away at the crowd, like all possessed. His straight, black hair was parted down the middle of his forehead, and his mustache rose and fell like fury as the words of warning came like red-hot shot through his lips.

"Who is that?" says I to Cousin Dempster, who was listening with all his heart.

"That," says he, "is Corbett, the young fellow who shot Wilkes Booth through the crevices of the old barn in which he had taken shelter."

I shuddered all over, and I'm afraid the spirit of prayer had a shock.

That young man was about the last person I should have expected to see praying, storming, and exhorting at a camp-meeting. He told us all how he had become so sanctified by the Lord, that small-pox could not touch him, though he went into the midst of it and nursed people down with the deadly disease, right straight through.

In fact, he seemed to think sanctification a certain preventative against small-pox, only I suppose you must be sure to get the genuine thing, just as he had got it.

Then another little fellow got up and told us that he had been an awful bad boy in his early days, and learned to chew tobacco and drink cider-brandy when he wasn't more than knee-high to a grasshopper. That the cider-brandy and tobacco had stuck in and defiled him through and through, till nothing but saving grace could have washed him clean and made his soul white as a lamb, which it then was, Glory hallelujah.

All the congregation chimed in here and struck up a solemn chorus of Glory, Glory, Glory, Glory, which ended in a rejoicing " Amen," when the young man informed us that religion had reformed all his depraved tastes, and now he both hated and despised cider-brandy, tobacco, and all the abominations he had formerly hankered after.

Before the young man sat down, another was on his feet, brimming over with sympathy.

" I too," says he, " have got an experience which urges me to bear testimony that what our precious brother says is true. I know it. I feel it in my own soul, for I, too, have met with regeneration, whereby all things with me have become new. Why, brethren, before I got religion I couldn't bear the sight of tomatoes, cooked or raw. They were an abomination to my unconverted mind; but now that I have got religion, there isn't a wigitable that grows, which I set store by as I do tomatoeses. So I can testify that old things pass away, and everything becomes new."

After bearing this testimony, the man wiped his mouth with one hand, and sat down, his head meekly bowed.

"Cousin," says I to E. E., "as camp-meetings do not belong to our special persuasion, and as I do not feel the regenerating spirit grow strong in my bosom just at present, supposing you and I go back to the tent? Don't you see it is getting to be after dark now, and we have had an awfully warm day in all respects."

Cousin E. E. arose, looking heavy-eyed and worn out.

"Yes, Phœmie," says she, "I have gone through a good deal, and feel the nothingness of everything but religion. Oh, cousin, if one could always feel as we do here."

I shook my head, but only answered:

"Come, cousin, we can hear the still, small voice better alone in our tent."

She yielded, and we started to make the best of our way out of the crowd, but five or six thousand persons swarmed around that regenerating camp-ground, and it was some time before we got safely into our own tent. Then I sat down by Cousin E. E., drew a deep, long breath, and said, "Thank goodness," with all my heart.

LXXXV.

THE SECOND DAY.

DEAR SISTERS:—I have been two days at this camp-meeting, fasting, because I have given up the fight about something to eat, and awake all night because the hot weather almost drove me into the anxious seat, from dread of a hotter place.

I hope you are satisfied with the way I have been walking this straight and narrow path of missionary duty. I wish I could say quiet path, but, being of an honest turn of mind, I must say it is both steep and noisy. · Just at this minute a prayer-meeting and revival is going on in the next tent to ours and the groaning and shouting is enough to drive one crazy. The tent is crowded full of women and children, and I don't know which jump the highest or make the most noise.

Well, I am not a wife—which you know is not my fault; neither am I a mother, which, under the circumstances, I am grateful for; but why little boys and girls should be brought here, and put in the way of a second birth, puzzles me. One event of that kind ought to be enough for any family of moderate ambition. · In fact, I know of people who would do without any, with Christian fortitude. But here we are—men, women, and children—trying to save each other with all our might, and doing it in a way that brings strangers together with a jerk sometimes.

Just as we were coming into the camping-ground this morning, where the whole road was beginning to swarm again, a nice old lady, in a gray dress, and with a little, white muslin shawl pinned over her bosom, came up to me, and, lifting her meek eyes from under her sugar-scoop bonnet, informed me that the Spirit was upon her. She was exercised with a sense of duty regarding my sinful condition, which was miserably apparent in the white feather that curlecued itself around my hat, and the cut of my gaiter boots that had heels enough to send a dozen souls to everlasting ruin.

I looked down at my boot, which is a scrumptious one, and said, with thankfulness, that I couldn't see anything in them that should carry the souls off; besides, they could be heeled again.

The woman shook her sugar-scoop bonnet at me, mournfully, and said something about a wicked and perverse generation, as if all mankind were standing in my gaiter boots, and she was rebuking it in a lump.

" Oh, sister ! " says she, " if I could only make you see with my eyes, and hear with my ears ! Why will you be so per. verse ? Have you no fear of the eternal flame that burneth and burneth forever ? "

"Fear!" says I, a-looking up at the hot sun, and wiping my forehead. "I should think so! If all creation has a hotter place than this, I'm too big a coward to hurry that way. If there is an ice-house in the neighborhood, I should prefer that by all manner of means, by way of a punishment, if I deserve any."

"Ice!" says she, solemnly. "Ice! have you never read the Scriptures?"

"Several times," says I, with sarcastic forbearance. "My father had a book of that kind, which he sometimes opened."

She could not understand the delicate irony of this answer; but pressed forward like an old camp-meetinger as she was.

"Did that good father never read of a place where a drop of water could not be found to cool a certain person's tongue?" says she. "If not, your paternal ancestor fell short of his duty. It is no wonder his child should have gone half through life without a ray of saving grace, and with a white feather in her hat."

Sisters, I was riled. "Half through life," says I. "Madam, do you know how old I am?"

She looked at me half a minute, with all the eyes in her head; then, with the cool air of a woman counting money, said, "about for—"

Sisters, I *cannot* repeat the audacious falsehood of that creature's calculation. It was enough to rile up venom in the heart of a born cherubim. If ever a fiend took the disguise of a sugar-scoop bonnet, I have encountered one. A heart of stone lay under the innocent folds of that muslin half-shawl.

"Madam," said I, with a look of overpowering indignation, "you must have begun and ended your arithmetic in multiplication. Take off half of the years you have mentioned."

The woman smiled so knowingly, that I longed to — Well, no matter, she smiled, and says she:

"At any rate, you are not too old for the mercy-seat."

"I should think not," says I.

"Look yonder."

I looked at half a dozen children jumping, kneeling, praying, and singing before the revival tent, which had been so full of worrying noises all night long, that none of us had got a wink of sleep.

"Look," says she; "unless you are born again, and become like one of these, there will be no chance that you will ever enter the kingdom of Heaven."

I looked at the lovely children, and I looked at her.

"Excuse me," says I, "the object don't seem quite equal to the trouble. I have no notion of going backward in my life. In the first place I was too handsome a baby in the beginning to hanker after a change, and since then—I say nothing; but really, I have seen a good many people that claim to have been born again, and, so far as I can judge, they don't look a mite better, or a day younger, after taking all the trouble, which is discouraging."

"Discouraging!" said the woman; "why, you are talking of regeneration! Come—come with me to the anxious-seat—hundreds are flocking there now."

"Excuse me," says I, "if you please. Crabs may change their shells, and snakes creep out of their skins—I rather think they do sometimes—but born-again females look so much like the old pattern, that it don't seem to me worth trying after one is grown up."

"Many an older person than you are has been born again," says she.

"You don't say so," says I, a-fanning myself with a palm-leaf, for every drop of blood in my body grew hot when she talked about my age, and I was mad enough to bite a tenpenny nail in two with my front teeth.

"Yes, I do say so, humble as I am," says Sugar-scoop. "Look out there. See those women in Israel—three precious souls, just gathered into the fold. For two days they have been constantly at the redemption-seat. The spirit is upon them now. Their souls are struggling to be free. Before another morning they will be born again."

15*

I looked at a group of women she pointed out, and the human nature within me yeasted over. They were three of the homeliest creatures I ever set eyes on—long and lank, with faces like sour baked-apples.

"Oh, my beloved sister," says Sugar-scoop, a-laying her cotton-gloved hand on mine; "can you look on that heavenly sight and not pray to be like unto them?"

I shook the cotton glove from my arm, and the hand that was in it, just as St. Paul shook off the viper.

"Like them, madam—like them! If I were one-half as lank and homely, I should want to be born again once a week, at least."

Sugar-scoop lifted both hands in awful horror.

"There are souls," says she, "given up to eternal darkness, I fear. Oh, sister, how I tremble for yours!"

I was trembling with indignation. What right had this woman to assault me in this fashion? I did not know her; she did not know me. My white feather was a badge of noble patriotism; my gaiter boots fitted a foot that has been an object of encomium with every shoemaker who has been honored by taking its measure—to say nothing of a glance given it by imperial eyes. Does religious zeal justify uncivil intrusion? What right had this sugar-scoopy woman to exhort me? How did she know that my heart was not already in the right path?"

I asked this very question:

"Madam," says I, "by what right do you pretend to teach me, a stranger, of whose life you can know nothing?"

"I'm in the service of the Lord," says she, "looking up lost sheep. When I find one, torn and draggled with sin, it is my duty to drive it into the fold, where its fleece can be worked white as snow."

"But how can you tell? By what authority do you claim the right to judge of a person you have never seen?"

"Are we not told to go out into the highways and the hedges, and force them to come in?" says she.

" Whether they want to or not ? " says I.

" Exactly," says she; " their not wanting to come into the fold shows the state of wickedness into which they have fallen."

" But how do you know that I *am* wicked ? " says I.

She looked at me a long time, as if the idea were new to her. She had been so eager in raking up sinners, that it seemed to hurt her feelings to think that any human being she met wasn't on the high road to—well, what's its name ?

" That feather," says she, " isn't a mark of regeneration."

" No," says I, " but it is the badge of a patriotic idea."

The creature didn't take in this delicate political hint. In fact, anything fine or keen is sure to puzzle your woman of one idea.

" Where do you go to meeting ? " says she, as abrupt as a cracked stick.

" Where my father did, generally," says I.

She looked at me queerly from under her sugar-scoop.

" Haven't backslid, nor nothing; because, if you have, re- member, before it is too late, that the last state of a backslid- ing sinner is worse than the first."

LXXXVI.

THE BLACKSMITH'S CONVERSION.

EFORE I could answer that audacious woman, a man came along with green spectacles on his eyes, and a broad straw hat on his head.

" What, sister, hard at work ? got hold of a case, I reckon ; but press forward to the mark of the prize."

" Oh, brother," says Sugar-scoop, " can't you stop a moment, and sow a morsel of seed on this barren rock. This is a precious sheep."

" Lamb, if you please," says I, quickly.

" No," says she, as smooth as oil, but no doubt boiling over with inward spite, " I have eyes, and can see. Sheep is the word. She is a precious sheep that, perchance, has once been in the fold, but is wandering far away from the straight and narrow path."

" A backslider," says he, eying my face over his spectacles.

" Hardened,". says she.

" Take her to the anxious-seat. Brother Blank is just the man for her case. You've heard of Brother Blank, just from the West, and burning with zeal. Heard of the way he converted a blacksmith out there—a great, stout, burly, unregen-. erated fellow. Why, compared to him, this poor, sinful creature is just nothing. That was a mighty work. What, you never heard of it? Well, I was there, and heard all about it on the spot.

" You see, Brother Blank, who belongs to the Methodist wing of this camp-meeting, was sent out by the conference to a sparse Western district, where the meeting-houses were a good way apart, and there was any amount of horseback riding to be done. On the cross-roads, near one of the stations, there was a blacksmith shop, where a great, two-fisted, tough old sinner was blowing up red-hot coals into red-hot flames, morning and night, which ought to have reminded him of the eternal fires which threatened him, but only kindled his wicked soul into fierce rebellion against God.

" Now this fellow had an awful spite against the ministers, and never let a new one pass his shop, without going out with his leather apron on, and a hammer in his hand, to scare the pious soul half to death with abuse, if nothing worse. When Brother Blank came on the district, he had to ride by the four corners like the rest; but he was a brave soldier of the Cross, and rode a first-rate horse, besides. being a tall, powerful man in body as well as in spirit. I rather think he had heard of the blacksmith, but that made no difference to him, he neither rode faster nor slower when he came in sight of the shop, but looked straight ahead, and trusted in the Lord.

"The moment Brother Blank came in sight, that miserable heathen brought his hammer down on the anvil with a crash, flung it across the shop, and went out with his fists clinched, his great bony chest bare, and his eyes blazing like sin.

"'Hallo!' says he, standing right in the middle of the road.

"'Hallo!'

"Brother Blank drew up his horse, and says he:

"'What's wanting, my friend?'

"'I want you to just tumble down from that saddle, and pay toll,' says the old sinner. 'No minister passes this corner without stopping to take a thrashing from these.'

Here the blacksmith held up two clinched fists, hard and black as sledge-hammers.

"'No nonsense; but get off, I say,' he bellowed out.

"Brother Blank had a heavy whip in his hand, with a short plump lash, which he began to play with.

"Get down, I say!"

"Brother Blank got down and laid the bridle on the neck of his horse.

"'Now step out here and take it like a man,' says the blacksmith. 'The last two ministers were such puny fellers, there was no fun in thrashing them; but you're something worth while. Stand out, I say.'

"While he was talking, the fire-blowing wretch rolled up his red flannel shirt-sleeves to the elbow, and went at Brother Blank with both fists.

"Now, sisters, Brother Blank is a true Christian—meek as a lamb in prayer and persuasion, but the sight of that audacious old sinner riled up the natural man in him awfully. He stepped back. His right arm swung out, and that whip-lash curled round the fellow's bronzed neck like a garter snake. Again and again the lash fell, now across the red face, now across the naked arms, but generally left great red welts, like the bars of a fiery gridiron, across his chest.

"Blind with the blows, and crazy with rage, the fellow struck out fiercely, but the lash stung him at every point, and at last he was glad to yell for quarters. Then it was that Brother Blank remembered that his mission was to convert sinners.

"'Down upon your knees,' says he, pointing to the dusty road with his whip—'down upon your knees, and pray the Lord to forgive your sins.'

"Down the fellow went, plump on his two knees, and down Brother Blank went beside him right in the dust of the street; and the way he wrestled for that blacksmith's soul was a lesson to all faltering Christians.

"'Lift those blood-shot eyes to Heaven and pray,' says he, and his voice was tender with compassion.

"'I won't. Pray for me,' says the sinner.

"He did pray. All the old Adam had left Brother Blank's soul when he laid down that whip. It was flooded now with the milk of human kindness. In a voice, strong as his right arm and clear as his conscience, he poured forth a petition to Heaven, so loud, so powerful, so full of Christian force, that the blacksmith began to tremble on his knees, the two hands that had been clenched like sledge-hammers clasped themselves, till the palms met and were uplifted to Heaven as a child pleads with its mother.

"By and by another voice—hoarse, deep, and earnest—joined with the prayer of Brother Blank. All that it said was, 'God be merciful to me a sinner;' but that was enough, for there was that stout old reprobate with his face to the earth, his broad chest swelling with repentance, and great tears making furrows through the cinders and ashes on his cheeks, penitent as a child, and meek as a spring lamb.

"When Brother Blank saw this, his feelings came forth in a grateful shout, tears leaped down his own cheeks, and in one voice these two men thanked God for the soul that had been saved."

When the man with green spectacles had finished his story, he took out a silk handkerchief from the crown of his hat and wiped his own eyes; then turning to the Sugar-scoop, says he:

"Let this encourage you to persevere to the end, for 'while the lamp holds out to burn, the vilest sinner may return.' If this person is hardened in the perversity of a depraved nature, think of the blacksmith, and do not despair."

"Did that heathen blacksmith hold out?" says I, so interested in the cindery wretch that I passed over his comments about my perversity.

"Hold out!" says he; "I saw him at a camp-meeting three years after, and heard him tell the story with his own lips. Brother Blank himself was sitting on the speaker's stand, and the blacksmith pointed him out to the people, and called on him to say if it was not his prayers that had snatched him as a brand from the burning.

"Brother Blank got up and walked with a lazy motion down the platform. Putting both hands behind him he smiled benignly down on the agitated face of his old enemy. Then he looked around on the congregation, and spoke:

"'Yes,' says he, 'I really do believe that I was the humble instrument of mauling some grace into that precious brother's soul.'

"Sisters, that was a glorious moment for Brother Blank; think of it—a human soul turned heavenward in the midst of its wrath; persevere with this one. Leave her not till she is brought to the anxious-seat, and so by regeneration to membership with the church."

"But I am a Church member," says I.

"A Church member?" says the man with spectacles.

"Certainly," says I.

"In good standing?" says the woman, dropping her underlip.

"A missionary from one of the first societies in the world," says I, with becoming dignity.

The woman with the sugar-scoop bonnet looked at the man with spectacles, and the man with spectacles looked at the woman with the sugar-scoop bonnet. Before they could begin again I bowed my head with a lofty and dignified air, and walked away; which, I take it, was something of a rebuke to people whose religious zeal runs ahead of their good breeding.

I have left that camp-ground and descended a hundred or two feet nearer the earth again, without feeling the worse or very much the better for it. The path of duty is sometimes awful steep. I found this precipitous to a wonderful extent. I really think nothing but the saving grace of church-membership kept me from the anxious-seat; but the opportunities of a new birth are not unlimited, and when one is folded and tethered among the lambs, there is a little awkwardness when you are exhorted to have it all done over again by a new minister and another church. Fortified with a certificate of church membership, I passed through the whirlwind and storm of this camp-meeting, with that graceful dignity which has won the high post you have kindly imposed on me.

True, sisters, the pressure brought to bear upon me was long, strong, and persistent. A fierce raid was instituted against my back hair and the soft puffings of my frizzes in front. My white hat was a terrible source of trouble to those who want regeneration in nothing but religion; and the feather seemed to get more notice than the preaching did wherever I happened to take it.

LXXXVII.

THAT OVATION OF FIRE.

ISTERS:—I give you this little dash of camp-meeting, because I wish to level myself gradually and gracefully down to the gay sinfulness of Long Branch again, where the salt air is revivifying, and our return is a source of complimentary jubilation at this no-end of a hotel. We came here in the ten o'clock boat—that floating mansion-house, which Mr. James Fisk left as a memorial of the public good a splendid sinner can do when he is active and oriental in his taste.

I am used to these things now; but it was gratifying as we drove up in Dempster's carriage from the railway to hear a glorious burst of music swell out from a round summer-house on the lawn. A serenade of that kind was what I had not expected, and my heart swelled with not unworthy triumph when I listened. The moment that crowd of musicians saw my white feather, they struck up "Lo, the Conquering Hero comes," with a soft and touchingly subdued sweetness, which threw an exquisite femininity into the air, and plainly marked out its object.

Feeling this, I bowed a graceful recognition to those superior performers, who answered with a prolonged blast from the most curlecued of the long toot-horns as our carriage swept down the curving road that forms a horse-shoe—just a little broad at the heel—in front of Messrs. Leland's hotel.

Feeling that many admiring eyes were upon me, I stepped with dignity from the carriage, and walked with a downcast look, which I did my best to make unconscious, through the gay crowd that had gathered in front of that long portico, only just to get a glimpse of me as I went in.

Sisters, I had compassion on these people, and walked with slow gracefulness through their midst, determined to give even the humblest a chance to see how true genius can deport itself when ovations of music and respectful admiration recognize its greatness.

There was a great publisher present when we got back to the hotel. I have no doubt that he listened to the music of that band when it gave me this harmonious reception, and I hope he indirectly felt the compliment reverberate back on himself. It was an honor he deserved to share with me, or any other high-bred, intellectual person to whom he had opened a golden pathway to the Temple of Fame through his numerous art jour-nals.

I had an idea of the gentleman in my mind, and tried to single him out from the crowd of persons standing in silent homage on the balcony as I passed into the hotel, but I think he was not there.

Before the day was out, I could give a good guess at the reason why he did not appear to claim the honor of my acquaintance. He was meditating a delicate little surprise for me—one of those poetic fancies that take root only in highly artistic minds. By and by you will hear what it was.

In Washington, and at the Grand Duke's reception at Sandy Hook—why that strip of salt water, which lets ships in and out from New York to the Atlantic Ocean, is called a hook, I cannot make out, for the life of me; and as for its being sandy—well, in my opinion, it is deep, salt water, and nothing else. But, as I was a-saying, in Washington, and at Sandy Hook, the largest guns of the nation did me homage. Here I am received with bursts of music from the middle of a home-lot belonging to the hotel; but this evening the crowning glory of an ovation was given me by the great publisher, who, unseen, and with the most delicate attention, startled me into a wild enthusiasm of gratitude.

By guns on the water, by guns on shore, and by enchanting strains of music, my appearance in society has been heralded. Now the cap-sheaf has been placed on all these honors by a compliment of fire combined with the most exhilarating music. On Saturday nights, every hotel along the beach is crowded from ground-floor to gable, and gay as a spring morning. Then the husbands and brothers and beaux come down from New York, till all the trains run over with masculine humanity. When the cars come in, it really is a sight to behold. Out from a long train of cars rushes a swarm of men, with here and there a feminine sprinkling, carrying carpet-bags, satchels, umbrellas, and little baskets of fruit. Then they cluster in a thick, black cloud around the depot, like bees swarming from their hives.

The streets all around are choked up with carriages, hacks, omnibuses, wagons, and all sorts of wheeled things, in which drivers sit, on the sharp watch, and ladies and girls wait for their men folks to get in and be drove away. I beg pardon—driven away.

On Saturday night, every female seems to own a mate of some kind, and be on the watch for him. Then the engines give a snarl, and carriages make a grand start and go off in a line, stringing down Ocean Avenue a mile or so, and leaving clouds of dust rolling along the beach, each driver going it as if he were crazy to leave all the other fellows behind.

Well, this fills the whole Branch with delightful confusion. The ladies put on their most scrumptious dresses, and the masculines blaze in red and blue and green neckties that almost set you on fire.

Everybody dances on Saturday night. Streams of music pour upon you in cataracts if you walk up the beach after dark. All the doors and windows are open, and you feel dizzy with the idea that all creation has got into one grand whirl. This is Saturday night at Long Branch, as a general thing; but the particular Saturday night after we came from the camp-meeting, was the beatinest thing of all. Early in the evening the people seemed to flock in crowds to this hotel. They came afoot; they came in carriages; they came by the omnibuses, load after load. Cousin E. E. was astonished, and couldn't understand it. "Never," says she, "have I seen such a crowd before. What can it mean?"

I said nothing, but kept a deep and satisfied thinking. What did it mean? Hadn't *I* just arrived? Hadn't the news spread? Was not this a popular uprising—a great wave of homage to the worth and genius of a woman whom I did not care to mention? These thoughts were in my mind when a great storm of music broke out from that summer-house in the front home lot. Then whiz went a fiery snake, clear up into the sky, where it bent its head, opened its mouth, and poured a stream of burning stars down over the people.

Mercy, what a great crowd those falling stars lighted up! The street in front of the hotel was black with people. The long, long stoop was swarming with them—the ladies all in scrumptious dresses; the gentlemen with red and blue ribbons on their hats, and the same colors glowing at their throats. This I saw by the light of the gas-globes and of those shooting stars that dropped like great jewels through the still air. The sight of that fiery snake frightened me; I jumped like a pea on a hot shovel, and gave a little scream.

"What does it mean? What temptatious snake is it?" says I, a-trembling all over.

"It's a rocket," says E. E.; "a publishing gentleman is going to compliment the ladies with a display of fireworks."

"The ladies!" thought I, in silent irony. There is but one lady to whom so noble a compliment can be paid, and that lady—is—but no matter!

I did not say this in words. Let E. E. have her vanities and her little delusions. She does assume a few airs on account of our relationship, but I seldom notice it—let her make her little mark in society. It pleases her, and does not hurt me. Only, an ovation like this—to think she, or any one else, could share that with me, is asking a little too much.

Out went another snake, curling along the grass, shooting straight up, with a venomous blue light in its folds that was enough to frighten one; but it sort of melted away in sparks, and then a great wheel of fire—crimson, blue, green, yellow, rainbowish in every line and spoke—began to whirl round and round at the other end of the home lot, sending out great curving plumes of sparks, and twisting them into ten thousand rainbows, all winding, whirling, and shooting fire like a great wheel of jewels and revolving stars.

Another broke out, and began to whirl close to one of the mammoth flower-vases, raining light down upon it, till the great white vase shone like snow, and all the flowers it held were frosted over with a beautiful light.

Then another wheel—another and another—kindled and burst

out, sending torrents of fire every which way, changing, flashing, shooting out gorgeous flames of color, till the grass was all aglow with light, and flashed under the vivid rain of sparks like a meadow full of lightning-bugs.

Now the whole front of the hotel was blazing with wheels, and the air was alive with fiery serpents that spit forth a storm of great jewels before they died. Between the wheels, tall thickets of fire started up, and rose into quivering trees, and shot golden fruit of many colors into the air, lighting up the crowd like ten thousand gorgeous lamps tossed upward and broken as they fell.

All this time the music was swelling through the fiery display, and the crowd clapped hands, as if enough honor could not be done to the occasion. My heart swelled—I felt this homage intended by this display, and the wild sympathy of the crowd filled me with a tumult of grateful feelings.

I arose, and, with one hand on my heart, bowed profoundly every time the crowd clapped its multitudinous hands. It was a glorious moment. I longed to meet the publisher face to face, and tell him how profoundly his generosity had touched my soul; but, with that modesty which ever accompanies true merit, he kept in the background, and hid away from the thanks my soul was panting to give.

Oh, Sisters, I wish you had been here in a body to see how this great white house—a half a mile or so long—was turned into a snow-white palace by the flood of fire in front of it. Then the sea—the great, heaving sea—on the other side of the road, was red as blood, and bright as gold, when the flames shot highest. I tell you, the golden gates of the New Jerusalem could not have been more beautifully luminous.

Earth, sea, and air were kindled with light, and full of shooting-stars for a whole hour. Then, as the fires began to wane, and the jewels to melt, two great, tall balloons, striped red, white, and blue, were illuminated, and sent sailing up and up in the air, each with a trail of shooting-stars dropping along its path. Up and up, higher and higher, the balloons rose, with a slow, graceful movement, and drifted away to sea—away, away, away—till they shone like little stars, and went out in the distance.

Then a great shout went up from the pleased multitude, which increased to frenzy when I once more showed myself.

My white hat was on; the feather floated out in the air like a banner. In my hand I held a fan. In the fervor of my emotion I pressed it against my bosom. The people saw it, and the storm of applause that burst from them fairly took me off my feet. Emotion overcame me; I retired from that long stoop.

Cousin E. E. followed me. She hasn't been herself since the camp-meeting; and when I asked her if it was not a beautiful ovation, she shook her head and answered, that all flesh was grass, which I don't believe any more than I believe that grass is flesh, which I know is not the fact, each being itself independent grass and independent flesh.

"Well," says I, "call it grass, or anything you please, but wasn't the whole thing perfectly gorgeous."

"Yes," says she, "it was a pretty compliment to the ladies of the hotel."

Sisters, that jealous, provoking woman said "ladies of the hotel," not "the lady of the hotel." She is an aggravating creature, sometimes; I do believe she is jealous of the homage which is lavished on your missionary. At any rate speeches like this look like it. Don't you think so?

I said nothing. A tart reply trembled on my tongue, but the atmosphere of that camp-meeting still clung to me, and I forbore to rebuke her.

Sisters, I was too lenient; somehow or other E. E. has spread her selfish idea through this hotel. The ladies were all carried away by the fireworks—no, excuse me, that would be dangerous to such as had tindery tempers, but they could talk of nothing else, and made a great fuss about the compliment paid to them. To them—as if any man who has an appreciative soul would think of diffusing a compliment among a crowd of ten thousand people; but the vanity and presumption of some females are just disgusting. But for the secret consciousness that no one could have been intended but myself, their conceit would provoke me. As it is, let them have their conceity illusions. Others may think what they please, but I have an inner consciousness that is satisfaction enough.

LXXXVIII.

LET HIM GO.

DEAR SISTERS:—You know, or can guess, at the anxious state of mind in which a sensitive female-woman must have found her experiences since the great Grand Duke left this country. I am told that the Imperial Court of Russia is hard to please in the way of marrying its sons—that nobility is not considered enough, and nothing but the child of an emperor or of a king will satisfy the pride of Czar Alexander.

But emperors are not to be found, like huckleberries, in the woods, and those among them that have lots and lots of children can't always find mates ready cut-out and made-up for all of them in the very uppermost crust of all the world.

When emperors are scarce, and imperial children plentiful, is it strange that some of them should be sent to a free country, where the highest royalty in all the world is to be found waiting for orders.

Republics have but one kingly order, that of individual genius, which ranks above kings all over the world, and is aspired to by queens, whenever a queen is gifted with superior ambition, as little Victoria Guelph was when she wrote her book of travels, and the life of her first-class husband.

That which a queen hankers after, the son of an emperor may be glad to mate himself with. Is it wonderful, then, that a

Grand Duke of all the Russias should aspire to the first femi-nine genius of a free land, and to a certain modest extent re-ceive encouragement from her?

A union between an archduke and the first lady writer of this country—excuse me, but truth is stranger than fiction—was a consummation that you as a Society ought to expect, and this nation, in its administrative capacity, ought to have in-sisted upon. If an aspiring and unprotected female cannot re-ceive the support of her own Government, where can she go for it.

Sisters, this union between ·Sprucehill and Russia is a great national question, which ought to have agitated this country from the shores of the two oceans, the Mississppi and Rocky Mountains inclusive.

There has been considerable of an internal rumbling sort of a convulsion, earthquaky and threatening, in various sections, which ought to have given timely warning of what the true national feeling was; but somehow Russia don't seem to un-derstand it, and I'm beginning to think that there is secret treason here at home—deep, double-dyed treason—of which your missionary is the object.

It is a shameful fact that the Government has taken no sort of interest in an engagement which would have linked the two great social centres of Russia and Sprucehill in a close and lov-ing union.

From the day my Alexis had an interview with President Grant my heart-history has been allowed to drag like a lazy funeral train. Before, all was bright and luminous, with beautiful aspirations; but from that time suspense has coiled around me, hope has flared up, blinked, and almost died out. I did not understand it then. It seemed to me that fickleness was in the heart of the great Grand Duke.

But I did him a cruel injustice. If our two hearts and des-tinies are severed, it has been by the underground machina-tions of this Administration. General Grant saw what was going on, and has cruelly circumvented two young and unsophisticated hearts that were knitting together, like ivy round an oak sapling.

I am determined on ·it. The country shall hear of my wrongs. Sprucehill shall have redress for the insult put upon her favorite daughter. In all that General Grant has done· in the way of omission, nothing approaches the inactivity which has wrung my heart, as wet blankets are twisted in the strong hands of a washerwoman.

He has not written me a line. His letters must have been interrupted. Evil machinations have been at work. The Government detectives are everywhere scattering slanders and distrust. I shouldn't wonder a bit if they have been to our old homestead on Sprucehill, mousing among church registers, and interviewing family physicians. Well, let them. Since I learned to write, some figures have been changed in the old Family Bible, and, thank goodness! old Doctor Perry is dead. The keenest detective won't find much difference between 1830 and 1850. It only requires that the curve of tha three should be rubbed out, and a dash sharpened to a point added. If they look for eighteen hundred and thirty there, I can tell them it isn't to be found. Let them search—that's all !

This was my state of mind three days ago. Now I am revivified with extra animation. Hope has perched on my white hat and sits there waving its feather like a pennant.

I am glad from the bottom of my heart that I didn't follow the duke across the ocean. After all a duke is only a man, hard to catch and expensive to cage. Why should we trouble ourselves about princes and dukes and lords, when we have the most genuine of all manly articles right under our feet. Dukes are scarce and hard to scare up, but there are as good fish in the sea as ever came out of it. That's my motto to-day.

16

LXXXIX.

DONE UP IN A HURRY.

ISTERS:—the atmosphere of Long Branch is propitious, not to say exhilarating, for close by this half-mile of a hotel is another, crowded full at this time of the year, in which we can hear fiddling and dancing every night of the week. The hotels at watering-places are celebrated for several things, particularly low ceilings, widows, youngish ladies, and girls like our Cecilia, who wonder every day of their lives how their mothers ever got along decently till they were born to tell them how.

Well, the most enterprising of these hotel accompaniments are the widows. Their superior advantages of experience is just overpowering, and these advantages are used with unscrupulous freedom. I say this with feeling, being one of the class that suffers from such unwarrantable competition.

A widow was in the hotel I have spoken of. Yes, what might be called two widows rolled into one, for she had put two husbands into their little beds, and tucked in the sods comfortably before she came to Long Branch in search of a third.

Sisters, she found him; her little traps and lines and baits had been all out to no sort of purpose for three or four weeks. She danced in the parlor, exhibited all the lines of a plumptitudinous figure at the bowling alley, which is a place I never saw, but have heard about; walked on the beach with a Leghorn hat on, curled up at the ears, and in front too, and Japanese umbrella, brown outside and yellow in the interior, which looked as if she had lots of money and meant to put it on the market with a dash.

There was a great deal said about this widow. Some observed that she was handsome. Some said she wasn't— mostly ladies. Some observed how graceful she was, at which others smiled and shook their heads. One person persisted in it that she was awful rich—two or three hundred thousand dollars, at least. Then that was contradicted. Forty thousand was more than any one could prove she had. Others persisted that her wealth, like her virtues, was unlimited. In fact, being a widow, she made the best of it and let people talk, minding her snares and traps and things all the same.

Last week a strange man came to that hotel. It was Saturday morning, and the first object that his eyes fell upon at breakfast was this widow, without the sign of a cap, and with a long curl straggling down to one shoulder, very fluffy and enticing. He looked at the curl; then his eyes wandered up to the widow's face. That face had smiled through a couple of matrimonial campaigns, and received the first battery of admiring eyes with a sweet, downcast look, innocent as blanc-mange. Then she lifted her eyes with slow modesty, and glanced wonderingly at her admirer, as if she were sort of be-wildered by his looking so much that way.

The stranger did not smile, but a light came over his face when he caught that childlike glance. Then both these inno-cent creatures fell to eating. Then he happened to look up again. So did she—a romantic coincidence that sort of affini-tized them to a great extent, before anybody saw what was going on.

After breakfast the stranger hunted up some one who knew him and the widow also. An introduction brought the two halves of that pair of scissors together, and the blades fitted beautifully. All they wanted was the rivet. But wait.

At twelve o'clock that day the stranger ventured to ask a favor. Would the widow give him a little music?

The widow said she would. The sweetness of a whole boil-ing of maple sugar was in her smile as she sat down by the parlor piano, and sent her two little hands fluttering over it like a pair of white pigeons with love-letters under their wings.

The widow flew her fingers; the widow looked at the stranger from under her eyelashes, and her voice thrilled through him till he began to think of magnolias and mocking-birds and other ornamental things which soften a man's feelings down to the fluffiness of a feather bed.

When she had done singing, he asked her to walk with him on the beach. She gave another slow lift of her eyelashes, said she would, and ran upstairs after the Leghorn and the Japanese umbrella, brown and yellow, with as many bones in it as the first April shad.

They walked the beach up and down, she leaning heavier and heavier on his arm at each turn. Then they sat down on the sand with their faces to the sea, and held the umbrella so as to shade off the people on the bank—they didn't care for the sun a bit—and in that condition they sat and talked and talked and talked.

By and by he got up from the sand. She lifted her eyes with a pitiful look of helplessness. He reached out his hand, and she rose to it gracefully, like a trout to a fly. The hand clung to his more than a minute after she got up—the sand was so uneven, you see. The stranger bore this with Christian fortitude, and really seemed as if he rather liked it. In fact, he encouraged her to hold on; and she did, with her sweet widowed face lifted to his just long enough to set his heart off like a windmill, when she dropped it again.

When they came up the flight of wooden steps that leads down from the bank, both her white hands were clasped over his arm as loving as the soft paws of a kitten, and he looked like a fellow that had been out shooting doves, and had come in with his net full.

They went in to lunch, and ate spring chickens; then they ended off with silly-bubs, which is a sweet froth that melts to nothing on the tongue—delicious, but not exactly hearty food.

Two hours after lunch, the stranger asked the widow to ride out with him; which she did, in the puffiest and silkiest of dresses, and with a lace parasol, lined with pink, between her and the sun. This was one of her snares, for she depended on

that pink lining for her blushes, having left them a good way
behind her somewhere about the first wedding.

The drive was paradisical. They talked, they smiled, they
said the loveliest little things to each other with delicious
reciprocity. He drove, and divided his manly attentions between her and the horses, giving her a generous share, which
was creditable to him as a man.

It was nearly twelve o'clock that night when those two people went up to their neglected couches—nothing but a widow
would have stood the shock of such impropriety among the
critical of her sex ; but she didn't care a mite.

Early the next morning, which was Sunday, these two persons were seen coming out of the little cubby-houses under the
beach in the queerest sort of dresses—I cannot describe them,
because, up to this time, beach flirtations have been forbidden
subjects with me.

But they came out on the beach, clasped hands, and walked
right into the biggest waves they could find.

What she said to him there I cannot tell, but by and by they ·
came back to the hotel, the sneakiest-looking creatures you
ever set your two eyes on.

I don't know when it was that she brought him to the point,
but the widow had netted him so close that he didn't even try
to flounder.

That night there was sacred music in the hotel parlor, and,
somehow, a minister of the Gospel dropped in, with a white
cravat on, and waited for something, looking as if butter
wouldn't melt in his mouth.

He hadn't been there long before the strange gentleman
came in with a swallow-tailed coat on, a white vest and cravat,
with ball-gloves on his hands.

Hanging on to his arm was that widow, in a long, white
dress, that streamed after her in windrows, and with a shower
of lace falling over her.

The minister got up, and opened his book. The people
hanging about hushed their talk, and in less than ten minutes

a third gold ring was chucked over the other two that weighed down the widow's finger, and she walked off with number three as proud as a white peacock.

It took this widow just two days and part of a night to spring her traps and draw her hooks—but, then, she *was* a widow.

Sisters, there is a good deal of commotion in our hotel just now. Rural single ladies talk of going over to the other place.

I had a little hankering in that direction at first, but, come to think it over, mean to stay where I am. It isn't the house that has done this, but the bland atmosphere of Long Branch. If that sort of thing is indigenous to the place—and I mean to test it thoroughly—Russia is welcome to the Grand Duke; a whole-souled American is good enough for me. Besides, Russia is an awful cold place, and I don't think I ever could bring myself to eat cabbage-soup or the roe of a sturgeon.

Sisters, if this sort of thing lies in the atmosphere, don't you think it would be a good thing for the whole Society to come down here next summer? A generous diffusion of masculine energy into the course might be a desirable change. For my part, I don't mean to leave this place till frost comes. I believe this thing is going to be an epidemic at the Branch, and when contagions rage I am sure to catch any disease that is going. I have had the measles twice, and two pretty severe tugs with the scarlet-fever. In fact, I was celebrated, as a child, for catching double. One thing is certain—I never ran away because a disease was catching, and I'm not going to do it here. On the contrary, I am making over one of my old alpaca skirts into a bathing-dress. If I know myself I shall fight it out on that line, if it takes all winter.

CHAPTER XC.

THE YELLOW FLAG.

EAR SISTERS:—I have gone and done it! Now let me give you a little wholesome advice. It comes out of my superior knowledge of the world, and experience of the human heart. Never say that you won't do a thing, because if you do, just as sure as you live it is the very thing that you are sure to plunge into, whether you want to or not. Besides, people who know enough to doubt themselves, understand that men and women are made up principally of human nature. Now human nature is a great fraud, and isn't to be trusted when he's found in the interior of your own heart, or anywhere else.

In one of my reports, I expressed myself as shocked out of a year's growth, when I heard about gentlemen and ladies going into the salt-sea waves together, and submerging themselves like mermaids in the swell and foam of the ocean. I said, in the heat and glow of modest feminine shrinkitiveness, that nothing on earth, or in the water, should induce me to do it; but circumstances alter cases, and the capacity of eternal change is the essence of genius, which is always making new combinations and discarding old prejudices.

I say it with reluctance, but truth demands frankness. Sometimes I am a little hasty in my conclusions.

Have I said enough—need I go on to explain that the result of a thing proves its propriety?

Now, bathing in company, in the abstract, does seem—well, peculiar. I might add other words which at one time came uppermost in my mind; but, looking toward results, I feel constrained to say nothing on the social aspect of multitudinous ablutions, but go into the high moral question which has slowly presented itself to my understanding.

Isn't there a passage of Scripture somewhere that speaks

about " fishers of men " ?   I think there is, and I am inclined
to see that kind of business from a high moral stand-point.   If
men are to be legally caught with a dripping dress and an old
straw hat for bait, who shall say that the thing is wrong?   If
men are told to go down to the sea in ships, what should pre-
vent a female woman from going down in a four-cornered
straw hat, a flannel tunic, and—well, pantalettes on?   Everything depends on the point of view from which one sees a thing.

As a marine picture, salt-sea waves rushing in upon a sandy
beach can hardly be considered complete without throwing a
little life into the foreground; but when that life is composed
of a flock of old straw hats, and a lot of staggery, blinded, dripping people under them, I can't say that I hanker after this
particular marine view.

From an artistic stand-point then I reject the whole subject;
but as the means of catching a heart afloat, that same picture
offers numerous facilities.

Well, sisters, as a social institution I no longer sneer at sea-
bath flirtations.   When two days of them end in matrimony, it
isn't worth while to fight out the question on that line any
longer.   I give in.

Such engagements may be unstable as water, but a damp engagement is better than none at all.

With these sentiments, I finished off my bathing-dress, and
put a red ribbon over a high-crowned, square-brimmed hat,
coarse and clumsy, which was to keep my face from the sun,
and my flowing tresses from the briny ocean waves.

Early in the morning I went out into the veranda, and
took a survey of the ocean—the broad infinite expanse of
waters into which I was about to plunge in search of—well,
health.

In front of the veranda, on the high bank, was a pole, like
the liberty-poles we run up on almost every village green of
New England.   On that pole a pale yellow flag was flying.

A chill ran over me, and I know that my arms must have
been roughened like a grater.

"The yellow-fever." I knew it was in the harbor, shut up there by the authorities. Had it escaped through Sandy Hook, and come poisoning the waters along shore? Now that I was ready for the first plunge, were my best hopes to be frustrated? Had I sat up all night sewing red braid on that tunic, and those—well, Turkish pantalettes, for nothing? Had I conquered a great New England prejudice, to be conquered myself by careless health officers? Why hadn't they taken an example by some of the old stock, and divided the whole thing among them in perquisites? I only wish they had.

Sisters, it was a keen disappointment. I was looking at that yellow flag, with tears in my eyes, when Cousin E. E. came on to the veranda.

"Come, Phœmie," says she, bright as a May morning, "where is the new bathing-dress? It will be splendid bathing!"

I looked at her, I looked at the ocean and at the path that led down to the beach, along which half a dozen real nice-looking gentlemen were picking their steps like rabbits toward a sweet-apple trap. It was tantalizing.

"Yes," says she, as contented as a lamb, "it will be lovely bathing this morning; I mean to try it."

"Try it," says I; "haven't you read that yellow-fever is in the harbor?"

"Well, what then?" says she. "It won't hurt us."

"Won't hurt us," says I. "Did you ever hear of poison getting into water that could be washed out? No, if it is in the harbor, some of it will drift down here. Look, you can see it sweltering in the waves now."

She looked out on the ocean, where a faint yellow tinge rippled and shone with treacherous temptatiousness

"Oh, that is only the sunshine," says she.

"But the fever," says I, "I know it is in the harbor, for the newspapers said so. They have run up the yellow flag wherever it is to be found. See there."

Cousin E. E. sat down and dropped both hands in her lap.

16*

"Cousin Phœmie," says she, "I really don't know whether you are a real genius or the greatest goose that ever lived. You are just a puzzle to me.   Who ever heard of yellow-fever in the water?"

"I have," says I, "in the harbor, and isn't the harbor all water?"

"Yes," says she, "that is true."

"Then, isn't it dangerous to bathe in that water, and don't that flag give us warning not to do it?"

"Cousin," says she; "as I said before, you know too much for common ideas to make an impression.   Now do try to understand.   There is one ship in the harbor that has yellow-fever on board—that is all.   It will not be allowed to spread from that one ship."

"Oh," says I, drawing a deep breath, "then it has not poisoned the water."

"Not at all."

"But the yellow flag?"

"That means good bathing, and plenty of it.   Come along. Don't you see people crowding down to the shore?"

CHAPTER XCI.

THE MAN THAT SAVED ME.

RAN into my room, and came out with a bundle in one hand and a coarse straw hat in the other.   That group of gentlemen was just dropping down the bank out of sight, and after them went a crowd of girls, with their parasols flaming in the sun like a bed of poppies.

"Come," says I, all joyful animation, "I am dying to begin."

E. E. spread her parasol, and off we marched.

We came to the steep bank, and went down a flight of wooden stairs to the sandy shore. Right under the bank was a long row of cubby-houses, made of boards.

"This is ours," says E. E., "come in."

I went in. Sisters, what happened in the privacy of that board sanctuary, is not for the public—let this satisfy the curious.

Two ladies went into that little retreat, with bunched-up skirts, beehive bonnets, and a general assortment of dry-goods, such as weighs down the ladies of the present generation to an extent that approaches martyrdom.

Two persons came out skimped down into nothingness. They had grown tall and slim, not to say spooky. There was a deficiency of glossy ringlets under the two hats that squared off in front and behind, and were flapped down over each ear.

E. E.'s plumptitudinous figure was mostly lost and gone, and I—well, I felt like a church steeple on a very high hill. I say nothing, the subject being one of great delicacy ; but from my experience in those Turkish—well, pantalettes—the female that begrudges her husband that class of garments, must hanker after change more than I do. When I came out of the little house, Dempster stood on the sand with a pair—well, of garments like mine, only more so, on, and a flaming red upper garment, bright enough to set the waves on fire, covering his broad bosom.

Another gentleman stood near him—blue and brown in his sea-outfit, youngish, and with eyes that made me wilt like a poppy the moment they fell upon me.

My goodness, how I did feel in that dress ! It was all I could do to keep from kind of scrouching down to hide my bare feet; but it was of no use, so I dug them deep into the sand, and felt myself blushing all over, while that gentleman in blue fixed his eyes upon them.

Anyway, there was nothing to be so mightily timorous about, for, according to my calculation, two smaller or whiter feet didn't leave their prints in the sand that day, though I do make that assertion with my own lips, that ought to be mute.

Cousin Dempster came forward, took both E. E. and my trembling self by the hand, and led us to the water.

I took one glance: a swarm of straw hats, a crowd of men, women, and children were floundering, swimming, screaming, laughing, tumbling through the waves, that lifted them up, flung them down, pitched them forward, and behaved in a way that no well-bred ocean would have thought of doing.

I shrank—I shivered—the heart seemed to die in my agitated bosom when the first wave kissed my feet; I gave a little scream, but checked myself bravely. The waves were full of men, some of them were looking at me.

I determined to act bravely, and be the heroine of the occasion. I let go of Dempster's hand. A wave struck me, my head went down and my feet went up. In my fright and anguish I remembered their size and whiteness, and found consolation in the thought while I strove to right myself.

It was in vain; while I staggered with one big wave, another took me unawares, like a thief in the night, and dragged me under, like a wild beast growling over some poor helpless lamb —it tore me away. I shrieked—I plunged—I fought madly for my life. Up through the vivid green of the waters the sunshine came toward me like light upon beaming emeralds. I clutched at it. I tried to scream; but my mouth filled with water, green flashes shot through and through my eyes. I began to pray. The Green Mountains, the farm, and all my life there shot through my brain; things I had forgotten came uppermost, and those thoughts grew pleasant while the waters seemed roaring me to sleep.

Something came toward me, bluish. Was it a monster of the deep hungry for the life that was so fast dying out?

It seized me. I was born upward on a great wave, and swept off into the light. The claws of some monster, or the arms of some friend, held me close. Which was it?

Some power of good or evil, beastly or human, had dragged me into the sand, where white foam curled around me, and the sun struck down upon my eyes like fire.

Some man was thanking another for a great favor; a crowd of people came swarming around me. I attempted to open my eyes, but the water dripping down from my hair came into them sharp and salt.

"Is she sick? Is she afraid? Do tell who it is?"

These questions came from women who had rushed up from the waters, and flocked around me like mermaids. I did not care about them, but by and by it came to me that men might be there as well. I lifted my hand, swept the wet hair back from my face, and, with a smarting pain in my eyes, saw my deliverer.

His blue garments were black with dripping water, the thick hair streamed over his forehead, his bare feet looked hard and powerful on the sand. It was the man under whose admiring eyes I had blushed and trembled.

"My preserver!" said I, clasping my wet fingers in an ecstacy of gratitude; "shall I ever live to thank you for the poor life you have saved?"

He smiled, he shook his head; I am afraid he laughed, such was his joy and exultation; yet the modesty of true greatness possessed him still.

"It is nothing," he said. "A wave knocked you head-foremost—that was all."

I knew better. It was the inherent greatness of a noble soul that impelled him to make nothing of his own heroic act. He must have supported me miles on miles in those stalwart arms. No protest of his could lessen the bravery of his action or the force of my gratitude. If woman's gratitude and woman's love are anything, his reward shall be great.

They bore me into that weather-beaten cubby-house, and there, with the help of E. E., my dripping garments were taken off, my wet hair done up snugly under the braids that had been left behind, and, filled with tender gratitude, I walked up to my hero in blue before going to my apartment in the hotel.

"Let me see you to-morrow," said I, pressing the hand of

that heroic man. "Then I may find language to express my life-long gratitude."

He bowed; he drew his hand, with evident reluctance, from my clasp, and retreated.

Ah, sisters, my destiny has come! I feel it in every breath I draw, in every sweet thought that haunts my brain. To-morrow I shall see him again. To-morrow!

Oh, sisters, he has just left me. Alas! alas! for human aspirations. I had written thus far when he came.

I received him in my room, looking pale, and, I think, interesting, for the sweet romance of my feelings left its imprint on my features. He came in with hesitation, and sat down on the edge of his chair, looking ill at ease, as if wishing to escape a mention of his own heroism. I felt a glow of admiration, a thrill of tender gratitude.

"You have saved my life," I said, clasping my two hands, "and from this hour I devote that life to your happiness. Tell me how I can begin to repay you."

He sat uneasily; he shifted in his chair. Then he murmured:

"Anything you please; I never thought of asking. It was only my duty."

"Heroic man!" I exclaimed; "and brave as modest. It is my pleasure to be more than grateful. Never, never can I repay you save with the warmest and sweetest emotions of a woman's heart. I owe you—ah, how much—how much!"

My hands were clasped, my eyes were uplifted; emotion prevented me finishing my sentence. He spoke, while my soul halted for words—

"Well, if you think so much of just helping you out of the way of a seaward wave, supposing we say five dollars. It is my duty, as bathing-master, to help people up from the sand when they get face downwards, as you did; but as you insist, I don't mind a fiver."

Oh, sisters!

XCII.

PLEASURE BAY.

EAR SISTERS:—I really do think that Cousin Dempster is one of the best creatures that ever lived. He seems to understand all the wounds and pains that a female woman's heart is exposed to, and sort of eases them off, so that you are cheated out of half your natural suffering.

I cannot say that the bathing in the salt-sea waves was not a failure as a matrimonial speculation; but that is my luck. In some respects, the future to me is like a mirage—I put my hand out hopefully, and grasp nothing but fog.

That bathing-master was a fine-looking man until he opened his mouth and attempted to sit down on a chair. He created a pleasant delusion in my bosom for a few moments, and then —well, we will say nothing more about that—the private sanctuary of a female woman's thoughts are too sacred for a Report.

If I wept in the stillness of the night, no one but the angel that records broken love-dreams will ever know of it. With this precious angel I am in full sympathy. He has done too much of that kind of writing for me not to feel the cruel pangs of the long list of disappointments with which his books are blotted.

Well, I arose the next morning after my experimental bath, heavy-eyed, heavy-hearted, and altogether blue as indigo. Cousin Dempster saw this, and his generous heart seized upon a remedy.

"Let us go down to Pleasure Bay," says he. "What do you think of a day's crabbing?"

"Crabbing?" says I, "just as if I didn't feel crabbed enough already. Do you want me to keep it up all day?"

Dempster laughed; so did E. E.; just as if I'd said something awful funny, which I wasn't in the least conscious of, not having a spark of fun left in me since that salt-water deluge and its consequences.

"Oh," says he, as good-natured as pie, "there is nothing like Pleasure Bay when one has the blues—a lunch under the trees, and a boat before the breeze."

I stopped him ; the dear, good fellow was launching off into poetry without knowing it; association with genius is doing everything with him. There is no knowing where he might have ended, if I hadn't lifted my forefinger, for a whole gust of poetry was riling up in his earthly nature like yeast in a baking of bread.

"I'll go to Pleasure Bay," says I, "but, for goodness sake, don't try that sort of thing again ; genius isn't catching, and though you have married into our family, don't expect that it will spread like an epidemic into yours, because it won't."

"Why not?" says he; "is there nothing in association?"

"Well, I can't exactly decide," says I; "strange things do happen in that direction. I have heard of young women marrying literary men who never wrote a line worth reading before, who burst out into full-blown geniuses right in the honeymoon. But it is wonderful how much their style was like their husbands'. Of course, those must be cases of especial affinity. When a woman has ransacked a poor fellow's heart, she naturally begins to pillage his brain, and I reckon he must like it at first ; but after that, he subsides into himself, and she subsides into herself, and somehow she writes just as she did before, and so does he ! "

"Then there are plenty of young ladies who carry their ambition and their flirtations in among the newspaper people and stray Bohemians," says E. E., kindling up to the subject; "for every time they get into a new flirtation, which is once in about three months, their style changes, giving them a wonderful versatility of talent that, somehow, dies out after awhile, as she grows old and homely."

"That is," says Dempster, laughing, "every time a literary

lady of this stamp changes her lover, she changes her style, too."

"Exactly," answers E. E., "and where she hasn't any good-natured lover she retires into modest privacy till one comes along."

I just listened, holding my breath.

"What," says I, "does fraud and deception creep into the sacred literature of our country? I cannot believe it."

"Can't you?" says E. E.; "but you have never been in Bohemia."

"No," says I, "that is a part of Europe that I hope to visit, but never have. Is it a popular place for Americans?"

"Oh, wonderfully popular, for people who dash off things here and there, write for this and that, and are willing to give half that they earn and know to any adventurer that comes along, free gratis for nothing; or, on occasion, sell reputation by the line, and for a price. Oh, Bohemia is a splendid place for adventurers and adventuresses to forage in!"

"What!" says I, "genius sell itself?"

"Yes," says she, "and its readers, too."

"Cousin E. E.," says I, "you slander the grandest, the purest, the most sublime people on the earth."

"Do I?" says she, nodding her head and laughing. "Wait and see."

"Remember—you are speaking of authors, the first and purest aristocracy known to our free nation."

"No; I speak of would-be authors—guerillas in literature —men and women of erratic ability, who adore inspiration and scorn work; for authorship, I am told, and believe, requires the hardest work of any calling in the world."

"I'm afraid it does," said I, drawing a long breath, "but then such work brings its own prompt payment. The power to write is happiness in itself."

"But what has this to do with Pleasure Bay?" says Dempster; "we mean to go there—not to Bohemia."

"Just so," says I, a-tying on my bonnet.

We got into Dempster's carriage, and after a delightful drive, we came down on the edge of a little bay, with green grass growing close down to the shore, and great, tall trees clumped here and there all around it.

I was so charmed with the scenery that I didn't realize where we were till the carriage stopped before a white house, with a long wooden stoop in front, when we got out and walked right away down to the shore, where a plank platform ran out from the land, and a cunning little boat, with white sails, lay dipping up and down like a duck in the water.

Sisters, I'm not timersome, but getting into a boat that rocks like a cradle in the water tries me, I must own to that. With what holding on and keeping your dress well down upon the ankles, one is seized with a sense of being awfully unsteady. This riles up the constitution to a state of dizziness that makes your ears buz like a bumblebee's nest.

I was thankful to get seated at last, and, tucking up my dress, prepared at once for a long sea-voyage. E. E. had slung a great straw gypsy hat on her arm, by the strings, when she left Long Branch, which she bent down over her head like an umbrella with herself for a handle; over that she spread a broad yellow parasol that blazed in the hot air like a great sunflower.

"Phœmie," says she, a-looking up from under her straw tent, "didn't you bring a flat? "

"No," says I; "the young fellows of that stamp didn't happen to be about when we started."

"Dear me! you'll burn your face up," says she; "that beehive is no protection."

"About as much as one of your York flats would be," says I. "But supposing I hoist my parasol, too—one don't need a beau for that."

The sun was pouring down like blazes, and I was mighty glad to spread my parasol, I can tell you; so I did it, and settled down on the same bench with E. E.

Dempster had been awful busy on shore, pulling out fish-lines, looking up nets that swung like a great hang-bird's nest, on the end of a pole: and now he was on his knees, hacking a fish into chunks, which he tied to a line and dropped into the bottom of the boat. At last he lifted his great straw hat, wiped the blazing warmth from his face, and jumped in.

CHAPTER XCIII.

NETTING CRABS.

OH, sisters! judge of my feelings, when directly after Dempster, came a splendid gentleman—a creature of romance, shaded from the vulgar gaze by a felt hat, and dressed like a mariner along-shore. He lifted his hat to me, and also to E. E.—with a lofty reservation in her case.

"Mr. Burke," says Dempster, with a degree of carelessness that, I am sorry to say, is characteristic—"he will teach you how to catch the creatures; for there is an art in it."

"Then I shall never succeed," says I, in a low, gentle tone of voice. "Where anything but pure nature is expected, I must always keep in the shade. You know, Cousin E. E., what an artless young thing I always was."

E. E. smiled—not at me but right up in the face of that strange gentleman. I declare, I never saw anything so bold in my life! But it was of no use; he came and sat down close to me. In fact, he took the parasol from my hand with a gallant air that made my heart beat like a partridge on a log. In one respect that movement wasn't an advantage: the parasol was not large enough to shade two, and he held it carelessly, as was natural to a dashing, splendid creature like him; but somehow the shade always fell on his side. I felt dreadfully certain that freckles were falling like split peas all over my face.

Still he smiled so sweetly and looked so magnificent that, freckles or no freckles, I was ready to give him up my beehive, too, if he had only looked as if he wanted it.

Dear me, how that boat did heel up and rock as we went sailing off down to a green grassy point, where the gentleman told me the crabs swarmed like lady-bugs around a full-blown rose—pretty simliar, wasn't it, sisters, and so original?

I was dying to know what sort of a fish a crab was, never having seen any in our brooks. Were they like sun-fish, rainbowish and flat; or like trout, sparkled over with dripping jewels; or small and silvery, like shiners and pin-fish?

I did not like to ask that magnificent stranger about this, and let him believe that crabbing had been an amusement of my childhood up in the Green Mountains—not that I said so outright—but my idea of discretion is to say nothing of a thing you don't understand, but wait and find out. What is the good of telling the world how much you don't know?

Well, I hadn't the least idea what a crab was, but the name made me feel a little rily. The water was full of them; I was pretty sure to find out; so I waited.

By and by, Dempster flung a great stone co-slash into the water, and tied us up just below a little green point of land that took the sunshine in its long grass till it seemed full of drifting gold which spread out upon the water in soft, shiny ripples.

E. E. shut down her parasol. Mr. Burke shut mine. "Now," says he, "for the lines."

With this he took up a lump of raw fish, gave it a swing and a splash into the water, and handed me the other end. Dempster gave another line and a chunk of fish to his wife, and then took one of the hang-bird nets and stood by as if he meant to do business.

By and by I felt a sort of hungry nibbling at the end of my line, and gave it a jerk just as if it had been a brook trout, hard to catch.

" Oh, goodness! " I just dropped the line and screamed like

everything, scared half to death.   If ever an innocent female caught a claw-footed imp, I came near doing it then.   Why the animal, varmint, double and twisted serpent—I don't know what to call it—clung to the bait till I hauled him clear out of the water, and then fell back with a big sprawl and an awful splash, sinking down again like a great mammoth spider that made the water bubble with disgust.

"What was it?   What was it?" I said, turning my scared face on Mr. Burke.   "What kind of young sea-devil is this?"

He laughed, and laid down the net he had just taken up.

"You pulled too quick," says he.   "Crabs are like women."

"Like women," I shrieked.   "What, those horrid things? Sir, I thank you!"

My voice shook so I could hardly get the words out with proper irony.   A generous rage in behalf of my sex possessed me.

"You did not hear me out," says he, pleasant as a sweet apple.   "I was going to say crabs were like women in this respect.   They must be led along, enticed, persuaded up to the bait."

"Oh!" says I, "that is a sentiment I can appreciate, but the comparison is dreadful."

"There is hardly anything in nature which would not be dreadful compared to some females that I know of," says he.

I laid one hand on my bosom and bowed, but the next instant I felt one of those scraggly fiends pulling at my line, and I drew it softly in, hand-over-hand.   Oh, how the beastly thing crept and crawled, and spread its scraggles as it nibbled and rose with the bait!   I declare it made the flesh creep on my bones.

"That's right, draw gently—lure him up.   Ho!"

As he spoke Mr. Burke just slid his net under the varmint, and flashed him up into the air, bait and all.

Sisters, there is no use in talking; if these creatures they call crabs ain't great salt-sea spiders, no such animals exist; and eels ain't fish, that's all.

Oh, I wish you could see them crawl up through the sea-grass and spread themselves. I declare it is just awful.

Well, down went this crab—which they all gloried in, being a great big gridiron of a fellow—into a hole in one end of the boat, and out went my bait after another.

At one great pull I brought up two wapping big fellows at a time, and trolled them on while Mr. Burke scooped them up. Chasing dragon flies in the old times was nothing to it.

E. E. was busy as a bee on her side of the boat, Dempster ladled the animals up for her, till we had a couple of dozen trying to creep away, and fighting each other like chickens in a coop.

By this time I could see that E. E., like a good many other people I could mention, was getting sort of restless for other attentions than those her husband could give. She kept casting side-glances at Mr. Burke, and at last says she to Dempster:

"Dempster, it isn't expected that a man should always be a-hanging about his wife. It's time for you to do some netting for Phœmie."

E. E. said this almost in a whisper, but I heard it, and all the temper in me riled up to my throat.

Sisters, this married woman was just dying to change off her husband for the beau that was devoting all his energies to me. I felt that the crisis had come that self-interest and a high moral standard demanded that I should keep this man from the lure of a married woman. I owed it to myself, to Dempster, and, above all, to the cause of morality, to hold that man firmly to his post.

"Phœmie," says Dempster, coming up to me and looking as if butter wouldn't melt in his mouth, "let me scoop for you?"

Before I could speak Mr. Burke took that nefarious hint and went over to E. E.

I gave Dempster a look of withering contempt, and flung my bait out with a splash that must have scared all the crabs out of a year's growth.

"No," says I, "you may be willing to desert the marital outposts, but I will not help you. Go back to your wife; I can catch all the crabs I want without help."

"Well, just as you like," says Dempster, and, settling down on the bow of the boat, he pulled his hat over his eyes and went to sleep, then and there.

Three crabs come up to my bait—nibble, nibble, nibble. I drew in the line, they crawled through the water after it. Still I drew and drew. Three great plump fellows came to the top of the water. It was a good chance to call Burke away. He was leaning over E. E. and whispering, while she listened.

"Here, here!" screamed I, "three at a haul. Will nobody help me?"

That man did not seem to hear me, but kept on whispering, while E. E. listened with a smile on her lips and her eyes half shut. The sight made me awful mad.

"I'll catch them myself," says I, and down I plunged my hand into the water. I meant to grip the crab, but he gripped me.

Oh, mercy, how he pinched and bit, and screwed his claws around my hand. It seemed as if he were twisting it into a corkscrew. I shrieked—I yelled—I tried to shake the varmint off—to dash him to atoms against the side of the boat. It was of no use: his sharp claws dug into me in fifty places; he bit like fury. The blood ran down my fingers, my voice grew weaker, but it broke up that flirtation. It was a cruel price, but I paid it cheerfully. While I retain my moral sense, no married woman shall degrade her sex by a flirtation in my presence. Never, never!

Yes, my screams broke up that well-arranged plan to delude Mr. Burke from my side, and it broke up the crabbing party too.

Dempster woke up and hauled in the lines. We had thirty crabs floundering in the hold, all fighting like imps of darkness.

"We'll have them for dinner," says Dempster, ferociously, "they won't be so lively half an hour from now."

He was right, it took us just fifteen minutes to sail back to that white house with the long stoop. Fifteen minutes after that, every crab was in water so hot that they gave up clawing and began to turn furiously red.

Half an hour after we sat around a long table out under the trees, with a great platter of those scrawny creatures lying with their red shells uppermost, a good deal easier to catch than they had been, I can tell you.

Mr. Burke was busy as could be, telling me how to put in my knife under the red shell, so as to lay the sweet white flesh open.

I say nothing, but it seemed to me there was one jealous female around those premises, and that female certainly was not me.

The meat of those creatures is just delicious—what there is of it.

Take it altogether, sisters, it seems to me that catching and eating crabs is an amusement which promises better than bathing.

If I am not very much mistaken, Mr. Burke held my hand longer than was quite necessary when he said good-night after we reached the hotel. I saw E. E. looking at us sideways, and I let it rest—rest lovingly in his clasp long enough to wring her heart. What right has she to have any feeling about it, I should like to know? Isn't she married?

CHAPTER XCIV.

EXTRA POLITENESS.

DEAR SISTERS:—Life is a pleasant thing to have when its chariot-wheels revolve in smooth places. I went to bed last night angry with Cousin E. E. Ever since Mr. Burke was introduced into our party she has exhibited a desire for gentlemen's attention which I think entirely unbecoming a married lady. I do not wish to be severe or captious; such feelings should be left to maiden ladies of an age that I have not yet dreamed of reaching. But a married woman who hankers after any other man's society than that of her own lawful husband is—well, not to speak harshly, an example that some people may follow, but I won't.

This morning, as we sat on the long stoop of the hotel, gazing out on the broad expanse of the boundless ocean, Mr. Burke came gently to my side, and spoke:

" Miss Frost."

My heart beat; my eyelids dropped, but I lifted them, in shy innocence, to his face, inquiringly, wistfully. What would he say next ?

" Miss Frost, have you ever seen a clam-bake ? "

I reflected a moment. Were clam-bakes indigenous to our Vermont soil ? Were they a product of the mountains, or a spontaneous growth of the river vales ?

" I do not think I have ever seen them growing in Vermont," says I, at last; " yet there are few roots or vegetables, wild or tame, that I don't know something about. There is wake-robin, on the mountains, with its spokes of red berries; and snake-root, and adder's-tongue ; but I don't remember clam-bakes among them, and I know they are not cultivated in our parts as garden-sas, I beg pardon, as vegetables."

Mr. Burke smiled out loud, and his black mustache curled down on each side of his lips delightfully.

" I fancy you have never seen anything of the kind in Vermont. Clam-bakes are only found at the sea-side—principally around Rhode Island. I don't think they prevail much in the mountains, as yet."

" You don't say so ! " says I. " Then they are a salt-water plant ? "

" Principally found in the sand and mud."

" That don't seem to me very remarkable," says I; " most vegetables are found in one or the other. Watermelons, for instance, grow best in a bare sand-bank : perhaps your new-fangled vegetable is of that species ? "

Again his black mustache gave a lovely curl, and his black eyes looked into mine so tenderly, as if something I had said tickled him almost to death.

" You *are* an original creature," said he.

I put one hand on my heart, and bowed.

" People about Sprucehill, especially the Society of Infinite Progress, have done me the honor to think so," says I.

" But about the clam-bake—if you like it, we must start for Pleasure Bay at once," says Mr. Burke.

" Do they grow down there ? " says I.

" Not as a general thing, but we shall make out to get one up, with a little trouble."   .

" Do they grow so deep ? " says I.

" You will see when we get there.   Mrs. Dempster is ready, and the carriage is waiting."

To please that man I would have done almost anything; but it did seem a wild-goose chase for a lot of grown people to rush down to Pleasure Bay for the fun of pulling up a lot of the strangest vegetables that ever grew.

" Do make haste ! " cried E. E. through the green slats of her window-blinds.

I got up and shook out my dress.

" It will be such fun ! " she called out.   " Mr. Burke has been so kind as to invite us, so don't keep him waiting."

I lifted my eyes to the dark orbs of that noble-looking man, and he must have known from the expression that I did not mean to keep him waiting in any respect.   Gently bending my head, I withdrew.

I came from my room like a moving picture, with my black alpaca newly flounced, and surmounted by that fleecy white jacket with great buttons and double-breasted in front.   Then my white hat, curled up victoriously, and the feather waving above it and curlecued around it, was enough to tantalize a minister.

Mr. Burke smiled graciously when he saw me come forth clad in the whiteness of my principles, and I knew that the sympathy between us was national as well as individual.

E. E. came out of her room flaunting a red jacket and a long black plume. Dashy for a married woman! But I said nothing. Let that young woman work out her own destiny; I am not her husband. I caught her sending sly glances from under her eyelashes at Mr. Burke. I wish Dempster had been close by, to see for himself, that's all.

If there is anything on earth that I detest, it is a flirty married woman.

We rode down to Pleasure Bay, four in the carriage, with that child perched up alongside of the driver. E. E. wanted to sit opposite to Mr. Burke, and, seized with a fit of extra politeness for that occasion only, insisted on it that I should get in first—which would have brought me face to face with Dempster. But I, too, was suffering under a sudden epidemic of good manners, and stepped back, bowing till the white feather shaded my face. She kept waving her hand; but I would not be persuaded into pushing myself before a married woman, and at last she got in, biting her lips as if she had a tenpenny nail between her teeth. I followed, looking innocent as a cat with cream on its tongue, and away we went.

CHAPTER XCV.

THE CLAM-BAKE.

TWO carriage-loads of people were at Pleasure Bay, wandering about under the trees in front of the hotel. Down between them and the bank was a lot of men piling up a heap of round stones and crossing sticks of wood over them till a high sort of a cross-beam pinnacle was built, to which one of the men set fire. Mercy, how it blazed up and flashed through the cracks in the wood! They seemed to enjoy the blaze, and worked like beavers around it—though I don't know how a beaver works, never having seen one.

Some of the men went down to the water, and, dragging up great armfuls of dark green and yellow grass, swelled out here and there with bulbs and blisters, laid it in a heap before the fire. Some of the others sat down on the rocks, with pails of potatoes and sweet corn between their knees, which they began to wash and tie up in their husks.

I was awful curious to know what all this was about, but made up my mind to wait and see; for Mr. Burke seemed so anxious and busy that I didn't want to stop him by asking questions.

When the wet weeds, potatoes, and corn came on, I thought that the next thing would be some clam-bake; but instead of that, a fellow came down from the house with a lot of young chickens, picked clean, which he carried by the legs, and another loafed up from the water with three great horrid green monsters, like crabs swelled out—green as the sea-weed, and so dreadfully crawly that the very sight of them made me creep all over.

" What on earth are those creatures ? " says I to Dempster ; " mammoth cockroaches that have taken to a seafaring life, or what ? "

" Why, lobsters," says he.

" Lobsters! " says I. " Not a bit of it. All the lobsters I have ever seen were bright red, and still as mice."

" That was after they were cooked," says he. " Wait till these come out, and they'll be red enough, I promise you."

Well, I waited and watched, for what these men were up to was more than I could make out. When the wood was all burned down they brushed the coals and ashes away with an old broom, and two colored men came up from the shore, carrying a two-bushel basket full of little longish-round creatures, hard as stone, and with a long black sort of a knot hanging out of one end. They were dripping wet, and pieces of sea-weed clung to them, as if they grew in the water like the crabs and lobsters.

Well, when the ashes were swept away, and nothing but the hot stones were left crowded close together, the two nig—well, colored persons, lifted that great basket between them and poured the round creatures among the hot stones till they sissed again. Then they piled on a heap of sea-weed, and a cloud of steam came pouring through. Then another layer, and over that the potatoes and corn were poured down and laid on. Then another layer of weeds, and the chickens and three great large fish, done up in cloths, were laid out for a steaming, and with them those live, green lobsters. Oh, mercy! how they did spread their claws and crawl through the sea-weed! It was enough to make you creep all over; but the men soon smothered them with steaming grass, which heaved up and down for a while, and then sank off, till the lobsters lay as dead as the chickens, and made no more fuss about being roasted alive.

By this time the whole heap—grass, chickens, corn, lobsters, and other shell creatures—was big as a small haystack. At last the two colored persons came down with a long tin pail, in which was a roll of butter and some vinegar. They sunk the pail down into the steaming sea-grass, clapped the corn on, and buried it with all the rest. Then more sea-weed and an old boat-sail flung over all, and that little mountain of roasting things was left to steam and sizzle while the whole party went to take a walk along the shore.

Mr. Burke kept by my side, and part of the time he carried my parasol, shading my face with it in the tenderest way.

He said something about the clam-bake, but I had really got so sick of everything in the fish, fowl, or vegetable line, that a curiosity, more or less, was of no consequence, so I said I should know how I liked clam-bakes better when I had seen one.

He answered that would be soon, for half an hour was enough to put one through.

Sisters, I was in no sort of hurry about it, for the rest of them were busy chatting and talking, so that we were just as good as alone, and the moments were precious as gold sands in an hour-glass.

By and by some one set up a shout. Mr. Burke wheeled right round, and says he:

"They are going to open the clam-bake; come and see it done?"

CHAPTER XCVI.

THAT CLAM BAKE.

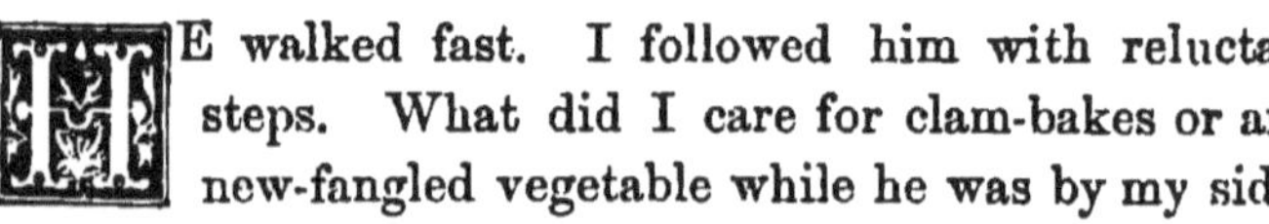

HE walked fast. I followed him with reluctant foot-steps. What did I care for clam-bakes or any other new-fangled vegetable while he was by my side?

The crowd were all around that heap of sea-weed when we came up. Men, women, Irish help, and nig—well, colored freemen, with eager eyes and open mouths, were waiting for the sail-cloth to be taken off. On the grass, under the trees, a great long table was set out with plates, glasses, castors, and things. At the end, two pails of ice, with the necks of a dozen bottles peeping up like hungry birds in a nest, stood ready for somebody to uncork.

Well, the nig—freedman gave that sail a jerk, and a cloud of salty steam rolled up from the sea-grass. Then he raked away a winrow of that, dug out a pail of melted butter and vinegar, and held a lobster up by one claw, looking red as a British soldier's jacket. The creature had given up fighting, and hung in his hand meek as Moses. The poor thing was green enough when he went in, but came out blazing red and steam-ing hot.

More sea-weed; chickens dripping with gravy; heaps of corn; potatoes, mealy, and broken open; fish, and then those longish-round shell things, heaped in plates and dishes, were carried off to the table. We followed those dishes; we sat down to eat. Those longish hard-shelled creatures had all burst open, and something that smelt delicious lay inside, with black heads sticking out.

I watched to see what the rest did with those animals, then seized one by the head, drew him out, soused him in the melted butter, and dropped him softly into my open mouth.

"Delicious, scrumptious, beyond anything I ever ate in my life," says I, when Mr. Burke leaned toward me and wanted to know how I liked it. "But what are these black-headed things with shells, called?"

"Oh, soft-shells—the best part of the clam-bake, I think," says he.

"I reckon you are right," says I, taking another little fellow by the nape of the neck, and biting him off at the shoulders. Then I drank a glass of the sparklingest cider you ever tasted, and went in for an ear of corn, smoking hot, and the breast of a chicken.

Mr. Burke wanted me to eat some of the red lobster, but the thought of it made me creep all over, so I asked to be excused, and said I preferred a dozen or two more soft-shells.

There was a good deal of first-rate cider drank around that table, and we left a bushel of open shells under the trees, besides a heap of lobsters, clams, and chicken bones, well picked.

Then we went back to look at the place where they had been cooked, and found nothing but a heap of smoking stones, a ring of burnt grass, and a pile of steamy sea-weed. Somehow, the sight of it all made me feel sort of faint, and it didn't seem to me that I should ever want to eat or drink again.

We went home from Pleasure Bay in the carriage, feeling lazy and kind of half sea-sick.

That night I dreamed that a whole regiment of green lobsters were crawling over my bed, clawing at me fiercely as they went. Then I thought that Mr. Burke came and shoved them off with both arms flung out, and invited me to breakfast on a heap of empty shells, dipped in butter, which set awful heavy on my stomach.

In fact, I had a worrying night, and got up feeling as if I had been feasting on tenpenny nails and roasted flat-irons.

XCVII.

ONE HOUR OF HEAVEN.

EAR SISTERS:—You haven't the least idea of what warm weather is in Vermont. Why, if one of your mountain trout streams could have runt hrough New York, it would have boiled over and cooked the poor little speckled creatures that live in its waves. You never saw anything like it in your born days. The sea breezes at Long Branch seemed to come over an ocean of melted lead, blasted up by some old furnace of a volcano. For one whole week I was just dying of envy, when I thought of the pigs roving loose in our village, with such lovely mud puddles to lie down in, without caring a sumarke whether their clothes were mussed —excuse that word, I got it here in York—or not.

While I was panting for breath on the sea-shore, I could think of them, with home-sick longing, up to their throats in the soft, mushy fluid of a delicious puddle, with swarms of yellow butterflies rising, floating, and settling around them, as if a bed of primroses had got tired of growing in one place, and had burst off on a grand spree through the air, settling down for a drink now and then.

Yes, sisters, I was brought, in the hot blast of those summer days, to a state of unchristian envy, and would have been glad to swap places with flounders, or have slept in some cellar, with a block of ice for a pillow.

But nothing that I ever saw lasts for ever, or if it does I haven't lived long enough to prove it. Still, one gets restless in weather like this, when human beings are dropping down dead in the streets of a city close by in dozens, from sun-strokes.

This morning I sat in my room, with a short gown and not over many skirts on, looking through the green slats of my door, and watching the sunshine shimmer down on the waves where the little white vessels were folding their sails, and going to sleep like birds too lazy for flying, when a colored person came to my door, and says he :

" Mr. Burke's compliments, and will Miss Frost take a walk with him on the beach ? "

I started up, and, says I:

" Won't I ! " Then I composed myself, and sent back compliments, and Miss Frost will have great pleasure in complying with Mr. Burke's polite invitation.

When the—colored messenger was gone, I sat down in the Boston rocker, clasped my hands, and drew a deep, deep sigh of esctatic expectation. Then I remembered that *he* was waiting, and sprang to my feet.

With my two shaking hands I fastened the other woman's hair over my own, that would neither curl nor friz worth a cent that awful hot day. Then I put on a white muslin dress, that looked seraphically innocent, and tightened it up with a plaid silk sash, that circled my slender waist and floated off like a rainbow breaking through a cloud.

Then I took my parasol in one hand, held my flowing skirts up with the other, and went forth to meet my destiny. Oh, how my feet longed to dance!   How my girlish heart beat and fluttered in this innocent bosom.

He was waiting for me in the long stoop, leaning against a post, and fanning his manly head with the broad brim of his Panama hat. Oh, how majestic, how—but language fails me here.

Arm in arm we walked along the beach.   He leaned toward

me, I leaned with gentle heaviness on him—delightful reciprocity—eloquent silence. A soft breeze blew up from the ocean, and kissed us both with refreshing softness.

"Ah!" said the noble man by my side, "this is delicious."

"Deliriously so," I murmured.

"You feel the revivifying effect?" says he.

"Exquisitely," says I, leaning a little more confidingly on his stalwart arm.

He bent his stately head and looked down into my eyes. Sisters, the thrill of that glance shook my delicate frame as bumble-bees set a full-blown rose to trembling when they swarm in its heart.

"Shall we go down to the sands?" says he; "the incoming tide is dashing them with coolness."

I understood the delicate meaning conveyed in these words. Nothing could be more exquisitely suggestive. The tide—what was that but his own noble self? The sands—pure, white, untrodden—in my whole life I never heard anything more typical.

"If you desire it," I said.

"If I desire it. Ah! Miss Frost, it is for you to say."

My heart leaped to this as a speckled trout snaps at a fly. Nothing so near a proposal had ever reached me before. But a New England woman is modest; she does not snatch at the first offer—far from it. I pretended not to understand the badly hidden meaning of his metaphor. A little art of this kind is feminine and excusable, even in a young girl dignified with Society membership and a mission. I felt that he could appreciate it. He did. Some people were below us on the sands. They paused to look up as this noble creature handed me down those wooden steps. The effect must have been artistical. My cloud-like skirts floated softly on the zephyrs. My scarf streamed out like a banner. I am afraid the curve of my boot might have been seen from below, for many admiring faces were turned that way, and Mr. Burke cast his eye downward in a fugitive manner.

At last we reached the sands, on which both the sun and waves were beating luminously.   By a ridge of white sand he paused.

"Shall we sit here ? " says he, with tender questioning.

" Anywhere," says I, with sweet feminine complacency.

Then I dropped down on the sand ridge, and sweeping my skirts together, cast a timid glance up and around.

That noble man was spreading a silk umbrella.   There was a hitch in the spring, and, such was his eager impatience to occupy the seat I had so delicately suggested, that a real naughty word broke from his lips—a word I, as a missionary, never could forgive, if it hadn't been the proof of such loving impatience.   As it was, like a recording angel, I blotted it out of my memory with a forgiving sigh.

That refractory umbrella was hoisted at last, and its owner placed himself on the sand beside me, holding it not seaward, but like a tent, shading us two from the whole world, while the sun took care of itself.

" This," says he, " is a sweet relief.   Don't you find it so, Miss Frost ? "

I answered him with a sigh, soft, but audible.

" Yes, one can draw a full breath here," says he.   " I was sure you would enjoy it."

" I do, indeed," says I, playing with the sand in the innocence of my heart.

Evidently embarrassed by deep feeling, he too began to sift the white sand through his fingers, which came so near mine that they made me catch my breath for fear he might clasp them.   On the contrary, he gave up the temptatious exercise, and throwing a generous restraint on himself, began to talk metaphorically and metaphysically about many things, especially about gathering maple-sap, of which he questioned me tenderly, veiling the hidden meaning in his heart, by a seeming interest in our trees.

He asked me, with infinite meaning in his voice, at what period the sparkling sap began to mount up from the curly roots of our maples, and vivify the trunk, twigs, and branches of that noble. tree.

I understood his meaning, delicately veiled as it was. He wished to reveal his contempt of young saplings compared to the vigorous tree. It was a poetic way of comparing young snips of things with whole-souled girls, who had all the bloom of youth, and all the strength of maturity.

I spoke my mind on the subject. I said that strength, greenness, a full-grown trunk were necessary before sweet wholesome sap could circulate from root to top of a sugar maple. That saplings amounted to just nothing at all. In fact, they kept absorbing, but gave forth nothing; that a rich maturity was desirable before the maple became important as a forest-tree or an object of wealth.

I think he understood me—or rather he understood that I, with the exquisite intuition of genius, understood him. For right off, on that, he said that he would like to live in Vermont, and own maple-trees himself; that native sugar was a sweet business, and must have a softening tendency upon those who entered into it.

He sometimes bought it of little boys in the cars, and always felt a soothing influence after eating it, that made him long to drink the native sap fresh from the tree. In fact, he took a deep interest in Vermont and all its institutions.

While we were talking on these sweet subjects, quite a breeze sprang up from the water.

Things brighten around us. The sky looked blue. The heaving waves of the ocean began to swell and sparkle as if a diamond mine were breaking up in their depths. I am satisfied that Long Branch is all that it has been cracked up to be—and more too, when kindred souls meet on its sandy shores.

" How bright! how beautiful!" says he, backing off suddenly from the maple question, which had covered a world of hidden meaning, and looking out to sea, with a delicate wish, no . doubt, to spare my blushes.

"Some persons have been kind enough to think so," says I, "but it isn't for me to say."

"I love the fitful changes—the soft transparency: nothing can be more lovely," says he.

The occasion required downcast eyes and shrinking silence. I gave him both. There could be no better answer for a speech so personal and yet so poetic.

"I hope you share my feelings in this."

That moment—that precious, precious moment—was broken in upon in a way that makes me clench my teeth as I write. Up the sands, racing forward like a young colt, came "that child," with her flat flying back by the strings, and a broken parasol in her hand; up she flew toward Mr. Burke.

"Come here," says she, "I want you to whip that boy out there within an inch of his life. I broke my parasol over his head, but it wasn't half enough; I want you to give it to him good."

"But what has he done," says Mr. Burke, no doubt riled to the depths of his noble heart, as I was.

"Done enough, I should think. He mimicked the way I carried my parasol, and said some folks wanted to be young ladies before they could read—that's what he has done," says the creature, flaming out like a bantam.

"Perhaps we had better go in," says Mr. Burke, lifting himself out of the sand.

"Not till you've given him hail Columbia," says the creature, taking a new grip on her broken parasol.

"I rather think he has got that," says Mr. Burke, reaching out his hand to help me up.

I arose. I jerked that Leghorn flat by the strings, and tied it under the creature's chin with a pull that made her scream. Then I took Mr. Burke's arm and mounted the wooden steps, with a feeling at my heart that is not to be described by mortal pen. What a world of bliss that wicked little wretch broke in upon. His soul was verging towards mine so beautifully. The final words were burning on his lips when she rushed in. Still, memory is left, reason is left. I know what was in that noble heart, and that knowledge is bliss.

I felt this: I knew his meaning. To a common woman he might have said, "I love you dearly. I wish above all things to spend my life with you;" but to a creature made up of sensitive pride and poetic niceties, unclothed proposals of this kind must be quite out of place. Of course I understood all that, and felt the refinement of his conduct deeply.

What more *could* a man say than this? In order to be delicately personal, one must talk by comparisons. To praise the State one is born in, is to praise one's self. To seize upon any material thing for a poetical comparison with a human being, is to be intensely complimentary to that being.

For the first time in my life I feel the sweet certainty of duplication. My heart swells with the beautiful faith of hope deferred. Those heavenly lines we have sung so often together in our meeting-house come back to my mind—

" To patient faith the prize is sure—"

I dare not go farther and complete the rhyme, because human sensation should not encroach on the divine; but the spirit of that hymn sings in my heart; for if there is anything on this earth that woman should be grateful for, it is love.

Yes, my sisters, at last I feel that I am beloved. A ray of sympathetic feeling has darted from a grand and noble soul to mine, changing that dull, sandy coast to Elysium.

Last night, when I retired to the secrecy of my chamber, it seemed to me that if ever a woman's heart—beg pardon, a young girl's heart—was born again, mine had become more tenderly infantine than it was when I lay one week old in my loving mother's arms.

The moonlight was streaming through the muslin curtains of my room when I entered it. It was an ovation of silvery light dawning upon the new life that opens before me. I do not know how other people feel when the crisis of fate is on them, but in my heart there is room for nothing but infinite thankfulness.

Yes, sisters, I think you can conscientiously congratulate me. Virtue does sometimes meet with its own reward, especially when it is combined with youthfulness, elegance, and high mental attributes.

XCVI.

C. O. D.

DEAR SISTERS:—The cruelty of one female woman to another is something awful. As a general thing, E. E. Dempster is a good-natured, amiable person, but her conduct on the very day after that heavenly season on the shore was worthy of the Spanish Inquisition. She has lacerated the heart in my bosom, and torn me away from this place like a ruthless highwayman. That is what she has done.

Early in the morning, while I was dreaming sweetly of the sea-shore, that unfeeling female rushed into my room.

"Phœmie," says she, "you can't sleep any longer. We are packing up for the city. Cecilia has been insulted here, and I won't stay another hour in the place."

"What! what is it?" says I. "How could you! He was just giving up metaphor and coming squarely out in the sweetest way."

"You will have no more than time to pack your trunk before the train starts," says she.

"Starts—what for! where?"

"For New York, and after that to Saratoga; Cecilia insists on it, poor, sweet darling."

"For New York?" says I.

"On the way to Saratoga."

"But—but who is going. Is—is— ?"

"Why, you and I, Dempster, and that sweet, ill-used child. Would you believe it, that rude boy's father refuses to whip him, and said.a girl that could give a black eye with her parasol was—well, I can't find the heart to repeat it. At any rate, she doesn't stay another hour under the same roof with that little fiend."

"But is that all—Oh, tell me is no one else going?" says I feeling as if a ton of lead had been heaped on me.

"Dear me. There is no one else to care for the poor child. Of course, no one will take it up but us. So make haste."

Out she went, leaving me just heart-broken and ready to give up. How could I go? how could I leave him and "the Branch," as if my soul were fleeing from his?

It was of no use. E. E. was set upon going, and I couldn't help myself.

Well, sisters, two hours after I left that bed we had packed up bag and baggage, given a cart-load of trunks for the express-men to smash or carry, just as they liked, and then took a little run of railroad, and a sail in a steamboat so grand and airy, and no ending, that we began to feel sorry that James Fisk was dead, or that his splendid ghost didn't roam along the steamboat track and keep things ship-shape, as he left them.

Well, in that steamboat we reached New York, warm, rest-less, and nigh about ready to give out, or take a friendly sun-stroke and be peaceably carried away to a cool vault in some shady graveyard.

I mentioned this alternative to Cousin Dempster, but he shook his head and answered that some of us might find our-selves waking up in a more uncomfortable place than the streets of New York; which I thought impossible, but said nothing.

Well, we had a few hours to stay in the city before a boat would be ready to take us to Saratoga Springs—a name that sounded so cool and refreshing, that I longed to get there and breathe again.

Cousin E. E. said, when we went ashore :

"Phœmie," says she, "there are a few hours before us; sup-pose we go a-shopping? I want ever so many things. Sara-toga is a dressy place, and I haven't a thing to wear."

Then, before I could object, says she to Dempster :

" A check, my dear, or if you have the funds on hand."

Dempster gave a sigh that shook his manly bosom through and through, and says he :

" There," drawing a roll of bank bills from his vest pocket, " will that do ? "

E. E. unrolled the bills and sorted them out.

" Ten, twenty, fifty, ten, ten, ten, fif— Why, Dempster, what do you mean? How far will a hundred and fifty dollars go? I want to spend more than that on Valenciennes lace for Cecilia's dress. The child must have something to wear."

She spoke in a grieved, half-angry way, that touched Dempster to the heart. He took out his pocket-book, but not another sign of money was in it. Then he felt in three or four pockets with the air of a man who was tormented with doubts of finding anything. At last he stopped looking.

" I haven't another red cent about me, dear. Indeed I haven't."

" Dear me, what am I to do? There is a guipure sacque at Stewart's that I must have."

" Couldn't you get along without it ? " says Dempster, with such pathetic earnestness that I really felt sorry for him.

" Get along without it ! How can you ask ? "

" That Brussels lace thing," faltered Dempster.

" What, that ? I have had it six months at least; besides, I saw another just like it at the hotel, and that is enough to disgust one with anything. If people will pattern after me, I can't help it. Then again one gets so tired of the same thing."

" But I have no more money."

" Can't you draw a check ? "

" My check-book is at the office."

" Always so when I want anything. Now, Dempster, this is too bad."

" Well," says Dempster, desperately, " get the thing, and tell Stewart to charge it ? "

Cousin E. E. turned her face away. It was awful cloudy, and I could see that she was biting her lips. She had an awful long bill at Stewart's already. Then her face lighted up.

"Can't I have them sent C. O. D., by express? You will have time to get plenty of money before then," says she, as soft as silk weed.

"I hate the system," says Dempster; "money in hand is the only way a lady should make purchases. Then she knows what she is about. Everything else leads to extravagance. I hate bills as if they were copperheads; they are things I never will forgive."

I saw that E. E. turned pale, and a red flush came around her eyes as if she were just ready to burst out a-crying.

Dempster thought it was because he had stood out about the money and gave in a trifle.

"For this once," says he, "have the things charged, but bring the bill with you. I must know what I am about in these matters."

"But I mightn't find them all in one place. Hadn't we better make it a C. O. D., just for once?" says she, pleading for her own way as if her mouth were full of humble pie.

"Do as you please for this once," says he, half out of patience, "but remember, I am set against bills and running accounts—pay as you go along, is my motto."

E. E. drew a deep breath, and, putting the money in a little mite of a leather satchel fastened to her side by a belt, took up her parasol and prepared to march off.

Cecilia followed after, surveying her little toadstool of a parasol, and stooping forward as she walked, like an undersized kangaroo.

I only wish E. E., or even Cousin Dempster, could see that child as I see her. But they can't. Where she is concerned, they seem born fools, both of them.

Well, off we went one way, and Dempster the other—he to get the money, and his wife to spend it. I looked on, and wondered how any man living could afford to get married. The whole thing made me down-hearted, and half-ashamed of my relationship with a woman who could worry money out of her husband like that, and not feel how mean she was—could not my cousin see that she was poisoning the soul of her own child by an example which she was just as certain to follow as she was to live.

Well, we got into a carriage and drove up Broadway; but instead of going to Stewart's great marble building, E. E. stopped at some other places, and kept buying and buying till I got tired out, and sat on a round stool by the counter, saying nothing, but thinking a good deal. Each place we left, I heard her say, " Grand Union Hotel, Saratoga : C. O. D.," till I got tired to death of the word.

At one place my cousin and that child had a grand set-to in the store. Cecilia wanted a bright-red silk dress to wear under her lace one ; but E. E. liked blue best, and ordered it. Then Cecilia declared she didn't want any dress at all, broke her new parasol striking it against the counter, and ended off by flinging herself down on a stool and drumming her feet against the counter—so mad that she cried till everybody in the store heard her.

Of course E. E. gave in, just to pacify her, while I would have given fifty of the brightest silver dollars ever issued by the U. S. Government, for the happiness of giving her the neatest little trouncing she ever got in her life. But luxuries like these, I can hardly expect just yet. How that cousin of mine can give up a parental prerogative so tempting to the hands I cannot imagine. I really would not put so much pleasure off an hour.

XCVII.

TAKEN IN.

ELL, after trapesing about from one store to another till I was nigh about tired to death, E. E. concluded that she had got through her shopping, except a few things that we could carry in our pockets, which kept us rushing in and out of every little shop we came to for an hour longer. Then she said we would stop into Purssell's and get something to eat, for she was beginning to feel hungry. This had been the case with me ever so long; not that I hankered much in hot weather for hearty food, but I felt a sort of faintness; and when she said something about Purssell's having delicious peaches, I knew that they were exactly the thing which would appease all the internal longing of my nature.

But just as my mouth was beginning to water, E. E. took out her watch and gave a little scream.

"Why," says she, "who would a-thought it? We have but just fifteen minutes to reach the boat in?"

My heart sank. The taste of those peaches had almost got into my mouth, but now a taste of dust came in their place. I could just have sat down and cried.

"Never mind," says E. E.; "we can get dinner on board."

"Dinner on board!" Thin soup; hot meat down in the bottom of a steamboat, with a smell of oil, sour water, and musty linen all around you—that is what "a dinner on board" means, and nothing else. The very thought made me feel rily about the temper—all that I wanted was, some peaches.

You will not wonder, sisters, that I hankered after this delicious fruit, which is about the only good thing that grows which we do not have in the old Vermont State. Only think of them—round, plump, juicy; with the redness of a warm sunset burning on one side, and pale-gold glowing on the other; cool, delicious, melting away in the mouth with a flavor that just makes you want to kiss some smiling baby while it is on your lips! Think of them! then imagine my feelings when I was hurried into a hack, and rattled off to the steamboat with the promise of a hot dinner in its internal regions. We saw peaches on every hand as we drove along—in stores, on street tables, in baskets carried by Irish women, who looked up at the carriage-window pleadingly as we drove along.

"Wait one minute," says I, as a woman came up with her long basket brimming over with the luscious fruit; "I must have some peaches."

"Not a second," says E. E.; "don't you see Dempster beckoning from the deck? The last bell is ringing. Come, come!"

The Irish woman lifted up her basket, and stood there enticing me. E. E. rushed up the plank, calling out: "Make haste, make haste!"

Cecilia sung out: "Come along, Phœmie!"

Two men had hold of the plank bridge. I had to cross then, or be left behind. I cast one yearning look towards the basket, rushed up the plank, and stood panting, by the side of Dempster.

"Oh dear, it is too bad!" says I.

"What is it, Phœmie?" says Dempster.

"Peaches!" says I. "Those delicious peaches—see how they glow in the sunshine!"

"Oh, nonsense! There is plenty on board," says he; "I'll go and get some."

"Not yet," says E. E.; "the deck is so crowded."

Dempster got seats for us and a stool for himself. The crowd was packed so close that one could hardly breathe. I was thirsty, I was tired out, and just ready to cry. E. E. was tired also, and a little cross. Cecilia was just as she always is —a nuisance. I felt like thanking Dempster when he jumped up, and says he:

"Now for the peaches!"

Away he went, just as good-natured as could be, calling back for me to keep his seat for him. I laid my parasol on it, and kept my hand on that ; but a minute after came a great heathen of a fellow and attempted to take the stool.

"It is engaged," says I, pressing down my hand.

"What of that?" says he, jerking the stool away, and throwing my parasol on to the floor. "Every one for himself, and no favors."

I was blue as indigo before that. At another time this creature would have riled me into a tempest, but now I felt more like crying. But there he sat, plump on the stool, looking as self-contented as if butter would not melt in his mouth.

Dempster came back. I looked up longingly. His hands were empty.

"I am very sorry," says he, "but there isn't a peach on board."

Well, there I sat, with the sun pouring down on me, while E. E. read the illustrated papers, and that child made herself generally numerous among the passengers. After awhile I got up to look over the side of the vessel, when that horrid wretch snatched up my seat and carried it off, looking back at me and laughing.

I said nothing—what was the use?—but leaned against the cabin-door, holding my satchel, the most forlorn creature you ever saw. Just then some one spoke to me. I looked round. It was a roly-poly, oldish woman, who spread considerably over her chair, and held a travelling-basket on her lap. She had found an empty stool, and asked me to take it.

I sat down while she smiled blandly upon me.

"Never mind that fellow," says she. "Some men are born animals of one kind or another, so let them go."

Her words were kind—her manner motherly. I liked the woman. She is not elegant, I thought, but who could be with all that breadth of chest and brevity of limb? I smiled and thanked her, wondering who she was.

"Pretty scenery," says she, pointing to the bank on which some cottage-houses, and a wooden tavern with red maroon half-curtains at the window, seemed to set the whole neighborhood on fire. "Now I would give anything for a house like that. Snug, isn't it?"

She might have been looking at the wooden tavern, or at a cottage close by with a beautiful drapery of vines running along the porch. "Of course," thought I, "she means that."

"Yes," says I, "it looks delightfully quiet."

She nodded, and opened her basket, a capacious affair, quite large enough to hold half a peck of peaches. My mouth began to water. Perhaps—

"Take one," says she, handing over a cracker.

I took the disappointment, and tried to eat, but with that hankering after peaches in my throat it seemed like refreshing one's self on sawdust. She noticed this, I think, and, with a little hesitation, looked into her basket again, then closed it, and, looking towards me, whispered—

"That's dry eating. Come down to the cabin, and I'll give you something nice."

"Something nice!" I felt my eyes brighten. "Something nice—peaches, of course. What else could she have but peaches?" I thanked her with enthusiasm; my eyes gloated on her basket. Peaches and plenty of them—delicious!

The stranger arose, smoothed down her dress, and led the way downstairs. Her presence was imposing, her step firm as a rock. Assuredly my new acquaintance was no common person —a little stout, certainly, but so is the Queen of England.

I followed her eagerly, thinking of the peaches, longing for them with inexpressible longing. We went through the cabin —on and on—back of some curtains that draped it at one end. Here she paused, set her basket on a marble table, and proceeded to open it.

I did not wish to show the craving eagerness which possessed me, and delicately turned my eyes away. Then she spoke in a deep mellow voice, as though she had fed on peaches from the cradle up.

"Look a-here," says she. "Isn't this something nice?"

I looked! the basket was open. She held a tumbler in one hand and a bottle in the other, from which a stream of brandy gurgled. That rotund impostor came toward me, beaming.

"There," says she, "take right hold. It's first-rate Cognac."

All the Vermont blood in my veins riled suddenly. I drew myself up to the full queenly height that so many people have thought imposing. Disappointment sharpened virtue's indignation.

"Madam," says I, "you have practised a hospitable fraud—in Christian charity I will call it hospitable—on a New England lady, who looks upon temperance as a cardinal virtue. Put up your bottle. Maple sap and sweet cider from straws are the strongest drinks I ever indulge in."

"Maple sap," says she, with a rumbling, mellow laugh, which ended in a cough as the brandy went down her throat. "Sweet cider, through straws! Well, every one to her taste."

Here she filled the glass again and held it out, smiling like a harvest moon.

"What, you won't take the least nip, just to save it, you know?"

I turned my back upon that rotund tempter, and walked with a stately step to the deck, followed by a rich gurgle from the second glass as it went down that perfidious creature's throat:

"Goodness gracious! What a surprise!"

This was my exclamation when I saw Mr. Burke coming towards me, across the deck, with a small basketful of the most delicious peaches in his hand.

There he came, smiling so blandly, and held out the basket for me to help myself. He was going to Saratoga, he said. The hot season had driven him to seek mountainous air. O sisters!

THE END.